THE FAMILY PRIDE

THE FAMILY PRIDE

(The Zero Enigma, Book VI)

Christopher G. Nuttall

ISBN: 9781082474873

The Family Pride
(The Zero Enigma VI)
Christopher G. Nuttall

Book One: The Zero Blessing
Book Two: The Zero Curse
Book Three: The Zero Equation
Book Four: The Family Shame
Book Five: The Alchemist's Apprentice
Book Six: The Family Pride

http://www.chrishanger.net
http://chrishanger.wordpress.com/
http://www.facebook.com/ChristopherGNuttall

Cover by Brad Fraunfelter
www.BFillustration.com

All Comments and Reviews Welcome!

HISTORIAN'S
NOTE

The Thousand-Year Empire dominated the twin continents of Maxima and Minima through two advantages, an unmatched command of magic and the development of Objects of Power, magical weapons and tools that made them seemingly invincible. But the Empire fell and the secret of making Objects of Power was lost.

Hundreds of years later, a young girl—Caitlyn Aguirre—was born to a powerful magical family. Caitlyn—Cat—should have been powerful herself, like her two sisters, but she seemed to have no spark of magic at all. She lacked even a sense for magic. In desperation, her parents sent her to Jude's in the hopes that exposure to magical training would bring forth the magic they were *sure* lay buried within her. There, she met Isabella and Akin Rubén, children of her family's greatest enemy. Isabella became her rival, while she formed a tentative friendship with Akin.

Cat developed no magic, but she discovered something else. Uniquely, as far as anyone could tell, she had no magic at all. She eventually discovered that a complete lack of magic was necessary for forging Objects of Power. Far from being useless, her talent made her extremely valuable and utterly irreplaceable. Cat was the only true 'Zero' known to exist. This led to her—and her friends, Akin and Rose—being kidnapped, then targeted by Crown Prince Henry and Stregheria Aguirre, Cat's Great Aunt, when they launched a coup against the Great Houses and the King himself. Their subversions—which turned Isabella against her family—nearly led to complete disaster…and perhaps would have done so, if Cat and Akin hadn't become firm friends.

In the aftermath, Cat proposed that she and Akin should be betrothed, creating a marriage bond between their families and making it impossible, at least for the next few years, for the two houses to come to blows. This was—reluctantly—accepted, with the proviso that either Cat or Akin could refute the agreement if they wished, when they came of age. Cat left Jude's to found her own school, where other Zeros—when they were found—would be taught.

Meanwhile, the Great Houses had to deal with the repercussions of the attempted coup and the sudden shift in the balance of power. Isabella Rubén, condemned as a traitor, was exiled to Kirkhaven Hall, where she discovered a secret her family had sought to bury…and a new secret, one of her own. Others took advantage of the chaos to stake a claim to power themselves, plots that were only foiled through sheer luck and outside intervention. The city remained unstable…

That was six years ago.

Now, as Akin Rubén goes back to school for his final year, his marriage to Cat is starting to loom…

I am so proud, if I allowed,
My family pride to be my guide.
I'd volunteer, to quit this sphere,
Instead of you in a minute or two.
But family pride, must be denied,
And set aside, and mortified.
And mortified...
Pooh-Bah, The Mikado

PROLOGUE

ONE

When I was a child, one rule was drummed into me from the very start. *Anything, for the family.* It was very clear. The family was my home, my tribe. It sheltered me, protected me, empowered me. And, in exchange for everything it gave me, I was to always put the family first. I could leave, if I wished; but if I left, I gave up everything. The family came first. Always.

Isabella, my twin sister, and I had grown up together, and been told—practically since birth—we were expected to be a team, against both the outside world and the family itself. The family might show a united front to outsiders—Father had made that very obvious, during his long and tedious lectures on politics and family loyalties—but we bickered amongst ourselves in a constant, genteel struggle for power. My sister and I—as the Patriarch's sole children—were expected to inherit, yet we could lose that position in a moment if we showed ourselves to be unworthy. In truth, I wasn't sure I cared. Isabella might enjoy the drive for power, she might strive to establish herself as a leader amongst our generation…but I did not. I was always more interested in forging and magic than in playing power games. It didn't matter if I wanted to inherit or not. I was going to inherit anyway. Father had it all under control.

I was ten years old, a year short of going to Jude's for the first time, when I finally realised just how far apart Isabella and I had become.

It was a long hot summer, dominated by endless lessons from our teachers and supervised playdates with children from other aristocratic families. The games might have been fun if they weren't so tightly controlled; I might have enjoyed it, just a little, if we'd been allowed to run free, like children who had no aristocratic parents to disappoint. Instead, we were expected to act like miniature adults, demonstrating our manners on one hand and our magic on the other. The playdates were boring. I found myself sneaking off as soon as possible. It was worth the lecture from Father just to be alone for a few, short hours.

I was sitting in my study, reading a book on advanced forging techniques, when Isabella burst into the room. I looked up, alarmed. We'd both practiced unlocking the other's door, but it was generally understood that neither of us would actually *enter* the room without permission. Our bedrooms were *ours*, the only rooms in the mansion that were truly private. Even our *governess* was supposed to knock. There had been times when I'd kept my mouth firmly closed, when she knocked on the door, and waited for her to go away. It worked. Sometimes.

Isabella and I looked alike, naturally, but—as we grew older—we had started to diverge. Her blonde hair, the same colour as mine, hung down in a single long braid, while mine was cropped close to my skull. Her blue eyes, I fancied, were a little sharper than mine, although our parents claimed they were identical. The green dress she wore was a copy of one of Mother's gowns, a dress so complex that it was difficult to put it on without magic; I, thankfully, was allowed to wear shirts and trousers. Isabella couldn't wear trousers. The old ladies of the family would throw their hands up in horror at the mere thought, then subject her to *very* astringent criticism. A young lady of House Rubén wearing trousers? What was the world coming to? Horror of horrors!

"Akin!" Isabella looked flushed, as if she had been running. "You have to help me!"

I stood up, glancing out the opened door. I half-expected to see Madame McGinty—our governess, a woman who would explode with fury if we forgot to call her *Madame*—charging down the corridor in a towering rage. Isabella had been picking fights with the governess more and more as we grew older, constantly struggling against the governess's dictates as she fought to establish herself as a young girl. I was on her side, naturally. Madame McGinty was not a nice woman. But the corridor was empty.

The door closed at my command. "What happened?"

Isabella held up a book. "I...ah...*borrowed* this," she said. "You have to help me."

I swallowed, hard. "You...you took that from *Father's* bookcase?"

Isabella nodded, her head bobbing so rapidly that her braid swung loose. I stared, unable to help myself. Father had made it clear that we were *not* to touch the books on his private bookcase. Some of them could be very dangerous to the unprepared. I had no idea how Isabella had managed to circumvent the locking charms, let alone steal the book without being frozen in place or zapped into a frog or having *something* unpleasant happen to her. She'd always been better at charms than I, yet Father was *much* older and far more experienced. I didn't spend as much time as I would have liked with my Father—he was always busy, managing the family—but I had a healthy respect for his powers. He'd been practicing magic for longer than I'd been alive.

"He'll kill you," I said, horrified. Not literally, I hoped, but Isabella would be in a *lot* of trouble. Father would hit the roof. Isabella would be grounded for so long that her grandchildren would still be trapped in her bedroom. "Why did you...?"

Isabella met my eyes, her blue eyes wide. "I had to *know.*"

I winced in perfect understanding. We *had* been taught to be curious, to study magic and develop our knowledge as far as possible. It seemed almost a *crime* to ignore books, even dangerous ones. I'd read hundreds of textbooks and tomes that had been intended for older children, although I hadn't been permitted to try any of the spells. I understood perfectly why Isabella would want to read a forbidden text. They were forbidden. That was half the fun!

"He's coming," Isabella said. She was always pale, but now she was so white that her skin looked almost translucent. "He'll find me and..."

Her voice trailed off. Isabella was already in trouble. She'd mouthed off to Madame McGinty earlier in the day and the governess had *not* been pleased. Mother wasn't going to be pleased either, when she came home from her society meeting. It really would not *do* to have a young lady showing anything less than the proper respect...Mother would be angry, Isabella would be grounded, and it was a horrible ghastly mess.

"What can I do?" I looked at the book. The title was faded, which meant it was old and probably very rare. "Isabella..."

"Tell Father *you* took the book," Isabella said. "*Please.*"

I blinked. "You want *me* to lie to Father?"

"He'll kill me," Isabella pleaded. "But he won't kill you."

I heard the bitter frustration in her voice and winced. Isabella would never be Heir Primus, let alone Matriarch. House Rubén was *always* led by a Patriarch. I might inherit my father's titles and position, but Isabella...the best she could hope for was marrying into a position of power. She would have power, I'd been assured, just as Mother had power...it wouldn't be *hers.* It was a sad irony of our lives that I, who didn't want power, was going to inherit it. And my sister would never have power in her own right.

I would have traded places. Gladly. Isabella actually *wanted* the power.

"He won't kill you," I pointed out. "The worst that will happen is that you get grounded..."

"Yeah, but I have to attend the Lancet Party," Isabella said. "It's *the* event of the year, before school. I have to go, just to solidify alliances..."

I rolled my eyes. Yes, I knew alliances were important. Yes, I knew it was vital to have friendships before we went to school. Yes, I knew that who one *knew* could be very important in later life…but I didn't really care. I'd been surrounded by sycophants for most of my life. Isabella, on the other hand, was determined to be a social queen. She'd started training for the role at a very young age.

"Please, Akin," Isabella pleaded. "I need this. I'll repay you…"

There was a solid knock on the door. I blanched, feeling my stomach starting to churn. Only one person knocked like that: Father. I looked at Isabella, at my sister's pleading face, and made up my mind. I took the book, then cast a simple spell. The door opened. My father stepped into the room.

"Akin, Isabella." His voice was very calm, so calm I *knew* he was angry. My father rarely showed any display of temper. "Would one of you care to explain…?"

I held up the book. "It was my fault, Father."

Father eyed me for a long moment, his face utterly implacable. I couldn't tell if he believed me or not. I wasn't a good liar and Father had been running the family since well before I was born. But his face showed no trace of his feelings. Isabella was going to owe me *big*. I made a mental note to ensure that she paid through the nose.

"Your fault," Father said, slowly. His face was expressionless. "And why did you take the book?"

"I was curious." I could have kicked myself. I hadn't thought to take a look at the book before Father had arrived. I could have come up with a convincing *reason* to borrow the book if only I knew the subject. "It was the first I touched."

"Indeed." Father's gaze moved from me to Isabella and back again. "Give it to me."

I held out the book. Father took it, his eyes never leaving my face. I knew, with a sickening certainty, that *he* knew I was lying. But he said nothing.

"I'm sorry, Father." My voice shook, although I wasn't sure if I was afraid or angry at Isabella for getting me into this mess. "I just wanted to know."

"Curiosity killed the cat," Father said, quietly.

"Satisfaction brought it back." Isabella gave him a charming smile. "Father…"

I shot her a sharp look. This wasn't the time to be flippant. It never was, when Father was concerned, but now was a *particularly* bad time.

Father gave her a stern look. "I believe Madame McGinty is looking for you, young lady."

Isabella paled. "Oh."

"And you can go find her, afterwards," Father continued. "Akin, I am very disappointed in you."

I looked down. "Yes, Father."

"You will report to my office after dinner, where we will discuss your punishment." Father's voice brooked no disobedience. "And you will remain in your room until dinner."

"Yes, Father."

Father studied me for a long moment. I was fairly sure he *knew* that ordering me to stay in my room wasn't much of a punishment. I had books to read, experiments to plan…and a perfect excuse to avoid everyone until dinnertime. Cousins Francis and Bernard had been nagging me to play hide-and-seek with them. I liked them both, but they were a bit much when I was trying to study.

"Good," Father said. "And the next time you want to read one of my books, ask first."

He turned and swept from the room. The door closed behind him with a sharp thud. I sensed the spell a moment later, keeping me firmly *in* my room. Anyone else could come and go as they wished, but I…I was stuck, until Father lifted the spell. I…

Isabella gave me a hug. "Thank you, thank you," she said. "I owe you my life!"

"Hah," I muttered. I hugged her back, very briefly. Dramatics aside, it was nice to know our relationship wasn't *totally* lost. "Anything, for the family."

CHAPTER

ONE

The corridor leading to my father's office seemed endless.

Isabella and I used to joke, in happier times, that Father used magic to deliberately extend the corridor. It wasn't impossible. House Rubén was so old, magic had seeped into the very bones of the mansion. The inside was bigger than the outside, in places; there were staircases that went up to the basement and corridors that twisted in odd ways, threatening to go in directions the human mind couldn't grasp. Father could have extended the corridor for miles, if he had wished, but I doubted it. I simply didn't want to reach the far end.

I felt my heart pounding in my chest as I made my way along the corridor. Isabella and I—and all the other children—had been told, in no uncertain terms, that we were *not* to enter the office floor unless we were specifically invited. And we were only invited when we were in trouble. I didn't *think* I'd done anything that might get me in trouble, certainly not in the last few weeks of summer, but...I couldn't help reviewing everything that had happened, wondering what Father might have found offensive. Perhaps someone had seen Cat and I exchanging brief kisses, when we'd last met. We might be betrothed, yet there were limits to how far we could go. We'd been chaperoned, but...

That was two weeks ago, I reminded myself. *Father would have told me off by now, if he was going to tell me off at all.*

I pushed the thought aside as I came to the first set of family portraits. The first one showed my parents, Lord Carioca Rubén and Lady Jeannine Rubén, on their wedding day. I stopped to look at them for a long moment, before heading on. Everyone said my father and I looked alike, but I couldn't see it. Father was taller and more dignified than I would ever be. The next portrait showed Isabella and I as children. We'd been five when the portrait had been painted…I smiled, as I walked past a series of portraits, each one painted a year after the last. Isabella and I really *had* looked alike, back then. We'd joked that we could swap clothes and no one would notice the difference.

My good humour faded as I reached the eleventh portrait. It was the last one that showed Isabella before her disgrace. She looked young and pretty, dressed in her school uniform…I swallowed, hard, as I remembered the House War and Isabella's role in it. She'd betrayed the family, she'd thrown her lot in with Stregheria Aguirre…she whose name was never spoken. Isabella had been young, young enough to avoid execution, but not young enough to avoid punishment. My sister had been in exile for the last six years. I'd only seen her once in all that time. Her letters had been upbeat—reading between the lines, I thought she'd found something to do—but something was missing. A little of her fire, her passion for life, her determination to be great, had died with Stregheria Aguirre.

And the Crown Prince, I thought. *He died, too.*

I swallowed, hard, at the thought. I'd *killed* the Crown Prince with the family sword. It was currently resting in a scabbard attached to my back, the scabbard charmed to make the sword difficult to see unless someone's attention was drawn—specifically—to its presence. I had the right to wear it—the blade had bonded to me, once Cat had repaired it—but not everyone liked the idea of me carrying a priceless Object of Power everywhere I went. It was silly—it wasn't as if students my age didn't know a handful of killing spells—yet...there was no point in arguing. Besides, the sword was—technically—a betrothal gift. It was going to get sticky if the betrothal fell through and Cat's family demanded the sword back.

I touched the hilt—it felt reassuringly solid against my skin—and forced myself to walk further down the corridor. The portraits changed, showing me—and me alone. There was no sign of Isabella. I might as well be an only child, for all the acknowledgement my parents made of their daughter. She was lucky they'd kept her childhood portraits. I knew that some of the family elders had demanded they be destroyed. Isabella had betrayed the entire family. They would forgive a great deal, but not that.

And if they hadn't pushed so hard, Father might have given them what they wanted, I thought, as I reached the final portrait. *He couldn't let them browbeat him into submission.*

I stopped and stared up at the final portrait. Cat and I stood together, flanked by both sets of parents. Cat's sisters were missing, no doubt a diplomatic measure to conceal Isabella's absence. We both looked older than we were, but...I smiled, feeling a rush of affection. I'd always known my parents would choose who I married, yet...I'd been lucky. Really, I had been lucky to *know* Cat before our match was arranged.

My father's door was solid wood. Privacy charms—some basic, some quite nasty—crawled across the wood, their mere presence daring me to tap the door. I braced myself, then lifted my hand and knocked. There was no sound, but I could *feel* the vibrations as they echoed through the aether. There was a long pause, just long enough for me to wonder if Father had been called away on short notice, before the door swung open. Uncle Davys stepped out.

"Akin," he said, sternly.

"Senior." I bowed, quickly. Uncle Davys—my father's twin brother—was *very* insistent on proper protocol being followed at all times. It was no surprise to *me* that Cousin Francis, Davys's son, was a little hellion. "Father summoned me..."

"Quite." Uncle Davys didn't sound pleased. I knew he'd been one of the loudest voices demanding that Isabella's sentence be made permanent. "You may enter."

He walked past me and strode down the corridor. I glared at his retreating back, resisting the urge to stick my tongue out. My father and his brother had fallen out long ago, before they'd married and had kids, but they couldn't ignore each other. Uncle Davys had been the Heir Primus, until I was born; even now, he still had power and position within the family. I was surprised that Francis and I got on, most of the time. It helped, I suppose, that we were very different.

I turned and stepped into my father's office. It was an immense room, the walls lined with mahogany and studded with bookcases and cupboards. Two comfortable armchairs rested in one corner; another was dominated by an oversized wooden desk and a chair that looked like a throne. A large portrait of the entire family—Isabella included—hung from one wall. There were no windows. The light came from a handful of glowing crystals embedded in the ceiling. I schooled my face into careful impassivity as my father stood to greet me. He looked tired, tired and old. For the first time, it struck me that my father really *was* old.

Not that old, I told myself as I bowed. *He's only in his early fifties.*

"Akin." My father sounded tired too. "Take a seat, please."

He indicated the armchairs. I allowed myself to relax, slightly. If I'd been in trouble, I would never have been allowed to sit. I'd have had to stand in front of the desk and listen while he told me off for whatever I'd done. I sat, leaning back into the comfortable chair. My father sat on the other, resting his hands on his lap. Even when he was at home, even in his office, he wore fancy suits. It had never ceased to puzzle me. No one would dare say a word if Father chose to wear something *comfortable*.

"You're going back to Jude's in a week," Father said, shortly. There was never any small talk with him, not when he had something important to discuss. "Are you looking forward to it?"

"Yes, Father." It was true. I was. I'd miss the mansion—and my private forgery—but I was learning a great deal at school. The chance to work with Magister Tallyman was not to be tossed aside lightly. I'd already started to plan how I'd ask him for an apprenticeship, after I finished my final year at school. "It should be fun."

"You should be more concerned with your exams, not with *fun*." Father made the word sound like a curse. "Your exam results will dominate the next decade of your life."

"Yes, Father," I said.

Father nodded, slowly. "You will be Head Boy, of course."

I blinked. "What?"

"You will be Head Boy." Father sounded irked. He didn't like repeating himself. "You'll share the honour with Alana Aguirre, who has been appointed Head Girl."

"Father…" I stared at him. "Father, I didn't ask to…"

"Of course not." Father snorted, as if I'd said something stupid. "You are a *Rubén*, son, and Heir Primus. It would be surprising indeed if you *weren't* Head Boy. It would be quite difficult, quite difficult indeed, if Alana had been a boy too…"

"I didn't earn it," I protested. "I don't *want* it."

"You don't become Head Boy through merit," Father pointed out, dryly. "And whether or not you *want* it doesn't matter. You are going to be Head Boy, Son, and you are going to be *good* at it."

"Father…"

My father held up his hand. "The decision has been made, Son, and favours have been called in. It cannot be changed."

I scowled in mute resentment. Father hadn't *asked* if I wanted it. Why would he bother? He'd been making decisions for me—and the rest of the family—for years. But then, if he'd asked me, I would have said no. I didn't *want* to be Head Boy.

Father met my eyes. "Are you feeling up to discussing this rationally?"

"Yes, Father." It was hard to keep the anger out of my voice. I was *seventeen*, not a baby who couldn't be trusted to keep his hand out of the fire. "Why?"

"You are aware, of course, that there have been some...*rumbles*...of discontent amongst the family." Father's face was very cold. "On one hand, they have been...*concerned*...about me and my rule ever since Isabella...left us. There have been suggestions whispered—and not very quietly, either—that I am not up to the job. And, on the other hand, they have been deeply worried about the alliance between us and House Aguirre. They would prefer not to see the alliance become permanent."

I frowned. "Father, House Aguirre has the only known Zero. They are..."

Father cut me off. "I am aware of the advantages"—he shot me a smile that made him look years younger—"and also of your...*feelings*...regarding your betrothed. I have no reason to doubt that a *permanent* alliance would be good for the family, for *both* families. Less so, of course, for the *rest* of the city."

"But who cares about them?" I spoke with more bitterness than I intended. "The family comes first, always."

"Quite." My father studied his hands for a long moment. "They are also concerned about you."

"Me?"

"You," Father confirmed. "You have many strengths, Akin, but you also have weaknesses. There are...concerns that you are unable to manage the responsibilities that come with being Heir Primus and, eventually, Patriarch. And your betrothed has similar issues. It isn't as if you're betrothed to Alana."

I blanched. I liked Cat—Caitlyn Aguirre—but Alana? She'd grown up a lot, in the years since I'd first met her, yet she still had a sharp edge and sharper tongue. She and Isabella had been very alike, in a great many ways. Isabella had envied Alana, as well as hated her. Alana didn't have a family that stuck to the old traditions, even though they'd died with the

Thousand-Year Empire. She could succeed her father and take control of her family. And I pitied the poor bloke who married her.

"I have the family sword," I pointed out. I tapped the hilt, drawing his attention to the blade. "Doesn't that prove something?"

"The family council would object, loudly, to the suggestion that receiving the sword as a betrothal gift qualifies you for anything," Father countered. "You were merely the first one to touch the sword, after it was repaired. It could have been Francis or..."

"Or Isabella," I finished. "She could have taken the sword."

My Father's face darkened, as it always did when my sister was mentioned. I knew he loved her, even though he found it hard to show it; I knew he regretted sending her away, even though he hadn't been given a choice. He had to wonder, deep inside, if he'd failed as a father. His daughter had turned traitor. It was a wound that cut to the quick.

"Quite," he said. "The family council is lining up possible candidates right now. We have to move fast." I leaned forward. "Why bother? I don't want the job, and..." Father glared me to silence. "The family gives you many things," he said. "You have safety and security, wealth and power and education"—he waved a hand in the vague direction of Water Shallot -"that the average commoner could never dream of having. The family gives you a sword and a shield so you may fight for the family. And in exchange, you will serve the family. It is your duty."

"Yes, Father." I did my best to hide the sarcasm in my tone. It might drive him over the edge. "Anything, for the family."

The look Father gave me suggested that I hadn't managed to hide the sarcasm. "You should know, by now, that everything has a price. And the price the family demands, for what it gives you, is service. It is your duty to complete your education, marry well and—eventually—lead the family."

"And if I don't want the job?" I pressed on before he could explode. "What if Cousin Shawn or Cousin Alcamo would do a better job?"

"Well"—Father's voice dripped poison—"on one hand, that isn't very loyal to our branch of the family tree. Is it? And, on the other hand, reshuffling the succession will cause all manner of resentments. There will be endless disputes over just who should succeed me if you refuse the honour. That would be very bad, would it not?"

I knew the right answer. "Yes, Father."

Father eyed me. "And so, you must prove yourself worthy of the title you carry before my enemies can muster enough votes to challenge the succession. You must do something that will convince the doubters that they can support your succession, rather than trying to unseat you before I die or retire. No one expects you to be me, not yet, but they do want to see signs of promise."

It was hard not to give a sarcastic answer. "I don't think that being Head Boy will be that impressive, not to them. How many strings did you pull to get me the job?"

Father seemed oddly pleased by my comment. "Too many. But you're right. The family council will not be impressed. You're going to do something else."

I felt a flicker of fear. What could he have in mind? Marrying Cat clearly wasn't good enough. Cat and I had been betrothed for years. The arrangement might be a legal fiction, at least on paper, but it couldn't be dismissed. It had to be treated as real—as legitimate—right up until the point Cat and I grew old enough to marry...or say no. The fire-breathers who wanted to restart the House War couldn't do anything until the betrothal was formally ended.

"It also has to be done quickly," Father added. "There is a push, even amongst my allies, for you to be declared an adult immediately after you leave school. Cat, too, meaning that you will be expected to marry in a year or two. The ones who want to unseat you will have to act fast—and that means you'll have to prove yourself this year too."

I scowled. I knew the betrothal was important, but I didn't want to think about it. "What do they want me to do? Fight a dragon?"

"No," Father said. "You might fight a dragon, you might even *kill* a dragon, but that wouldn't prove anything. Your detractors might even claim that just going out to fight a dragon is proof you're an idiot. And they might be right. It would be very stupid."

"Yes, Father," I said.

Idiot would be the right word, I supposed. Dragons were nasty, immensely strong flying monsters that breathed fire and were practically immune to conventional weapons. Thankfully, they rarely flew into civilised lands, preferring to haunt the Desolation. Dragon hunters were amongst the bravest men in the world. They also had the highest death rates. It was rare for a man to stay in the profession after he'd brought down a single dragon. The skin alone would be more than enough to make him wealthy for life.

"You need to demonstrate the skills to run the family," Father said. "Everything from strong and skilled magic to leadership and teamwork. And you have to do it in a year. Less than a year, really. You cannot fail."

His voice was very firm. "You, Akin, are going become Wizard Regnant."

CHAPTER
TWO

I stared at him. "Wizard Regnant?"

"The Challenge," Father said, as if he felt he shouldn't have to explain. "You are going to take the Challenge—and you're going to win."

I found myself with nothing to say. Isabella would have come up with a glib comment, something that would have annoyed our father beyond words, but me? I had nothing. I knew about the Challenge, of course, and I knew that most young magicians *wanted* to be crowned Wizard Regnant, but not me. It was an honour, I'd been told, but…it wasn't one I wanted or needed. Cousin Francis or Isabella would have liked to complete, I was sure. Not me.

"Father," I managed. "I don't have *time* to take the Challenge."

My father's eyebrows crawled up. "I've studied your school reports very carefully," he said. "You are not such a poor student that you need to spend your final year studying…"

"But I have too much else to do." I found myself struggling for excuses. "You've lumbered me with the Head Boy job and…"

"Most people would be grateful to be named Head Boy," Father pointed out, smoothly. "It *does* open doors, in later life."

"Not for me," I countered. "I'm the Heir Primus of House Rubén and…"

"Yes. And you can lose that in a moment, if the family council votes to replace you." My father lifted a hand in warning. "Akin, this is not a game.

You have a position you won by luck, by an accident of birth, not by proving yourself. And now you *do* have to prove yourself, if you want to keep the position."

His voice rose. "And I will *not* have you throw everything away, not now. I've worked too hard to ensure that *my* bloodline remains prominent amongst the family line."

I swallowed. "Yes, Father."

Father glowered at me for a long moment. "To the unintelligent, the Challenge seems thoroughly pointless. It appears to be of no more import than football or dodgeball or one of a thousand other games where the cranially impaired throw balls around and bore everyone to death with tales of famous goals they scored or matches they saved through their sole efforts. You would be right to dismiss a man my age, Akin, who bragged about his victories on the field at school. They are so far in the past that no one really gives a...no one really cares."

Isabella wouldn't agree, I thought. My sister had joined the netball team back when we'd been firsties, back before her disgrace. I'd always assumed it was a chance to network, rather than for the joy of the game, but her letters made it clear she missed the sport. *Cat, on the other hand, would agree with you.*

"However, to the more discerning, the Challenge has greater meaning." Father held me in place with his eyes, his demeanour making it clear that I'd better pay attention—or else. "It is impossible to win through luck, or personal skill. The only way to win is to demonstrate the skills required of a patron, which—by astonishing coincidence—are the skills required to run a Great House. On a smaller scale, of course, but still...if you do well at the Challenge, and become Wizard Regnant, you will be accepted as Heir Primus without further argument. And that is what you are going to do."

"It isn't a coincidence at all," I muttered.

"No, it isn't." Father smiled in approval. I would have enjoyed it more if he hadn't been setting me up for trouble. "The Challenge is just like a war game, only slightly more genteel. *Slightly.* You'll face the same sort of challenges"—his lips quirked into a smile—"as I do on a daily basis. And if you do well, you'll demonstrate that you have the potential ability to take my place. No one expects you to be perfect, right from your first day. You should see the list of mistakes *I* made in my first year. But they will be a great deal more tolerant of your mistakes if they think you have the potential to overcome them."

"I see," I said.

"Everyone knows the winner will go on to great things," Father insisted. "And it will win you time to establish yourself as Heir Primus."

"Yes, Father." I wasn't sure I wanted it, but...I knew I couldn't say no. "Anything, for the family."

"Indeed," Father said. "Anything."

I looked down at my hands. I'd have to read the rules—I'd never bothered to study them religiously, unlike some of the sportier boys in the dorm—and see if I could find a way to win without too much effort. Or wasting too much time. In theory, I didn't need to study *that* hard to pass my exams; in practice, I knew I had to work hard if I wanted to impress Magister Tallyman and convince him to take me as an apprentice. Or another Forger, if Magister Tallyman refused to take me. Magister Tallyman's recommendation would go a long way, if it was given freely. There was no way I could *force* him to recommend me.

"I'll do my best," I promised.

"I want you to do more than your best," Father said. "I want you to *win*."

"Yes, Father." I looked up. "And Father, if I do this, can we recall Isabella from exile?"

My father's face darkened, just for a second, before it went completely impassive. "You *do* realise she might be happier where she is?"

I scowled. Isabella was in exile, trapped at Kirkhaven Hall. She was a very long way from the closest city, let alone Shallot. I couldn't believe she was *happy* there. She was practically in solitary confinement. The girl I remembered, the social queen who'd built a circle of friends and clients, couldn't possibly enjoy being on her own. I was sure she wanted to come back as soon as possible.

Although all her friends and clients abandoned her even before she was disgraced, I thought, sourly. I hadn't failed to take note. If Isabella could lose her friends so quickly, over something as minor as losing a duel, I could lose mine too. And I had never been the most sociable of people. *If she comes home, how many people will welcome her?*

Father seemed to read my mind. "She would be effectively confined to the hall," he said, nodding towards the walls. "No one would invite her to parties, no one would take her as an apprentice…no one would want to have *anything* to do with her, even for us. She would be ostracised, right from the start. She would be about as welcome in polite society as Lady Younghusband."

I blanched. I had no idea what Lady Younghusband had *done*—the grown-ups had spoken of it in hushed whispers, when I'd been around— but it had been serious. It must have been. She'd had to close her mansion, dismiss most of her servants and retire to her country estate, where she spent her days doing…what? I didn't know, but it didn't matter. High Society didn't care what she did, as long as she did it a long way from Shallot.

"Isabella is a lot *younger* than Lady Younghusband," I pointed out. "And…"

Father cut me off. "And if Isabella hadn't been so young," he said, "she would have been beheaded."

I shuddered, helplessly. The thought of my sister laying her head on the block…

"People will forget that, once they see her seventeen-year-old self." Father's voice was remorseless. "They won't remember that she was a young girl. They'll think of her as an adult, old enough to make her own decisions and take the consequences; they'll think she knew what she was doing and ostracise her."

"She was a child!" I protested. "Father, she was *young*."

"And now she's practically an adult," Father said. "Can you imagine *me* as a little boy?"

I shook my head. It was impossible to believe, truly believe, that my father had once been a little boy. I knew it must have been true, once upon a time, but...I didn't really believe it. I just couldn't accept, emotionally, that my father had ever been young. The tales some of my older relatives had told about my father...they couldn't be about *him*, could they? He could never be a child to *me*.

"Of course not." Father smiled, thinly. "And there will be people who will not accept that Isabella could *ever* have been a child."

"It doesn't matter," I insisted. "Even if she's back here..."

"Confined to the mansion?" My father quirked an eyebrow. "What sort of life is that?"

I had to admit he had a point. I'd never really *liked* going outside, not when there were books to read and magic to perform, but Isabella had always been an *active* girl. She'd learnt to ride when she was a child—it had taken me considerably longer to master the beasts—and she'd explored the city with her friends long before she'd gone to school. Madame McGinty had once spent *hours* screaming at her for climbing a tree in the grounds and ruining an expensive dress. Isabella might see the mansion as nothing more than a prison cell. A luxurious cell, to be fair, but a cell nonetheless.

"And besides, the family council will never agree," Father said. "And even if *they* did, the *king* will never agree."

I scowled. "Father, it was I who killed the Crown Prince..."

"And it took me *months* of negotiating to keep the king from demanding *your* surrender," Father snapped. "Yes, the brat was a traitor who betrayed his own father. I know it and you know it and everyone *important* knows it. But the king cannot admit it, not publicly. He was furious..."

He stood and started to pace. "If we didn't have that betrothal contract, if we didn't have your betrothed's family helping us, we might have been in some trouble. I could have lost you as well as your sister."

"Father..." I found myself, again, at a loss for words. "I thought...if I hadn't killed him, I..."

"I know," Father said. "And so does the king. But he lost a son."

He turned to face me. "You'll understand when you have children. You'll go through times when you wish you'd never had them, you'll go through times when you'll want to strangle them with your bare hands, but...you'll love them and, in the end, you won't want anything *bad* to happen to them. You'll find it difficult to refrain from jumping in, the moment your kids encounter a problem, and solving it for them. Childrearing is a lot harder than it looks."

You hired nurses and governesses to do the heavy lifting, I thought. My parents had been distant figures, when I was a child. Mother and Father had been there for us, but...we'd spent most of our time with the help. *You didn't see us as much as we would have liked.*

I felt oddly disturbed, in a manner I found almost impossible to articulate. There had been times when my parents had been angry at me, there had been times when they'd imposed discipline with a heavy hand, but... I'd never felt they didn't *want* me. Or Isabella, even after everything. It had never occurred to me that there might have been times when my parents regretted having children. Or that they'd been trying to do me a favour when they'd left me to sort out my problems for myself.

"Yes, Father," I said, finally.

Father snorted. "You say that now. Just you wait till you and Cat have kids."

I blushed. I couldn't help myself. "Father..."

"Grandchildren are the reward for the grandparents, and the punishment for the parents," Father added. "I'm sure Cat's father will agree."

I wanted to vanish. Or melt into the floor. Or simply turn invisible.

"Just you wait," Father said. He made it sound like I would be executed in the evening. "Just you wait."

"I'm sure I can do a better job," I said, nettled. "I learnt from *you*."

Father laughed. "I said that to your grandfather," he said. There was a hint of rueful admiration in his tone. "And I never realised how much he did for me until I had children myself."

"Yes, Father," I said.

"But, right now, it is politically impossible to bring Isabella back, even if we keep her confined to the mansion." Father sat down, resting his hands on his knees. "We couldn't convince the family council to let us bring her back and, even if we did, we would still have to convince the king. If Isabella had been a few years older, she'd be dead."

"You said," I muttered.

"And even though we played her up, as much as possible, as a victim of Stregheria Aguirre's manipulations, it still made her look very bad." Father shook his head. "We can't bring her back anytime soon."

I looked down at the floor. "Yes, Father."

"And it would cost us a great deal," Father added. "Have you been following the news from Magus Court?"

"No, Father," I said. "I…"

Father let out a long, angry sigh. "You should. You really should."

"Yes, Father."

"Right now, the Great Houses are waiting to see if our alliance with House Aguirre is formalised when you and Caitlyn become adults." Father met my eyes, silently daring me to look away. "If we *do* become permanent allies, it will have a serious effect on the balance of power. The other Great Houses will combine against us, because they will *not* accept permanent submission. We know they're looking for a Zero of their own. Sooner or later, they'll find one."

I nodded. Cat could not be unique.

"And they're also working on ways to bell the cat." Father smiled, as one does at a pun that isn't really funny. "They're giving Magus Court more power, legal and practical; they're strengthening the City Guard and appointing a High Inquisitor, with authority to investigate and punish warlocks.

They *say* it's for the good of all, and some of them may even believe it, but *we* know it's an attempt to put restraints on our power. A smooth succession, when I die or retire, is a must. It is vitally important that you are prepared to take my place."

"Yes, Father," I said, sweetly. "Wasn't that the problem with Crown Prince Henry?"

Father looked unamused. "Quite. But believe me, there will be a *lot* of work for you to do."

I stared. "Father, I want an apprenticeship…"

"Your apprenticeship will be with me," Father said, bluntly. "You'll learn to row, young man, before you take the helm."

My heart sank. "Father, I…it isn't what I *want*."

Father's voice was surprisingly gentle. "We don't always get what we want, Akin. You were born to power and that brings responsibilities…"

"But I don't want them!" I knew I sounded like a child, but I couldn't help myself. "I don't want my life decided for me…"

"I know," Father said. He reached out and rested a hand on my shoulder. It was so out of character for him, it caught my attention immediately. "If Isabella was still here, without a shadow over her, I might consider teaching her too, so she could…*advise*…you. And if there was someone else I trusted to serve, I'd teach him instead. But I cannot. I have to teach you, my only son. There's no one else."

"Perhaps we shouldn't keep power." I wanted to scream. It was all I could do to keep from tearing off my family ring and throwing it in his face. "I don't want it…"

"And if it was clear that you weren't going to succeed me, either through removing yourself from the line of succession or being removed from it, there would be a power struggle to determine who would take my place." Father's eyes bored into mine. "And, right now, that would be disastrous. It would destroy everything our ancestors worked for, over the last few centuries. I will not allow it."

I stood, trying to keep him from seeing my pain. My family could trace its lineage all the way back to the days before the Thousand-Year Empire, to a time that was as much myth and legend as hard fact. I could recite the entire family tree, from a half-forgotten tribal headman to...well, *me*. My ancestors had been so haughty, they could trace their ancestry right back to the very first men and women known to exist. And yet, the family had hit hard times. We—my family—were a branch of a branch of the *original* family. It had taken us centuries to climb back to the very pinnacle of power.

The portrait on the wall seemed to be laughing at me. I glared at it, feeling a wave of bitterness. I loved my family, really I did, but...I didn't like the obligations that came with being part of the house. I envied Cousin Francis and Cousin Penny more than I cared to admit. *They* could find masters, if they wished; *they* could build careers for themselves, they could make their own lives...

But Father was right. I *had* to succeed him. There was no choice.

"When I was your age, I wanted to be a sailor," Father said, quietly. "I do understand."

I glanced at him, understanding—suddenly—why he'd invested so much money in foreign trade. It was hard to imagine that my father had wanted to sail to the Silver Isles, or distant Hangchow, but...I believed it.

"Yes, Father." I turned to face him and bowed, formally. "Anything, for the family."

CHAPTER

THREE

The family library was immense, taking up nearly two entire floors of the mansion. Isabella and I had only been permitted to enter under supervision as young children, a restriction that had only been lifted after we'd gone to school. Indeed, the library had been a good place to seek solitude over the years. Most of my peers were either banned from the library, on the grounds they weren't *that* closely related to the core bloodline, or disinclined to spend time reading when they could be playing instead. Cousin Francis would sooner be seen dead than reading in the library.

Twit, I thought, as I stepped through the door. Powerful wards curled around me, then faded once they'd confirmed my identity. *Knowledge is power, and all the knowledge of the world is stored here.*

I calmed down as I looked around the stacks. That wasn't true and I knew it. The family never threw anything out, which meant there were books and magazines and newspapers that dated back centuries…the books, at least, almost certainly outdated by now. It was interesting to know what our ancestors had thought, years ago, but modern magic had moved on. I shook my head slowly, then walked into the reading room. The librarian kept a handful of modern textbooks, academic journals and law books there, expecting we'd use them more than anything else. I rather thought he was right. There weren't *that* many of us who were interested in digging into the past.

"Akin, my boy," Uncle Malachi said. He was sitting in a comfortable armchair, half-hidden amongst the piles of books. "How are you?"

I blinked in surprise. Uncle Malachi had been in the hall for years—he had his own suite and everything—but it was rare to see him in the library. He spent most of his time wheeling and dealing, schmoosing with my father, Uncle Davys and everyone else who haunted the mansion. Indeed, he was one of the few people who managed to remain on good terms with *both* my father and his brother. It helped, I supposed, that he wasn't *really* family. He'd married my Aunt. He might be an Uncle, but he'd never inherit anything.

"Uncle," I said. He'd given me permission, long ago, to call him *uncle*, rather than *senior*. "It's been a long day."

Uncle Malachi waved to the armchair next to him. "Come and tell me all about it?"

I sat, resting my hands on my lap. Uncle Malachi looked jovial and stout, unlike my father and his brother. And he wasn't blond. His brown hair flopped over a face that was starting to show the effects of too much good food and not enough exercise. He'd always been friendly, always been willing to advise me and my sister…he'd always been a friendly ear, someone willing to *listen* to us. Most adults had wanted us to be seen, but not heard, when we'd been children. Even now, it was hard to believe that any of them would take me seriously. They'd known me as a child. But Uncle Malachi had always listened.

"Father wants me to take the Challenge," I said, numbly. "I don't even know where to *begin*."

"At the beginning," Uncle Malachi said. "Why *does* he want you to take the Challenge?"

"To prove myself," I said. "It…I don't want to do it."

Uncle Malachi looked pitying. "You know your father took the Challenge, when he was your age?"

I blinked in surprise. "My father?"

"Your father," Uncle Malachi confirmed.

If it had come from anyone else, I wouldn't have believed it. My father's disdain for sports—and everything related to sports—was well-known. He'd reprimanded Isabella for kicking a ball around the grounds, instead of spending her time developing her magic and learning how to be a proper young lady. My father...but then, he *had* insisted that I take the Challenge. And he'd given good reasons, too. It was suddenly easy to believe that *he'd* had the same problem. My grandfather might have ordered him to take the Challenge too.

"Oh," I said. "And what happened?"

Uncle Malachi looked...vague. "Something happened. There was some sort of...scandal. It got hushed up at the time, but...your father was never crowned Wizard Regnant. Or anything, for that matter. Everyone involved was sworn to secrecy."

I blinked. "Everyone?"

"Everyone," Uncle Malachi confirmed. "Whatever happened was pretty bad."

"And it was bad enough that everyone had to be sworn to secrecy?" I shook my head in disbelief. Asking someone for an oath was...bad manners, at the very least. At worst, it was an outright demand for complete and total surrender. "Was it something to do with Uncle Joaquin? Cat's father?"

"I don't *think* so," Uncle Malachi said, slowly. "But you won't find anyone who'll discuss it with you."

I frowned. I couldn't believe my father could be so petty as to hold a grudge over a sporting event. I knew the Challenge was important, but... there was a new Wizard Regnant every year or so. Wasn't there? Or...

"And everyone has been sworn to secrecy," I mused. "Why is it so important?"

"Are you really that naïve?" Uncle Malachi met my eyes. "The Challenge is more than just a game, Akin. Everyone knows the winner is marked out for great things."

"Father said the same," I said.

"He may not have explained it properly," Uncle Malachi said. "The Challenge is important—and very far from *fair*. Cheating and outright sabotage is perfectly legal, as long as people cheat in the approved manner. And there have been quite a few contests where *no one* emerged victorious. There doesn't *have* to be a winner."

"And Father didn't win," I commented. "Why not?"

"The details were hushed up, as I said," Uncle Malachi reminded me, without the irritation Father would have shown at repeating himself. "But... it must have been bad. The Challenge is *important*. Enough leaked out, I think, for your father to wind up with egg on his face. It would have made his early years as Patriarch difficult. If you win...it will reflect well on him."

"Oh," I said.

"The Challenge is really a mirror of inter-house politics," Uncle Malachi added. "Whoever puts together a winning team is destined for greatness."

"My father lost...and he's still great," I pointed out, sardonically. "What happened to the other losers?"

"Some got points just for trying," Uncle Malachi said. "Others...vanished, after they graduated. But Akin...everyone who *won* went on to great things."

"So you keep saying." I wasn't that impressed. "Where do I find a copy of the rules?"

"They haven't changed in the last fifteen years," Uncle Malachi said. He pointed a finger at a handful of volumes, resting on the bookshelf. The closest was marked with Jude's logo. "You'll probably find the latest there, if you look. Check when you get to school, just in case there were any changes over the last year. They may be revised again."

I frowned. "Again?"

"There was a really big cheating scandal sixteen years ago," Uncle Malachi said. "You would have been a baby at the time. I'm not sure what happened, really. Someone found a way to cheat that was against the spirit of the rules, but not the letter. In any case, they revised the rules carefully to prevent it from happening again."

"And they didn't *tell* us what they did?" That sounded odd, to me. "Why not?"

"They probably didn't want to give future contestants ideas," Uncle Malachi offered, after a moment. "There's cheating and then there's *cheating.*"

He stood. "I have a meeting with your uncle in twenty minutes," he said. "But if you want to chat, afterwards, I'm available."

"Thanks, Uncle," I said. "I'll see you later."

I watched him walk out of the room, then stood myself and reached for the latest copy of Jude's rules and regulations. I'd read it once, when I'd gone to school, but I hadn't paid much attention to the sporting rules. They'd never really interested me. A handful of warnings about not turning Magisters into toads, casting mind-control spells on fellow students and the dangers of drinking concentration potions before an exam greeted me as I opened the cover, reminding me that the rules *did* change fairly regularly. I wondered, idly, just which student had managed to turn a Magister into a toad. *That* would have been an impressive feat. Anyone who taught at Jude's would be an above-average magician, no matter *what* they taught. I found it hard to believe that even an upperclassman could turn a Magister into a toad.

Maybe it was Madam Ruthven, I thought, uncharitably. The historian had the unearthly gift of being able to suck the fun out of her subject, as if she were a vampire and history lessons were her prey. *It isn't as if anyone has seen her do much magic.*

I felt a pang of guilt—Cat couldn't do *any* magic, and it certainly didn't make her any less of a person—and pushed the thought aside as I flipped through the book. Rules on how to treat lowerclassmen, rules on how to handle upperclassmen...detailed instructions for cleaning and pressing one's uniform jacket? I was starting to think that whoever had written the book had been paid by the word. They always used five words where one would do. I was starting to feel a little frustrated by the time I reached the correct section. Irritatingly, it had been separated from the rules governing football, netball and all the other sporty wastes of time...

... And the very first paragraph was a warning that the Challenge could be deadly.

I felt my heart skip a beat as I read through the section. The Challenge had rules—the writer had said, without bothering to elaborate—but even within the rules, contestants could die. A girl had died, four years ago...I'd been in second year at the time, hadn't I? How had I *not* heard about it? And a boy had died three years before that...others had been badly injured, including one boy who would never be the same again. The book didn't go into details, which I found more than a little ominous. Magic could heal almost any sort of physical damage. What had happened to the injured student? Perhaps he'd gone mad.

And Father wants me to compete, I thought, as I turned the page. *Perhaps he's gone mad.*

Once I was past the harrowing warnings—and the blunt statement that anyone who competed knew the risks—I finally reached an outline of the rules themselves. They appeared to be relatively simple, something that worried me. I could compete on my own, if I wished, or form a team of up to ten students—all upperclassmen. Lowerclassmen were specifically forbidden from taking part. I supposed that made sense. There weren't many lowerclassmen, myself included, who could have matched magic against an upperclassman.

And we're not allowed to ask for help from anyone significantly older, I mused. The rule was clearly designed to prevent us from enlisting adult help. *No parents, no teachers, no one from outside the school...*

I frowned. Cat and I were the same age, but—depending on how I looked at the rules—enlisting her help was probably out of the question. Uncle Malachi had pointed out that there was cheating and then there was *cheating*. The rules weren't too clear on where the limits actually *were*, but asking for Objects of Power from my betrothed was probably too blatant for the staff to tolerate. No one else would be able to do it. And there was no clear explanation of what we'd actually have to *do*. I assumed we wouldn't be kicking a football around the field, but…what *would* we be doing? The rules weren't clear.

It could be anything, I thought, slowly. I could ask Father, but if he hadn't volunteered the information it was unlikely he'd give it to me. *What do they want us to do?*

I considered for a long moment. Something that required a team…yes, I *could* do it alone, legally, but I had the feeling that would be asking for trouble. A magical duel, trading spell for spell? Or…or what? A set of tasks that had to be completed in a given time? I'd done group projects at school, working with my handful of friends. Maybe the Challenge was the same thing, on a bigger scale. I didn't know.

Shaking my head, I closed the book and surveyed the remaining shelves. The earlier editions weren't any help, although one of them went into gruesome detail about an accident that had been expunged from later versions. I returned the original book to the shelf, then turned and walked out of the library. It was late afternoon, nearly dinnertime. Thankfully, I'd been told I could take it in my rooms.

Isabella would have done a better job, I thought, as I walked up the stairs. *She'd have loved the Challenge.*

I felt a pang of guilt as I reached my room, passing a pair of lesser cousins—both too young to go to school—on my way. They seemed so happy and carefree…it made me wonder if Isabella and I had been so innocent, once upon a time. I heard their laughter as I opened the door, the sound cutting off abruptly as the door closed. I'd warded the suite against sound years ago. I had never been able to get used to hearing noises while I slept and worked.

My dinner was already waiting on the table when I arrived, concealed neatly under charmed covers that kept the food in stasis. The maid had come and gone…thankfully, she hadn't entered my bedroom or my study. I'd had to explain to her, years ago, that she couldn't tidy my desks and shelves.

Everything was ordered. It was just *my* order, impervious to lesser minds. Cat had laughed, when I'd told her. Mother had been much less amused.

Isabella was much the same, I thought. *She had her own way of doing things too.*

I sat down and removed the covers. The kitchen staff had outdone themselves, cooking a meal of roast lamb, roast potatoes, vegetables and gravy, with sticky toffee pudding for dessert. My father had hosted a dinner for lunch, if I recalled correctly. I wondered, suddenly, just who he'd been hosting and why. It couldn't have been a big family gathering or I would have been forced to attend. Maybe it had been a friend or…or Uncle Joaquin, coming to discuss plans for the wedding. I felt my stomach sink at the thought. I liked Cat. Really, I did. But I wanted our wedding to be more than just a family event, more than just the glue that bound our alliance together. I wanted…

What you want doesn't matter, a voice said, at the back of my head. It sounded very much like my father. *Anything, for the family.*

I scowled. I knew the problem. As long as Cat and I were children, we couldn't get married. Of course not. And that meant that the ultimate question of whether or not we'd actually get married was moot. But, once we were declared adults, we would have to make an actual decision. And I knew we wouldn't be allowed to delay for long…

Being betrothed did have its advantages, I reminded myself, sourly. Normally, I would have spent my summers being introduced to suitable young women—and being chaperoned, heavily, as we talked about absolutely nothing. But that couldn't happen as long as I was betrothed. I didn't have to worry about filling out a dance card either. It would be insulting to my betrothed to dance with anyone else. *Now, though, the time has come to pay the piper.*

I ate my dinner, put the plates to one side—the maid would collect them later—and walked into my study, closing and locking the door behind me. I was fairly sure my father could get into the room if he wanted—he was the mansion's wardmaster—but everyone else would have real problems breaking into my room without setting off alarms. I glanced around, quietly making sure everything was where I'd left it, then sat down at my desk and reached for paper. I'd promised myself I'd write a letter to Isabella before I went back to school...

And I'm going to have to be careful what I write, I thought, sourly. The family council read the letters I wrote to Isabella, on the grounds an exile had no right to privacy. They'd wanted to read the letters I sent to Cat, too, but Father had overruled them. *Who knows what they'll conclude from my scribbling?*

I rolled my eyes, wrote the letter and placed it in an unsealed envelope. There was no point in charming it shut. If the family council couldn't open it, they'd toss it in the fire. They'd made that clear, long ago. Uncle Davys had been *very* firm about it. I had never understood why he'd been so angry at Isabella, but he'd made his point. The nasty part of my mind wondered why he couldn't simply remove the charm, read the letter and replace the charm himself. He wasn't a poor magician, whatever else he was. It wouldn't be that much of a hassle.

Perhaps he just wants to make it clear that she's in trouble, I thought, as I placed the letter in the box and headed into my bedroom. *Or perhaps he's just a pain in the neck.*

My lips quirked. I knew worse things to call him. But if I said them too close to Mother...

Bedtime, I told myself, firmly. *Tomorrow will be a very busy day.*

CHAPTER
FOUR

I felt the ward jangle as someone opened the door, jerking me out of a sound sleep. I sat up, rubbing the sleep from my eyes. The maid—she was new, barely a year younger than me—started backwards, almost dropping the tea tray. I'd slept in the nude, as I usually did. Her face went so red I was *sure* she expected to be fired on the spot. I smiled at her as reassuringly as I could. I didn't *think* I had the power to fire a maid. Mother ran the house with a rod of iron and she would be furious if I presumed to tread on her toes.

"Just put it there," I said, covering myself as I indicated the table. "I'll put it outside when I'm done."

The maid placed the tray on the table, curtseyed delicately and retreated backwards out of the room. I tried not to stare. She was a very pretty girl and the maid's outfit suited her, but Mother had made it very clear the maids were not to be touched. Given that she'd actually *hit* a distant uncle with wandering hands—and banished him from the household shortly afterwards—I wasn't inclined to take liberties. Besides, Cat would kill me.

I stood, stumbled over to the table and inspected the tray. Coffee and milk, nothing else. Mother expected me to join the others for breakfast, then. I sighed—it was really too early in the morning for Cousin Francis—and drank my coffee, savouring the weak taste. I'd never been able to understand how my father could drink coffee that was darker than Cat or Uncle Joaquin. His coffee tasted so foul that I'd spat it out after I'd taken a sip. Maybe it was an adult thing. I'd discovered, over the last year, that a lot of things I'd considered unbearably disgusting—when I'd been a child—were actually tasty to the adult palate.

They'd have to be, I mused, as I finished the coffee and headed into the shower. *Otherwise, no one would eat or drink them.*

The thought made me smile. Father had told me, when he'd been in one of his better moods, that people didn't buy and serve expensive dishes for the *taste*. They did it to show off their wealth. A man who could serve his guests roast griffin or boiled harpy was a man of wealth and power, if not taste. Beef, lamb and chicken might taste better, but they were *common*. I snorted as I washed and dried myself, then donned a simple suit. Thankfully, *men* weren't expected to wear a new dress every day.

I carried the tray into the living room and put it on the table for collection, then headed down to the small breakfast room. It felt odd to be eating there, now I was seventeen, but I wasn't -- yet—a formal adult. Kids didn't eat breakfast with their parents, not in a house governed by rules that dated back over a thousand years. We ate alone, in a room that had been designed for us. The wards on the walls kept us from making a mess...I sighed, as one of the maids hurried over to pull out a chair for me. It wasn't as if I was *seven*.

"Hey, Akin." Cousin Penny was sitting at the table, eating a bowl of porridge. "How are things this morning?"

I sat down. It was too early in the morning for Cousin Penny, too. Uncle Malachi's daughter was two years younger than me: blonde, beautiful, and disgustingly cheerful. She wore a green dress that reminded me of Isabella... *she* reminded me of Isabella, save for having a face that was a little more rounded than Isabella's. Her dress was pushing the edge of what was socially acceptable for a young girl, a little bit too tight around her breasts. I had a feeling she'd be ordered to change the moment Uncle Malachi or Mother saw her. There was no way she'd be allowed to leave the mansion looking like *that*. She was lucky her mother had stayed on the estate, rather than returning to her family home.

"Tiring," I said, shortly. The maid brought me a plate loaded with bacon, eggs and potato cakes. "How are you?"

"Oh, just fine." Penny's smile—somehow—grew wider. "Auntie has been teaching me special spells."

I rolled my eyes. There was no shortage of rumours, exaggerations and outright lies about spells that could only be cast by women, spells that were passed from mother to daughter by word of mouth and never written down. I doubted they were *really* that special. It wasn't that hard to unravel a spell designed for women and adapt it so it could be cast by a man, if someone had crafted such a spell in the first place. Most spells were designed so that anyone could cast them, if they had the power.

"Don't mock," Penny said. "They're very interesting spells."

"I'll take your word for it," I muttered. If the spells were *that* secret, why wasn't Aunt Petal teaching her daughter? Mother was only a Rubén by marriage. "Are you looking forward to going back to school?"

"I'm going to be a dorm monitor," Penny said, excitedly. "I'll be in charge!"

"My sympathies." I swallowed a piece of bacon, then poured myself more coffee. "You'll find it hard work."

"Not me." Penny sounded confident. "I'll just tell them what to do and they'll fall in line."

I heard a crashing sound outside and turned, just in time to see Cousin Francis hurry into the room looking innocent. I *knew* he'd done something. No one looked *that* innocent in our family, not unless they'd done something Not Allowed. I glanced past him, half-expecting to see an angry adult bearing down on him. Uncle Davys was so strict he made my father look like Uncle Malachi. No wonder Cousin Francis was such a tearaway.

Francis closed the door and sat down, without waiting for the maid. "So…what's up with you?"

I studied him for a long moment. He was blond—like everyone else who shared the family bloodline—and devastatingly handsome, to the point where he was the envy of nearly everyone in my year. Girls adored him, boys wanted to *be* him. He was the kind of person to whom almost everything, from academic honours to sporting victories, came easily. I would have envied him myself, perhaps, if I hadn't already been betrothed. It was something of a puzzle that we actually got on.

"I'm taking the Challenge," I said, bluntly. "It's going to detract from my schooling."

"Oh, hard luck old bean." Francis affected an accent that made me want to grind my teeth. "Why not just throw the contest? Sit down and do nothing until time runs out."

"Father will kill me," I said. If I *did* lose my position as Heir Primus, Francis was on the short list of possible candidates to take my place. "I'm very attached to my life."

"And Catty won't be impressed if you just flunk out," Penny pointed out. "She'll think you're a..."

I glared at her. "Cat. Or Caitlyn. Not *Catty*. Treat her with some respect!"

"You'd better," Francis added. "Lady Caitlyn will be running this house, one day."

Penny flushed. "I...she won't have *time* to run the house. Not if she's forging every day."

That was a good point. I chose to ignore it. "You will treat her with respect," I said, stiffly. Penny was no longer a lowerclassman, and I could no longer give her lines, but I wasn't going to let that pass. "She is my betrothed, and she is going to be my wife, and you will not..."

Penny held up her hands in surrender. "I yield. I'm sorry."

"I think you should do some more toadying, maybe a little kowtowing," Francis said. "Then we'll know you're sincere."

"Oh, shut up," I told him. Father had taught me that it was dangerous to back someone into a corner, to force them to surrender or fight to the death. Penny had apologised. "Just let it go."

"Everyone was talking about your victory on the field," Penny said, quickly, to Francis. "What happened?"

Francis beamed so brightly that I *knew* he'd just been waiting for someone to ask that question. "Well, it was the last few seconds of the match," he said. "The scores were perfectly even. Half the team has been sent off for turning their opponents into footballs and tossing them in all directions. The referee was clearly biased against us, after someone who shall remain nameless had hexed him when his back was turned. And we had to win..."

He made sweeping gestures with his hands as he retold the story. "I took the ball from Gavin and ran forward, inching it towards the goal. The goalie got ready to kick it back and I hexed the ground under his feet, turning it to mush. He ended up flat on his back, looking like a right plonker. And I kicked the ball right into the goal. Goal! The crowd went wild. They cheered and cheered and cheered.

"The captain of the other team must have swallowed a dictionary. He shouted a whole list of insults at his goalie, calling him a nincompoop, a nitwit, a...somewhere in the middle, the referee yanked him off the pitch and put him on the bench. The crowd pointed and laughed. I took the opportunity to score a second goal! Goal! And then the time ran out. We won!"

I snorted. I didn't believe half of the story, although I was fairly sure that Francis *had* scored the winning goal. He wouldn't have tried to lie about something that could be easily checked. I knew people who would find his bragging so irritating, they'd happily spend hours trying to catch him in a lie. Francis wasn't really given to lying, in any case. He was more likely to bend the truth in creative directions.

"And you managed to win the game." Penny's eyes were shining. "What are you going to do for an encore?"

"There'll be matches this year," Francis said. "And afterwards"—for a moment, he looked lost—"I don't know."

I felt a flicker of sympathy, mingled with amusement. It was rare for someone to make a living through football. Uncle Davys would certainly refuse to let Francis *try*. He'd probably disown his son if Francis chose to waste his adulthood playing sports instead of studying magic. And yet...if anyone could make it, Francis could. He was irritating, at times, and easy to envy...but I didn't really hate him. No one did.

"I'm sure you'll be fine," I assured him.

"You never come to the matches," Francis pointed out. "How do you know?"

"Yeah," Penny said. "You ought to show your loyalty by attending the matches."

I shook my head, firmly. Team sports were bad enough when *playing*. I'd never liked them and I'd dropped gym class as soon as I could. But watching was worse. If I'd wanted to watch a bunch of idiots running around on a muddy field, I could have sat on the roof and watched the neighbourhood children at play.

"You could always watch the netball matches." Francis elbowed me. When I looked at him, he winked. "You never know what you might see."

I felt my cheeks redden. "I don't have time."

"Excuses, excuses," Francis said. "Just because you're betrothed doesn't mean you can't *look*."

"No," I said, more sharply than I'd intended. "But that doesn't mean I *should* look."

"I'm going to be a dorm monitor," Penny said, quickly. "Isn't it wonderful?"

I could have kissed her for changing the subject before it went somewhere—anywhere—I didn't want it to go. "I don't know. Is it wonderful?"

Francis smirked. "Do you think we should tell her? Or should we let her innocence be shattered like everyone else?"

Penny scowled at him. "What do you mean?"

"Well," Francis said. "If youth and beauty wishes an education from old age and beauty..."

"You're two years older than me, not two decades," Penny snapped. "You're not even *two* years older than me! More like nineteen months!"

"And yet, I look down at you from my lofty perch." Francis stood and made a show of looking down his nose at her. "So young, so tender, so ignorant..."

Penny pointed a finger at him. I sensed a spell building under her skin. "Talk."

Francis, just for a second, looked as if he was going to dare her to hex him. I hoped she'd have enough sense not to try. Francis was much stronger and far more experienced than she was—I supposed his cheating on the football field had given him some useful skills after all—but whoever won, we'd all catch it from our parents. Mother would be furious if we destroyed the breakfast room. I couldn't see Uncle Davys or Uncle Malachi taking it lightly either.

"It's really very simple." Francis affected an unconcerned drawl, but I could see him readying a shield charm under the table. "You think you're going to sleep easy, in a dorm full of brats who've probably never spent a night away from home? Some of them will want their mummies. Some will want their teddy bears. Some will want you to do their homework for them... and believe me, you're the one who will get into trouble if they don't do their homework. The ones who come from powerful families will sneer at you, like this"—he affected a truly awful sneer—"and the scholarship kids will need to be taught how to behave before they mortally offend someone with their lack of manners."

He smiled. "And guess who gets to *teach* them?"

Penny lowered her hand. "I'll find others who can teach them."

"It's *your* job," Francis jibed. "If you ask Akin's friend—you know, the pretty redhead—to teach them, *she'll* get the credit. Not you. You'll get pointed questions about why you couldn't do your job, followed by being marked down. You won't become Head Girl, for sure."

"Pretty redhead?" Penny eyed Francis, sardonically. "I thought you were dating Dinah."

Francis's face fell. "Dinah dumped me at the end of last term," he said. "She wanted...well, she wanted..."

"Someone who cared for her?" Penny stuck out her tongue. "Or someone who could actually keep his eyes to himself?"

I kept my *thoughts* to myself. It wasn't uncommon for upperclassmen to date, but...it was easy to get into real trouble. My father had warned me, when I'd gone into the upper years, that I had to be careful. I was betrothed. Anything I did wouldn't just reflect badly on me and my family. It would reflect badly on Cat as well.

"She wanted a betrothal before she...well, before she'd accept my suit." Francis reddened. "And that wasn't in the cards."

"I see," Penny said, drawing out the words. "How...*charming*."

I nodded in agreement. Francis was a catch, I supposed, but...Dinah came from a good family. She wouldn't be inclined to get close unless there was a formal betrothal contact, a promise of marriage...I felt a flicker of sympathy for both of them. It was definitely easier to have a betrothed already. But then, if I'd disliked Cat, it would have become a nightmare very quickly.

"So I'm free," Francis said. "Hurrah! No ball and chain for me!"

Penny pulled a notepad out of her dress pocket. "Note to self," she said, as she pretended to write. "Warn all girls to stay away from Francis."

"Oh, go off and boil your head." Francis elbowed me. "You want to be my wingman? We're allowed to go out of the school this year, you know."

I lifted an eyebrow. "And you haven't been sneaking out every night since we became upperclassmen?"

"Maybe not every night," Francis said. "Every second night, perhaps."

The door opened before he could continue. I looked up and saw the butler enter the room, carrying a silver tray. A blue envelope rested on the tray, addressed to me. I took it, nodded my thanks and turned it over and over in my hands. The back was covered with Jude's logo, just like the books.

"Wow," Penny said. "I got one of those. You're going to be a dorm monitor too?"

"I can't see it happening," Francis said. "He could be a sports monitor, but..."

"No." I opened the envelope, carefully. "No one would appoint *me* sports monitor."

"Nah," Francis agreed. "You'd never do anything with the role."

I didn't bother to deny it. Instead, I pulled out the letter. It was short, straight to the point. I would have been impressed if it hadn't been bad news.

"I'm Head Boy," I said.

"Hah, hah, very funny," Francis said. He produced a screeching sound that *might* have been a laugh, if someone used their imagination. A great deal of their imagination. "The very thought..."

I offered him the letter. "Read for yourself."

Francis took it, then pretended to gulp. "Well, so long Jude's. It was nice knowing you—and the pile of rubble you become."

Penny narrowed her eyes. "How did *you* get the job?"

"Oh, the usual," Francis said. "A few thousand crowns to the Triad, a few thousand more to the Castellan, a couple of hundred to the Magisters, a bottle of cheap rotgut to the poor bugger who's in charge of cleaning the school..."

"That isn't fair," Penny protested.

Francis winked at me. "You can give her lines, you know? And there aren't any limits. You could make her write out a *billion* lines."

"I never wanted the job," I said, as Penny paled. "And I..."

"Tough cheese, dear boy," Francis said. "You'll just have to enjoy it. Or do it so badly your father puts you out of everyone else's misery."

It was a line that deserved a snappy response, something that would put him firmly in his place. Isabella would have thought of one, I was sure. But I didn't.

"Oh, shut up," I said.

CHAPTER

FIVE

My mother was delighted when I showed her the letter, so delighted that she almost convinced me *she* believed I'd become Head Boy though merit, rather than Father bribing all and sundry to get me the post. She promptly ordered the staff to start preparing a family banquet, loudly bemoaning the fact that there wasn't time to invite half the city. I wasn't too bothered, even though I would have liked to see Cat before I went back to school. It was a lot easier to talk to her when we weren't being chaperoned by adults who listened carefully to whatever we had to say.

And then report it back to both sets of parents, I reminded myself, as I packed my trunk for school. *Whatever we say, they'll hear.*

I groaned at the thought, then finished packing. It hadn't been easy to convince Mother to let me do my own packing, rather than leaving it to the maids. She'd only relented after I'd become an upperclassman, although she *had* insisted on giving me a list of things to pack and to check it twice. I couldn't help thinking she was worrying over nothing. Seven pairs of black trousers, seven black jackets, seven white shirts, seven pairs of black socks and black underwear…and a single, neatly tailored suit for special events. It wasn't as if I *needed* seven pairs of everything. Besides, I didn't attend many formal dances. Being betrothed, I could only attend if my betrothed *also* attended. And Cat and I had grown very ingenious, over the years, at coming up with excuses for one or both of us not to attend.

Francis tapped on my door, an hour before the banquet. "Guess what I got?"

"An offer of marriage from Sonia Graceland?" It was mean-spirited, but I couldn't resist. The poor girl had been on the marriage market for so long that her odds of making a good match were low. I'd heard too many of my relatives gossiping about her. Sonia could pass for forty-three, apparently, with the light behind her. "Or something more serious?"

"I made Sports *Captain*," Francis said. He waved a letter under my nose. "Read it and weep!"

"Those poor sporty fools," I said. "Sports Captain, huh? How many people do you think Uncle Davys bribed to get you *that* slot?"

Francis coloured. "I earned it myself."

"Oh, dear," I said. "They *really* must be scraping the bottom of the barrel."

"You know perfectly well I earned it," Francis snapped. "Besides, who else *could* they pick?"

I shrugged. Francis might be right. He *was* captain of two different teams—football and dodgeball—and…well, I had to admit he'd led both teams to victory. They wouldn't have tolerated an incompetent in his place, whatever his connections. I could easily see Francis being appointed Sports Captain purely on merit. I just didn't believe it.

"Good luck," I said. "Is it true the Sports Captain gets ritually debagged if his team loses?"

Francis snapped his fingers. Sparks darted in all directions. "I'll make anyone who tries very sorry."

I slammed my trunk closed, placed a couple of locking charms on the latch and pushed it into place for the manservants to collect, later in the day. Mother *might* insist on checking—she still talked to me as though I was a little boy, even though I was nearly an adult—but I had no doubt she could unlock and replace the charms for herself, if she wanted. Besides, I hadn't put anything *too* personal in the trunk. *That* was reserved for my carryall.

"Don't forget to pack your supplies for the Challenge," Francis said. "You could bring anything you wanted."

"A guaranteed win would be nice," I said, dryly. The dinner bell rang, summoning us to the dining hall. "But I don't know how to pack that."

I checked my appearance in the mirror, making sure I looked as presentable as possible, then headed to the door. If there was one advantage to the banquet being held at such short notice, it was that I wasn't expected to don my finest clothes. Only *family* would see me. I could let my hair down, if only metaphorically. The thought made me snort. If Penny or Cat let their hair down in public, before they were declared adults, it would be a major scandal.

Francis fell into place beside me as we walked down the stairs. "Any thoughts on strategy yet?"

"None." I sighed. "I don't even know what we have to *do*."

"Win." Francis elbowed me. "That's all you have to do."

I snorted, rudely. Francis was entirely correct, but…I put the thought aside as we walked into the dining room. It was a very light gathering for a family banquet. Only forty-seven adults and nineteen children, ranging from five to seventeen. I was surprised when Mother pointed to a seat at the adult table, right next to my parents and Uncle Davys. I was being considered an adult? Even discovering that Francis had a chair right next to mine wasn't enough to dull my delight. I'd been too old for the children's table for years.

"Penny looks green with envy," Francis said, in a whisper that was designed to carry. "She's still trapped with the toddlers."

Uncle Davys gave him a sharp look that would have quelled *me* in an instant. Francis puffed up, looking ready to argue with his father in public. I nudged him, quickly. If Francis spoilt the banquet, Mother would be furious. Uncle Davys might have to banish his son from the mansion. Forget treason and betrayal. Ruining a family banquet was unforgivable. My eyes found the empty chair, on the other side of the table; I sighed, feeling a pang of bitter regret. Isabella should be sitting there…I wondered, grimly, where she was. She wouldn't have received my letter yet.

Father called the banqueters to order and then made a short speech, praising me for being appointed Head Boy. I did my best to look modest, convinced that *everyone* in the room knew I hadn't earned the post. Beside me, Francis waved cheerfully when his name was mentioned. I tried not to roll my eyes. Sports Captain wasn't a minor position—it wasn't as if he'd been appointed ink monitor—but it wasn't a gateway to greater things. Unless…perhaps Francis could make it a gateway. He certainly had the wit to succeed.

The crowd drank to my health, then started to eat. Mother—perhaps wisely—had ordered that neither Francis nor I were to be offered alcohol, even though we *were* being treated as adults. I didn't really blame her. The wine was strong and…I didn't want to make a fool of myself in public. My one encounter with alcohol had been enough to convince me that I had no head for wine. Father had promised he'd teach me how to be a wine snob, when I left school, but I wasn't looking forward to it. I'd sooner talk about forging, if I had to make pointless conversation with strangers. At least I might be able to make intelligent conversation.

Auntie Danni caught my eye as we moved on to the second course. "So, when do you think you'll be an adult?"

I flushed. I knew what she meant. When would Cat and I be getting married? I looked down at the table, trying not to show my embarrassment. I'd be declared an adult soon, perhaps as soon as I left school. Cat…I wondered, suddenly, when *she'd* be declared an adult. It wouldn't be long for her, either. Both sets of parents were running out of excuses to delay matters.

"I don't know," I said. "It depends on my parents."

I heard the same question, time and time again, as the banquet wore on. I'd known the adults engaged in a *lot* of pointless chatter, but I'd never really grasped that the pointless chatter could hide conversational attacks and verbal manipulations. I felt naked and unprotected, convinced that whatever I said would wind up being used against me. I honestly didn't know why my father put up with it. Or why Isabella *wanted* it. My life would be so much easier if I served an apprenticeship, then set up shop as a forger. A skilled forger—and I knew, without false modesty, that I *was* a skilled forger—could make a very good living.

It was almost a relief when the banquet finally came to an end. Penny, Francis and I were sent upstairs to shower and change into our travelling clothes, while the adults headed into the smoking room for after-dinner drinks and conversations. Father had told me that a great many decisions were made in smoke-filled rooms, between movers and shakers of both genders; now, I believed it. A banquet wasn't *just* an excuse for a good time. Father and his peers would use the banquet as a cover for private chats and deal-making.

I showered, changed, picked up my carryall and knocked on Francis's door. "You decent?"

"No, but come in anyway," Francis called. "Ready to go?"

"Yeah." I pushed open the door and stepped inside. Francis's rooms were smaller than mine, but not by much. "You?"

"Ready," Francis said. He snorted. "We could just walk to school, you know."

I nodded. It wouldn't be *that* long a walk, even if night was starting to fall. We wouldn't be in any danger, but…tradition was tradition, not to be gainsaid by mere mortals. We were to drive to school in a carriage, wearing travelling clothes rather than school uniforms…I rolled my eyes. The cloak I wore over my suit felt uncomfortably warm. I muttered a spell to cool myself as Francis led the way downstairs. Our trunks were already in the carriage.

Penny met us at the bottom of the stairs, wearing a long cloak over a dark blue outfit. She didn't look pleased, but kept whatever was bothering her to herself. I nodded to her and led the way out the door. The carriage was already waiting in the driveway, a pair of manservants standing beside it. They opened the door as we approached, pulling down a tiny staircase to allow Penny to board without damaging her dress. I felt a flicker of sympathy. Her dresses had made it hard for her to take part in our childhood games.

The carriage rattled into life as soon as we took our seats. I leaned back in my chair, silently willing the other two to remain silent while we drove to school. The others, for a wonder, kept their mouths shut. They probably felt the same mixture of anticipation and fear that *I* did. The carriage rumbled over the bridge to South Shallot—I wanted to peer down at the boats on the river—and headed onwards. Outside, I heard people shouting and cheering. Shallot was the city that never slept.

"I want to be on the netball team," Penny said, suddenly. "You can do that for me, can't you?"

Francis smiled. "What's it worth?"

Penny coloured. "Francis!"

"Be nice," I said, reprovingly. As Sports Captain, Francis had the final say on who played in competition matches. "You want the best players on your teams, don't you?"

"Ah, but is she the best?" Francis smirked. "If she fumbles a ball…"

I pushed back the curtain and stuck my head out the window as Francis and Penny argued. Jude's was just coming into view, a cluster of buildings that had long-since been merged into one giant structure. Jude's had been expanding for years, according to the histories; one day, I thought, it would eventually absorb the whole city. And yet, I knew there were entire sections that had been abandoned, boarded up and eventually allowed to fall into disuse. I'd spent many happy hours exploring them with my friends.

The wards tingled as the carriage passed through the gate and headed up towards the main entrance. The walls were low, but were topped with steel spikes and charmed devices to present a challenge to any student who wanted to sneak out for a night on the town. It was traditional for upperclassmen to make their way through the wards, even students who had the right to come and go as they pleased. Francis had even boasted of giving a porter a black eye. I suspected he was telling the truth. Tradition *also* dictated that a student who managed to escape the porters was allowed to go free.

"And we're back," Francis said. The carriage rattled to a halt. "You know what the students from Roanoke said about Jude's?"

I didn't, but I could guess. I'd seen Roanoke—and a couple of other schools—and they'd been magnificent, towering buildings with more grandeur than a Great House. Jude's, by contrast, looked more than a little ramshackle, as if the school had no real pride in itself. But I wouldn't have traded Jude's for anywhere. There was something about the slapdash nature of the building that appealed to me. I wasn't sure what. A slapdash approach to forgery—or any branch of magic, really—was asking for serious injury or death.

A porter came up to us as we disembarked and looked at Penny. "You are...?"

"Penelope Rubén," Penny said. "I'm..."

"In fifth-year," the porter said. "Proceed at once to your dorm and remain there until breakfast."

Penny flushed angrily, but the porter ignored her. "You two are to make your way to the seventh-year suites," he said, turning to me and Francis. "Your trunks will be sent along in due course."

"And mine?" Penny didn't react well to being dismissed. "What about...?"

"You're still here?" The porter gave her a sharp look. "One demerit for not following orders and one demerit for being cheeky."

Penny glared at him, then turned and marched to the entrance. I tried not to laugh. Penny was an upperclassman now, but there was still a strict social hierarchy. She was probably the lowest-ranking student right now, at least until the lowerclassmen arrived tomorrow. And yet...I shook my head, hoisted my carryall over my shoulder and headed towards the entrance myself. Behind me, I heard the porter barking orders to his staff. They'd move the trunks—Penny's too—to the dorms before we had a chance to miss them.

"Ah, poor Penny," Francis said. "I knew her."

"She isn't going to be killed," I pointed out. Two demerits on the first day were bad, but I'd had worse. I was sure Penny had had worse too. "She'll get over it."

Jude's felt...*odd* as we made our way up the chairs. The corridors felt *empty*, even though I could hear faint sounds in the distance. The majority of the upperclassmen had either already arrived or would join us tomorrow, accompanying their siblings amongst the lowerclassmen. I hoped they'd remember to keep their distance once they reached school. Upperclassmen and lowerclassmen didn't socialise, even if they were siblings. It was social death to be seen with someone significantly younger. Last year, I'd had to pretend I didn't know Penny when she'd been given detention.

Another porter met us at the top of the stairs. "The Head Boy and Head Girl share the princely suite," he said, pointing to a gold-edged door at the near end of the corridor. "The Sports Captain gets a room of his own."

"Hard luck," Francis said, cheerfully. He leaned closer to whisper. "Do you share the same..."

"Shut up," I hissed. I didn't know if the porter could give demerits to *us* and I didn't want to find out the hard way. And I *really* didn't want rumours getting around. "You..."

The porter cleared his throat. "You're expected to report for breakfast at nine o'clock tomorrow, then attend upon the Castellan in his outer office at eleven."

"Nine o'clock," Francis said. "They're letting us sleep in."

"Just you wait," I muttered. Upperclassmen had to set their own alarm spells. "We'll be getting up at seven the rest of the year."

The porter shrugged, then motioned for us to walk past him. I felt the wards crackling as I led the way down the corridor, strong enough to make it clear that this was upperclassmen territory, yet too weak to actually keep lowerclassmen out. It made sense, I supposed. The Head Boy's suite was also his office, his place of work. A lowerclassman might have to visit without an invitation. I wasn't allowed, I guessed, to bar the outer door.

Francis stopped in front of his door and glanced at me. "See you tomorrow?"

"Yeah," I said. "Sure."

I hurried down the corridor and stopped outside the Head Boy's suite. A handful of charms rested on top of the wood, ranging from a basic locking charm to a complex spell designed to prevent scrying. I puzzled over it for a moment, then decided there would probably be students who'd want to spy on the Head Boy. They'd get into awful trouble if they were caught—a boy had been expelled for trying to scry the female changing room—but I knew that probably wouldn't stop them. The students were ambitious. They wouldn't have come to Jude's if they weren't.

The door opened when I pressed my hand against the wood, the charms retreating back into the aether. I pushed the door wide open and surveyed the room. It was strange, an odd mixture of homey and official. Two large wooden desks were placed against the wall, with solid wooden chairs; a pair of sofas had been placed in one corner…it reminded me of my father's office. And yet, it was mine. Mine and…

Alana was sitting on one of the sofas. "Well, hello," she said. Her voice was very calm. "Come on in."

CHAPTER
SIX

I felt my heart begin to pound. "Hello."

Alana sat upright, crossing her long legs. "Close the door and come on in," she said, a deadpan expression on her face. "We have to chat."

I pushed the door closed behind me, then placed my carryall against the wall. I liked Cat—I missed Cat—but I'd always been wary of her sister. Alana had grown up a lot, in the years since the House War, yet she remained sharp-tongued, devilishly clever and magically powerful, always willing to avenge slights with hexes and even borderline curses. Cat had told me enough about her childhood to ensure that I never wanted to turn my back on her sister. And yet...now we had to share a suite?

"I suppose we do," I said. The Head Boy and Girl were exempt from society's rules about fraternisation, as long as they were careful. I was lucky she was my prospective sister-in-law. "What do we have to talk about?"

I sat down on the sofa and studied her for a long moment. Alana was tall for a girl, with very dark skin and long dark hair bound up in a single loose braid that looked as if it were threatening to come undone at any moment. She was pushing the edges of acceptability, for a girl of her age, but I doubted anyone would say anything. She *was* her family's Heir Primus, after all, and I would be very surprised if her hair *did* come down in public. Alana was more than skilled enough to make sure it remained firmly in place.

She and Cat—and Bella, the third triplet—were fraternal siblings, but… they didn't really *look* alike. Alana's face was sharper, her eyes were darker… I thought. They lacked the warmth of Cat's eyes. And her black dress was just a *little* too tight, too daring. Cat had never worn anything like it, even when—particularly when—we'd been chaperoned. Alana was definitely pushing the limits as far as they would go. I wondered, absently, what her parents had said about it.

"You're Head Boy." Alana shot me a wink. Her voice was sardonic. "Congratulations. I'm sure you earned it."

"And you're Head Girl," I pointed out. "I'm sure you earned it too."

"Well, *quite*." Alana smiled, revealing a set of very white teeth. "I'm sure we *both* earned it."

I yawned, suddenly. "Are we going to spend the rest of the evening lying to each other about what we *earned*?"

"Why not?" Alana managed an elaborate shrug. "It's what all the *important* people do."

Isabella would probably have agreed, I thought. *And she would have taken part too.*

Alana rested her hands on her knees. "Let us be brutally honest. We don't like each other very much. Your family and mine have been enemies for billions upon billions of years."

"A gross exaggeration," I said.

"Whatever." Alana shrugged, again. "That said, on one hand, you are betrothed to my sister and so I have to be nice to you. Or at least *polite* to you. And, on the other hand, we have a shared responsibility. We have to be polite to each other."

"I can do that," I said. Mother had taught me how to cut someone dead without ever stepping outside the bounds of good taste. "And…"

Alana held up a single dark hand. "And, as you must be aware, the alliance between our families is uniting others against it. You and I…will probably be pressured to do something stupid that will be used to harm our families. It is *important* that we at least pretend to get along."

She smiled. A true smile. For a moment, I could truly believe that Cat and Alana were sisters. "All you have to do, if you care about the alliance, is do everything I say."

I snorted, dryly. "I have a better idea. You do everything *I* say."

Alana giggled. "Fat chance. But you see the point? In private, we can disagree as much as we like. But in public, we have to pose a united front. No hexing or undermining where the baddies can see us."

"Agreed," I said. She was right, as much as I hated to admit it. We were allies, forced together by circumstances and familial manoeuvring. "In public, we will be the best of friends."

"That won't be easy," Alana said. "We're also rivals. You're taking the Challenge, are you not? So am I."

"Ouch," I said. I could have kicked myself. *That* had never crossed my mind...and it should have done. A girl as ambitious as Alana would take the Challenge. Of *course* she would take the Challenge. No one, not even her father, could have forbidden it. "So, we're rivals too?"

"Yeah." Alana looked pensive, just for a second. "I can't join your team and you can't join mine."

"I know," I said. Neither of us could take a subordinate position. We would be team leaders, or nothing. "I trust you'll excuse me if I don't wish you good luck?"

"I don't need luck," Alana said. "And I have plans."

She leaned back against the sofa. "We can cooperate, as Head Boy and Head Girl. Have you seen your rooms?"

I shook my head. "I've only just arrived."

"The rooms are identical," Alana said. "You have a large bed and a bathroom...you can use your room for whatever you like, as long as you don't disturb me. I won't rat you out if you don't rat *me* out. The main room"—she indicated the office with a wave of her hand—"and the private kitchen are shared. Clean up your mess, keep control of your guests and I won't complain."

"Likewise," I said. Alana had clearly put some thought into sharing a suite. I wished I'd had the foresight to do the same. "If we're supposed to use this space as an office, we'll just have to share it."

"Quite." Alana shrugged. "Pick a desk, any desk. I've already chosen my room."

"Either one," I said. "Now, if you don't mind…"

Alana held up a hand. "Are you still carrying the sword?"

I nodded, shortly. "I take it everywhere."

"May I see it?" Alana cocked her head. "I won't touch."

Her eyes opened wide as I reached back and drew the blade from the scabbard. It glowed faintly in my hand. I could *feel* the sword yearning to be used, demanding to be tested…I'd discovered, over the years, that it could cut through wards as if they weren't there and guide my hands as I fenced with blademasters. It was too dangerous to use for practice duels, I'd been told. The sword wanted to *win*.

"Impressive," Alana said. She leaned forward. "How do you carry it? Doesn't it dig into your back?"

"It's barely there," I said. The scabbard was an Object of Power, a present from Cat. I didn't pretend to understand how it worked. The sword wasn't just hidden, it was…practically intangible until I touched the hilt. I could press my back against the chair and feel nothing, thanks to the magic. And yet, I could never quite forget it was there. "Magic."

Alana smiled, but it didn't quite touch her eyes. "Cat's work?"

"Yeah." I nodded. "She forged it for me."

"You'd better get her something *very* good for her birthday," Alana said. I thought I caught a hint of regret in her voice. "And not the formalised gift either."

I shrugged. Mother had supervised the formal gift-giving, insisting that—as my betrothed—Cat was *not* to be subjected to *my* taste in presents.

She'd made me give my betrothed a whole string of birthday gifts, ranging from the faintly absurd to the inappropriate. My private gifts had been much more personal, I thought. Cat clearly felt the same way. Her private gifts had actually been *useful*.

"I'll try," I said. "Has she complained?"

"No." Alana smiled. "But I'll let you know if she does."

There was a knock on the door. I stood and opened it. A pair of porters were waiting outside, with our trunks. A familiar face stood behind them. I smiled and stepped to one side to allow them to enter. I hadn't seen much of Rose over the summer, but she hadn't changed much. Her long red hair, tied in a neat braid, hung down over a white dress that managed to be both simple and elegant. Cat's mother had done wonders for Rose's sense of style.

"Akin," Rose said. She glanced at Alana. "And Alana…"

"Ah, the chaperone," Alana said. "Cat's not here, I'm afraid."

Rose blushed. I looked away, in the hope that neither of the girls would see me blushing too. Rose had been our chaperone, but she'd been a very *understanding* chaperone, always willing to look away at the right times. Not that Cat and I had done very much, of course. A handful of kisses…it wasn't really that bad. Was it?

"It's good to see you again," Rose said, as the porters placed the trunks in our room and departed without a word. "I've missed you."

"I missed you too," I said, honestly. I liked Rose, if only because she didn't have a secret agenda. Everyone else I knew had ambitions, even the younger kids. Rose just wanted to be a Healer. And she'd make it, too. Patronage from both our families would see that she had all the opportunities in the world. "What were you doing all summer?"

"Studying with us," Alana said. She motioned for Rose to sit next to her. "And learning all sorts of interesting spells."

"Lady Aguirre is a good teacher." Rose sat, as far from Alana as she could while sharing the same sofa. "And she told me all sorts of things."

"Including some spells that are normally kept within the family," Alana said. "I was quite surprised."

I wasn't. Rose was Cat's best friend, as well as a client of two families. Cat's mother had excellent reason to teach Rose a handful of spells, even if they *were* supposed to remain in the family. Rose was practically *part* of the family. I wondered, idly, what my own mother had taught Rose. I'd seen them chatting together, when Rose had visited the mansion. It was a shame she couldn't stay with us.

"They were very *interesting* spells," Rose said. She crossed her legs. "I also heard something from Lord Aguirre, something that…are you taking the Challenge?"

"So it seems," I said, dryly. *Rose* knew about the Challenge? I was surprised. She'd never struck me as particularly sporty. She certainly hadn't wasted her time playing netball when she'd been a lowerclassman. "I wasn't given a choice."

"It *is* very important," Alana pointed out. "And that is why I will be Wizard Regnant."

"Says you," I said, without heat. "What happens if you lose?"

"I won't lose," Alana said.

Rose cleared her throat. "I understand you have to form a team," she said. "Cat…Cat suggested I should join."

I blinked in surprise. Cat had never liked sports either, although—in her case—she couldn't play properly. She'd be unable to hex the other players—or keep herself from being hexed, right from the start. She *could* produce Objects of Power to even the odds, but…I had a feeling they'd be confiscated. There were *rules* against using Objects and Devices of Power on the playing fields. I'd never seen the point, personally. The players had few qualms about bending the rules in order to win.

"She did?" I knew I sounded stupid. "I…"

"She did," Rose confirmed. "And I think I could take part…"

"You can't." Alana was trying to sound regretful, but she wasn't succeeding. "You can't take part in the contest."

Rose gave her a sharp look. "Why not?"

I echoed her. "Why not?"

Alana met my eyes. "Rose is a client of both houses," she said. "By competing against me, she is taking sides against my house...mortally offending one of her patrons. And you know what that will do for her reputation."

Rose looked from Alana to me and back again. "That's not true..."

"It is," Alana said. "Akin?"

I forced myself to think. Father had drummed it into my head, time and time again, that patrons and clients had certain responsibilities to each other. A patron was supposed to assist his client, in exchange for support and obedience. A patron and a client could break up, amiably enough, and no one would think less of either of them, but outright betrayal...I cursed under my breath, using a word Mother would have slapped me for even *knowing*, let alone saying in front of two young ladies. Alana was right. Rose couldn't join my team. She couldn't join *either* team. It would be seen as a betrayal.

Uncle Joaquin might be fine with it, I thought. *Rose could certainly ask his permission to play on my team. But even if he said yes, it would destroy her reputation as a reliable client...*

"It's true," I said, slowly. "You can't join my team. Any team."

"Even mine," Alana said. This time, she actually sounded regretful. "You'll just have to sit on the sidelines and cheer loudly."

"If they let us cheer," Rose said. "You know there's no actual description of the Challenge itself? Nothing written down, as far as I can tell."

I nodded. "Just a handful of vague hints," I agreed. "Nothing actually *useful*."

Alana stood. "Perhaps they want us to be ready for anything," she said. "Or maybe they just want to test our skill at improvising."

"Or maybe they just make the rules up as they go along," I said. I'd played *that* game as a child, although I'd quickly grown bored of it. "We might get told, an hour before we start, that all of our plans and preparations were worse than useless."

"Maybe." Alana sounded disturbed. "But that doesn't make sense, does it?"

"Why not?" Rose grinned. It made her look stunning. "You can't expect the world to play by the rules, can you? The rules can be rewritten. On the spot, if necessary."

"Then there would be no point to the Challenge," Alana insisted. "How could we prove ourselves as…well, *anything*…if the rules change at will? We might as well get onto the field to play netball, then get told we're going to play football instead."

Francis would be pleased, I thought. *He always said netball was a game for girls.*

But I took her point. The Challenge would be pointless if it didn't map onto the patron-client game we'd be expected to play as adults. It was a test of one's ability to build a team, to make alliances and work out the best way to make *use* of one's teammates…I felt a flash of regret that Rose couldn't join me. She might lack family connections—blood connections, at least—but she had a hard core of common sense. Francis and Penny and many others I knew lacked it. Francis was more interested in playing games than preparing himself for the future.

"We'll see," I said. "The Castellan wants to see us tomorrow, doesn't he?"

"Yeah," Alana said. "He'll tell us what he wants us to know."

And leave us to figure out the rest for ourselves, I thought.

"I'm sorry," Rose said, looking at me. "I thought it could help…"

"Don't worry about it," I said. I thought, briefly, about writing to Uncle Joaquin anyway, then dismissed the idea. Whatever he said, whatever he did…it wouldn't matter. Rose would be blighted anyway. "But thanks for offering."

"I'm sorry too," Alana said.

"I bet you are," Rose snapped.

She stood, smoothing down her dress. "It's late," she said. "And we have to be up early tomorrow."

"Not *that* early," Alana objected. "We're getting a late breakfast."

"And then we have to study," Rose pointed out. "Our *real* classes start on Tuesday, remember?"

"I won't forget," I assured her. "And I'll see you tomorrow."

Rose left the room, closing the door behind her. I watched her go, then turned to look at Alana. She was looking half-amused, half-apologetic. I wondered, sourly, if she'd really set out to do Rose a favour...or simply throw sand in my gears. It could easily be both. She'd managed to maintain a level of plausible deniability...I would have been impressed, if it hadn't been aimed at me. Uncle Joaquin's successor was devious, cunning...she'd pulled off a coup and even *I* had to thank her for it.

"Bedtime," I said, firmly. "See you tomorrow?"

"Of course," Alana said. "Take a look around before you go to bed."

I peered into the kitchen and smiled. There was a kettle, a stove, a food preserver...I couldn't cook anything more complex than scrambled eggs and toast, but I wasn't much of a cook anyway. A collection of jars held everything from tea leaves and coffee grains to sugar and cereal. I nodded to myself, then picked up my carryall and stepped into my bedroom. It was huge, easily large enough for two or three people. The bed alone was massive.

And the bathroom could easily have come from home, I thought. I had a bath, as well as a shower and a washbasin. A mirror hung on the wall, charmed to show my reflection from any angle. *They're treating us well...*

I sobered. The room came with a price, one I had to pay. I was Head Boy—and I had to be a *good* Head Boy. If I failed, if I screwed up, my family would be shamed. Father would be furious. And how could I blame him?

Anything for the family, I reminded myself, as I undressed and clambered into bed. It was soft and warm, certainly when compared to my old dorm mattresses.

Anything at all.

CHAPTER
SEVEN

"So." Francis sidled up to me as I loaded my plate with bacon and eggs. "Did you have a good night?"

"It was a comfortable mattress," I assured him. I knew what he meant, but I wasn't going to rise to the bait. "And I would have overslept, if I hadn't set an alarm spell."

"You know what I mean," Francis said. "Did you have fun?"

"We're in separate bedrooms," I said, tiredly. If Alana overheard him, Francis was going to have a miserable year. "And you should know better than to suggest otherwise."

Francis snickered. "Just a joke," he said. He took a plate for himself, then followed me to the table. "You should see the humour in it."

I rubbed my eyes. "I'm sure I could see the humour in turning you into a frog, if I tried. Or an earthworm."

"I'm sure you could too," Francis said. He looked around the room. "I'm sure there are more than a dozen of us, you know?"

"They're still in bed," I hazarded. I'd set my alarm, but others—who normally relied on parents or maids to wake them—might have forgotten. Or perhaps they just didn't feel like eating. They were going to bitterly regret that, later in the day. "Does it matter?"

"You never know," Francis said. "The ones who get up early might be the ones to beat."

I surveyed the room for a moment. There was no sign of Alana or Rose, but Bella—Cat's sibling—was sitting at a table, munching her way through an immense plate of bacon and eggs. She had her back to me, so I didn't wave. Bella was nice, but in a vague kind of way. Cat had said that Bella was strong in magic, yet too lazy to *really* aim for greatness. Beside her, I saw a pair of clients. The nasty part of me wondered if they were doing Bella's homework.

"Maybe," I said. "You got up too early, didn't you?"

"I already took a look at the sports hall," Francis said. "This year is going to be *great*."

I shrugged and started to eat. The bacon tasted fine, but the eggs were a little overdone. The cooks needed to turn out as many as they could, rather than cooking them to perfection…I shrugged and ate them anyway. Rose had made it clear that the simple breakfasts we endured at Jude's were the height of luxury, compared to breakfasts in peasant villages and sailing ships. I supposed she was right. I didn't have to walk very far to see poverty. The people who lived in Water Shallot rarely had two crowns to rub together.

"I have a different question," Francis said. He leaned forward so he could stage-whisper in my ear. "Have you made any progress on picking out a team?"

"No." I shook my head, bitterly. "Rose can't join, and…"

"Too bad," Francis said. "It would have been lovely to have her with us." I blinked. "Us?"

"I'm joining you," Francis said. "Did you think I was going to let you face the Challenge alone?"

"I didn't think about it," I admitted. In hindsight, I should have asked. "Did your father give his blessing?"

Francis snorted. "I could do everything my father wants, so perfectly that even *he* couldn't find fault, and you know what? He'd find fault anyway. I haven't bothered to ask him. If I volunteer, and you accept, he can't yank me out."

I nodded, slowly. Francis wasn't a declared adult, not yet, but…he was too old to be unceremoniously yanked out of a team. It would be the clearest possible demonstration of his father's lack of regard for him. Uncle Davys had enemies. They wouldn't hesitate to take note. Crown Prince Henry wasn't the only son who'd turned on his father. He was merely the one unfortunate enough to be a prince when it all came apart.

"I'd be happy to have you," I told him. I wasn't lying. Francis and I were very different, but I'd never doubted his nerve. I'd once watched him pick his way through a series of wards, any one of which would have done him serious injury if he'd tripped it. "And that means I just need eight others…"

"I don't think you need the full ten," Francis said. "But you have to be careful who you pick. I think a lot of upperclassmen are either patrons or clients already."

I felt my heart sink. Isabella was good at making friends and building networks. Me? Not so much. I was on cordial terms with most of my fellows, but…I wasn't *that* close to any of them. And I hadn't even been *trying* to build a patronage network. I'd assumed it would come to me, automatically, when I succeeded my father. I'd been a bloody idiot.

"I'll ask around," Francis assured me. "It doesn't matter if *I* get egg on my face."

He grinned. "Just don't ask Dinah. She hates me."

"She's a smart girl," I said. "But I think she's a Bolingbroke client."

I slowly ate my breakfast, watching as the dining hall filled with upperclassmen. Penny stepped into the room, accompanied by two of her friends. She shot a glance in my direction, but otherwise ignored me. I understood. In public, we didn't know each other. Behind her, I saw a handful of familiar faces; Alana, Rose, Clarian Bolingbroke…and Lindsey, the only other betrothed girl I knew. Alana seemed to be dominating the group, of course. I wondered, sourly, just how many of her followers were her clients.

"She's pretty," Francis said. I thought he was talking about Alana. "Lucky so-and-so."

"She'll turn you into a frog if you make even the *slightest* hint of an improper suggestion to her," I said, turning back to my food. "And if she does, don't expect me to undo the spell."

"That's alright." Francis made a show of puffing up his chest. "I like a challenge."

I finished my breakfast without incident, then checked the clock. There was still an hour to go before we saw the Castellan, so we wandered the school and checked out the library. It was closed. Francis laughed at my stunned face, then pointed out that the librarian was probably still on holiday. She wore herself out, each term, trying not to scream at users who damaged books. Rumour had it she'd *killed* a student who'd dropped a book in the toilet. I was fairly sure it wasn't true.

"We can see the sports field instead," Francis said. "Coming?"

I shrugged and followed him towards the east side of the school. I'd never *liked* the sports section—a combination of playing halls, games fields and running tracks—but it felt different now I was an upperclassman, someone who didn't *have* to play games. The girls were lucky. Games weren't compulsory for *them*. The air felt cold as we made our way through the bleachers, Francis giving a running commentary on what he was going to change when he took office. I think the sports masters used wards to keep the air cold deliberately. It was the sort of sadistic thing they'd do.

"Time to go inside," I said, an hour later. "The Castellan is waiting for us."

Francis nodded. We walked back inside and through a maze of corridors and stairs to the Castellan's outer office. It was a large room, seemingly bigger on the inside; it held the entire class of seventh-years comfortably, rather than cramming us all into a tiny space. I looked around to see if anyone was missing, but it looked as if we were all here. Rose came over to join us, looking relieved. She didn't have that many friends, either. That had always puzzled me. Rose was friendly enough—and well-connected. I knew that quite a few families had tried to lure her into a marriage contract.

And they'd be lucky to have her too, I thought. *She'd bring more than just family connections to the match.*

The Castellan stood on a small podium. He spoke quietly, but his words carried. "Thank you for coming," he said. He waved a hand at the door, which shut with an audible *thump*. "I won't keep you for long."

He paused, just long enough for us to quiet down. "This is your last year with us, unless—by some mischance—you repeat the year. Some of you have already been declared adults. The remainder will almost certainly be declared adults, upon graduation. You will find that, in this year, we will largely *treat* you as adults. You will have freedoms that the students below you will *not* enjoy."

"Poor souls," Francis whispered.

I hissed at him to be quiet as the Castellan kept speaking. "You have already completed your first set of exams, but your second and *final* set of exams will be decisive. Your futures, if you intend to continue to develop yourselves"—he gave Francis a pointed look—"will depend upon your results. You *may* be allowed to repeat the year, but you'd better have a very good excuse. Please bear in mind that slacking off is *not* considered a suitable excuse. You will be treated as adults. *Adults* do not need to be kicked out of bed and forced-marched to the study halls. If you can't motivate yourselves, too bad. We're not going to do it for you.

"This year will also see the Challenge. As seventh-years, you have the right to form a team, join a team or try to take the Challenge alone. You do not *have* to do it—don't let anyone tell you differently—but a good showing, even if you don't win, can be beneficial in later life. If you want to take part, inform me within the week. Anyone who tries to sign up after next Monday will be given detention instead."

There were some chuckles. I wondered if I could find a way to delay matters until time ran out. But Father would be furious.

"Cheating has long been a part of the Challenge, as you may have realised," the Castellan added. "It isn't uncommon for teams to harass the other teams. It is all perfectly legal, if it is conducted in the proper and acceptable ways. However, I must warn you"—his cold gaze swept the room—"that the proper and acceptable ways do *not* include the destruction of school projects, schoolwork or anything that might seriously impede your victim's ability to pass their exams. Anyone caught doing that will be flogged."

Someone chuckled. The Castellan's gaze hardened. "It may amuse you to note that the ban on corporal punishment, through a loophole that may have been deliberately written into the rules, doesn't cover acts of misbehaviour conducted as part of the Challenge. Yes, you *will* be flogged. And then you will be expelled. Do *not* try us on this."

"So we're allowed to injure our fellow students," Francis whispered, "but not destroy their schoolwork?"

"Quite right, Mr. Rubén." The Castellan had very sharp hearing. "And *please* bear in mind that they can injure you too."

I glanced at Francis. "Shut up!"

The Castellan smiled, humourlessly. "You may look for recruits amongst the upperclassmen, from fifth to seventh years. You may *not* try to recruit a lowerclassman without specific permission, which will probably not be granted. You may use anything you produce for yourself, or can obtain from your fellow students; you may *not* ask for help from anyone outside the school, without—once again—special permission. I might add that such permission, again, will probably not be granted."

Which means I definitely can't ask Cat, I thought. It wasn't a surprise, but it still stung. *And I can't buy anything from a forger either.*

"Finally, you will notice that the descriptions of the Challenge are a little bit vague," the Castellan said. "You will not know what you are *actually* meant to be doing until just before the Challenge actually begins. This will force you to think, I believe. All I will tell you, here and now, is that we will give you a task to perform. And if you fail, you fail."

I swallowed, hard. The room was very quiet.

"And now for better news," the Castellan said. "Akin Rubén, Alana Aguirre, come forward."

I glanced at Francis, then walked to the front of the room. Alana stood next to me as we turned and faced the crowd. She made the school uniform look good. But then, so did most of the other aristocratic girls. The ones who could arrange for private tailoring had done so. I knew Francis had done the same. I hadn't bothered, myself.

"After much careful contemplation, Akin and Alana have been appointed Head Boy and Head Girl," the Castellan said. "They will wield the full authority of their role, subject only to myself. I trust you will make their assumption of the position an easy one."

No one even *pretended* to be surprised. They'd probably heard through the grapevine, if they hadn't seen Alana and I go in and out of our suite. And it didn't take a genius to work out who was most likely to be appointed. Our families were the most powerful in the city, at least for the moment. It would be more remarkable if one or both of us *didn't* get the job.

"You will assume your full duties from this moment onwards," the Castellan added. "Good luck."

My mouth was dry. "Thank you, sir."

Alana smiled sweetly, but said nothing.

"There is a sign-up list outside my office," the Castellan said. "If you want to form a team, take a new sheet, add your name to the list and then write the names of your teammates underneath. People who are *not* listed as being part of your team will *not* be allowed to join the Challenge. That said…you can keep adding team members right up until the moment the Challenge is formally announced. At that point, you're committed."

His eyes swept the room. "If you want to undergo the Challenge on your own, you can. But the odds of victory are very low. Consider yourself warned."

There was a long pause. "Mr. Rubén, Miss Aguirre, remain behind. The rest of you are dismissed."

I glanced at Alana as the room emptied. Francis was the last to leave, throwing me a jaunty salute before hurrying out. I had a feeling he was going to wait outside, just so he'd be the first to hear the news. Or maybe he'd go back to the sports field. He had work to do, organising the team captains and planning the first competition match...I felt a sudden burst of gratitude. Francis could easily have begged off joining my team. Instead, he'd been the first to commit himself.

The Castellan turned and led us into his inner office. I couldn't help looking around with interest. I'd never been inside, as students were only allowed to enter when they were in serious trouble. Cat had been inside, back in her first year, when she and Rose had been threatened with expulsion for conducting dangerous experiments. I wondered, as I took the indicated seat, just how many strings Uncle Joaquin had pulled to keep the two girls from being unceremoniously kicked out.

And it was lucky he did, I reminded myself. *Cat might never have discovered what she was if she'd gone home...*

"Here are your handbooks and punishment books," the Castellan said. He passed us each a pair of notebooks. "As you may be aware, you have the right to punish upperclassmen as well as lowerclassmen. However"—he shot a sharp look at Alana—"there will be dire consequences if you are caught abusing your power. You will *not* enjoy them."

Of course not, I thought. *Punishment isn't meant to be enjoyable.*

"Your exact duties are specified in the handbook, but there are a handful I need to bring to your attention." The Castellan turned his gaze to me. "You are responsible for supervising the monitors, from dorm and homework monitors to lunch and hall monitors. You are responsible for handling problems facing younger students; if they come to you, you are to help them. You will also be responsible for organising committees, at least until you can find someone willing and able to handle the task. And you will be responsible for giving the final speech on Graduation Day."

"Both of us?" Alana leaned forward. "Or just one of us?"

"You'll write the speech together," the Castellan said. "And if there are any…consequences…you'll face them together too."

I had to smile. I'd sat through six Graduation Day speeches from successive Head Boys and Girls and they'd all been bland, boring and tedious. But there had been one, given a couple of years before I'd been born, that had brought the house down. The students had laughed, if rumour was to be believed; the important guests hadn't considered it anywhere near as funny. I had no idea what had happened to the Head Boy, but I doubted it had been pleasant. I knew Magisters didn't *like* being played for fools.

"We'll be careful," I said, dryly.

"Very good," the Castellan said. "The lowerclassmen will start arriving this afternoon. You can assist the porters. I suggest you spend the morning reading your handbooks so you know what to do."

"Yes, sir," I said.

"Good," the Castellan said. "Dismissed."

I glanced at Alana, then led the way out of the room. The sign-up list was already pinned to the notice board, with a handful of names already written down. Ayesha and Zeya McDonald, Hamish Bolingbroke, Adam Mortimer…the latter, I noted, seemed bound and determined to complete the Challenge on his own. He'd already torn away the space for names to be entered beneath his own.

"Interesting," Alana mused. "I didn't expect Hamish to join."

"You'd expect Clarian to join," I agreed. Hamish was a Bolingbroke, but from a distant branch. Clarian was from the main bloodline. Her brother was the Patriarch. "But she's obsessed with potions."

I sighed as I picked up the pen. It didn't matter.

Shaking my head, I signed my name.

CHAPTER

EIGHT

In all honesty, I hadn't realised just how much work went on behind the scenes.

Mother had made sure I knew the basics of household management, of course, but *she* had the butler and a small army of servants to help her. Jude's had the Head Porter and *his* assistants, yet there was still a great deal of work for the upperclassmen. I understood, now, why senior upperclassmen were so willing to hand out hundreds of lines for the slightest infraction. The lowerclassmen had a nasty habit of producing hundreds of problems for the upperclassmen to solve.

Alana and I barely had a moment to catch our breath before the firsties began to arrive. We showed them into the Great Hall, where the Castellan welcomed them to Jude's, then supervised as they were sorted into halls. I couldn't believe just how young they looked, young and nervous and utterly unsure of themselves. Had I ever been that young? They looked like little kids, kids who'd borrowed clothes from their older siblings and were pretending to be grown up. A handful were snivelling, trying not to cry openly. I hoped they managed to control themselves. No one would forget a firstie who cried for his mother on his very first day. I told myself, firmly, that I hadn't felt even a *flicker* of concern at sleeping so far from my parents. It wasn't as if my bedroom had ever been right next to theirs.

The firsties milled about, their eyes getting wider and wider every second. I almost envied their youth and innocence. They'd make their closest friends and greatest rivals at Jude's…perhaps even meet their future partners. I allowed my eyes to skim over them, noting which wore tailored uniforms and which had purchased trousers or skirts from the thrift shop. The latter would likely be commoners, commoners who'd either won scholarships or convinced their parents to take out loans to fund their education. It wasn't a bad bet. A student who completed the first four years of schooling would be in a good place to make an excellent living, even if they never took the final three years or served an apprenticeship. I'd known quite a few "new men" who'd climbed to power, some even winning seats in Magus Court. They deserved every bit of their success.

And I'm supposed to be looking out for talent, I reminded myself. It seemed futile. The firsties were so young—the youngest was probably no older than eleven—it was impossible to tell which of them would be great. I'd just have to watch and wait…no, *Penny* would have to watch and wait. I wouldn't be around long enough to watch the firsties develop. *She'll be the one who picks the next generation of clients.*

The sorting finally came to an end. Alana glanced at me, then shrugged. I'd never really *liked* public speaking, even though Father had made me take rhetoric classes over the summer holidays. Francis had been good at it, of course. He might not be able to put together a complete argument, certainly not a written argument, but he was glib. He could argue with the best of them. It helped, I supposed, that he was popular. People wanted to believe whatever he had to say.

I stepped forward. "Raven Dorm, follow me. Hawk Dorm, follow the Head Girl. Everyone else, remain in the hall until called."

The Ravens shuffled forward, their eyes downcast. I groaned inwardly, reminded myself that most of them wouldn't have spent more than a night or two away from home, then commanded them to follow me. They'd been sorted at random, ten total strangers…all girls. Alana would handle the boys. I cast my eyes over them once again, then beckoned for them to follow. It took several minutes for them to form a proper line.

I tried to see the school as they saw it, as I led them up the stairs. I'd spent years exploring the structure, trying to grasp the underlying logic... if, indeed, there *was* any logic. They'd probably get lost, the first time they tried to make their way from the dorms to the breakfast hall. The Magisters would be quite understanding the first few days, then increasingly sarcastic. The poor firsties would have to learn their way around very quickly if they didn't want to get into trouble. A few nights in detention would convince any sluggards to learn the rules.

They're so young, I reminded myself. I wondered, suddenly, if this was how my father saw me and my sister. So young, so innocent, so...I shook my head. I didn't want to think about it. *They'll learn, in time.*

I heard a voice behind me, so weak I could barely make out the words. "Who's that?"

The girl flushed when I glanced back, cringing as if she expected a blow. I wondered, idly, what sort of horror stories she'd heard from her parents and older siblings. My older relatives had told all sorts of stories, terrifying Isabella and I until Mother had overheard Uncle Remus and pointed out—very sarcastically—that no one would have *survived* such treatment, with or without magic. If Mother hadn't made it clear that he was talking nonsense...

I followed her gaze. She was pointing at a portrait, hanging from a wall. A dark-skinned girl, her lips curved in a mischievous smile that suggested she knew something we didn't. I could believe it. I knew her story...

"That's Caitlyn, the Zero," another firstie said. "She's..."

"It isn't." I had to struggle to hide my amusement. "That's Anna the Artificer."

I motioned for them to keep walking, leaving the portrait behind. The firstie girl wasn't *that* far wrong. Anna the Artificer *was* one of Cat's ancestors, a very distant relative. But she hadn't been a Zero. I didn't know *that* much about her—reading between the lines, I was sure she had been a natural-born child—but no one had had any trouble duplicating her work. Cat, on the other hand, was unique. No one else could make Objects of Power.

As far as we know, I reminded myself. *Someone could easily have found another Zero and kept their existence to themselves.*

We stopped as we reached the entrance to Raven Dorm. "As you enter," I said, "place your hand against the Raven. The door will recognise you in the future, allowing you to come and go as you please."

As Penny pleases, I added, silently. *Sneaking around may be tradition, but you have to sneak.*

The door opened. Penny was standing inside, looking stern. I could practically *hear* the firsties gulp. Penny looked so strict that *I* almost quailed. I winced, making a mental note to keep an eye on her. The dorm monitor was supposed to supervise the firsties, true, but she was also supposed to teach them the ways of the school *and* be the first port of call if they needed help. Penny should have refused the post if she didn't feel capable of handling it. But then, if she'd refused…it was pretty certain she'd never be offered another.

I met Penny's eyes. "Good luck."

Penny shot me a look that said, very clearly, *get out.* I made a show of looking around—there didn't seem to be any real difference between the male and female dorms—and then turned and retreated, leaving the firsties to their fate. They seemed worried as they watched me go, very uncertain of themselves. I didn't blame them. They were equals now, at least in theory. And they had to learn to get along.

Poor kids, I thought.

I headed back downstairs, collected the second group of girls and led them to their dorms. This group seemed a little livelier, probably because they'd had a chance to chat while waiting. I smiled at some of their jokes, glancing back to see the first friendships being formed. I hoped they'd last, once school settled down. There was no way to avoid dorm room politics, even if you came from the bluest of blue blood. If someone wound up at the bottom, permanently, their life would not be worth living. I'd never really enjoyed the endless struggle for prominence.

But you never really had to play, either, I reminded myself. *Your family was so high and mighty that you never had to worry about being on the bottom.*

I put the thought aside as I returned, once again, to the Great Hall. There were four groups of female students this time, forty in all. I took the remaining two to their dorms, introduced them briefly to the dorm monitors and then met Alana at the bottom of the stairs. She looked tired, even though it was the middle of the day. I didn't blame her. The girls had been quiet, but the boys might have been rowdier. They might also have been more inclined to challenge a Head Girl's authority.

Alana laughed, softly, as she saw me. "Were we ever that young?"

"Of course not," I lied. "I sprang into being at the tender age of sixteen."

We shared a brief laugh. I didn't really miss my days as a lowerclassman, although I missed *Cat*. We'd had so much fun together, developing our forging skills. No one else came close to either of us, not even Francis or Rose. They'd both need years of additional instruction before they caught up with me. Trying to catch up with Cat was hopeless.

Alana leaned against the wall. "There was one young boy who reminded me of my cousin," she said. "Can you believe he actually tried to cast a spell on me?"

I couldn't. "Really?"

"An itching spell." Alana snickered, rudely. "Quite a nice little cast too. He's going to be a prankster in future, you mark my words."

"Oh." I disliked pranksters. They thought their pranks were funny. Their sycophants generally agreed. Their victims, on the other hand, weren't laughing. "Did you set him straight?"

"Five hundred lines," Alana said, with heavy satisfaction. "And detention on the weekend, which I will have to supervise."

"How uncommonly generous of you," I said, dryly. "I'm surprised you didn't give him something worse."

"It's his first day." Alana shrugged. "And I made it clear that he could expect worse if he went around hexing upperclassmen."

I nodded. Upperclassmen were not permitted to *start* a hexing war with lowerclassmen, but they *were* permitted to finish one. Any lowerclassman who hexed an upperclassman had better be ready for the hexing of his life, followed by lines and detentions. Alana *had* been remarkably merciful. I wondered if she'd seen something of herself in the little brat. She'd been willing to throw hexes around freely as a firstie too.

"The girls behaved themselves," I said. "A handful looked unhappy to be at school, away from their parents…"

"They'll get over it, if they don't want their dormmates making fun of them," Alana commented. "And they'll see their parents soon enough, at half-term."

"If they can afford to go home," I countered. I'd never given it any thought, at least until I'd met Rose. "A poorer student might have to stay at school over the holidays."

"How unfortunate." Alana shrugged. "Better to live here than go back to a hovel."

I opened my mouth to point out that commoners didn't *always* live in hovels, then decided it was pointless. Alana knew Rose too. If she hadn't drawn the right conclusions by now, she probably wouldn't draw them at all. Instead, I glanced at my watch. It was nearly dinnertime and felt like bedtime. I didn't have any official duties until the weekend. Perhaps I could get away with skipping dinner and going straight to bed.

The door opened. Francis walked in, looking depressingly cheerful.

"Akin," he called. He glanced at Alana, then managed a deep bow. "My Lady!"

Alana looked unimpressed. "What do you want?"

"Well, I have a list, if you're interested." Francis grinned, broadly. "But I actually came to borrow my cousin."

"My sympathies," Alana said, to me. "Good luck."

"And I was wondering if you'd like to go to town this weekend," Francis added. "I'll show you a time you will never forget."

"I have no doubt of it," Alana said, her tone leaving no doubt that she didn't mean it in a good way. "I have detention this weekend."

Francis opened his eyes, wide. "Detention? What did a girl like you do to deserve detention?"

Alana held up a hand. I saw a hex dancing around her fingertips before she thought better of it. I wasn't sure who'd win, if they started hexing each other, but it didn't matter. The Magisters would be unimpressed. Alana and Francis could be stripped of their posts at will, if they misbehaved. They hadn't even been Head Girl and Sports Captain for a week!

"I can give you lines, you know," Alana growled. "And I will, if you insist on being stupid."

She turned and strode off. Francis made rude gestures at her back as she stepped through the door, closing it behind her. I sighed in exasperation. One day, Francis was going to get himself in very real trouble. I had no idea what Uncle Joaquin would say, if Alana had walked out with Francis, but I doubted it would be anything good. Francis was hardly a suitable partner for an Heir Primus.

"That girl has a stick up her…backside," Francis said. He gave me a jocular wink. "They're the best, you know."

"No," I said. I didn't want to hear it. "I have to work with her…"

"I could do a lot more with her," Francis said. "And if I were…"

"Shut up," I said. I was too tired for banter. "What do you want?"

"I've just been addressing the sports teams," Francis said. "We lost a bunch of players last term. A third graduated, you know. The rest decided that schoolwork was more important, the traitors."

"How terrible," I said. "To think that their futures are more important than kicking a ball around a muddy field."

"I'll have you know that the field isn't *muddy*," Francis protested. "It's covered in grass!"

I shrugged, unconcerned. "What do the sports teams have to do with me?"

"Well, no one would expect you to play football," Francis said. "They might as well expect Blair to play football."

"How lucky for me," I said, sarcastically. Blair wasn't a bad sort, but he was quite alarmingly fat. I didn't know *why* he hadn't brewed or bought himself a slimming potion and drank it. "What do you want with me?"

"Well, it turns out that the Head Boy has to write a note, requesting additional resources for the sports team," Francis said. "You have to countersign it, at the very least."

I blinked. "I do?"

"Yeah." Francis smiled. "You're not going to say no, are you?"

"You should have asked Alana," I pointed out. No one would trust *my* opinion on sporting matters. Did the teams need new equipment? I didn't know. Nor did I care. "Preferably *before* you tried to ask her out."

Francis snorted. "Ah, you know her. She'd refuse to sign anything I put before her."

"She does have a working brain," I said. "And she likes sports too."

"It's important," Francis insisted. "I have to have teams lined up before the end of the month or we won't be able to join the leagues…"

"How terrible," I said. "I…"

"It *is* terrible," Francis said. "We'd be laughingstocks."

"Jude's is a school of magic, not a school of sports," I said. "No one judges us by the quality of our sporting teams."

"Yes, they do." Francis leaned forward. "Our players cast spells to help them play, remember. The spells they devise often have practical uses. Remember Wilberforce? He got a charms apprenticeship because of the sporting spells he invented."

That was true, I supposed. It had never really impressed me—one could invent spells without playing sports—but I could see the appeal. And sports did have a greater impact on the school than most people realised. It probably wouldn't hurt if I played a role, no matter how minor, in procuring supplies for the teams. It might even work to my advantage.

"Give me the list." I met his eyes. "And be *reasonable*. They're not going to shell out a million crowns for sporting equipment."

"I'm only asking for half a million crowns." Francis grinned at my shocked face. "I kid, I kid. A hundred thousand crowns."

"And if they *give* you a hundred thousand crowns, in cash or credit, I'll run naked through the school," I said. Francis would be lucky to get a *thousand* crowns. "Put forward a reasonable request and I'll countersign it. Put forward something that makes us both look like utter idiots and I'll use it for toilet paper."

"Maybe if I submit two requests," Francis mused. "One for you and one for Her Mightiness, the Head Girl. The Castellan might not notice…"

"He would," I predicted. The Castellan's secretary, a sour-faced prune who'd been horrible to Cat during her early months at school, was renowned for never missing anything. She'd spot the trick instantly and report it to her superior. "And then the *three* of us would look like idiots."

Francis smirked. "We don't already look like idiots?"

"You're the one kicking a ball around the field," I said. "You tell me."

"Hah," Francis said. "So…any thoughts on who we should ask to join us?"

"Not yet," I said, yawning. I wanted dinner and bed. I'd settle for bed. "But I'm working on it."

"Better hurry," Francis advised. "All the good students are already taken."

CHAPTER

NINE

Francis, I was starting to realise as I followed my peers into Magister Niven's classroom, had had a point. Indeed, he might have been more correct than he'd realized. There were forty students in my year and nearly all of them were spoken for, one way or the other. Not everyone was taking part in the Challenge—unsurprisingly—but even the ones who *weren't* still had connections that make it difficult, if not impossible, for them to take my side. And even *asking* them was a severe breach of etiquette.

I sat next to Francis and watched as Magister Niven strode to the front of the room. He was dressed in an outfit that had been fashionable hundreds of years ago, but now made him a laughingstock...or would, if we didn't know him so well. Magister Niven delighted in forcing us to question assumptions—his first *class* had been called Questioning Assumptions—and we knew very little about him. I honestly wasn't even sure if he was male or female. I assumed he was a man, but...I didn't know. He wore male clothing one day and female clothing the next. It was impossible to say anything for certain.

Cat loved him. I found him annoying.

Francis nudged me. "He looks like a giant fruit trifle."

I hid my amusement. Magister Niven might overlook the cheek—he'd overlooked things that would make other Magisters explode with rage—or he might not. He liked being unpredictable. And besides, his class was always interesting. He was one of the rare teachers who allowed us to talk back, who expected us to openly debate. We just had to be able to back up our words. I respected him for it, even if I didn't like him very much. The other Magisters never admitted their faults.

Magister Niven waved a hand at the door. It slammed shut. The click of the lock was audible in the sudden silence.

"Be seated," he said, as if we weren't already. "Class is now in session. Latecomers will be hexed."

He paused, allowing his words to sink in. "This—our final year together—will be a little different from the norm. I have done my best to teach you to think for yourselves. If you haven't mastered the art by now, you are unlikely ever to succeed and thus have doomed yourself to a lifetime of mediocrity. You must be careful who you follow, for they will always have their own interests—not yours—at heart. And if you remember nothing else I teach you, this year, remember that. It will save you much heartache in the future.

"But if you are here now, you presumably know how to think. I won't test your fragile little brains any further."

His words hung in the air. "This year, your final year, is centred on Shallot itself. We have studied the history of the city; now, we will study the politics. Some of you"—his gaze rested on me for a long moment—"will have learnt this at your father's knee. Others will have picked it up over the last few years. And still others will have chosen to blind themselves to politics. That is a mistake. As a great sage observed, you may not be interested in politics, but politics is always interested in you. It is my job, in my final year, to make sure you have the background knowledge you need to navigate the political world."

"So he's going to teach everyone how to play," Francis muttered, to me. "That'll make life harder…"

Magister Niven had sharp ears. "Francis. Perhaps you could explain why I *shouldn't* teach politics?"

Francis stood. We had to stand when answering questions. I wondered, idly, what sort of response he'd give. It would be difficult to justify *not* teaching politics…

"Yes, sir," Francis said. "With all due respect, you are a Magister. You are not a politician. Your lessons, therefore, are theoretical. They are not rooted in experience. You cannot explain how politics work because you have never *worked* in politics."

"An interesting answer," Magister Niven said, as Francis sat. "Would anyone care to make a rebuttal?"

Louise—I barely knew her—held up her hand, then stood when Magister Niven nodded at her. "You might not have experience, but you do know how the system works. You can teach us to use it even if you haven't used it yourself."

"Very true," Magister Niven said.

"And you can make sure we're all on a level playing field," Louise continued. "No one will have an unfair advantage."

Francis nudged me. "Where does she think she is?"

The class snickered. Louise flushed, angrily. Magister Niven fixed Francis with a sharp look, then motioned for Louise to sit down. She did, her face red. I felt a flicker of sympathy, mixed with irritation. Louise was a know-it-all who knew everything, apart from basic manners. I didn't think she had any real friends in our year.

"She drank too much Clever Dick Potion," Francis muttered. This time, he had the sense to keep his voice low. "Lots of brains, no friends at all."

I gave him a sharp look, then studied Louise as Magister Niven started to draw a diagram on the blackboard. She was a tall, auburn-haired girl who would have been pretty if she'd bothered to put any effort into her appearance. Her parents were merchants, if I recalled correctly; wealthy enough to send their daughter to Jude's, but probably not wealthy enough to buy her some etiquette lessons. She was smart—no one could deny it—and she wanted everyone to know it. No one could stand her for long. I'd heard through the grapevine that she'd practically been kicked out of two separate dorms by her dormmates. I had no idea why.

"Shallot was originally founded in the Sixth Century of the Thousand-Year Empire," Magister Niven informed us. "A number of Great Houses took advantage of the founding to establish themselves as movers and shakers in the field outside the Eternal City. Others, already well-established in imperial politics, made sure to plant branches in the new city. This was lucky, as it ensured they survived the collapse of the Thousand-Year Empire. Those branches found themselves the last survivors of their families."

I shivered. My family had been one of those branches.

"Our historical records of *precisely* what happened after the Fall are somewhat lacking," Magister Niven continued. "However, it is fairly clear that the Great Houses managed to retain control of the city and defend it, once the civil wars began. Their eventual alliance with the kingdom ensured that they would no longer need to fear an outside threat, at least for a few hundred years. Their independence was a *fact*. However, this presented them with the problem of running the city. On one hand, they had power. On the other, they had to figure out a way to keep it."

He gave us a toothy smile. "Power is a curious thing. On one hand, it can be enforced—by the mailed fist and spellcaster, if necessary. But, on the other hand, it relies on a certain degree of acquiescence from the disempowered. Those who are at the top find themselves in a lonely spot, while those who are below them work to undermine their power and claim it for themselves. To govern, one needs the consent of the governed. And when the governed withdraw their consent, chaos follows. The Great Houses needed a reasonable degree of consent in order to function. But why should anyone *offer* that consent?"

His gaze swept the room. "Anyone?"

Alana stood. "We were the ones who saved the city," she said. "The power was ours by right."

"Your ancestors saved the city," Louise said, without standing up. "*You* didn't."

"Silly girl," Francis muttered.

"She has a point," I muttered back. "And…"

"Quiet," Magister Niven ordered. He gestured to Alana. "Answer that, please."

Alana shot Louise a look that promised trouble later. "The Great Houses saved the city and passed what they'd saved to their descendants. Over the years, they amassed great wealth and power which they *also* passed down to their descendants. It was theirs. They could do whatever they liked with it. And they passed it down to their descendants. What I inherited from my ancestors is mine by right."

Magister Niven nodded, slowly. "Louise? Rebuttal? And stand, this time."

Louise stood, valiantly ignoring the snickers. "We're not talking about private property or possessions," she said. "We're talking about power over *people*."

"A very good point," Magister Niven said. He motioned for Louise to sit. "The Great Houses might feel that the power was theirs by right. But they also knew that everyone *outside* the aristocracy would feel differently. How, then, did they invite the commoners to join the political structure? How did they give the commoners a stake in the city without conceding too much power?

"It was not easy. Too little democracy and a large percentage of the population would be effectively disenfranchised. Their interests would not be heeded, as they did not have the vote. The enfranchised, for want of a better word, would organise the government to suit themselves. This would lead to resentment, unrest and eventual revolution. But, on the other hand, too much democracy would be equally destructive. The voters would vote for bread and circuses, which would give rise to a class of politicians who would promise to satisfy their demands...they would not offer good government, but seek public approval by giving the mob whatever it wanted. This would eventually lead to collapse."

Louise stood. "People aren't *stupid*."

"No, they're not." Magister Niven nodded. "But they are self-interested. And the lure of getting something for nothing is one that has seduced many a bright spark. Rationally, one might understand that there are limits. Practically, not so much."

He paused. "Eventually, they established Magus Court.

"There are one hundred seats in Magus Court. Each one represents a tribe—and every adult citizen within the city is enrolled in at least one tribe. A sailor, for example, is enrolled in the sailing tribe, with a right to vote for his representative. Indeed, the sailor may *also* be a member of a different tribe, with a right to vote there too. It isn't uncommon for someone to be a member of five or six tribes. I myself have four different memberships, thus four different representatives.

"Each tribe is allowed to govern its internal voting structure as it sees fit. The systems are transparent, by law. The sailing tribe, for example, gives more weight to captains and officers than it does to ordinary seamen. The Potion Masters Guild, on the other hand, treats all of its qualified members as equals. Once someone qualifies, they have the right to demand enrolment—and the guild, which is a tribe, does not have the right to turn them away."

He paused, significantly. "And what are the Great Houses? Tribes."

I nodded as a rustle ran around the room. I'd known that, but I'd rarely heard it stated so bluntly. The Great Houses controlled, directly or indirectly, around sixty to seventy seats on Magus Court. Individual houses might come and go—we'd lost power and regained it—but the system itself would go on. It was fiendishly clever, I acknowledged. The commoners—from dockyard workers to merchants and traders—had a vote, but their vote didn't count for very much. They could better themselves, if they worked hard...yet, if they did, they often got absorbed into the system. A large-scale reform movement was simply impossible.

Because once someone has reached the top, Father had said once, *they don't want to bring the system crashing down.*

"That is the key to understanding the stability of our system," Magister Niven informed us, calmly. "It is not impossible to climb the ranks, to become a 'new man.' It is, indeed, a great honour to *be* a 'new man.' But the price for climbing the ranks is becoming one with the system. It is very difficult to work outside the system. Those who do are often criminals."

Louise stuck up a hand. "Because they're working outside the system?"

"Because they're committing criminal acts," Magister Niven said, dryly. "Did you ever hear of a Thieves Guild? A Kidnappers Tribe? A society for people who cross the road without regard for oncoming traffic?"

"That's not what I meant," Louise said.

Magister Niven cocked an eyebrow. "And what *did* you mean?"

Louise reddened as the class tittered. "I meant…what if someone doesn't want to join a tribe? Or a guild?"

"At the very least, any adult citizen would be enrolled in one of the residential tribes," Magister Niven said, quietly. "But why would they *not* want to join one of the working tribes? Or found a tribe of their own? It isn't impossible."

"A tribe could bar someone from joining," Louise insisted.

"Not legally," Magister Niven said. "If you met the criteria for joining a tribe, they could not reject you. Nor could they rewrite the rules to reject you, unless they somehow managed to exclude you without excluding current tribesmen. And if they do, there are ways to complain."

"If you have money to take it to court," Louise said.

"Quite," Magister Niven said. "And might I remind you, *again*, that you should stand when you have something to say?"

"Twit," Francis muttered.

I nudged him. Oddly, despite myself, I felt a twinge of respect for Louise. She wasn't liked, not really, but...she hadn't tried to change herself in order to fit in. Rose hadn't managed that, nor had any of the others...I wondered, suddenly, if it would be worth the effort of getting to know her a little better. She was irritating, but smart. And she was clearly determined to go places.

But not if she keeps alienating people, I reminded myself. Father had made it clear that people would *remember* whatever we did at school. *If people remember her as a horror, they won't give her any chances once she leaves school.*

"The patron-client system pervades the political structure," Magister Niven said, addressing the entire class. "A patron offers support to his clients—everything from money to positions and promotions—and, in exchange, expects the unstinting support of his clients. A client in a powerful position—a tribal representative, for example—is expected to favour his patron, not—perhaps—the people who voted him into office. He is therefore required to perform a careful balancing act between the interests of his patron and his voters. A wise patron will not put too much pressure on his client. A client who fails because he is unable to maintain the balancing act is useless."

"That's not fair," Louise muttered.

Magister Niven gave her a sharp look. "Of course it's not fair," he said. "The *world* is not fair. We are not equals, right from birth. Some people have advantages, others disadvantages...a person can be as smart as a whip and still be denied promotion, forced to watch helplessly as people with better connections are promoted over their heads. And luck—good or bad—plays a role. A moment of bad luck can bring your entire world crashing down."

He met her eyes. "I have spent *years* teaching you to question your assumptions. And one you *must* question, one you must discard, is the belief that life is *fair*."

"It could be worse," Francis said.

"Yes, it could be," Magister Niven agreed. "And yes, you could try to make it better. But if you want to make something better, you have to start by understanding why things are the way they are. There is nothing to be gained by flailing around at random. Learn to row before you take the helm."

He scowled. "And remain behind, after class," he added, looking at Francis. "I want a word with you."

I nudged Francis. "You got in trouble!"

"Hah," Francis said.

Magister Niven raised his voice. "For your homework tonight, I want you to contemplate an age-old riddle. There is a gate, standing alone, in the middle of a field. It appears to be completely pointless. Should the gate be removed? I want your answers by the end of the week, before our next class. And there will be a prize for the one who gives me the best answer."

Francis grinned. "Do you think it will be something worth having?"

I shrugged. Magister Niven gave all kinds of rewards. And then he forced us to try to understand why he might have given us *those* particular rewards. Some of the things he'd given me, over the years, were so pointed that he might as well have stabbed me with a knife.

"Dismissed," Magister Niven said. "I'll see you next week."

"I'll see you at lunch," I told Francis. I didn't think he'd be in *real* trouble—he'd probably just get a punishment essay, in addition to his regular homework—but that wouldn't stop me rubbing it in. "And then we have Defence."

"That's always fun," Francis agreed. He stood and started to amble towards Magister Niven's desk. "Be seeing you."

I nodded as I picked up my carryall, my eyes seeking Louise. She looked downcast as she packed up her books, alone in the middle of the crowd. She…I made a mental note to approach her, when I had a moment. It was unlikely anyone had secured her services already. Hardly anyone could stand her. Clever as she was, her personality drove everyone away.

And I don't have many other choices, I reminded myself. *All the good ones are taken.*

82

CHAPTER
TEN

"I see I didn't manage to drive you away," Magister Harmon said, when we gathered in his classroom after lunch. He gave us all a toothy grin. "I'll just have to work harder, won't I?"

We shuddered in unison. Our first five years of Defence—Protective and Defensive Magic, according to the school handbook—had been conducted by Magistra Solana, a stern but decent teacher who'd instructed us in the fundamentals. I'd liked her, more than I cared to admit. She'd put us all on solid ground when she'd taught us magic. But now, as upperclassmen, we were instructed by Magister Harmon, the roughest and toughest teacher in the school. He was a good teacher, I supposed, but he was also horrible. He seemed intent on driving as many of his students as possible into fleeing his class and never coming back.

I tried to keep my face impassive as I listened. He was a short muscular man, with a scarred face and hair shaved so close to his scalp that he was practically bald. He'd been a soldier in the King's Life Guards and never let anyone forget it, although rumour had it that he'd been kicked out for unacceptable brutality. I'd asked Father about it, after I'd met Magister Harmon for the first time, and Father had laughed. Unacceptable brutality, apparently, was how someone got *in*.

"We'll be spending the afternoon making sure you haven't gone soft over the summer," Magister Harmon informed us. "And then we will start on some *really* interesting spells."

I shivered. The classroom was freezing. I think he charmed it deliberately. The shorts and shirt I wore—that we all wore—didn't provide anywhere near enough protection. He'd told us that suffering built character, but personally I thought he was just a sadist. Making us suffer was part of his job. I honestly didn't know how he got away with it.

Probably because he's an equal opportunity sadist, I thought. *Everyone suffers at his hands.*

"I trust you brought your sword," Magister Harmon said, addressing me. "You're going to be needing it."

"Yes, sir," I said. I reached back and grabbed the hilt. "I'm ready."

"Very good." Magister Harmon pointed towards the line of training dummies, positioned against the far wall. "Here we go."

He snapped his fingers. The training dummies jumped to life, their inhuman forms snapping into attack position. I drew the sword in one smooth motion as the others grabbed swords off the walls, whispering curses as hexes started to fly. The dummies moved with inhuman speed. I had to let the sword guide me in snapping their hexes out of the air. Two students were knocked to the ground—hard—before they could muster a protective charm.

"Don't clump up like that," Magister Harmon barked. "Defend yourselves!"

A dummy lunged at me. The sword darted out, guided by its formidable magic, and sliced right through the dummy's chest. It fell to the ground, in pieces. I saw sparks of magic darting around it as another dummy appeared, trying to hex me. I deflected the spell, then stabbed it with the sword. It collapsed too, emitting an inhuman sound. I shivered as I ducked another hex.

"Here," Francis called. "Quickly!"

I covered his back as he matched blades with another dummy, forcing it to lower its guard before he hit it with a fireball and blew it into bits. I saw Alana and Bella, also fighting back to back as the dummies closed for the kill. One appeared, ready to move into Alana's blind spot and hex her; I sliced it in half without thinking, watching the pieces fall to the ground. She shot me an unreadable look, then nodded her thanks. I grinned at her, then moved on to the next target.

And then, suddenly, everything was over. The dummies were all gone.

"Form a line, those who can." Magister Harmon didn't sound impressed. "How many of you lost?"

I glanced at the students on the ground. Eight were down, held in place by magic. "Eight, sir."

"I have two points to make," Magister Harmon said. "First, if that had been a real fight, eight of your comrades would be dead."

I swallowed, hard. There were only twelve students in the class. Only four of us had lasted long enough to defend ourselves.

"And second," Magister Harmon continued, "don't assume…"

A spell slammed into my back. My arms and legs locked, painfully. I tumbled forward, catching sight of Bella falling too. Someone—I think it was Francis—landed on my back as I hit the ground. The impact hurt, even through the spell. I struggled, trying to cast a counterspell, but it was impossible. I couldn't even focus my mind well enough to call on the sword.

"… That the battle is over until the fat lady sings," Magister Harmon said. "Can you hear singing? I can't."

An invisible force gripped me, flipping me over. I landed on my back, looking up at the dummies. They'd reconstituted themselves the moment our backs were turned, then hexed us. I cursed under my breath. Magister Harmon had deliberately set us up to fail. Of course he had. He wanted us to learn a lesson.

Magister Harmon snapped his fingers. The spell holding me broke. I sagged, my muscles aching painfully. My jaw hurt from where it had hit the ground. I scooped up the sword and forced myself to stand. It was a mistake to show weakness in Magister Harmon's class. He could practically smell it. Beside me, Alana staggered to her feet. Her face was set in an expression of pinched determination. And yet, she looked subdued. Even *Francis* looked subdued. There were no whispers in *this* class.

The dummies turned and ambled back to the wall. I watched them go, then turned my attention to my classmates. Bella looked badly shocked, but otherwise unharmed; Louise's cheeks burned with humiliation. Beside her, Saline—another girl, one I barely knew—seemed unmoved. Her face was slack, as if she wasn't quite there. I wondered, suddenly, if she'd caught the brunt of the hexes. Should she go see the healers?

Magister Harmon didn't seem to think so. "I trust you all understand," he said. "You cannot take anything for granted."

He looked at me. "Put that sword away," he added. "The rest of you, return your blades to the wall."

I did as I was told, even though I wanted to keep hold of the blade. I could trust it to defend me, although it wasn't very good at telling the difference between a mock attack and something that was actually deadly. If the dummies had been real people, they would be dead. I let go of the hilt, feeling my body sag as I broke the connection. The sword didn't just guide my blows. It boosted my endurance too.

"Divide into teams," Magister Harmon ordered. "No, I'll do it for you."

I glanced at Francis, who shrugged as he was paired with Bella. I expected to be paired with Alana, but instead…Magister Harmon pointed Saline towards me. I saw a flicker of concern cross Louise's face—I wondered, just for a moment, if I'd been wrong about her not having friends—as Saline joined me. I didn't know either of them that well. They'd both been in different classes, over the last two years. But they'd survived two years with Magister Harmon. They had to have *something* going for them.

"We will practice blocking exercises," Magister Harmon informed us. "I trust that you remember how to cast a block?"

"Yes, sir," I said.

"Good," Magister Harmon said, once the others had agreed. "Go. Find a space and go."

"A pity we can't find a space on the other side of the school," I said, to Saline. "It would be fun, wouldn't it?"

She eyed me for a long moment, as if she hadn't understood what I said. I met her eyes, trying to see if they were unfocused. If she was concussed… I'd have to tell Magister Harmon, I'd have to take her to the healers. But then she smiled, brightly. It made her face light up.

"Yes, it would be." Her voice was very soft. She sounded a little like Cat. "But *he* would object."

I studied her as we found a space and faced each other. She was shorter than me by about a head, with light brown skin, dark brown eyes and long hair that hung down in two neat braids. Her shirt was loose, but…I would have found the sight more interesting if the room hadn't been so cold. She wore a pair of glasses, somewhat to my surprise. It wasn't *that* difficult to fix someone's eyesight. And the belief that a disability somehow led to greater strength in magic had been disproven long ago. No one let their children remain disabled these days, not if they had the money or magic to fix the problem.

"Do you want to block me?" I looked down. "Or should I block you?"

Saline hesitated, just long enough to make me wonder about her. Again. "I'll block you," she said. "Please…"

I nodded. "It's fine with me."

She smiled, then started to cast the spell. Her movements were slow, but sure. I had a feeling she'd be in some trouble if she ever had to cast the spell in real life. I hoped Magister Harmon hadn't noticed. He'd knock her flat on her back if he did, then point out just how much worse it would have been if she was facing a *real* attacker. He had never bothered to pretend the world was a decent place. I respected Magister Harmon for that, even though I didn't like him. I had too many relatives who believed children shouldn't be told the truth.

I mustered the fireball, then threw it at her block as hard as I could. The air in front of her seemed to solidify as my spell struck it, exploding into a sheet of fire as it slammed into her magic. A wave of heat gusted across me, fading quickly as the room's temperature reasserted itself. I saw her smile again—it was oddly endearing—and then threw the second fireball, right at her block. It shimmered in and out of existence as I pounded it, again and again. I focused my magic, pushing her as hard as I could.

And then, the block shattered…

Saline dropped to the ground and rolled over as the remnants of her magic flew in all directions. For a horrible moment, I thought I'd really hurt her. It was possible. Magister Harmon didn't bother with the safety wards Magistra Solana cast before every lesson. But instead…she sat up, giggling. It dawned on me that she'd allowed herself to drop before the block finally crumbled.

"Good," Magister Harmon said. "But what was wrong with it?"

I jumped. I hadn't realised he was behind me. I certainly hadn't heard him…I turned slowly and wished, a second later, that I hadn't. He was so close that I would have slammed into him, if I'd not jumped back. It was a wonder I hadn't heard him.

"It held," I said, surprised. Saline was strong, whatever else could be said about her. "I had to batter it down."

"Really." Magister Harmon didn't sound impressed. "Raise a block. Saline can batter it down."

He stepped to one side as I raised the block. It was a simple spell, on the surface, but it required a great deal of concentration and power to hold it firmly in place. There were simpler defensive spells, from shield charms to personal wards, but none of them would last long on the battlefield. Most killing spells, I'd been warned, would cut through them like a knife. And there were times when ducking and dodging weren't options.

I raised the block, then waited. Saline was taking her time.

"Now, if you please," Magister Harmon ordered. "I don't have all day."

Saline lifted her hand, then snapped it down as she cast a fireball. It wobbled as it flew towards me, veering from side to side so rapidly that I was half-convinced it was going to hit Magister Harmon before it struck my block. And yet…there was a *lot* of power tied up in that fireball. The force of the impact nearly pushed me back. I closed my eyes and concentrated, feeding as much power as I could into the block. It solidified rapidly, a second before the next fireball hit it. The third destabilised, exploding midway between us.

"You stupid girl," Magister Harmon bellowed. "What were you *thinking*?"

Saline looked as if she wanted to cry, but didn't quite dare. Magister Harmon bawled her out, pointing out just how dangerous it *was* to cast an uncontrolled fireball…I felt my heart wrench in sympathy as he finally turned away, his glare lighting on me. I knew I was in trouble. I just didn't know why.

"So," he said. "What's wrong with the block?"

"It worked, sir," I protested. Behind him, I could see Saline wiping away a tear. "It worked…"

"Of course it worked." Magister Harmon sneered, as if I'd said something very stupid. "If it hadn't worked, our Head Boy would be a blackened corpse on the ground."

And you'd probably love that, I thought. Logic told me it wasn't true, but it was very hard to believe. *One less stupid student to worry about.*

Magister Harmon took a step back. "Raise the block again," he ordered. "Now."

I hurried to do as I was told. Saline was in no state to cast another spell. And that meant…

Magister Harmon raised his hand and cast a fireball. I barely saw it before it slammed into my block with terrifying force. It was all I could do to hold the spell together. My magic *screamed* in pain as he hit the block a second time, bursts of heat leaking through as the block began to come apart. I tried to stumble back, or drop to the ground like Saline had done, but my legs felt rooted to the spot. And then a third spell hit the block, shattering it into a million pieces. A wave of force picked me up and threw me towards the far wall. I knew I was dead…

… And then I hit a safety ward and bounced.

Magister Harmon strode forward as I fell to the ground, landing on my bottom. "What went wrong?"

"You broke the block," I managed. My bottom hurt. "You hit it too hard."

"Obviously." Magister Harmon sneered, again. "But what *really* went wrong is that you allowed the block to hold you in place. You poured too much magic into it, instead of planning for what you'd do if—when—the block collapsed. And what happened?"

"The block collapsed," I said, dully.

"Correct," Magister Harmon said. "Tonight, I want you to think about what you should have done. You'll have another chance tomorrow."

"Yes, sir," I said.

He strode off to bully Francis and Bella, who'd been knocking each other around with great abandon. I watched him go, then looked at Saline. Louise was standing next to her, whispering words of quiet encouragement. I felt a sudden rush of warmth, mixed with pity. I wasn't sure what was wrong with Saline—if *anything* was wrong—but it was nice of Louise to help her. And her suggestions weren't bad either.

I took a breath, then walked over to join them. "Are you okay?"

Saline nodded, shortly. She was breathing heavily—and I could see a tear in her eye—but she was holding herself together. I wasn't sure Isabella would have done as well. But then, even Magister Harmon would have hesitated to shout at Isabella. A word in my father's ear would have ruined Magister Harmon's career.

"You did well," I said. "You nearly took down my block."

Louise glared at me. "What do you want?"

I felt a flicker of irritation and suppressed it, ruthlessly. "I have an offer for you, for both of you," I said. "If you're interested, come to the Head Boy's suite after dinner."

Louise's eyes narrowed. "And if we're *not* interested?"

"Then don't come," I said. I could have ordered her to come, but I had the feeling that would be a mistake. "But you might find it useful."

I looked at Saline. "You too."

"... Maybe," Saline said. Her voice was dreamy. "Maybe we will."

"And maybe we won't," Louise said. Her eyes were sharp and cold. I knew she was looking for the sting in the tail. I hoped she'd realise there wasn't one to find. "I..."

Magister Harmon's voice echoed through the giant classroom. "Over here, now!"

I nodded to the girls, then turned and hurried back to the front. Magister Harmon had finished reviewing the blocks and was handing out homework assignments. I sighed as he passed me a sheet of paper, with instructions to read a dozen sourcebooks by the end of the week. It was going to keep me busy, even if I didn't get any more homework from anyone else. I had too much else to do.

Francis nudged me as class was dismissed, not a moment too soon. "What did you have to say to dumbo and the know-it-all?"

"I thought I might convince them to join us," I said, airily. "And you'd better be nice to them too."

Francis blinked. "Really?"

"Yeah," I said. I sobered as the enormity of what I'd done began to dawn on me. "And now I just have to think of how to convince them."

CHAPTER
ELEVEN

It wasn't easy to plan a meeting.

I hadn't realised that, either, until I'd had to do it myself. My mind ran in circles as I tried to decide how best to proceed, what sort of offer I could make…Isabella would have done a much better job. Francis, of course, was no help at all; Alana, who'd kindly agreed to leave us alone for an hour or so, wouldn't have given me advice if I'd asked. It was bad enough that we were going to be unchaperoned. People would talk, even though there were four of us in the room. I just hoped Cat let me explain if she ever caught wind of it.

Francis arrived as planned, taking the seat on the sofa I offered. I could invite all three of them into my bedroom, but I thought that would be a bad idea. Louise and Saline would already be nervous about visiting me, even if it was just a friendly chat. Besides, technically, there was nothing wrong with inviting them into my sitting room. Alana could come back at any moment.

Of course, none of the Grande Dames will accept that explanation if they want to make an issue of it, I thought, as I heated water in the pot. *They could make things really difficult for all four of us if they wished.*

There was a knock on the door. I exchanged glances with Francis, then hurried over and opened the door. Louise and Saline stood there, the former looking nervous and the latter…curiously unconcerned, as if she was drifting through life. I glanced past them—the corridor was empty—and motioned for them to step into the room. They'd clearly put some thought into the meeting too. Louise wore a long blue dress, her hair in tight braids; Saline had remained in her school uniform, but redone her braids to make it clear that they *wouldn't* be coming down easily. I wasn't blind to the underlying meaning. I wondered, absently, if it would matter. We all had enemies.

"Take a seat," I said, indicating the other sofa. "Tea? Coffee?"

Louise shot me a sharp look, as if she was wondering just what I had in mind. "Tea would be lovely, thanks. Saline?"

"Yes, please," Saline said.

I nodded as I went to get the drinks. Louise had picked up *that* much etiquette, at least. If a guest was welcome, one offered a drink. I poured four mugs of tea, placed them on a tray and carried them back into the main room. Louise and Saline were sitting on the sofa, facing Francis. They still looked tense. I put the tray on the table and sat down myself. My mouth was dry. I wasn't sure how to proceed.

Louise broke the silence. "I'm sure you had a *reason* for inviting us here," she said, dryly. "Can we get to it?"

Francis snickered. "You have a more important social event to get to?"

Louise flushed, angrily. "If you called us here to mock us…"

"I didn't." I shot a sharp look at Francis, reminding him to be nice. "I had something else in mind."

"Indeed." Louise took her mug, but didn't put it to her lips. "And that would be…?"

I took the plunge. "I'm taking the Challenge," I said. "And I would like to ask you—both of you—to join my team."

Louise's face went very hard. "If this is a joke, I swear I'll…"

"It's no joke." I felt a pang of sympathy. Louise was abrasive—and bossy—but she had to feel very alone at times. She didn't even have dormmates any longer. Saline was the closest thing to a friend she had and…it couldn't be a very satisfactory friendship. "I could use both of you."

She studied me for a long minute. I tried to look as open and honest as I could. She'd probably been pranked before, by people who wanted to irritate her…she was, I suspected, one of the people who could *never* keep from rising to the bait. In some ways, she reminded me of Isabella. She'd never been very good at letting things go, either. But then, she'd also had power and position. Louise had none.

"And you want us," Louise mused. "Why us?"

"You should be honoured," Francis told her. "This is a great opportunity…"

"To have everyone laughing at me, again?" The bitterness in Louise's voice was almost palpable. "Why should I do *anything* for you?"

"Akin is an Heir Primus, soon to be Patriarch," Francis pointed out. "You should be honoured that he has chosen you for his team."

"Shut up," I said, before Louise could explode with rage or storm out. "What do you want?"

Louise blinked. "What do I *want*?"

"If you're on the winning team, you'll have…opportunities that normally wouldn't be open to you," I told her. I'd looked it up. The victorious team members often did quite well for themselves. "I can't guarantee a victory. But I can guarantee to make it worth your while. What do you want?"

Her face remained blank, but I could tell she was interested. She'd learnt to control her face, yet…she was leaning forward, betraying her interest. My mother would never have revealed so much to watching eyes. But then, my mother had nestled at the core of High Society for nearly four decades. Louise would always be an outsider, even if she married well.

"What are you offering?" The studied disinterest in her voice would have been insulting, if I hadn't known she didn't mean it. "What can you give me?"

I looked back at her evenly, daring her to put her cards on the table. "What would you like?"

"He can give you anything." Saline's voice was soft, but it cut through the air like a charmed knife. I'd nearly forgotten she was there. "Your dreams, Louise. He can give you your dreams."

Louise coloured. "Akin...are you serious?"

"Yes." I leaned forward. "What do you want?"

I saw a flash of bitterness, mingled with desperate hope, cross her face. "I want...I want to establish myself. I want to be something for *myself*, not because of who fathered me or my bloodline or...or anything. I want to be important. I want to do good and..."

"On your own?" Francis cocked an eyebrow. "No one ever accomplished anything on their own."

"I don't want to be dependent on others," Louise said. "I just want to be *me*."

I bit down the urge to point out that Louise was *already* Louise. "What sort of good do you want to do?"

"I want to make things better." Louise looked down at her mug. She still hadn't taken a sip. "I want to go into politics and make things better..."

"And everyone hates you," Francis said, snidely. "You *do* have a habit of rubbing people the wrong way."

"I have to make myself heard," Louise snapped. "Just because you have a list of titles as long as my arm..."

"That doesn't mean you have to treat people like idiots." Francis cut her off. "You talk down to people, all the time. And they resent it. You nag them to do something and they'll decide not to do it, even if it means cutting off their nose to spite their face. They'll hurt themselves because it's the only way to keep from giving in to you."

"I tell them what they need to hear," Louise insisted.

"And they resent you for it." Francis shrugged. "Why do you think you were never in the running for Head Girl?"

Louise glared. "Because *Alana* has a powerful family?"

"That's part of it," Francis conceded. "But you lack the ability to get along with your peers."

"But I'm *right*," Louise said. "I..."

"It doesn't matter." I met her eyes. "Being *right* isn't enough. If you want social credit—and influence, influence enough to get people to listen to you—you need to be *liked*. Or at least tolerated."

"And no one *has* to tolerate you," Francis finished.

"Including you, it would seem." Louise crossed her arms under her breasts. "What would you suggest?"

"You want to go into politics," I mused. It made sense. A merchant's daughter would have a reasonable chance of rising to power within the merchant's guild, particularly if she had powerful friends and connections. "My patronage would help, I suppose, but it would also be a hindrance. You'd want to appear as independent as possible."

I studied her for a long moment. "I'll help you learn how to make yourself respected, if not liked," I said. It wasn't going to be easy, but I could try. "And that would teach you how to build the connections you need if you want to go into politics."

Louise scowled. "I don't want connections," she said. "I want people to vote for me because they support me, not because of who I am."

"The two are intermingled." I let out a long sigh, silently grateful that my father had drilled the facts of political life into my head. "If people don't like you, they will be automatically prejudiced against anything you should happen to say. If you bombard them with facts and figures"—I'd read Louise's essays, when I'd been assisting Magister Tallyman—"they will start to tune you out. And your opponents will not hesitate to take advantage of it. They'll call you everything from a killjoy to a maiden aunt and mock you relentlessly."

"They do already," Louise said.

"Yes," I agreed. "And you never fail to rise to the bait."

"You don't have to like people," Francis agreed. "But you do have to fool them into *thinking* you like them."

"That's breathtakingly cynical," Louise objected.

Francis smirked. "But true."

"I can teach you," I said. I'd have to give that some thought, but I was sure it could be done. "And if you join my team, I will."

"I want something else," Louise said. "I want to be on one of the committees."

I hesitated. I could put her name forward—I could even insist on her being seated, if I was willing to horse-trade with Alana. But would it reflect well on *me*? Louise had many virtues, I admitted privately, yet she didn't play well with others. She'd either drive away the remainder of the committee, leaving her to do all the work herself, or push them into open rebellion. I'd heard stories about committee meetings that had turned into warzones, the staff being forced to intervene…I scowled. That would *not* look good on my record. And yet, she had to start somewhere.

"I'll see," I said, carefully. "Which one did you have in mind?"

"I'm not sure." Louise sounded surprised. Perhaps she'd thought I'd reject the idea out of hand. "Perhaps the TA committee? Or the Graduation committee? Or even the Yearbook committee?"

"I'd have to think about that," I mused. It would be difficult to get Louise on the TA committee, particularly as she hadn't *been* a TA. The other two… perhaps. I'd have to discuss it with Alana. "They start operating after half-term, so you'd have to wait anyway."

Louise met my eyes, challengingly. "You give me your word to do your best," she said, "and I'll join your team."

Saline nudged her, sharply. "Be careful…"

I held up a hand. "I'll do my best," I said. "But I can't guarantee anything."

Francis nodded. "And he can't put you on any of the sporting committees," he said. "That's *my* call."

Louise shuddered. "I hate sports."

"Really?" Francis leered cheerfully at me. "Looks like we've found you a bride."

I flushed in embarrassment. "I'm betrothed."

Francis laughed at his joke. Louise lifted her hand, as if she were about to hex him before thinking better of it. I was glad she didn't. Francis would have hexed her back and then…the entire team would have disintegrated before it ever got off the ground. Beside Louise, Saline looked as if she wanted to disappear. I didn't blame her.

I looked at Saline. "And what do you want?"

"She wants help," Louise said.

I met her eyes. "I'm asking her," I said. "Let her answer for herself."

Louise reddened, her eyes dropping to her knees. I winced, inwardly. It would take a *long* time to cure her of all her bad habits, time she probably didn't have. I made a mental note to see if I could find her an etiquette teacher. They were normally expensive, at least to commoners, but there were plenty of people in the family who could help. They'd do it for me, if I became Wizard Regnant. They'd know I'd be Patriarch one day.

Saline squeezed her friend's arm, gently. "I know the magic," she said haltingly, "but it only comes slowly. I need…I need to work on my spells. I want to make my family proud."

I studied her, thoughtfully. There was nothing wrong with her power, just her ability to use it. She wasn't stupid, just…slow. It was odd, to say the least. Maybe she'd been moved ahead too quickly. It was dangerous to advance without a solid grasp of the fundamentals, the aspects of magic my parents had taught me from birth. If Saline had lost her grip on the fundamentals, she'd never master advanced magic. Or maybe she'd simply peaked. There were a few rare cases where a magician had reached a certain point and simply stopped advancing. But someone would have noticed… wouldn't they?

"We can practice spells together," I said. If nothing else, she could help us practice *our* spells before we were thrust into the Challenge. "And perhaps we can work our way through the textbooks."

Saline gave me a shy smile. "That would be very good, thank you."

I smiled back. "Will you join the team?"

"We'll both join the team," Louise said, after a wordless glance with Saline. "And even if we lose…"

"You'll be able to make something of it," Francis said. "And if you don't… at least you'll have a chance."

Louise—finally—took a sip of her tea. "So. What do we have to *do* for the Challenge? Because I looked it up and there's next to nothing in the library, just a list of winners and losers and people who died during the game."

"You can't find *all* the answers in books," Francis said.

"You can at least find out what people *want* you to know," Louise countered. "Or think or believe or…or whatever."

I nodded. A liar wouldn't *lie* unless he wanted to be believed, Father had said. Knowing what someone was prepared to lie about was instructive, if one had time to think about it. I'd never really understood until I'd grown older. You could learn a great deal about someone by the lies they told.

"They want us to be surprised," Saline said, softly. "If we knew what we were doing, ahead of time, we could prepare."

"Obviously," Francis said. "So what do we do?"

I held up a hand. "They tell us that the whole game is a test of our abilities," I said. "I think they'd want us to do more than simply duel the other teams. There must be a goal, a victory condition…"

"Perhaps it's simply *last man standing*," Francis said. "There are four teams right now, counting us. Perhaps we're meant to fight it out with the others."

"I hope not," Louise said. "It seems a little pointless."

"Yeah." I nodded in agreement. "They'd want us to do more than just *fight*."

"And there would be no big secret around a fighting game," Saline pointed out. "The people who watch football know the rules as well as the players."

Francis smiled. "You watch football?"

"Sometimes." Saline blushed. It looked oddly endearing on her light brown skin. "It can be relaxing."

"You must come to my next game." Francis's smile grew wider. "You'll enjoy it."

Louise and I shared a look of perfect, mutual horror. It was not *our* idea of a good time.

I cleared my throat. "First, we practice our spells…both for duelling and everything else. Second, we work on preparing tools and equipment. We're allowed to take whatever we can carry onto the field, as long as we make it for ourselves."

Francis smirked. "I didn't make my clothes," he said. "Does that mean we have to play *naked*?"

"No." Louise crossed her arms. "Definitely not."

"Probably not," I said. "But we can't bring in weapons and supplies from outside."

Francis sobered, rapidly. "Does that include your sword?"

I blinked. I hadn't thought about it, but…did it include the sword?

"I don't know." I wasn't sure I wanted to check. I could claim innocence if no one *told* me I couldn't take the sword. "We'll see if they say anything about it."

"They may argue that bringing it is cheating," Louise pointed out. "You should ask."

"Maybe," I said. "So…we start planning and practicing on the weekend?"

"Saturday would be fine," Louise said. "I…"

"I have sports," Francis said, flatly. "Sunday."

"Sunday," I agreed. I had a vague plan for Saturday, if Rose was around. "Louise? Saline? Is that alright?"

"Yeah," Louise said. "And"—she paused, rethinking whatever she had been going to say—"thank you."

"You're welcome," I said. "And thank you too."

"Just don't let us down." Francis ignored the sharp look I sent him. "This isn't a game."

"Then perhaps you should take it seriously," Louise said, dryly. She stood. Saline followed her. "See you on Sunday."

"Well," Francis said, when they were gone. "This should be interesting, right?"

"Yeah," I said. It wasn't quite the word I would have chosen. "Interesting."

CHAPTER
TWELVE

"I thought you'd be too busy to explore," Rose said, after breakfast on Saturday morning. "I hear you have a team now."

I eyed her. "Where did you hear that?"

Rose shrugged. "Oh, here and there. It's no big secret, is it?"

"I suppose not," I said, as we walked down the corridor. "I wish you could join."

"I wish I could too," Rose said. "But it isn't possible."

I tried not to yawn. We'd only been back at school for a week and I already felt tired. The teachers had plunged us in at the deep end, barely taking a single period to review material we'd covered last year before leading us into the future. Advanced Potions with Magistra Loanda, Charms with Magister Grayson and Magister Von Rupert, even Forging with Magister Tallyman…I'd barely had any time to myself. And what little time I had was spent being Head Boy. I supervised detentions, lectured a handful of lowerclassmen caught in upperclassman territory and a dozen other duties I hadn't known about until I'd been given the job. No wonder it came with so much prestige. A successful Head Boy had a *lot* of work to do.

At least Alana is on duty this morning, I told myself. I was always on duty, in a sense, but we'd agreed on a rota for weekend duties. *She gave me some time to myself.*

I grinned at Rose as we hurried down the stairs and into the lower levels. Jude's was a maze of abandoned sections, hundreds of rooms and compartments that had simply been sealed off from the rest of the school and left to themselves. I'd spent much of the last six years exploring the underground passageways and I *still* didn't know them all. Some of the abandoned buildings were bigger on the inside. The internal geometry of the school seemed to defy logic and reason.

There's an Object of Power buried under the school, I reminded myself. Cat had told me about it, years ago. *That's probably warping the local dimensions out of shape.*

"They're going to offer me a healing apprenticeship next year," Rose said, as she fiddled with a locked door. It wasn't very secure. The staff had barely made even a token effort to keep people out of the underground. "You think I should do it?"

"I think you'd be good at it," I said. The door came open, revealing a darkened corridor beyond. A handful of light gems, embedded within the ceiling, glowed faintly, so faintly that they barely provided any illumination at all. "And it would give you an excellent start in life."

"I know," Rose said. "But I want to be more than just a healer."

I peered down the corridor, then cast a night-vision spell. "What do you mean?"

"Well, I want to help *everyone*," Rose said. "And not just the people who can pay."

It struck me, suddenly, that Rose and Louise had a great deal in common. "I think there would be nothing stopping you from helping everyone," I said. "You'd just have to have the magic."

"But not everyone can pay," Rose said.

I grinned as I started to walk down the corridor. "You have powerful connections, Rose. I'm sure you can get a stipend as you help the poor."

Rose followed me. "I spent part of the summer working in a clinic," she said. "And it was hard to see people who needed help being unable to get it, because they couldn't afford it. The healers worked for free, some of them, but they couldn't afford the potions they needed to treat the sick…"

I nodded, slowly. The economics of potions were very simple. The ingredients, even the very basic ingredients, cost money. And then one had to pay the brewer. It wasn't illegal to brew potions at home—the law would have been unenforceable, if it had been on the books—but healers were supposed to purchase their potions from guildsmen. It was the only way to guarantee quality. But it also drove the price up…Rose had a point. Even a very basic potion could cost two or three times as much as it should by the time it reached the patient.

"There must be some way to fix the problem," I mused. "Perhaps you and Louise should talk about it."

I *heard* the surprise in her voice. "Louise?"

"She wants to change things too," I told her. "You and her might get along."

I took a breath as we passed through a ruined door. The air tasted of dust. My throat was suddenly very dry. I took a drink of water from my canteen—six years of exploring had taught us to bring supplies—and cast a filtering spell on my mouth. Dust boiled up around us as we made our way further into the complex. I could *feel* it crawling into my clothes and running down my skin. I was going to have to take a proper bath when I got back to my suite. Alana was probably going to make sarcastic remarks about me trailing dust everywhere I walked.

"I'll see," Rose said. "But she hasn't shown any interest in *me*."

I winced, inwardly. The Great Houses didn't *have* to look down on the commoners. We were secure in our supremacy. But someone who was only inches above the poverty line, someone who was all too aware that a single misstep could send them plunging back into poverty…there was no one so aware of their place, and determined to keep it, as someone who lived *next* to a poor district. Louise's parents were probably more snobbish than *mine*.

"Give her time," I said. "Maybe she'll learn."

"Maybe," Rose said, doubtfully.

I nodded in wry understanding. Common-born or not, Rose had shown a willingness to learn—and enough power and promise for people to overlook her flaws. Louise had power and intelligence—more intelligence than power, I suspected—but she seemed to expect the world to change for her, rather than trying to adapt herself to the world as it was. It was an odd attitude for someone from a merchant family. I'd always thought merchants had a good grip on reality. Perhaps Louise had been spoilt when she was a little girl. Or perhaps she was just too stubborn to change. I could understand why someone might think *changing* was a kind of giving up.

We pushed open another door and peered into a small classroom. My eyes went automatically to the bookshelves—I'd found some interesting books under the school—but these shelves were empty. The classroom itself looked eerie. I could have believed that the students would return within hours, perhaps days, if the chairs, desks and tables hadn't been so dusty. I reached out and touched one of them. The dust was so deep that I was certain that no one had entered the room in the last few years.

"This would make a good place to practice spells and stuff," I commented. "We're meant to find a base…"

Rose snickered. "Should I know where your base is…?"

"I trust you not to tell," I said. The rules stated that we *had* to have a base, somewhere that wasn't a classroom, a bedroom or otherwise restricted in any way. We could secure it ourselves, if we wished, but we couldn't rely on higher authority to secure it for us. "You won't, will you?"

"Well…" Rose drew out the word. "What's it worth?"

I grinned, knowing she was teasing. "My appreciation?"

"I'll settle for a visit to the potions lab," Rose said. "Or a trip outside the walls."

"We could." I was surprised. "You can go on your own, you know."

Rose shook her head. "I'd sooner have someone with me," she said. "I feel ill at ease within the city."

"I'll come," I promised. "And we can try and take Cat too."

"I'll look the other way from time to time," Rose said. "But not *too* often."

I rolled my eyes. High Society wouldn't bat an eyelid at Alana and I sharing a suite, if only because we weren't sharing an actual *bedroom*. And the very *idea* of Rose and I doing something when we were alone wouldn't occur to any of them. But if Cat and I were seen in public, without a chaperone, we'd face some pretty astringent criticism. We couldn't even talk in private—just talk—without fuelling the rumours. I promised myself that I'd make any rumourmongers pay, if I ever figured out who they were. The really dangerous ones managed to hide themselves pretty well.

"Thanks," I said. "Perhaps we should go to the zoo."

Rose laughed and followed me through a series of twisting corridors. I honestly didn't understand why this part of the school had been abandoned. There were sections that seemed permanently on the verge of collapsing, perhaps sparking a general collapse as they tumbled into rubble, but *this* section seemed intact. Classrooms, dorms, a handful of offices…I opened a drawer in one of the offices and found coins dating back over a hundred years. I pocketed half of them, after checking to see if the coins were cursed, and gave the rest to Rose. It was possible they were worth quite a bit of money now.

"Everyone else will be setting up secret bases too, won't they?" Rose grinned as we started to make our way back towards the surface. "Are you going to look for them?"

I shrugged. Sabotage might be part of the Challenge, but…I didn't have anything *worth* sabotaging, not yet. The four of us—I'd have to look for at least one or two more—had barely gotten off the ground. I wondered, absently, what they'd think about sabotaging the other teams. Francis would be all for it, I was sure; Louise and Saline might have other ideas. Louise clung to the rules so tightly that I doubted she'd approve of any attempt to make things harder for the other teams.

But they'll start making things harder for us, soon enough, I mused. *And then we'll have to start pushing back.*

"I don't think I'm allowed to discuss it with you," I said, finally. "And besides, I have no grand plans either."

Rose nodded. "Alana said the same," she said. "She can't discuss her plans with me."

I smiled. "I'm just glad she doesn't have you," I said. "You'd tip the balance in her favour."

"Thanks." Rose reddened. "Be glad she doesn't have *Cat*."

"Yeah." I sighed, tiredly. "I am..."

I broke off as I heard the sound of crying, coming from further down the corridor. No, not crying. *Whimpering.* I glanced at Rose, then picked up speed. Something was dreadfully wrong. If someone was in trouble...the noise grew louder as I walked up the corridor, trying to determine precisely where we were. We were just outside the more well-travelled parts of the school, the corridors and passageways everyone knew about even if they didn't use...

"Let me go," someone sobbed. "Please..."

I clenched my fists as I turned the corner. Two beefy-looking boys and a girl—all three upperclassmen—were casting hexes on a pair of lowerclassmen. A girl was stuck to the ceiling, hanging from her hands and legs waving helplessly in the air; a boy was leaning against the wall, his face covered with painful pimples and bruises. He cried out, again, as a hex stuck his chest. They weren't just trying to humiliate him. They were trying to hurt him and...a rush of anger shot through me. How *dare* they?

"Stop." My voice thundered through the air. "Now!"

The upperclassmen jumped, then spun to face me. The boys looked, just for a moment, as if they wanted to fight; the girl glanced at the nearest door, as if she was calculating if she could make a run for it. I readied myself, suddenly unsure of my badge's ability to stop a fight. If I lost, my position as Head Boy would become untenable. I'd be a laughingstock.

I met their eyes, one by one. "What do you think you are doing?"

The girl looked defiant. "This is our territory," she said. "And…"

I made a show of looking around. "I don't see any markers. Do you?"

The girl coloured, angrily. "This is *our* territory. Everyone knows it!"

"Really? I don't." I glanced at Rose. "Do you know it?"

"No." Rose shook her head. "No one told me."

"We found this place," one of the boys said. "It's *ours*."

I glared at him. "Then you put locking spells on the doors, or traps to discourage intruders," I said. That, at least, was tradition. "You do *not* torture students who happen to enter anyway."

"It isn't torture," the girl protested. "It's just…"

I cut her off. "You're upperclassmen," I told them. "You're meant to set an example. A *good* example. Not engage in sadistic tortures, particularly not of lowerclassmen…"

"But…"

I ignored her as I drew the punishment book from my belt. "The three of you have detention," I said. "And you will write out a hundred lines, each. *I will not bully younger students.*"

"That's not fair," one of the boys said. "I…"

"Quite right," I agreed. "You can write out two hundred lines instead."

The girl glared at the boy, then looked at me. "We can't have detention…"

"Yes, you do." I stared her down. "Would you like to do *five* hundred lines instead?"

"… No," the girl said.

"Scram," I ordered. "And *don't* let me catch you bullying anyone, ever again."

They turned and ran as if they were being chased by men with whips. I watched them go, then motioned for Rose to help the girl while I tended to the boy. The upperclassmen had been cruel. The girl's weight could have pulled her arms out of their sockets, even if the bullies didn't do anything else to her. And the boy's face was bloated with hex scars and even a couple of minor curses…I cancelled them all, carefully. His face slowly returned to normal.

"… Thank you," he managed. He couldn't meet my eyes as he wiped away tears. I understood. He'd been utterly outmatched, but he still felt as though he'd shamed himself. I hoped the girl wouldn't tease him for breaking down. That would rub salt into the wound. "We were just exploring… we didn't know it was their room…we didn't…"

"They should have marked it," I said, gently. Rose and I had been chivvied away from rooms upperclassmen had claimed for themselves—and we'd tripped a handful of traps, which had been quite embarrassing—but we'd never been *tortured*. The upperclassmen had stepped well over the line. "If they'd wanted to keep it to themselves, they would have sealed it."

I patted him on the back, silently wishing I could do more. He could have been my brother. But then, if he *had* been my brother, no one would have thought less of either of us if I'd taught the three upperclassmen a lesson. A *real* lesson. But I couldn't help him so openly, not now. He was just lucky I'd stumbled across the scene. No one would call him a sneak.

Perhaps the rules do need to be changed, I thought, tiredly. *But how?*

The girl came over to me, rubbing her arms. "Thank you."

"You're welcome," I said. She looked painfully thin, with pale skin and stringy red hair in a loose braid that had nearly come apart…a commoner then, probably from the far north. I wondered, absently, if she knew Rose. "And just be careful where you go next time."

The girl nodded, her eyes lingering on my Head Boy badge. "Is it true you know Lady Cat?"

"He's going to *marry* Lady Cat," Rose put in.

"Lady *Caitlyn*," I corrected, sternly. One couldn't shorten a lady's name when one used her title. It was disrespectful. "And yes, I know her."

The girl nudged the boy. "Markus, you should ask him."

I frowned. "Ask me for what?"

Markus looked even paler. "I want to be a TA," he said. "Magister Tallyman's TA."

"You'll find him a demanding soul," I said, warningly. I'd spent four years as Magister Tallyman's TA. *Demanding* was being polite. A forger could not afford incompetence or sloppiness. There were no shortcuts—and anyone who thought otherwise was likely to injure or kill himself. "And if you make a mistake, he'll sack you."

"If you put my name in, I'll do anything," Markus said. "Anything, anything at all."

"Don't *say* things like that," I snapped. My mother had told me, during lessons, never to make *any* open-ended promises. They had a habit of coming back to haunt you. "But I can put a word in for you, if you like. How are your grades?"

"Good," Markus said. "I like forging, but…I don't have the background for an apprenticeship unless I TA or something."

I nodded, slowly. I could have had that apprenticeship, if Father hadn't said no. And if I couldn't have it…

"I'll put your name forward," I said. I'd been meaning to talk to Magister Tallyman anyway, when I had a moment. "But if you let me down, I'll be furious."

"He'll turn you into a toad," the girl said, cheekily.

Rose cleared her throat. "And who are you?"

"Isabel," the girl said. "Nice to meet you!"

I flinched. "Isabel," I said. It was suddenly very hard to speak. I knew I was being silly, but I couldn't help it. I had to swallow hard before I could continue. "Nice to meet you too."

CHAPTER
THIRTEEN

I had loved Magister Tallyman's giant classroom complex from the moment I'd first laid eyes on it. Even now, after six years of being a student and four years of being a TA, I still loved it. Magister Tallyman presided over a collection of workshops, from classrooms for large groups to tiny workrooms for one or two students, and a cluster of storerooms that held everything from common wood and metal to rare gems and elements that came from all over the world. Cat and I had spent many happy hours in the complex, when we were firsties; even now, without her, I still enjoyed sneaking into the workrooms and forging something for myself. It was a way to relax.

Magister Tallyman himself was sitting at a desk when I entered, staring down at a complex arrangement of lenses and gold threads. He hadn't changed much over the summer; he was still immensely muscular, his body giving the impression of being seriously overweight even though he was more beefy than fat. But then, he'd always been larger than life to me. He'd been the greatest forger in the city until Cat came along and *she'd* had an unfair advantage. It was greatly to his credit, I thought, that he had never taken it personally.

He looked up at me and grunted a welcome, then pointed to a stool. I sat down and watched as he returned to his experiment, studying his face with great interest. No one would ever call him *handsome*. His face was covered in scars—so were his hands and legs—and his eyes had a distinctly piggish look, as if someone had botched a transfiguration and been unable to undo the damage. I knew a number of students, particularly firsties, were scared of him, something I had always found a little unfair. Magister Tallyman was a perfectionist, an intensely demanding teacher…but I had never doubted his commitment to teaching—or to student safety. No one had died in his class.

"Akin," he said. His voice had grown gruffer, I thought. "Tell me what you make of this."

I nodded, then studied the device on the table. It was…odd, to say the least. A collection of lenses, held together by gold wire…I couldn't see what it was designed to *do*. A Device of Power? I couldn't sense any knot of magic surrounding it either. Beside it, a pair of makeshift Objects of Power sat on the table. I didn't need to ask to know that Cat hadn't made them. The Objects of Power were already coming apart. Magister Tallyman must have made them himself.

And he didn't put any real effort into it either, I noted. The forging had worked—the slow disintegration was proof that *something* magical had happened—but there was no elegance to it. *He didn't intend for them to last.*

"I don't know," I admitted, finally. Magister Tallyman wasn't the sort of teacher who'd mock a student for ignorance. Better to admit ignorance than try to make up an answer. "What is it?"

"A microscope," Magister Tallyman said. "Lawrence suggested it, damn the man."

I blinked. Lawrence? It took me a moment to realise he meant Magister Niven. I only knew his first name through reading one of his books. The average Magister wouldn't share his name—or anything *personal*—with his students. I didn't even know Magister Tallyman's first name.

"That is a microscope?" I leaned closer, puzzling it out. "There are no magnifying spells…"

"No." Magister Tallyman sounded more irritated than amused, although it didn't sound as though he was irritated with me. "There are no spells involved, just carefully carved and placed lenses. Lawrence was quite determined on that point. The less magic, the better."

"It works?" I found it hard to believe that anything as complex as a microscope could work without magic. "What do you see?"

"There are ways to produce lenses that correct eyesight problems," Magister Tallyman informed me, as if I hadn't already known it. "They're rare—eyesight can be easily corrected through magic—but they can be made. And they work. I just had to develop the concept a little further to make a magicless microscope."

"Impressive," I said. I didn't see the *point*, but it was impressive. "What do you see?"

Magister Tallyman stood. "Come and have a look," he said. "Close one eye and put the other to the uppermost lens."

I walked around the desk and did as I was told. The lens seemed to shift oddly as I closed my eyes—it was nowhere near as *simple* as a magnifying spell—but otherwise it seemed to work perfectly. Magister Tallyman picked up one of the Objects of Power and slid it under the bottom lens. My vision blurred, just for a second. And then...

I blinked. "What?"

The Object of Power was...*corroding*. I stared, trying to make out what I was seeing. The material—the combination of metal and wood—was coming apart at a molecular level, while the gemstone at the top was already dull and lifeless. I peered down at the gem, carefully tracing out the fragmented lines within the rock. It would be invisible to the naked eye, I was sure, but it was there. The Object of Power was already useless.

"It's coming apart," I said, in disbelief. I'd seen disintegration spells, but they worked very fast. This process, whatever it was, was happening so slowly that it was practically impossible to perceive. "What's happening?"

Magister Tallyman let out a short laugh. "I have no idea," he said. "But I've checked and rechecked. Every Object of Power I've forged starts to corrode almost immediately. The rate of corrosion varies, but the Object of Power is rendered useless very quickly. And the kicker, the *kicker*, is that the process accelerates when I try using magnification spells. It sped things up so fast, the Object practically exploded in my face."

I glanced at him, concerned. Were those new scars?

"Don't worry about it." Magister Tallyman dismissed my concern with a wave of his scarred hand. "There's always danger in research, as you know as well as I."

I nodded. Cat had nearly killed herself—and Rose—back in first year. I'd nearly blown off my own hands twice, the second coming very close to giving me a set of scars to match my teacher's. And there were forgers—and alchemists—who set out to make a whole new breakthrough, only to accidentally blow themselves up instead. There were a handful of places where the grass would never grow again, thanks to their experiments. No one knew what they'd been messing with—or why. No one had ever found their bodies either.

"I'm still studying it," Magister Tallyman said. "But it's curious. Your betrothed doesn't seem to have the same problem."

"No," I said. "Cat's Objects of Power *work*."

"Yes." Magister Tallyman studied the microscope for a moment, his eyes contemplative. "And she appears to be unique."

"She cannot be unique," I said. Father had argued as much, when he'd been convincing the family council to support the betrothal. There would be others and, given time, they would be found. "Once others are found…"

"If," Magister Tallyman corrected. "Lawrence had a theory about that, but…it isn't one I can share."

Cat can probably get it out of him, I thought mulishly. *And why wouldn't he share it with me?*

"I've been fiddling, trying to see if I can determine something useful about the corrosion effect," Magister Tallyman said. "But, so far, I cannot even determine *why* it exists. All I can say for certain is that it *does*."

"Cat has no magic," I reminded him. "And she has no problems with... corrosion. That cannot be a coincidence."

"Quite." Magister Tallyman nodded in agreement. "But I've been experimenting with working from a distance, both through magic and remote devices. Neither one has succeeded in producing an Object of Power. It may be a question of delicacy, as my remote hands lack the delicacy of my *real* hands, but it may also have something to do with the magic involved in their creation. If magic is required for potions brewing, forging may require a certain *absence* of power."

I frowned. It was hard to believe, but Cat was living proof there was *some* truth to it.

"What about Devices of Power?" I took another look through the microscope. "Do they have the same problem?"

"They *might*." Magister Tallyman seemed unsure. "Objects of Power last indefinitely, as long as they're not destroyed or purposely damaged. Devices of Power, on the other hand, do not. They can be repaired, but they can also be worn down through overuse. I've looked"—he shrugged heavily—"and I haven't been able to see any proof they *are* corroding. But they do decay, so *something* may be at work."

I tried to sound reassuring. "We'll figure it out."

"I certainly hope so." Magister Tallyman stood, brushing pieces of sawdust and metal filings off his apron. "Anyway, I assume you came here for a reason?"

"Yes, sir," I said. "First, I was wondering if I could continue to use the workshops...?"

Magister Tallyman stroked his misshapen chin. "For the Challenge, I assume?"

"Yes." There was no point in trying to deny it. "It would be very useful."

"Perhaps." Magister Tallyman made a show of thinking about it. "Yes, you can. And you can draw on the supplies, as you did before. Same rules and regs. But I would also have to give the same facilities to anyone else who thought to ask. Better to have them forging in here, where it's relatively safe, than have them do it in their bedroom."

"Yes, sir." I couldn't disagree. "I wasn't asking for exclusive rights."

"A good thing too," Magister Tallyman said. He shook his head. "Complete waste of time, you know. You should be proving yourself in other ways."

I wished I didn't agree. "It has to be done," I said. "Do *you* know what we have to do?"

"I've been sworn to secrecy." Magister Tallyman grinned, toothily. "I don't know why they bothered. There isn't a student alive who could *force* me to talk."

"No, sir," I said. "Did you take the Challenge yourself?"

"I was too busy learning my trade," Magister Tallyman said. He smiled in happy memory. "You know, I don't even remember who was crowned Wizard Regnant that year. But I do remember the first time I crafted a warding base for my master."

"Oh," I said. A thought struck me. Magister Tallyman was old enough to be my father. "Do you remember my father? As a student?"

Magister Tallyman shook his head, slowly. "He and his brother weren't in my year. I knew who they were, of course, but they didn't really impinge on me. They just weren't important."

Father wouldn't like to hear that, I thought, amused. Father was one of the most powerful men in the city. To be dismissed so casually…it was a little surprising. Father knew quite a bit about forging. Magister Tallyman should have known him better if they'd shared an interest in common. *But then, Father couldn't take up an apprenticeship either.*

I shrugged. "I don't suppose you know what happened when Father took the Challenge?"

"I didn't care enough to take note, at the time," Magister Tallyman said. "You'd be better off asking him. Or Hugh. He's been here since before the Fall."

"Hugh?"

"Magister Von Rupert," Magister Tallyman explained. "He was a teacher here when *I* was a lad."

Back in the days of the terrible lizards, I thought. I wasn't fool enough to say that out loud. Magister Tallyman liked me, as far as I could tell, but there were limits. *But if the old gent is that old, will he even remember?*

Magister Tallyman cleared his throat. "Was there anything else? Or do you want to help me forge another Device of Power?"

"I wish I had time," I said, honestly. "But yes, there was something else. I met a younger student"—I described Markus, quickly—"who wants to be your TA."

"Does he now?" Magister Tallyman seemed amused. "He does have potential, I'll give him that. But why do *you* care?"

I frowned. I honestly wasn't sure. There was a bit of me that felt a certain...kinship with Markus. We weren't related, as far as I knew, but we had something in common. And it wasn't as if we were competing. There was nothing to be gained by sabotaging Markus's schooling. Magister Tallyman couldn't make me his apprentice when I had to study under Father instead.

"I want to make sure that students have the best support," I said, carefully. It wasn't a lie, not really. "And a fourth-year might be more helpful than I."

Magister Tallyman looked as if he wanted to lift his eyebrows, if indeed he had any eyebrows *left*. "And is that true?"

"Sort of," I admitted.

It was true. It was rare—almost unknown—for a *firstie* to serve as a TA. I'd had problems with my own year, let alone older students. If I hadn't had the family name, I might have had as many...issues...as Louise. It was bad enough being lectured by another student without that student being two or three years younger than me. Markus, at least, wouldn't have that problem.

"And how much of your request comes from concern for me," Magister Tallyman asked, "and how much of it comes from a desire to build up a collection of favours owed to you?"

"A little of both." There was no point in trying to deny it, either. Father was right. I'd wasted the time I could have spent building up a patronage network for myself. "But that doesn't mean I'm wrong."

"True," Magister Tallyman agreed. "Tell you what. I'll test Markus. If he has the potential—enough potential—I'll give him the chance. If he doesn't, I'll take it out on you. Understand?"

"Yes, sir," I said.

"Good." Magister Tallyman gave me a toothy smile. It was far too easy to see that half of his teeth were missing. "Now go away, unless you wish to help."

I bowed, then hurried through the door. I'd gambled on impulse…Father had always told me to trust my instincts, but this could easily blow up in my face. Magister Tallyman hadn't been joking, when he said he'd take it out on me. A failure this early in my career as a patron would throw my entire future into doubt. And Father would be furious.

My legs carried me slowly up towards my suite. Someone had pinned a list of team leaders and members on the noticeboard at the top of the stairs. I stopped and scanned it thoughtfully. Alana had five listed team members already, while Ayesha and Zeya McDonald had three. I reminded myself that was still five. The McDonald twins were close, so close they were practically a single entity. Neither Cat nor I had ever had *that* sort of relationship with our siblings. Below them, Hamish Bolingbroke and I both had four team members each. Adam Mortimer was still on his own.

Four teams, I mused. *Five, if you count Adam.*

I shook my head slowly, then made my way down to the suite. If we had no way to know what was coming, we'd just have to try to prepare for everything. And we'd have to do our best to cover all the bases. But how *could* we? Did we need to bring food and drink as well as weapons and tools? Medical supplies? Or could we count on the spectators coming to our aid?

My blood ran cold. *People have died during the Challenge...*

I pushed open the door. Alana was sitting at her desk, working her way through some paperwork. The hall monitors list, from what I could see. I rubbed my eyes. I was going to have to patrol the halls myself, at some point. Tuesday, probably. I didn't have any classes until the afternoon, so I could sleep in afterwards...she looked up at me and smiled, tiredly.

"I hear you put Puce and her suitors in detention," she said. "What happened?"

"I caught them being bullies." Puce...Puce Harkness. A minor house, without much influence, but strong ties to Bolingbroke. I wondered if Hamish or Clarian were going to give me a hard time over it. I found it hard to care. "They can flirt while writing lines."

Alana's smile widened, just for a second. "Well put."

I shrugged. "Can I ask you a question?"

"Ask any question you like," Alana said. "I don't promise an answer."

"Hah," I said. "Is it just me...or is the Challenge really silly?"

"An easy question." Alana grinned. "It's just you."

"We could *die* on the field," I reminded her. "Our bodies might never be found."

Alana considered it for a moment. "If you didn't want to take the risk, you shouldn't have signed up in the first place."

I glared. "I didn't have a choice."

"There's always a choice," Alana said. "Dad taught me that, after... everything."

She shrugged. "Take the Challenge. Do everything in your power to try to win. Or choose to back out, now, and deal with the consequences. There comes a point where there is nothing to be gained from whining. Either you up and play the game..."

"Or get called a coward by all and sundry," I said. "If it was just me…"

"Then ditch the jock, the smartass and the dumbo," Alana said. "Go alone, if you must."

"I can't do that," I objected.

"Then stop moaning," Alana told me.

"Really," I said, as I headed for my bedroom. "You can talk."

She gave me a sweet smile. "And do. Frequently."

CHAPTER

FOURTEEN

"This...*this*...is where you want to practice spells?" Louise sounded as if I'd made an indecent suggestion. "This dusty old tomb?"

"It's a classroom, not a tomb," I pointed out.

"Practically identical, I would say." Francis laughed. "Do you have a better idea?"

I looked around, trying to see it through their eyes. The classroom had been abandoned decades—perhaps centuries—ago, the bookshelves and cupboards long since stripped of anything useful. Thirty desks sat in neat rows, their tops open to reveal that the compartments underneath were as empty as their matching chairs. I was surprised someone hadn't removed the desks and put them somewhere else. They might be decades out of fashion, but they were still usable. They didn't *seem* to have soaked up enough magic to make them dangerous. The room itself was perfectly usable.

But it was covered with dust, so much that it was clear no one had entered the room in years. Ours were the only visible footsteps. There were no hints that anyone else even knew the room existed, let alone that they'd bothered to visit. I imagined the scavengers would have been through years ago, then left it alone. Or maybe it had simply been stripped bare when it had been abandoned.

"We should find a safer room," Louise said. "One with proper protections and wards."

"One where everyone will know where to find us," Francis pointed out. "And we won't be able to...protect the room, not properly."

"Hah," Louise said. "You really think someone is going to spy on us?"

"It's part of the game," Francis reminded her. "Didn't you read the rules?"

I rolled my eyes, then started to cast spells. The dust reared up at my command, gusts of controlled wind pushing it towards the far walls. Saline smiled and began to cast spells of her own. The dust congealed into dustballs, which slowly solidified until they took on the consistency of snowballs. They'd make good weapons, I thought, if we ever had to throw them at someone. If nothing else, it wasn't the sort of weapon anyone would *expect*. Francis looked down at his sports kit, then started to push the desks to one side. Louise joined him a moment later. The floor was slowly becoming clear.

"Pretty," Saline commented. "But dead."

I followed her gaze. Someone had drawn a complicated network of runes and sigils on the floor, a pattern that had once summoned and shaped magic. Now, it was dead. Whoever had sealed the room had made sure of it, cutting across the incantation lines to make sure that the magic had dispelled long ago. I reached out with my senses, making sure there truly was nothing there. There was no hint of magic, save for the ever-present background hum of the school's wards. I'd long since grown used to their presence.

"I'll be picking dust out of my hair and dress for *weeks*," Louise complained. "I hope this is worth it."

"You should have worn your gym kit," Francis said. "It's a *lot* easier to clean."

"I burnt it after I became an upperclassman," Louise said. "Four years of running around on a muddy field was *quite* enough."

"Hear, hear," I said. I hadn't *burnt* my gym clothes, but I'd taken a certain childish glee in leaving them at the hall when I'd become an upperclassman myself. "I quite understand."

"You'll just have to put up with the dust." Francis finished pushing the desks aside and came back to the centre of the room. "And next time, perhaps you should wear something you can *move* in."

Louise coloured, but said nothing. I had to admit—privately—that Francis had a point. Louise's dress would have looked elegant at a party, but it was utterly useless for anything that required physical activity. I honestly wasn't sure why she'd worn it. There were plenty of options that didn't involve trousers. Besides, Louise was a commoner. She wouldn't face *quite* so much comment if she dared to wear trousers.

I put the thought aside and started to cast privacy wards. Francis joined me a second later, layering one set of wards on top of the next. I had no illusions—a master wardcrafter would have no trouble taking them down—but the cluster of warning spells should at least *tell* us if we were being watched. Louise and Saline watched, Louise's hand twitching as if she wanted to help. I was glad she didn't. I'd never worked with her before. Our magics wouldn't mesh together properly.

We'll have to fix that, I mused. I finished casting the wards, keyed them to the four of us and sat down. *By the time we go into the field, we'll have to be ready.*

I cleared my throat. "I hereby call this meeting to order," I said. My father had said the same, often enough, although *he* managed to make it sound dramatic. I had the feeling that *I* sounded like a prat. "First order of business: deciding just what we're going to do."

"You're the boss," Francis said. "You *tell* us what to do."

"I didn't agree to that," Louise said, immediately. "If you make decisions for me, without consulting me, I reserve the right to disregard them."

"He's trying to get your goat," Saline said. She knelt beside Louise, brushing down her long black skirt. "And he's succeeding, too."

"We need to work together," I said, quickly. "I've been giving the matter some thought."

I took a breath. "There are obvious limits to what we can produce for ourselves *and* carry onto the field," I said. "And as we don't know what we'll actually be *doing*, it's hard to tell what we might need."

"We already know that," Francis said, dryly.

"I'm just setting the stage." I pulled my notebook off my belt. "I think we should concentrate on three things. Weapons, tools and food. And drink. We may discover that we're expected to spend days or weeks undertaking the Challenge."

Louise paled. "And they won't feed us?"

"We're meant to fend for ourselves," I reminded her. "Do *you* know how to conjure food from thin air?"

"No," Louise said. "Do *you*?"

I shook my head. It wasn't *impossible* to conjure food, but it required more power and discipline than I had. And the food had a tendency to vanish, shortly afterwards. Anyone who stuffed themselves with conjured food might discover they became hungry again, at the very least. At worst…they might find their lives at risk. It was easier and safer to transmute something I didn't like into something I *did*, but even that had its perils. I wouldn't care to rely on transfigured food when I might be miles from medical help.

"So we take some food and bottles of water," Francis said. He shrugged. "We don't know if there's water there either, do we?"

"No." I knew spells to clean water, but they'd be useless if there was no water in the first place. "But they can't want us to die of thirst."

Francis snickered. "Are you sure?"

Louise gave him a sharp look. "What do you mean?"

"Perhaps the *real* purpose of the contest is to *remove* magicians who might prove dangerous," Francis said. "If you're too good at magic, you die in the contest and no one bats an eyelid."

"… Impossible," Louise said. "Someone would have noticed!"

"Yes," I said. "Of all the paranoid conspiracy theories…"

"Just because you're paranoid doesn't mean that someone *isn't* out to get you." Francis leaned back, clasping his hands behind his head. "We know so little. We don't even know the *rules*."

"We know some of them," Louise said.

"Yes, but are they *all* of the rules?" Francis chuckled. "For all we know, they won't tell us about the rest of the rules until it's too late."

"That wouldn't be fair," Louise insisted. "They can't blame us for breaking rules we didn't know existed."

"Debate it later," I told them. "Right now, we have work to do."

I opened the notebook and showed them the first page. "It shouldn't be difficult to get our hands on food and drink. We can brew a handful of nutrient potions—I know they taste foul, but they'll keep us going. If we each carry a handful of vials, we should be able to cope if we lose one or two…"

"If they get stolen, you mean." Francis looked grim. "The other teams may be planning to take what they need from us."

Saline laughed. "If everyone is planning to steal from everyone else, there will be nothing *to* steal."

I grinned. "That would be unfortunate, wouldn't it?"

"Yes," Louise said, primly. "We'd *all* be in trouble."

"I understand you're good at brewing potions," I said, to Louise. "Can you brew these for us?"

"Yes." Louise studied the list thoughtfully. "I don't have the knack, I've been told, but I can make these."

"We should look for a brewer," Francis said. "We need at least two more teammates."

"Everyone who hasn't been snapped up has declared their neutrality," I said. "We can't ask them…"

"Then we look at the lower years," Francis said. "There are a couple of promising sixth-years…hey, we could ask *Penny*."

"That's a thought." I didn't think Penny would want to join. And even if she did, she would be two years behind most of the contestants. "I'll think about it."

"I can brew the potions," Louise said. "I just need the supplies."

"I'll see to it," I told her. I took back the notebook and flipped to the next page. "We'll also need a handful of medical potions and suchlike."

"We do have healing spells," Francis pointed out.

"Potions are more reliable," I reminded him. "And now…"

I turned the page, again. "I intend to forge a number of Devices of Power," I said. I held out the list. "Do you have any suggestions?"

"More spellcasters," Francis said. He frowned. "Why are you going with Tennant's Multitool when you could be going with Davidson's? Or Whittaker's?"

"Tennant's is more versatile," I said. "It isn't as *precise* as Davidson's or Whittaker's, but you can do more with it. If I knew what we were facing…"

I shrugged. "We have to cover as many of the bases as possible. And there are, as always, limits to what we can carry."

"It's a good list." Saline looked bored. "Are we going to practice magic now?"

"Yeah," Francis said. He jumped to his feet. "Let's cast spells, shall we?"

"I can forge all of these and store them here until we need them," I said. "But do we need anything else?"

"I'll think of something." Francis smirked. "But now…magic."

Louise clambered to her feet. "Where do we start?"

"Basic hexes and spells, then work our way onwards," Francis said. He winked at me. "That's how *I* do it on the sports field."

"I don't want to know what you do on the sports field," I muttered, as I stood. "Where shall we begin?"

Francis grinned and started to demonstrate a handful of first-years spells, including a couple of uses I'd never considered, Louise looked bored at first, then rapidly got interested as Francis talked about how they could be used on the sports field. Neither of the girls had any trouble mastering the spells, the handful they didn't already know. It wasn't until we reached fifth-year spells that they started to have problems.

"You need more power," Francis told Louise, flatly. "Your spellcasting is good, but you don't have the power to back it."

"And how do I *get* the power?" Louise grimaced, as if she'd bitten into something unpleasant. "You don't just *wish* for it."

"You work hard," I said. "And you practice."

I turned to Saline, leaving Louise and Francis to practice spells. It wasn't Louise's fault that she was underpowered, compared to the rest of us. Francis, Saline and I had been practicing magic since we were five years old. We'd developed power reserves Louise didn't even know existed. She would catch up, unless she'd already peaked, but...she would never be a match for Alana. She was skilled at making use of what she had, yet...

Intelligence can always beat raw power, I thought, remembering something my first tutor had used to say. *A person who knows what he's doing will always have the edge. But if that person is facing someone with more power who also knows what he's doing...he'll lose.*

Saline gave me a shy smile as she tried to cast a complex spell. I frowned as I watched, trying to see what was actually *happening.* Saline had the raw power to cast the spell, but she wasn't casting it quite *right.* There were odd little gaps in her spellcasting, flaws that weakened or neutralised the spell. I could *feel* the waves of raw power radiating out from her spellcasting. She had the power, all right. But she didn't have the comprehension.

"Try again," I said. "Do it piece by piece."

Saline nodded and started again. I sensed the magic starting to take shape, the building blocks of the spell falling into place. It was...crude, in many ways, without the elegance I'd come to expect from my peers. And yet, it worked. Saline just had to keep plodding, it seemed. She couldn't progress in leaps and bounds.

"Well done," I said, when she cast the spell. "It worked!"

She smiled at me. She was very pretty when she smiled.

"But she has to cast the spell quicker," Francis said. "Try it again."

Saline looked downcast, but went to work. The spell started to build… and Francis threw a hex at her, freezing her in place. The magic surrounding her faded back into the aether as I rounded on Francis. He looked utterly unrepentant, utterly unmoved by my anger and Louise's shock. Indeed, he was smirking.

"You utter…" Louise bit off a word young ladies weren't supposed to know. "What did you do *that* for?"

"She was taking too long to cast her spell," Francis said. He stepped past her and stopped in front of Saline. "In the time it took for her to cast the spell, I could have done a lot worse to her than simply freezing her in place. She would be first person taken off the field…"

"You don't *know* that," Louise snapped.

"Yes, I do." Francis tapped Saline's forehead. "You have played dodge-ball, have you not? The slowest players are always the ones taken off first."

Louise cast the counterspell. Saline stumbled forward, nearly losing her balance and falling to the floor. I put out a hand to steady her. Her eyes were wide with shock, but she wasn't angry. I wasn't sure why. I wouldn't have been happy if someone had attacked *me* like that…

"You should have let her free herself," Francis said. "It's the only way she'll learn."

"She needs practice," Louise insisted.

"Exactly," Francis said. "And you're not *giving* her the practice!"

I rubbed my forehead. "Have you ever tried casting spells together?"

"You mean, as a team?" Louise glanced at Saline, who shrugged. "I was…I was never allowed to practice."

"Odd." Francis frowned. "Did you ever *try*?"

Louise flushed red, but didn't rise to the bait.

"Try now," I said. "If Saline provides the power, Louise should be able to cast the spell."

Francis glanced at me. "This could prove dangerous."

I didn't believe it. "And when did you care about *danger*?"

"We'll cast a spell on him," Louise said. She walked around until she was standing in front of Saline. "Are you ready?"

Saline rested her hands on Louise's neck, her fingers touching bare skin. "Ready."

I stepped to one side as the power began to build. Saline was putting out a *lot* of power...my hair tried to stand on end as electric sparks flickered in and out of existence between the two girls. Louise started to cast the spell, the power rapidly taking on shape and form...Francis raised a shield charm, but it was too late. The charm shattered, pieces of magic flying in all directions. And Francis's body melted into a dog.

Saline giggled. "It suits him."

"It should have been a worm," Louise said. "Or a slug. But that would have been redundant."

Francis barked, loudly. I could tell he was trying to break the spell, but... it still took him several tries before the spell broke and his body snapped back to normal. He was on all-fours, looking incredibly silly...I bit my lip to keep from laughing as he stumbled awkwardly to his feet. The spell had been incredibly powerful. I'd sensed the overspill from metres away.

"Hah," Francis said. "I broke the spell."

Louise gave him a sweet smile. "And I could have stepped on you before you escaped, if I'd wished."

Francis glared at her. "I..."

"Good work," I said, cutting him off. We didn't have time for another argument. "Now, we need to practice..."

"Wait." Francis held up a hand. The alarm on his face was striking. "Check the wards. Can you feel that!"

I blinked, then reached out with my mind. The wards were pulsing around us, yet...something was wrong. No, an *absence* of something. I felt a flicker of alarm as I started to inspect the entire network. Someone had managed to slip a probe into my wards, carefully picking their way through the array of spells...someone was *spying* on us. I exchanged horrified looks with Francis. We used similar spells to protect our bedrooms at the mansion.

Saline caught my arm. "What's happening?"

Francis turned and ran towards the door. "Someone is *spying* on us!"

CHAPTER
FIFTEEN

I readied a spell as I followed Francis to the door, although I wasn't sure *what* I'd do to any intruders. Turn them into toads, perhaps, or objects? Or…there were limits, certainly before the Challenge actually began. Francis threw the door open and charged out, casting a powerful discovery spell. Anyone lurking in the shadows, hidden behind an obscurification charm or an invisibility cloak, should have been instantly noticeable. But the corridor was empty. Dust motes floated in the halflight, undisturbed by our presence. I listened as carefully as I could, but there were no retreating footsteps. We were alone.

Louise stepped up to me. "I can't see anyone."

"Nor can I," Francis said. "But I definitely *sensed* someone."

Saline caught my arm. "Perhaps we should move."

"Hell with that," Francis grunted. He shot me an unreadable look. "This is *our* room. We're not moving just because someone knows where we are."

I was tempted to agree. The abandoned classroom was practically perfect for our needs. Room to practice spells, cupboards to store our supplies… I didn't want to abandon it in a hurry. And yet, Saline had a point. Anyone who wanted to hamper our team had already found our base. It was just a matter of time until they managed to find a way to break our wards and slip inside.

"I don't know," I temporised. I stepped back into the room and reached out to query the wards again. There was no longer any sign of an intruder. If I hadn't sensed it—if Francis hadn't sensed it—I would have doubted the intruder had even been there. Whoever had probed our defences had been *good*. "This room is ours."

I forced myself to think as Francis closed the door and started tightening the ward network, piece by piece. How had the intruder even *found* us? We'd taken care to sneak through the corridors, making sure we took the long way around just in case we were being followed...perhaps we were being paranoid, but all was apparently fair in the Challenge. And we'd used scattershot spells to make it difficult for anyone to track us through magic. It wouldn't have been entirely impossible, but it would have been very difficult. It would have required blood magic, and blood magic was banned at school.

"We can keep the room," I said, finally. "But we'll double our wards and look around for somewhere else, if necessary."

Louise checked her watch. "I have to be in the library in thirty minutes," she said. "If you don't mind, I'll go for a shower and a change."

"You're cutting it fine," Francis teased.

"Hah." Louise, for once, didn't rise to the bait. "Saline? You coming?"

Saline nodded. "When do we meet again?"

"Tuesday evening," I said. "But feel free to come here and practice at any time."

"You *should* practice." Francis sounded stern. "You need to speed up your spellcasting."

Louise nodded curtly to me, then turned and walked out of the room. Saline followed, closing the door behind her. I shook my head slowly as I started to cast the next set of wards, warding the chamber as solidly as I could. The intruder had been very—very—good. It was hard to pick up traces of his presence now, as if he'd carefully repaired the damage he'd done when he slipped back into the shadows. It had been sheer luck we'd caught him in the first place.

Francis squatted on the floor and peered up at me. "How did he even *find* us?"

I shook my head. "I don't know. Maybe we weren't the first to find this room."

"Perhaps," Francis said. "Or maybe someone betrayed us."

"Who?" It didn't seem likely. Rose had been with me when I'd found the classroom, true, but she wouldn't have told Alana. Or anyone else, for that matter. "Who even knew we were coming here?"

"The girls knew," Francis said. "One of them could have betrayed us."

I snorted. "Francis, they didn't know we were coming here until we *led* them here. How could they give away our secrets if they didn't *know* our secrets?"

"Louise is smart," Francis said, dryly. "And Saline is dumb. Louise could have tagged herself so our intruder knew to follow her—Saline could have been tagged without her knowledge. Either way, they would have led the intruder right to our door."

"Saline isn't dumb," I said, hotly. "She's just a bit slow."

"That's *dumb*," Francis said.

I shook my head. Saline wouldn't have become an upperclassman if she was *dumb*. A student who'd reached their limits by the time they took their exams at the end of fourth year would have been gently advised to go elsewhere. They certainly wouldn't be welcomed into the upper classes. Saline's father could have bribed all and sundry, I supposed, but…I shook my head. *Cat's* father had pulled all sorts of strings to get her into Jude's. It was astonishing just how much people were prepared to overlook if they were insulted with a fairly considerable bribe.

Or so Father keeps saying, I reminded myself. *But surely there are limits.*

"She has the power," I mused. "But she cannot quite grasp the concepts without a lot of hard work."

"It sounds like she needs remedial education." Francis stood up. "Are you going to be teaching her the basics? Again?"

"If I have to," I said, evenly. I hoped it wouldn't be necessary, but if there was no choice…I'd do it. "She does have a lot of power."

"So you keep saying." Francis winked. "Do you have a crush on her?"

"I…*no*." I was genuinely shocked at his suggestion. "I'm betrothed!"

"Just because you're betrothed doesn't mean you can't look." Francis gave me another wink. "Saline is just the sort of girl you like. Cute. Sweet. Huge tracts of land…"

My face grew warm. "I don't know what you're talking about."

"Yes, you do." Francis smirked at me. "You like her."

"Enough," I snapped. "I'm betrothed!"

Francis shrugged. "And your betrothed is far from here. She'll never know."

"I'd know." I glared at him. "And I do care about her."

"How sweet," Francis said. He waved a hand at the wooden ceiling. "Do you realise what you're missing?"

"Enough," I repeated. "Right now, we have to get through the Challenge without being killed. Or being turned into dogs."

"Woof, woof," Francis said. He headed to the door. "You do realise that we're going to have to push back?"

"No," I said, as I followed him. "We don't know who spied on us. We can't go around hexing people at random."

Francis managed to sound genuinely puzzled. "Why not?"

I made a rude gesture at his back as I started to cast a series of wards, detection charms and booby traps. Anyone who tried to enter the room, unless they were already keyed to the wards, would find it very difficult. And, if they got through the first layer of keep-out wards, they'd find themselves caught in a network of booby traps. I made a mental note to come and check regularly. Someone might wind up trapped so thoroughly they couldn't get out.

Which would get us in trouble, if they didn't show up to class, I thought. *It would depend on who actually got the blame.*

"Nice work," Francis said. "I'd like to see the sorcerer who could get past *that*."

"No, you wouldn't." I snorted, rudely. "If we saw him, he'd be getting past it."

I took one final look, then turned and headed along the corridor. Francis followed, his footsteps echoing in the silent air. I looked from side to side, watching for signs of our intruder, but there was nothing. I didn't even see other footsteps in the dust until we reached one of the more well-travelled sections. Behind me, Francis cast a spell to hide our footsteps from prying eyes.

And someone else could have easily done the same to us, I thought, coldly. *Who knows?*

Francis nudged me as we reached the top of the stairs. "You talk to Penny, when you have a moment," he said, as we cast spells to remove the dust. "I'll see about a couple of other possible players."

"Check with me first," I said. "We don't want to make anyone fail their exams."

"Then they can retake the year." Francis chuckled. "They won't be the first and they won't be the last."

I gave him a sharp look. "Seriously."

Francis shrugged. "I'm expected on the sports field in an hour," he said. "I'll see you later."

"Later," I agreed.

I watched him go, then turned and walked towards the office complex at the heart of the school. It felt odd to be stepping through the wards as if I owned the place. I felt vaguely as through I was trespassing, even though—as Head Boy—I had a perfect right to enter as I saw fit. I'd sneaked in and out of the section a couple of times, when I'd been younger, but if I'd been caught...truthfully, knowing that I would be in trouble if I *was* caught was part of the thrill. Francis and I had more in common than I cared to admit.

The records room sat at the bottom of the corridor, guarded by heavy wards. I put my hand on the doorknob and waited for the wards to unlock before I stepped inside. The air inside was very cold, a sense of *potential* hanging in the air. I felt an odd little shiver. The feeling of being out of place, of being somewhere I really wasn't *supposed* to be, grew stronger. I told myself, firmly, that I was being silly. The wards would never have let me in without a fight if I wasn't supposed to be there.

And even though I do have a right to be here, I don't have a good explanation, I thought. *I'd better hurry before someone demands answers.*

The filing cabinets opened at my touch, revealing hundreds upon hundreds of files. I was tempted to peek at a handful—Alana's, Francis's, my own—but instead I merely sifted through them until I found Saline's. It was thicker than I'd expected—Alana's was surprisingly thin, given all the trouble she'd caused—and a pair of nasty charms snapped at me until I managed to counter them. I took the folder, put it on the desk and started to skim through it. I knew better than to risk taking the file out of the room.

Saline's permanent record was...odd. She'd clearly been a very bright girl when she'd started school, although—curiously—she'd done her first year at Roanoke. I supposed that explained why she didn't have many friends. By the time she'd transferred to Jude's, most of her peers had formed friendships and patronage networks that wouldn't have much room for a newcomer. And yet...she'd done well, up until she became an upperclassman. There was no hint that anyone had bribed the school to admit her. There had been no need.

And yet, she'd started to decline.

I read through the records—exam reports, essay marks, disciplinary referrals—and frowned as I tried to make heads or tails of them. There was no cause, as far as I could tell, but Saline had simply started to go downhill. She'd started having problems, which had led to more problems, which had led to her falling behind. The teachers hadn't noted any behavioural problems, but...I shook my head. Had she been pushed too hard? Or had she simply peaked?

And no one noticed? My thoughts mocked me. *That doesn't seem very likely.*

I read through the last notes in the file, then closed it up and returned it to the cabinet. Whatever had gone wrong had gone wrong very slowly, which meant...what? A charm? If she was under a charm...I considered the possibilities as I slipped out of the room and headed back to my suite. If she was under a charm, a spell designed to make it harder for her to learn...why?

Who would do that to her? I asked myself. *And why?*

Francis didn't think much of the idea, when I told him about it. "Every time we go home, we cleanse ourselves. It's common sense. Why would Saline's family not check her for spells whenever *she* went home?"

I had to admit he had a point. Louise was common-born—her parents might not be aware of the danger, let alone know what they needed to do about it—but Saline came from an aristocratic family. They'd been practicing magic for centuries. They might not have qualified as a Great House—if they had, I doubted she would have joined my team—but they were far from powerless. Saline's condition could hardly have passed unnoticed. If they'd had any reason to suspect long-term spell damage, or a charm someone had placed on their daughter, they would have turned the world upside down to find a cure.

"Maybe they can't find the spell," I mused. "Or it did its work and evaporated."

"There would still be something detectable," Francis pointed out. "You can't hide a curse."

"Not easily," I agreed. The really dangerous curses were designed to hide themselves, but the effects were noticeable even if the curse itself was invisible. "But it's odd to think that she slowly went downhill without anyone noticing."

"People don't always get better," Francis said. "Look at Lope. A terror on the minor fields, when he was a lowerclassman, but he came apart the moment he set foot on the major fields. I had to kick him off the team for actually *catching* the ball..."

"How terrible," I said, dryly. "Catching a ball someone kicked at you."

"He nearly cost us the game," Francis said. "Only the goalie is allowed to touch the ball with his bare hands."

"And then someone cheated by claiming that, as he was wearing gloves, he wasn't actually touching the ball with his *bare* hands," I said. I'd heard the story. "Didn't he get away with it?"

Francis grinned. "They had to rewrite the rules, just for him."

I snorted. There was a certain kind of pleasure, I supposed, in finding a loophole...even if the loophole was closed very quickly. But it still struck me as silly. If Francis put as much effort into his studies as he did into playing games, he would have left me behind long ago. He might even have bested Alana in the quest for valedictorian. She was pretty much at the top of the league.

"The minors are meant to be *fun*," Francis said, more seriously. "No one *really* gets mad if you make a mistake. But the majors? Oh, if you make a mistake, it will haunt you for the rest of your life. Lope just folded under the pressure."

"Fun," I repeated. "Let me tell you how much I *hate* sports."

Francis held up his hands in mock surrender. "You don't need to tell me again, really."

He shrugged. "But you know as well as I do that upperclassmen are under a lot of pressure. If you want an apprenticeship, this is your last chance to prove yourself worthy. If you're an Heir...this is your chance to prove yourself worthy too. How many students have trouble coping? And how many of them actually dare to show it? We'd be mocked if we showed weakness in front of the class..."

"True." I'd seen Janice break down and cry once, back in fourth year. She'd never been allowed to forget it. "But Saline is too good-natured to be under stress..."

"You *do* like her," Francis carolled. "I knew it."

I glared. "And she does pick up concepts, when people take the time to explain it to her," I insisted. "She's not stupid."

"She may be under a lot of stress you can't see," Francis said. "I know *you* think I'm being stupid, when I talk about the importance of winning games, but it's important to *me*."

"I suppose," I conceded. "Do you think we should bring it to someone's attention?"

Francis frowned. "That Saline needs help?"

"That something might be wrong," I said. "If she has been charmed, or spell-damaged…"

Francis cut me off. "First, you don't *know* she's been charmed. You'd need to have some kind of proof before you started hurling those accusations around. And second, if she hasn't been charmed, people will say you're showing an untoward interest in her."

"People like you?" I met his eyes. "She's a teammate, you know. We have a responsibility to help her."

"And we're not allowed to ask for outside help, or we might wind up being disqualified," Francis said. He shrugged. "Why don't you suggest she teaches Louise how to cleanse herself? It might get rid of any…unwanted spells on Saline too."

I gave him a sharp look. "You have got to be kidding."

"Take one for the team," Francis advised. He leered cheerfully in my general direction. "Probably literally, in this case."

"You…" I sighed. "It might work."

"Yeah," Francis said. "And while you're at it, you might also plan how you're going to teach etiquette to Louise. The way she's going, she'll spark off a House War just by walking in the front door. Or she'll be kicked out within seconds of the moment she opens her mouth."

"Another problem," I said. "But, fortunately, I have books to help."

Francis gave me a mock-appalled look. "You're going to make her read Lady Dancing Sunbeam's books on how the Decent Woman Should Comport Herself in Polite Society? Poor Louise! What has she ever done to you?"

I laughed.

CHAPTER
SIXTEEN

The school felt eerie after dark, as if familiar corridors and chambers became something strange and alien when the lights were out. I strode down the corridor, my footsteps echoing oddly in the shadows as I walked past a set of closed doors. The statues of famous magicians through the ages became twisted and warped in the semi-darkness; the stuffed and mounted animals on the walls became terrifying monsters...I knew them all, in the light, but I still got nervous as I caught glimpses of them in the darkness. They seemed to take on an entirely different aspect in the shadows.

And there are supposed to be ghosts in the school, I thought, as I walked onwards. *Who knows what might be lurking in the darkness?*

I shrugged, dismissing the thought. I'd never seen a ghost, not in Jude's, but everyone knew a friend of a friend who'd seen *something* after dark. I had a private suspicion that what they'd *really* seen had been an upperclassman on patrol. Some of my peers were sadistic enough to pretend to be ghosts, although that sometimes backfired. I'd been a fourth year when the Head Boy had come down to breakfast, sporting a magnificent black eye. The official story had been that he'd walked into a wall, but I knew the truth. Francis had been sneaking around the school and, when he'd been caught, had lashed out. By tradition, anyone who managed to escape had to be let go, but Francis had been lucky the Head Boy hadn't seen him clearly. I wouldn't have cared to be in Francis's shoes for the rest of the year if he'd been recognised.

And now I'm in the Head Boy's shoes, I reminded myself. *I'd better be careful.*

I yawned as I slipped down the stairs, listening carefully for the sound of tiny footsteps. It was uncommon for firsties to start sneaking around the school so early, but the other years…*they* might have started right from the start. Alana had told me that she'd caught a pair of third-years trying to break into the kitchen only a day ago. I wondered just what sort of reception they'd had in the dorms, when she'd marched them back upstairs. Their dormmates would have been expecting a midnight feast, not a hasty dive under the covers when the Head Girl walked in. The dorm monitor had probably received an earful too. Letting the younger students sneak out was bad enough, but getting caught at it was worse.

It was difficult not to yawn again as I reached the bottom of the stairs. Mondays were always busy, but this Monday had been bad. I would have swapped patrol duties if I'd thought anyone would be willing to exchange. I wanted my bed, not…I considered, briefly, just going back to bed anyway, before putting the thought out of my head. I had a duty and…I stopped, dead, as I heard scuffling from inside the kitchen. The door was ajar. A thrill of excitement ran through me. Someone was inside.

Got you, I thought, as I inched forward. The sound stopped, abruptly. Whoever was inside knew I was there. *And now…*

Sweat prickled on my back as I pushed the door open, a spell dancing over my fingertips. If whoever was inside took a swing at me, he'd regret it. And yet…nothing moved inside. I wondered, for a moment, if I'd been hearing things before I saw the shape standing in front of the cupboard. I laughed, despite myself. The hypnotic spell the kitchen staff used to defend the biscuit cupboard had claimed another victim. It was easy to avoid, if you saw it coming, but if it took hold of you before you realised you were there…I relaxed, slightly, as I inched closer. The lowerclassman stood there, dumbly. He must have walked straight into the spell when he was trying to hide.

I reached out and tapped his shoulder. He jumped, spinning around. The spell had practically frozen his awareness. He wouldn't have heard me coming up behind him. He wouldn't even have been aware of my presence. To him, I'd practically appeared from nowhere. He lost his footing a second later, crashing to the floor. I peered down at him, silently noting his face. A second-year, clearly. Old enough to know enough magic to get into the kitchen, but too young to be sensitive to the more dangerous traps…

"On your feet," I said, without heat. I wasn't really angry. Sneaking around school was an old tradition, after all. I'd done it myself as a lower-classman. "Name?"

"Um…" The lowerclassman paused, clearly trying to think of a fake name. "Daniel Morgan."

"Really?" I didn't believe him. "Danny is *real*?"

The lowerclassman flushed. It probably hadn't occurred to him that taking a name from a funny strip character hadn't been a good idea. I might have outgrown them a few years ago, but I still remembered. It wasn't as if I'd sprung into the world fully-grown.

"Simon." He lowered his eyes. "Simon Portage."

"That's better." I took the punishment book from my belt and scribbled down a note. "Write fifty lines. *I will not get caught when I sneak out of my dorm in the small hours.* Understand?"

"Yes, sir," Simon said.

"Good." I jabbed a finger at the door. "Go back to bed. And don't get caught again."

Simon hurried out the door and ran up the stairs. I smiled after him, then closed the kitchen door and resumed my patrol. There was no need for any further punishment. He hadn't done any real damage, after all. Besides, his dormmates would give him a very hard time, once he got back upstairs. They'd mock him relentlessly until someone else got caught.

The remainder of the patrol passed uneventfully. I returned to my suite at five in the morning, when the servants started lighting fires and cooking food for the students, and flopped into bed with a sense of relief. I needed to write a report, but it could wait. Besides, I was the person who was meant to *read* the report. I resolved to speak very sharply to myself later, then closed my eyes. My alarm spell went off a second later. It took me several minutes to realise it was noon.

I checked my watch, just to make sure, then stumbled into the shower before changing into a fresh uniform. It was nearly lunchtime…I picked up my bag, then hurried out of the bedroom, through the office and down the corridor. If I was lucky, I'd have a chance to catch up with Penny before she went down for lunch. We really *weren't* supposed to be speaking publicly, not given that there were two years between us. Or unless we had a very good excuse…

A trio of lowerclassmen hurried past me as I entered their dorm complex. Simon was amongst them. He lowered his eyes as he saw me, as if he was afraid of catching my attention again. I ignored him as best as I could. Upperclassmen were not supposed to notice lowerclassmen unless they were doing something naughty. It wasn't quite as easy as people made it sound.

I smiled at the thought as I passed through the wards to the firstie dorms, then frowned as I heard someone shouting in the distance. I picked up speed as the voice grew louder. It sounded like Penny. No, it *was* Penny. I rounded the corner to see Penny looming over a Firstie girl, who cowered against the wall. She was shouting loudly enough to be heard on the other side of the school.

"…uniform is a total disgrace!" she shouted. She looked as if she was on the verge of picking the girl up and shaking her. "And your braids…"

She reached out and tugged at the girl's braids. The girl yelped in pain as they came loose, blonde hair spilling down around her face. I felt my heart twist. She looked so much like Isabella that it was almost painful, even though her face was different…I knew, technically, that I should turn

144

and walk away. But I couldn't...the girl could have been my sister, if things had been different. If...

"And what would happen," Penny demanded, "if one of the boys tugged on your braids?"

I cleared my throat. "What—exactly—are you doing?"

Penny jumped. I saw magic darting over her fingers as she swung around to face me. Behind her, the girl started to splutter. She looked as if she wanted to turn and run. I'd caught her being bullied by her dorm monitor, her braids were down and...I didn't blame her for being horrified. If there was anything worse than being picked on, it was having people watching while you were being picked on.

"I was teaching Kate the ropes," Penny said. She stood upright, her hands resting on her hips. "Go away."

I cocked my eyebrow, then looked at Kate. She was utterly terrified. "Is that true?"

Kate looked from me to Penny and back again. "Yes," she stammered. Tears were streaking her face. "I'm..."

"Go into your dorm, get cleaned up and go down for lunch," I ordered. I knew Kate was lying, but I didn't blame her. No one could afford a reputation as a sneak, even if the people they sneaked on thoroughly deserved it. "And close the door as you pass."

Penny's face reddened. "How *dare* you?"

I felt my temper rise. "How dare *you*, you...what did you *think* you were doing?"

"She's *my* charge," Penny said, ignoring my question. "And she can't go out of the dorm looking like the common-born brat she is! I knew how to tie a tie when I was her age!"

"You had six years of education from a succession of governesses," I pointed out. Penny's governesses had tended to resign. I had a sneaking suspicion I knew why. "Kate's first introduction to etiquette came when she entered the school, ten *days* ago. Do you really expect her to know how to tie a tie?"

"It isn't difficult," Penny insisted. One hand went to the tie around her neck. "I know how…"

"It took me years to learn," I told her. In truth, I hadn't mastered it until I turned fifteen. I'd just figured out how to use magic to tie the tie. It had nearly strangled me, a couple of times, but it had worked. "It takes *time* to learn."

Penny ignored me. "You have absolutely *no* business butting in…"

I took a moment to compose myself. Francis might believe that Penny could join the team, and that she might be useful, but I didn't. I'd intended to give her the chance, yet now…I shook my head. She could take the Challenge herself, in two years, if she lived so long. I had the feeling the firsties were on the verge of mutiny already. And it had only been ten days!

"You seem to have forgotten who you're talking to." I channelled my father, as best as I could. He didn't shout, when he got really angry. His voice grew so cold that the air seemed to turn to ice. "I am the Head Boy, Heir Primus of your House. You do *not* talk to me like that. Not now. Not *ever*."

Penny paled as she realised just how badly she'd put her foot in it. Upperclassmen had freedoms lowerclassmen lacked, but they didn't include the freedom to be rude to the Head Boy. And I *would* be her Patriarch, when my father died or retired. I could make her life thoroughly miserable, if I bore a grudge. She knew she was in trouble.

She dropped to her knees, bowing her head. "I seek pardon," she said, formally. "And I…"

The door opened, behind her. I cursed Kate's timing as she hurried out of the door, almost tripping over Penny. Penny would *never* forgive Kate for witnessing her humiliation. It was bad enough to have to beg my forgiveness on bended knee. If word got out…

I said nothing, but jerked my head towards the corridor. Kate took the hint and practically ran past us and down the stairs. I hoped she'd have the sense to keep her mouth closed. If she talked…Penny would do something stupid. I was sure of it.

"I seek pardon," Penny repeated. I could practically hear her teeth grinding. "And I…"

I took a moment to centre myself. "You are the dorm monitor," I told her. "It is your job to help them settle into school, to teach them the basics of school life and etiquette…it is *not* your job to bully them, or to belittle them when they make mistakes…mistakes that shouldn't surprise you, as you made mistakes when *you* were a little girl."

My heart twisted again. Kate really *did* look like Isabella.

"It's my responsibility," Penny said, quietly. "What they do reflects on me…"

I let out a sigh. "No one expects them to be practically perfect in every way," I pointed out, as calmly as I could. "No one is going to blame you when they mess up."

"Really," Penny said.

"Really." I allowed my voice to harden. "They will blame you, though, if you treat them badly. Or if you lay hands on them."

"My dorm monitor slapped me," Penny said, dully.

"She shouldn't have done that," I told her. The nasty part of me found it hard to blame the poor girl. But…I was surprised Penny hadn't complained. Her father would have had something to say about it—and *he* was married to my aunt. "And you should have complained."

Penny lowered her eyes and said nothing. I looked at her for a moment, then shook my head.

"Get up," I ordered. I was tempted to leave her on her knees, but someone else might be along at any moment. "And listen to me."

I waited until she was standing, then met her eyes. "You are to treat your charges well. I'm not asking for you to be their best friend, or pretend you're one of them, but you are to treat them well. Show patience, when you try to teach them the ropes. And *don't* mistreat any of them. Do *not* give Kate a hard time because she saw you on your knees."

Penny reddened, again. "If she tells the world…"

"She won't," I said, although I had no way to be sure of it. Kate was a commoner. She had no way to understand what she'd seen—or why she should keep her mouth shut. Penny had sacrificed her dignity to plead for forgiveness. "Give her a chance. Give all of them a chance."

"You don't understand," Penny whined. "You were…"

"I was a dorm monitor," I reminded her. I hadn't enjoyed it—and there had been times when I'd wanted to strangle the little brats—but I hadn't bullied them either. "I coped. You can cope too."

"Yes, but you had boys," Penny said. "I have girls."

I blinked. "What difference does *that* make?"

"Your boys had all the freedom they wanted before they came to school," Penny argued, angrily. "My girls had no freedoms *until* they came to school."

"Really." It sounded like a weak argument to *me*. I'd spent half of my fifth year chasing boys who'd let their new freedoms go to their head. But then, I supposed Isabella might have agreed with her cousin. "It doesn't matter. You are *not* to mistreat them. Be their big sister, instead. Be *there* for them."

Penny looked unimpressed. "You've seen how Cousin Candy treats *her* siblings?"

"Then try and do better than her," I growled. "She's a bad example. Do better."

I turned, then stopped. "And if you do it again, I'll give you lines."

Penny flushed. "You *wouldn't*."

"If you act like a kid, I'll treat you like a kid." I lifted my hand in farewell. "Behave yourself."

I left her behind as I hurried down to the dining room. If I found Kate alone…I sighed inwardly, unsure of what I'd say to her. Kate couldn't be seen talking to me, particularly not now. The Head Boy talking to a firstie who wasn't in trouble? Some people would want to know why. Penny would think she *knew* why. And she'd take it out on Kate.

There was no sign of Kate as I entered the dining room. I frowned, hoping she hadn't decided to skip lunch. She'd have a rough time of it later if she had, unless she'd hidden some cake and treats in her trunk. I made a mental note to keep an eye on the situation and headed over to the upperclassman table. The staff had cooked curry for lunch. I took a helping and sat down, wondering what my mother would say if she knew I was eating curry for breakfast. It still *felt* like the early morning to me.

Francis came into the room ten minutes before the bell, collected a plate of food and sat next to me. His lips were slightly swollen, but he was grinning like a loon.

I glanced at him. "You alright?"

"Yeah," Francis said. His grin grew wider. "Things couldn't be better."

"Potions this afternoon," I reminded him. I had no idea what he was so happy about. Two hours of advanced potions were looming in the near future. "Things are rapidly growing worse."

"Hah," Francis said. He leaned closer, until he was practically whispering in my ear. "Guess what *I've* been doing?"

I rubbed my forehead. It was still too early. "I don't want to know," I said. "You can tell me later."

CHAPTER
SEVENTEEN

The next few weeks passed very slowly.

The team and I worked hard on our plans, brainstorming constantly in a bid to figure out what we might be facing and how best to counter it. Francis and Louise, surprisingly, made a good team as they practiced their spells, while I worked with Saline. She was definitely odd, I decided, although I still had no idea what was actually *wrong*. There were times when she was as calm and collected—and *there*—as the rest of us and times when she seemed to be in her own little world, unwilling or unable to return to reality. And she needed to work her way through the concepts practically from scratch before she could cast any new advanced spells.

Francis, somewhat to my surprise, hadn't argued when I told him that Penny would not be joining the team. Instead, he'd proposed two others; Tobias and Harvard. Tobias, a sixth-year with a remarkable talent for potions, had been as friendless as Louise before she'd joined us; Harvard, a fifth-year who was an excellent duellist, was thrilled to be taking part in the Challenge. I had to admit he was good. Francis claimed Harvard would make his way to the Duelling Circle one day. It would have been fun, I admitted, if the looming threat hadn't overshadowed our lives. We would have to take the Challenge soon...

... And we still didn't know who was spying on us.

Someone *was* spying on us, I was sure. The wards were regularly probed, time and time again. Whoever was poking at our defences was *good*, very good. We'd set some traps, in hopes of catching the intruder by surprise, and a handful of trackers that should have led us right to them, but nothing had worked. I was honestly starting to wonder if someone had enlisted a little adult help. It was against the rules, but—like so many other things—only against the rules if you got caught.

"Remember to keep moving," Harvard instructed us, as we mock-duelled through the corridors. "You don't need to waste energy on shielding yourself if you can keep from being hit in the first place."

I nodded, feeling sweat trickle down my back. I'd always been in fairly good shape, for a young man my age, but Harvard and Francis were both stronger and faster than I. It would have been a great deal worse if Father hadn't drilled me in the fine arts of duelling and fencing. It had seemed pointless, at the time—swords were barbaric, compared to magic—but I was grateful now. In hindsight, Father might have been trying to prepare me for the Challenge for years. But he could have done a far better job.

"I did keep moving," Louise protested. "You zapped me anyway."

"Then move faster," Harvard said. "Concentrate on making yourself as small a target as possible—and always throw something back, even if it's just a little itching hex. It'll upset him."

"And probably annoy him," Louise said.

"He's trying to get you anyway," Harvard pointed out. I think he was enjoying the chance to lecture an older student. It wasn't something that happened very often. "How much more annoyed can he *get*?"

He shrugged. "A person who is angry is a person who will make a mistake. You just have to be ready to take advantage of it."

"Just as you took advantage of Gavin in the last duel," Francis said. "You made his pants fall down."

"And then he tripped as he tried to get to me," Harvard said. "Someone who isn't thinking very clearly will make an easy target, if you're ready. So watch for the mistake when it comes."

Louise nodded, then glanced at Saline. "Isn't anyone going to unhex her?"

"She's supposed to unhex herself," Harvard said. "I *told* you to leave her alone."

I sighed, inwardly. Saline had absolutely *no* talent for casting motionless spells. It was odd—she should have mastered the art long before she joined the upper classes—but apparently true. A firstie who froze Saline would have Saline at his mercy...at least until the hex wore off or someone cancelled it in passing. I'd forced myself to practice, time and time again; I'd forced *everyone* to practice. Saline was the only one who hadn't made any progress.

"Well, we can't just leave her here." Louise rested her hands on her hips. "We have lunch in a few minutes."

"We can always skip lunch," Harvard pointed out. "And she won't get any hungrier while she's frozen."

"I can't skip lunch." Tobias's voice was strongly accented. He spoke as little as possible, if only to conceal his origins. No one would ever mistake *him* for an aristocrat. *Guttersnipe* had been one of the kindest words hurled at him before he'd learnt to fight back. "And I have the rest of the potions brewing in the lab. They require some care and attention."

"It won't kill them to stand a little longer," Francis said. "You don't need to put so *much* care and attention into them."

"But that's what will make him a great Potions Master one day," I said. It wouldn't be *hard* to get Tobias an apprenticeship, not if his marks were as good as he claimed. I could convince a couple of family brewers to take him on. They'd have to do something about his manners, but that wouldn't be hard either. I had the feeling that Tobias would want to leave the gutter in the shade. "He'll leave the rest of us far behind."

Tobias eyed me, as if he expected the compliment to be withdrawn—or turned into mockery—within seconds. I gave him my best encouraging look, which probably wasn't *that* strong. I'd given him my word that I'd find him a place, if he passed his exams with flying colours, but I'd be surprised if he truly believed me. Promises were cheap in Water Shallot. Keeping them could be expensive.

I nodded to him, then snapped my fingers at Saline. She crumpled to the floor like a puppet whose strings had been cut. Louise glared daggers at Harvard—he'd been the one to hex Saline—and ran forward, helping her friend to her feet. Saline rubbed her arms and legs vigorously. Harvard's spell hadn't so much frozen her as locked her muscles in place. She was going to have almighty aches and pains for the rest of the day. I made a mental note to speak to him about it. There was a line between intensive training and naked cruelty.

"It didn't work," Saline said. She tottered on her feet, as if she was going to fall over again. Her face was a picture of helplessness. "I just couldn't free myself."

"You need to work on it," Harvard said, firmly. "Right now, anyone can sneak up and hex you in the back."

"Yeah," Francis said. "And you also have to keep low too."

Louise gave me a sharp look. "Do we *really* have to go through all *this*?"

"Yes." Surprisingly, it was Tobias who answered. "To the Darkness with the rules. The other teams will stop at nothing to stop *us*."

"And *someone* has been watching us," Francis reminded us. "We don't even know who."

"We should be trying to spy on them," Harvard said. "We know where they're hiding."

"We *think* we know where they're hiding," I countered. "And what do we have to hide?"

Francis looked disbelieving. "Everything! Our base, our supplies, our tactics…"

"There's nothing here that's particularly important or unique," I pointed out.

"The sword is unique," Francis said, dryly.

"And if they watch our practices, what then?" I met his eyes. "Are they going to be afraid of us...or are they going to wet themselves laughing?"

"Don't be so sure." Harvard studied his hands. "Just knowing that Saline cannot cast motionless spells would be a *big* advantage, in the wrong hands. Or knowing that Louise is slower on the draw than the rest of us...yes, someone could take advantage of that. And Francis has a tendency to act without thinking and over-commit himself..."

"Go hex yourself," Francis said, rudely. "I'm still Sports Captain."

"Until the end of the year," Harvard countered. "And you're not Duelling Champ, remember?"

I winced. *Alana* was Duelling Champ, at least amongst the final-year students. They wouldn't let her duel now, not when she might lose to a *mere* sixth-year...I wondered, slowly, if Alana, Harvard and the other duellists held private contests of their own. They would never be entered in the official record—no one would ever take formal notice of them—but the duellists themselves would know. I could easily see Alana taking part in underground duels. She wasn't the sort of person to back down from a challenge.

Or a Challenge, I reminded myself. I had no doubt *her* team was functioning as smoothly as...as an Object of Power. Alana had known she would be taking the Challenge for months, unlike me. She could have organised her team and planned her tactics well before the rest of us knew we were entering. It was technically against the rules, but no one would say anything to her about it. *They'd have to prove she did it first.*

I held up a hand before Harvard and Francis could start hexing each other. "We do have a lot to work on," I said. "But we are making progress, aren't we?"

"Yes." Louise eyed me. "But you have a promise to keep."

"I will." My stomach rumbled, loudly. "I think we'd better go for lunch."

Francis nudged me as we cleared the room and reset the wards. "You should take her to the next dance," he said. "It would give her some practical experience."

I shook my head. "People will talk."

"They'll understand if you go as friends," Francis said. "I'll bash anyone who says otherwise."

"No," I said. In theory, it was a good idea; in practice, it would open a whole can of scorpions. "I'm betrothed. I can't take anyone to the dance."

"I'm sure Cat will understand," Francis said. "It isn't as if you're married."

I gave him a sharp look. "I have a responsibility to uphold the betrothal."

"Yeah." Francis looked back at me, evenly. "But is it also an excuse to avoid your social obligations?"

I nodded as we walked through the door, closing and warding it behind us. Francis was right. I hated social dances—I hated the pointless chatter, the requirement to dance with every potential partner, the simple fact that everything I did would be fodder for the gossipmongers—and being betrothed did give me an excuse not to attend. I couldn't attend without Cat and *she* had as little interest in going as I did. Besides, if she *was* able to go, everyone would be watching us anyway. They'd draw all sorts of conclusions from the way I held her on the dance floor.

We rejoined the others and walked back to the upper levels. Francis left us as soon as we passed through the door, claiming he had someone he wanted to see. I guessed he had a girlfriend, someone he wanted to keep quiet about for the moment. Or a boyfriend. I found it hard to believe—Francis had gone through a year when he'd been unable to keep himself from staring at every girl who crossed our path—but it was possible. He had good reason to keep *any* relationship quiet. People would talk.

And he's not betrothed, I reminded myself. I felt an odd twinge of jealously. *He can date whoever he likes without causing problems for the family.*

I pushed the thought aside as we entered the dining room and headed towards the upper tables. They were suspiciously empty—I guessed most of the upperclassmen had gone into the city for lunch—and we had no trouble finding good seats. The lower tables were crammed, as usual. I saw Penny instructing her charges on the proper way to eat in good company, her face cold and hard. The firsties appeared to be listening raptly. I hoped it wasn't because they were scared.

Louise nudged me. "Were we ever so young?"

"It's hard to believe," I said, as I ladled food onto my plate. "But…you know, it's been a long time."

"A very long time," Louise said. "Why do they have to learn better manners?"

"I suppose it depends." I considered the answer for a long moment. "Auntie Gladys used to say that manners were a sign of good breeding, that knowing what fork to use was a sign that someone was a gentleman. If you used the pudding spoon to eat soup, or the soup spoon to eat pudding, it was a sign you were *no* gentleman. And if you used your fingers…oh, that was a sign you were born in the gutter."

"It sounds silly," Louise said.

"It is, a little," I confirmed. "We were never allowed to use our fingers in polite company, even on picnics. We had to eat our sandwiches with knives and forks."

Louise giggled.

"Mother, on the other hand, said that good manners allowed people to get along, even when they disagreed with each other," I continued. "It was alright to call someone an idiot as long as you did it in a socially acceptable manner. And if you spoke nicely to people, instead of demanding they did whatever you wanted, they'd be happier with you. It's never easy to tell who'll bear a lifetime grudge for your bad manners until you find a knife buried in your back."

"A *real* knife?" Louise sounded concerned. "Or…or what?"

I glanced from side to side, then leaned closer to her. "Pretend you insult someone, here and now. They show no reaction, but they remember. Years later, you want a favour from them…and they tell you to go stick your head in a bubbling cauldron. Whatever you're doing is ruined because you insulted someone, so long ago that you might not even remember what you did."

"You make it sound charming," Louise said. She sounded as if she wanted to panic, her eyes flickering to her knife and fork. "Really."

"Father always insisted that we should think of the long term," I said. "And you never know who'll wind up on top, with power over you."

Louise looked at her hands. "It doesn't seem fair, somehow."

"You never know," I said. "One day, *you* might have the power."

Francis joined us just as we finished our dinners, grinning from ear to ear. He looked perfectly normal, but someone would notice...I was *sure* someone would. And then they'd keep an eye on him until they found out who he was dating. I wondered if I should ask him, before the truth came out. There weren't *many* students that Francis could date without having *really* bad repercussions.

"Don't forget to eat something," I told him. "We'll be doing more spell-casting after lunch."

"I haven't forgotten," Francis said. He took a potion vial from his belt, uncorked the lid and drank it, grimacing at the taste. "Judy agreed to take over my duties for the afternoon."

Louise coughed. "Judy?"

"She'll be Sports Captain next year, unless someone pays out *thousands* of crowns in bribes," Francis said. "She's almost as good as me."

"Oh," Louise said. "Is she as big headed as you?"

I elbowed her, gently. She flushed, perhaps remembering our conversation.

"Of course not." Francis took no offense. "My ego has a gold medal for being big. So does..."

"Oh, stop bragging," I said.

"I was going to say I also have the silver and the bronze." Francis winked at me. "*That's* how big my ego is."

"They couldn't fit anyone else on the stand," Harvard said, as he stood. "Shall we go back down?"

"Yeah." I stood too, picking up my tray. "Shall we?"

The school felt quieter as we made our way back downstairs. I wasn't too surprised. The lowerclassmen would be studying or playing sports, while the upperclassmen would be out of the grounds—and perhaps out of bounds—or training for the Challenge themselves. We saw no one, once we entered the lower levels. I was almost disappointed. It hadn't taken me *that* long to start exploring the school when I'd been a lowerclassman, and…

I stopped. Something was wrong.

"Wait," Francis said, sharply. "What's missing?"

"The wards," I said. "We should have crossed the wardline by now."

I lifted my hand, nearly reaching for the sword before I stopped myself. The wardline wouldn't have stopped *us*—we were all keyed into it—but we should have sensed it. And it was gone. I glanced at Francis, then motioned for the girls and Tobias to remain behind as the rest of us scouted forward. The inner wardline was gone, too. So were the trap spells that should have stopped any intruder in their path. And the door was hanging open.

Francis breathed a word he wasn't supposed to know as we peered through the door. The room had been devastated. The desks and chairs had been smashed into flinders, the cupboards had been pulled from the walls and thrown to the ground; I cursed out loud, bitterly, as I saw the shattered potions vials. The different brews had mixed together, creating a serious problem…they'd all have to be neutralised before they exploded or…or something…

I swallowed hard. I knew the rules. I knew that sabotage was perfectly legal. But…it was still hard to take. They'd wrecked a great deal of work, for what? I silently thanked the Ancients that I'd left most of the completed Devices of Power in the Workroom. They'd probably be untouched.

"Oh, no." Louise came up behind us. She sounded heartbroken. "Who did this?"

"I don't know," Francis said. The anger in his voice was terrifying. "But we're going to *get* them for it."

CHAPTER
EIGHTEEN

Tobias stepped into the shattered room. "How can we get them if we don't know who they are?"

"We'll figure it out," I told him. I looked at the potions mess and shuddered. It was only a matter of time before the liquids congealed into something dangerously unpredictable. "Can you deal with the mess before it goes foul?"

"Of course." Tobias sounded irked. "Give me a moment."

"It was the McDonalds," Francis said. He'd been studying the damage to the spells. "One or both of them. Probably both."

I glanced at him, sharply. "How can you be sure?"

"I share a class with Zeya McDonald," Francis said. "She's *very* skilled at manipulating charms—and I have enough of a sense for her magic that I can *feel* her presence. She was probably the one spying on us, right from the start. She's certainly good enough to do that without being detected."

"We *did* detect her," Louise argued.

"Yes, but we didn't know it was her." Francis snapped his fingers at the tattered remains of the wards, collapsing them back into the aether. "We had no idea who to blame. Not until now."

I thought about it. I didn't know the McDonald sisters that well. They'd shared a dorm with Cat and Isabella, back when we'd all been firsties, but they'd never been really close. How could they have been? House McDonald was a rival to both House Aguirre and House Rubén. The best anyone could have hoped for was polite neutrality. Isabella had told me, once, that the McDonalds had mocked her after she'd lost a duel to Cat. I had no trouble believing they might have ruined our supplies. It *was* part of the game, after all.

"We have to hit them back," Francis argued. "Now."

Louise frowned. "What do you have in mind?"

"Wreck their base," Francis said. "Do unto them as they did unto us!"

"We don't even know where their base *is*," Louise said. "Or do we?"

"We have a rough idea," Francis said. "Come on. We'll hit it now!"

Louise held up a hand. "It's absurd. If we get caught…"

"And if we do nothing," Francis said, "they'll do it again. And again."

I stared at the mess, feeling miserable. Francis was right. We had to hit back. Father had drilled it into me, more than once, that allowing an enemy to get away with something practically guaranteed they would do it again. Isabella hadn't stopped practicing her hexes on me until I'd started to hex her back. And yet, an inability to let anything go had practically *triggered* the House War. People had attacked and counterattacked and counter-counterattacked until the original cause, whatever it had been, was forgotten.

"You can't be serious." Louise looked at me. "Akin, tell him he's being stupid."

"We have to push back," I said. I hated the logic, but I couldn't deny it. "And quickly."

"And if we get caught?" Louise glared at us. "We could be expelled!"

"No," Francis said. "They can't expel us for playing by the rules."

"Hah," Tobias muttered.

"This is ridiculous," Louise said. She glanced at Saline. "Call us when you're feeling less stupid."

Saline shot me an unreadable look, then turned and followed Louise as she flounced out of the room. I didn't blame her for being uncertain and reluctant to go out on a limb. It wouldn't be easy to expel me—or Francis—but Louise was much less secure. Rose had nearly been expelled after she'd helped Cat perform a dangerous experiment. If Cat's father hadn't gone to bat for her, she *would* have been expelled.

"We don't need her." Francis sneered at the door. "We can do it ourselves. Just like old times."

"Quite." I looked at Tobias. "Can you finish cleaning up the potion, then attend to your brewing? We'll meet you later tonight."

Tobias looked relieved, just for a second. I guessed he'd had the same worries as Louise without being able to admit it. He'd be branded a coward, even if he was right. I shook my head in disgust, then glanced at Harvard. The duellist looked back at me, evenly. I had no doubt *he'd* go into danger without a second thought.

"Do you want to stay here," I asked, "or come with us?"

"I'll come, unless you want me to lie in wait here," Harvard said. "It's something to do."

I nodded, feeling my heart starting to pound. "Shall we go?"

Francis grinned. "Just like old times," he repeated, as he opened the door. "Let's go."

I gave him a sharp look. As kids, we'd sneaked around the mansion, testing our skills against the wards and locks as we tried to break into sealed rooms. Isabella had raided my room, time and time again; I'd raided hers… we hadn't stolen anything, of course, but we'd worked hard to make sure the other knew we'd been there. The risk of being detected —and turned into something—was part of the thrill. I'd caught Penny trying to sneak into my room two years ago, with a hex I'd carefully concealed under the rug. She'd still been trapped when I'd returned hours later.

And we were being prepared for school, I thought, as we slipped down the corridor. *The skills we learnt at home came in handy here.*

Francis stopped at the top of a disused staircase. "We have to be careful from now on," he breathed. "They'll be watching for us."

I nodded. No one would wreck our base without expecting retaliation. The McDonalds would have tightened their own wards, perhaps even pushing them as close to blood magic as they could without crossing the line. Ayesha and Zeya McDonald weren't just twin sisters. They were actually *friends*. Only one of them could be the Heir Primus, only one of them could take power, but…somehow, they were still friends. They worked together very well, better than Isabella and I had ever managed. Perhaps they intended to share the post, when their father died. Or maybe they thought they could simply swap places every so often.

They might get away with it too, I thought. No one would ever mistake me for Isabella—or Cat for Alana—but Ayesha and Zeya McDonald were practically identical. *No one will look too closely, for fear of what they might find out.*

The air grew colder as we made our way down the stairs. I reached out with my senses, trying to sense something—anything—that wasn't part of the background hum. This section had been abandoned long ago, but there were still flashes and flares of magic flickering around the wood and stone walls. The McDonalds could have hidden all kinds of wards and trap spells in the section, if they wished. Given proper preparation, the spells would last *years*. I'd stumbled across a handful of trap spells left behind by students who'd graduated when my father was a boy.

They really should clean out the lower levels properly, I told myself. *But that would spoil the fun.*

I froze as I felt…*something*…up ahead. A spell, twisting in and out of existence…I frowned, keeping as still as I could. It was a neat little trick, far too complex to have been cast by a lowerclassman. The spell didn't maintain a constant watch, as far as I could tell; it pulsed back and forth, the beats of magic coming too quickly for us to duck under its watchful eye and escape. I glanced at Francis, puzzled. The McDonalds would have keyed themselves to the wards, naturally, but how could they get close enough for the ward to recognise them without triggering the alarm? I was missing something, but what?

"There," Francis hissed. "Look at the floor."

I followed his finger. There was a device, a Device of Power, positioned on the floor, just under the spell. It was moving very slightly, magic pulsing around it...it took me a second to realise that the motions matched the pulsing of the spell. It wasn't *projecting* the spell, as far as I could tell; it was merely directing it. I felt a flicker of admiration as the pieces fell into place. They'd set up a feedback loop. If the spell failed, the Device would sound the alarm...

Or vice versa, I thought.

I lifted my hand and carefully, very carefully, cast a manipulation spell. The Device stopped moving, holding the watching spell in place. I could *feel* it protesting as I inched into the corridor, ducking low as I ran past the spell. Francis and Harvard followed me, keeping their heads down. My spell failed a moment later, allowing the device to move again. I tensed, but we were already past the guard. Anyone else would have real problems until they figured out how to keep the device from moving.

"Good work," Francis whispered.

We shared a smile, then inched further down the corridor. The abandoned classrooms on the far side of the watch spell looked as if no one had visited them for years, but that hadn't stopped the McDonalds scattering dozens of spells around to deter trespassers. We had to work our way onwards, sneaking around or dispelling the spells as we passed. I hoped the McDonalds hadn't done something *very* clever, something so brilliant that I didn't have a hope of anticipating it. Their inner spells were common, far too well understood for my peace of mind. Ayesha and Zeya McDonald were too smart to rely on them.

"There's more focused magic in there," Francis whispered. He jabbed a finger down the corridor, towards a metal door. It was covered in runes, each one carefully defaced to render them useless. "Harvard, you keep watch."

"Got it." Harvard slipped into the shadows, casting an obscurification charm on himself. I could barely see him and I *knew* he was there. "I'll alert you the moment anyone comes."

I glanced at Francis as we sneaked towards the door. Ayesha and Zeya McDonald—and their entire team—could be in there, right now. The thrill of being somewhere I shouldn't was still there, but now it was mingled with fear. Mother and Father had made it very clear that we *weren't* allowed to break into an occupied room, although I hadn't understood why until I was much older. Ayesha and Zeya McDonald had five other people on their team, all powerful and experienced…at least by student standards. If we walked right into their midst, we'd be lucky to escape unhexed.

And we'll be laughingstocks, I mused. There were two wards on the door, both very basic. I broke the first one effortlessly, then turned to the second. *That would be worse than anything else.*

Francis seemed unconcerned. I envied him. His life was so carefree. He could play his sports and court girls and enjoy himself without risking his future—and his family's future. The worst that could happen to him was… well, what? I couldn't think of anything permanent, unless there was a terrible accident. Francis could take a pratfall into a muddy puddle and people would laugh with him, not at him. I could forget to tie my tie properly and no one would ever let me forget it. And if I embarrassed myself…

I hesitated. It wasn't too late to back out. We could sneak out again, or simply trigger the spells as we left. Done properly, it would have freaked them out. If they couldn't find any evidence of what we'd done…they'd think they'd missed something. They'd waste their time looking for something, unaware there was nothing to find. It was tempting, but…I remembered the damage they'd done and gritted my teeth. I couldn't let them get away with it.

Francis pushed the door open with the tip of his spellcaster. No one shouted, or screamed, or chanted a spell. The room inside was quiet, as silent as the grave. I inched inside slowly, looking around. The chamber had probably been a potions lab, once upon a time. The stone walls had been thoroughly scrubbed, but they still bore traces of explosions and other accidents. It would be a long time before lichen grew there, if it ever did. I felt traces of magic flickering around me as I headed towards the backrooms and peered inside. The McDonalds had chosen well. They'd be able to hide all sorts of traps and tricks within the room, relying on the magical aura to conceal them.

"They must practice here," Francis said.

I nodded. The backroom was crammed with supplies, from dozens of potion vials to a handful of Devices of Power. They were crude, compared to mine, but they would work. They'd even enchanted a broomstick, although I wasn't sure why. The old legends of magicians flying on broomsticks had been disproven long ago. Cat was the only person who'd built a flying machine in living history and it had very nearly broken apart during its first and last flight.

She wants to build another one, I thought, feeling a sudden glow of warmth. *And we can do it together, afterwards...*

"You get the potions," Francis said. He opened a cupboard, revealing more potions. "I'll..."

I hesitated, feeling a pang of guilt. Someone had spent weeks brewing the potions. If I destroyed them...they'd destroyed ours, I told myself. I had to push them back. I checked for traps, then reached for the first vial. And realised, as I heard a *click*, that I'd made a terrible mistake.

"Get out of here," I hissed, as magic flared around me. It was a trap. It was...I felt threads of magic reaching towards me, as if they were ropes animated by a sorcerer's will. The McDonalds had done something clever or something stupid, and I wasn't sure which. It would have been easy to catch me with a simpler spell, but I might have noticed it in time and stepped aside. "Move!"

A warning spell glimmered in my awareness. Someone was coming. Francis turned and hurried towards the door, slowing as he reached the edge. I snapped at him to hurry as a thread of magic wrapped around my legs, trying to hold me in place. There was no point in us *both* being trapped. He took one last look at me, then fled through the outer room and into the corridor. I felt another thread of magic pulling at my arm, a spider's web of magic slowly forming around me. The faster I moved, the faster it grew. I tried to counter it, only to discover I'd made it worse. The spellbreaker on my belt was practically out of reach.

I grabbed for the sword and drew it. The blade sliced through the magic like it wasn't there, but the magic reformed with terrifying speed. I would have liked to study it, if it hadn't been trying to catch me. Instead, I cut my legs free and ran for my life. Behind me, the magic grew stronger. I had the nasty feeling it would keep growing until it ran out of power.

The outer door opened as I approached. Ayesha—or Zeya—McDonald. She was a tall girl, with long brown hair, a willowy body and a dress that showed them both off to best advantage. Her eyes went very wide as she saw me, her hand lifting to cast a spell. The sword snapped forward, practically of its own accord and deflected the spell with terrifying ease. I had to keep a firm grip on the hilt to keep it from skewering the poor girl. Sabotage was one thing, I reflected as I returned the sword to the scabbard. I couldn't start murdering the competition.

I braced myself. The McDonalds were good. But I might be able to fight my way out…

Ayesha—or Zeya—moved forward with striking speed and kissed me. For a moment, I almost melted into the kiss. Her lips were so warm and… and then I felt my entire *body* start to melt. The world spun around me. I tried, desperately, to cast a counterspell, but nothing worked. Ayesha—or Zeya—was growing larger…no, I was shrinking. She'd turned me into a frog! I tried to jump back as she reached for me, but it was already too late. We'd cut so many frogs up for potion ingredients that keeping one helpless until we butchered it was practically second nature.

"Zeya told me we should have guarded the room," Ayesha said, as she popped me into a bag. "She'll never let me hear the end of it."

I forced myself to concentrate as the bag started to move, suggesting she was taking me somewhere. Panic threatened to overwhelm me, time and time again, as I tried to break the spell. I'd been a frog before—it had been Isabella's favourite spell, when we'd been kids—but this spell was different. It twisted and turned like a living thing. And then the bag opened and she grabbed me by the neck.

"Have fun," Ayesha said, as she pulled me out of the bag and threw me into a room. "Bye, bye."

I heard the door slam closed as I twisted in the air, the frog's instincts allowing me to land safely. The room looked odd, through the eyes of a frog. Benches and chairs that would barely have reached my knee, as a human, were suddenly overwhelmingly huge. And my vision was skewed…it took me several moments to realise the thing hanging from an open locker door was a dress…

My blood turned to ice as I realised what she'd done. She'd thrown me into a changing room. The *ladies* changing room. And if they caught me…

… I was dead.

CHAPTER
NINETEEN

For a moment, panic nearly overwhelmed me.

If I was caught…I could *not* be caught. The scandal would utterly destroy me. I would be expelled…even if I wasn't expelled, no one would ever take me seriously again. I'd be branded a peeping tom, if the truth didn't get out…if it did, it might be worse. Ayesha would get in trouble too, perhaps, but…I'd be the one who was laughed at, I'd be the one who was the butt of all the jokes. And Cat would break the betrothal, if her family didn't do it for her. She'd have no choice.

I looked around, hastily. We'd joked about the girls' locker room being a place of wonder and mystery, but it didn't look *that* different than ours. A cluster of benches and lockers, showers and toilets…if I hadn't spotted the dress, I might not have realised the danger until it was far too late. I felt oddly disappointed, but…I put the thought aside as I checked the door. It was closed. There wasn't enough room for me to slip underneath, even as a frog. The wretched spell was making it impossible to cast spells myself. Perhaps I could hide…I doubted it. A paranoid girl might detect me and then…

There was a window, right at the top of the room. I braced myself, then jumped onto a bench and then up to the lockers. The window was small, opening into the bright summer air…I heard the door opening behind me and jumped, throwing myself right through the window and into the unknown. Girlish giggles echoed behind me as I tumbled into the gutter, rolling over and open as water carried me on; I hoped—I prayed—that they hadn't seen me. It would be hard to prove anything, if I didn't get caught, but I couldn't afford to have rumours like *that* floating around. Ayesha knew the truth. She could spread the word.

The world tilted around me as the gutter threw me into a pipe. I struggled to gain control as it carried me on, but the pipe was too slippery for me to catch hold and right myself. I silently thanked my ancestors that frogs could breathe underwater—I felt as if I was going to drown, even though I knew I was safe—as the pipe opened up again. I plunged down, falling into a cool pond. Instinctively, I swam deeper. The water felt safe, safe and calm and welcome and...

I caught myself, sharply. The frog's mind was gnawing at mine, threatening to subsume me. I hadn't realised the danger, not really. Childish spells—spells I'd learnt when turning some unsuspecting victim into an animal had seemed the height of humour—had safeguards, designed to prevent the victim from losing his mind. But whatever Ayesha had cast on me was different. It was hard, so hard, not to let the frog take control. Only the thought of being lost forever—or coming back to myself somewhere far from home—allowed me to keep myself together. The green water wasn't welcoming at all. It was a deadly trap.

Move, you idiot, I told myself. *Get up!*

I broke the surface and looked around. I'd been carried into the grotto, a pond half-hidden behind the rear of the school. It had been a long time since I'd walked through the tangled mass of greenery and skirted the lake—I'd been reluctant to return, ever since we'd been kidnapped and stolen from the school. Rose had never wanted to return, and Francis had been more interested in playing sports than walking for pleasure. The thought helped me come back to myself. Francis could have been caught. Or he and Harvard could be looking for me, right now. I swallowed hard as I concentrated, summoning all my reserves. I had to break the spell before it was too late.

And if someone threw Francis into the locker room, I thought bitterly, *he'd get away with it easily.*

The spell was still strong, twisting and turning as I tried to break it. I swore silently that I would never be annoyed at Saline again, not if I got out of this mess. The frog's body wasn't designed to cast spells, but that shouldn't have made a difference. I struggled and struggled and struggled, yet…it felt useless. I wondered if I shouldn't just hop back to school and announce myself. I knew the signs to prove I was a transfigured human, not a real frog. And yet, if I did, I would become a laughingstock. My position as Head Boy would be untenable, even if no one figured out who'd enchanted me or why. I hadn't wanted the post, but now…

Concentrate, I told myself. *Focus!*

I felt the sword, resting somewhere at the back of my mind. It had been transfigured too, but…it was still there. It was real, it was…the spell seemed to tense, snapping and snarling at the sword's sheer presence, then it broke. I found myself choking, swallowing foul-tasting water as I slipped below the waves. The water was suddenly very cold and clammy and…I kicked off my shoes and swam towards the shore, clambering onto a rock and sitting there, coughing up water. I'd never realised how deep the pond actually was. No one, as far as I knew, had ever swum in it before. The stories about monsters lurking at the bottom suddenly sounded very believable.

"Well," I managed. I silently thanked the ancients that I'd worn comfortable clothes, rather than my uniform or something expensive. "*That* was embarrassing."

I picked myself up and carefully cast a pair of drying spells, gritting my teeth at the unpleasant sensation of water trickling down my legs and pooling on the rocks. My clothes felt dry, now, yet I still looked a mess. I cast a summoning spell, hoping to recover my shoes, but nothing happened. They were too deep—or too stuck—to be yanked out of the water. I peered into the pond, but saw nothing beyond utter darkness. Perhaps there was a monster at the bottom after all.

Shaking my head, I turned and started to walk back to school. The grassy path was scratchy and unpleasant against my bare feet, but it could have been worse. I kept away from the nettles—and a handful of plants I knew to be dangerous, if treated without great care—as I slipped out of the grotto and walked towards the rear entrance. I could hear cheering in the distance, from one of the sports fields, but no one was in sight. I hoped I wouldn't meet *anyone* as I sneaked back to my room. It would be difficult to explain why the Head Boy was walking around without his shoes.

I passed through the door, then stopped dead. What if…what if Ayesha had reported me for being in the locker room? She wouldn't have had to *lie*. She could just have left out a few details and delivered the *coup de grace* to my reputation. The Castellan and his staff could be searching for me right now, bent on expelling me before the scandal broke…I tensed as I heard someone pound down the corridor towards me, then told myself it didn't matter. Ayesha could hardly admit the truth—not now—without admitting what she'd done too. I doubted her reputation would survive either.

Francis came into view, followed by Louise and Saline. "Akin! You're alive!"

"Yeah." I tried not to notice how they stared at me. I probably looked terrible. "And I need a shower."

"Yeah." Francis made a show of holding his nose. "I wasn't going to mention that, you know."

I glared at him, then led the way back to my suite. Thankfully, there was no sign of Alana as we entered. She was probably drilling her team, or having a day in town, or…or something. I didn't care, as long as she was elsewhere. It was going to be hard enough to tell my team what had happened without having to admit it to her too. Alana would mock me relentlessly for it.

"Wait here," I said. "I'll be back in a moment."

Francis nodded. "Can we burgle the Head Girl's desk while you're gone?"

"*No!*" After everything that had happened, I didn't think that was very funny. "Leave Alana's desk alone."

I hurried into my room, stripped bare, threw my clothes in the washing basket and showered as quickly as I could. My body was covered in stains from the pond…I muttered a pair of soaping spells, silently grateful that I'd let my governess teach me. I wanted a bath, not a shower, but…there was no time. I climbed out, dried myself and changed into a fresh outfit. The old outfit might have to be discarded. The laundry staff might ask awkward questions if they took a careful look at it.

At least it wasn't expensive, I told myself. I hadn't bothered to invest in expensive gym clothes or duelling outfits. Francis had spent half his allowance on kitting himself out for sports matches, but I hadn't seen the point. *I can buy another complete set if necessary.*

"So," Francis said, as I rejoined them. "What happened to you?"

I scowled. "What happened to *you*?"

"I sneaked out and hid," Francis said. "There were others on the way, so I slipped away and linked up with Harvard. The tracking spell we used on you kept spinning crazily until we finally found you. What happened to *you*?"

"Ayesha cast a spell on me," I said. I wasn't going to admit *how* she'd cast the spell on me. The feel of her lips against mine still tingled, even though she'd enspelled me. "She turned me into a frog and dumped me in the girls' locker room."

Francis stared. "You lucky…"

Louise reddened. "Lucky? You…you…"

I held up a hand before she could start hexing one or both of us. "I didn't see anything," I said, quickly. "I managed to make it out of the room and escape. The spell…just took a long time to break."

"Hours," Francis said, quietly. "What did she *do* to you?"

"She kissed you," Saline said. There was no accusation—or amusement—in her voice. "Didn't she?"

I flushed. "She just jammed her lips against mine…"

"Sounds like a kiss to me," Francis said. "How…*terrible*…that must have been."

Louise was looking at Saline. "She *kissed* him?"

Saline reddened. It was clearly visible, even on her brown skin. She mumbled something so quietly that I couldn't hear it, something that... something I couldn't follow.

"Speak up," Louise insisted. "What do you mean, she kissed him?"

I shot her a warning look. If I spoke to my friends like that, all the time, it wouldn't be long before I didn't *have* any friends. Louise ignored me, her eyes fixed on Saline. Saline seemed frozen before her stare. I opened my mouth to tell her that she didn't *have* to tell us anything, whatever Louise said, but she spoke before I could say a word.

"There are spells." Saline's voice was very quiet. "*Girl* spells. Some of them are taught to us before our first blood, spells to protect our lives and our virtues. Others are taught afterwards, when we"—she shook her head, as if she didn't want to talk about it—"one of the spells is designed to be cast when we kiss, if we don't *want* to kiss. Someone who tries to steal a kiss gets turned into a frog. I was told it couldn't be broken."

"It was very hard to break," I said. "She kissed me. Did that weaken the spell?"

"Mother told me the spell is powered by emotion." Saline sounded as if she wished she'd never said anything. "If she kissed you...yeah, the spell might not have worked quite right."

Louise had something else in mind. "How come...how come no one ever taught *me* those spells?"

"They belong to the Great Houses." Francis smirked. "I dare say your mother didn't know the spells. And if you didn't start studying magic early, you wouldn't have been able to cast them."

"That isn't *fair*," Louise protested. "Do you know how many girls get... kissed...or, or worse, against their will? Do you know...?"

"Then learn the spells," Francis said. "Oh right, you can't. No one will teach you."

"I can teach you," Saline said, quietly. "They're not *that* hard."

Louise looked doubtful. I didn't blame her. Saline meant well, but…she might not be a very good teacher. And with a spell that required a degree of intimacy to cast, Louise might never know she *didn't* know the spell until she tried to cast it and something went wrong. And then…I shook my head. Who *could* teach her? Penny? Or Alana? Or Rose? It was quite possible that Auntie Sofia, Lady Sorceress and Potions Mistress, had sat down with Cat's best friend and taught her the facts of life.

"Saline can teach you," I said. I was curious myself, although I would never have admitted it. "And if she doesn't, we can ask someone else."

"And then you can practice." Francis leered. "You can test the spell on me."

Louise reddened, again. "I'll leave you a frog, you…"

I held up a hand. "We can discuss that all later," I said. "For the moment…we didn't do *any* damage to the McDonalds. And if she tells everyone what happened…"

"She won't," Francis predicted. "She'd have to explain what happened and why. You could demand a formal inquest, if the rumours got out of control. And that would make sure that everyone knew she kissed you, rather than you forcing a kiss on her."

"She doesn't have to tell them that," I objected. "She can just say…"

Francis shook his head. "She has every reason to keep her mouth shut," he insisted. "At best, she will be confessing to putting a boy in the girls' locker room…they expelled someone for that, didn't they? And *she* had the excuse of being blackmailed into it. At worst…Ayesha did something that could break a betrothal contract. To *Cat*, the one Zero. She'd be disowned by her family, just to keep them from being permanently cut out of any future agreements."

He reached out and patted my shoulder. "You're in the clear, Cousin."

"I hope you're right," I said.

"And I hope it taught you a lesson," Louise added, primly. "Your lust for revenge nearly broke you."

"Things will go better next time," Francis said. "We learnt a lot from this experience."

Louise lifted her eyebrows. "Like...*don't do it again?*"

"Possibly how not to do it," Francis said. "We still have to repair the damage and replace the lost potions."

"We can do that fairly quickly," I said. "I think we'd be better served by trying to figure out what we have to do—and what we might need to do it."

"They might change things every year," Francis pointed out.

"Then they wouldn't bother to hide the records," I countered. "And besides, how many changes can they *make*?"

Louise snorted. "We don't know what the original rules are—or were. We certainly can't guess at how they might have been changed."

"True." I stared at my hands for a long moment. "We'll keep training, of course. And we'll see how much more we can learn before time runs out."

"You *could* ask your father," Louise said. She'd suggested it before, several times. "If he says no, then...well, you'd know."

"The rules say we cannot ask for adult help," I reminded her. "And Father is very definitely an adult."

"He's old enough to be your father," Francis cracked.

Saline gave him a shocked expression, then looked embarrassed as she realised it was a joke. I sighed, inwardly. It was a joke, but—in the wrong company—it could be very embarrassing. And dangerous, if someone believed it...or merely *pretended* to believe it.

"Maybe we could find a new way to cheat," Francis said. "Perfectly legal cheating, of course."

"No," I said. "We need to concentrate on our training. It's what'll get us through the Challenge."

"You could ask Magister Niven," Louise said. "He's teaching us about how the city actually works. He might be able to point us in the right direction."

I blinked. Louise didn't *like* Magister Niven. But she had a point. If the Challenge was a reflection of real-world politics, as played by the Great Houses, Magister Niven might be the person to ask. And if there was any Magister who might defy the Castellan, it was Niven.

"I'll see what I can do," I said, as the door opened. Alana stepped into the room, her eyes widening as she saw us. "Don't worry, we're on our way out."

Francis blinked. "We are?"

"Yeah," I said. "It's nearly dinner time."

Louise took the hint. "I'll see you at dinner," she said, standing. "Saline can tell me all about...well, everything later."

I watched them go, then glanced at Alana. She was watching me, a curious expression on her face. It struck me, *really* struck me, that she was Cat's sister. In that moment, the two girls looked very alike.

She smiled, wryly. "You do realise you're not supposed to plot and plan in here?"

"We were just having a chat," I said, flushing. Alana was right, technically. "You can have a chat too."

"With you listening in?" Alana's smile grew wider. "I think not."

CHAPTER

TWENTY

It was no surprise to me, over the next few days, that *something* leaked out.

It couldn't have been the truth. Francis was right. There was no way the staff—and our families—could have avoided doing *something* if they'd learnt the truth. But enough had leaked out to make Francis and I look like idiots. I gritted my teeth, trying to stay calm as upperclassmen pointed and laughed. It wasn't easy. The McDonalds had broken into our base, smashed our supplies…and we had made ourselves laughingstocks when we tried to fight back.

The only consolation, I supposed, was that the Magisters didn't seem to care. They kept piling work on us, from more advanced potions and charms to forging and wardcrafting. A couple seemed determined to drive their entire class into an early grave, forcing us to abandon our training program and spend most of our evenings in the library. And I had more duties than any other upperclassman. I envied Francis, more than I cared to say. The Sports Captain had subordinates who could run games for him. I had no one I could order to take my place.

And then there were detentions…

I'd hated detentions myself, even though I knew it could be worse. The *really* badly-behaved students were put in the stocks, when they weren't suspended or expelled outright. But there was something about being trapped in a classroom, after classes were meant to be finished for the day, that got to people. The lowerclassmen wrote their lines, or scribbled their punishment essays, while every so often throwing wistful glances at the bright sunlight outside. I sat at my desk and watched them, brooding. It was sheer luck, I supposed, that the rumours hadn't reached the lowerclassmen.

A motion caught my eye. "Fredrick, if you throw that hex at Daria, you'll get more lines."

Fredrick flinched. He'd thought I wasn't paying attention. I watched him until he returned to his lines, then returned to my brooding. I should have brought a book. Or a notebook. Or…something. I really should have known better. I'd taken detentions before. It was on the tip of my tongue to order one of the lowerclassmen to go *get* me a book, but I refrained. I wasn't meant to be drawing attention to the fact I *wasn't* paying—much—attention.

The thought made me smile as I opened the desk drawers and glanced inside. There were no notebooks, no sheets of paper…there weren't even any trashy novels, hidden at the bottom of the drawer. The detention room got checked every day, if I recalled correctly. There was little in the room, save for what we brought. I would have killed for one of the silly novels Isabella had used to read, despite our governess's disapproval; I would even have welcomed one of the books that was supposed to provide moral guidance to Young Children and—instead—bored them to death. The heroes were either paragons of morality or bumbling halfwits who ran into danger without thinking. I supposed I should have been paying more attention to those old tales. I'd run into danger—and near disaster—because I'd wanted revenge.

And because they wrecked a lot of our work, I said. My team hadn't said anything, not to me, but I could tell they were discouraged. We'd taken a hit—and we hadn't even been able to hit back. Francis talked about going back to the McDonald base and hitting it again, more carefully this time, but I was wary. We'd had a very close shave. *I don't want to go through that again.*

It wasn't a pleasant thought. My feelings were conflicted. There had been a thrill, yes, in being somewhere I wasn't supposed to be…yet, I knew—all too well—just how close I'd come to utter disaster. And…Ayesha had kissed me. I knew she'd done it to sneak a spell past my defences, but…she'd kissed me. My mind kept replaying it, over and over again. I had no idea how I was going to tell Cat. She might break the betrothal on the spot. Or she might laugh at me. I honestly wasn't sure which one was worse.

Being laughed at would be bad for me, I thought, dryly. I valued Cat's good opinion more than anyone else's. *But breaking the betrothal would be bad for the family.*

I looked up as the door opened. A latecomer? Very few students were *late* for detention, not when it meant more lines or a notation in their permanent records. Kate stepped into the room, looking…my eyes narrowed. Kate looked like a doll, one of the perfect china dolls my mother had owned and forbidden us to touch on pain of… well, she hadn't been explicit, but she'd made it sound pretty bad. Isabella had wanted one, I remembered. Mother had promised her one for her sixteenth birthday. I wondered, suddenly, if Mother had sent the doll.

Kate walked over to me, her eyes downcast, and held out a red slip. I glanced at it, sharply. Kate had been given lines for cheek—and orders to do them in detention, rather than doing them in her own time. I didn't have to look at the signature to know that Penny had written the slip and sent Kate to me. I looked up at Kate, feeling another pang—she looked like Isabella, in the days when we'd been displayed to prospective clients—and motioned for her to take a chair. She sat, looking terribly out of place. It was odd for firsties to get formal detentions. Their dorm monitors normally dealt with them directly.

I allowed my eyes to roam around the room, then glanced at the clock. Only twenty minutes had passed since the period had started…just twenty minutes? It felt like I'd been sitting in the chair for hours. I wanted to stand and pace, to march around the room and peer out the window, but I refrained. I'd always hated watching the upperclassmen prancing around when *I'd* been a lowerclassmen. One of them had always peered over our shoulders while we'd written our lines. I wouldn't have minded so much if his breath hadn't stunk. I really didn't want to know what he'd been eating. We'd joked that someone had cast a permanent halitosis hex on him.

Think, I told myself. *You can think, even if you can't do anything else.*

My mind ran in circles. Father had told me I'd be attending a potions fair, over the half-term. I had no idea why—naturally, he hadn't bothered to ask before making the arrangements. Rose would be coming with me, which was odd. I didn't need a chaperone if I wasn't going to see Cat...*could* I be going to see Cat? Her family was a little reluctant to let her out of their sight, but she was *seventeen*. There was no way she'd consent to remaining a prisoner forever, even if she wasn't betrothed. And a potions fair was something she'd enjoy. I allowed myself to hope I'd see her. Away from our families, with only Rose to chaperone us, we might actually be able to *talk*.

I had to smile at the thought. We were supposed to do nothing now, *but* talk. And yet, what could we talk about with the old biddies listening in? I couldn't have a normal conversation with Cat—about *anything*—when I knew that everything we said would be reported to our parents. Ancients alone knew what conclusions they'd draw, from our talks about Objects and Devices of Power. Perhaps they'd fear that we were planning to take over the world. It struck me as a little too much hard work.

Which didn't stop Stregheria Aguirre and the Crown Prince from trying, I reminded myself, grimly. I tried hard not to think about the Crown Prince—and how he had died at my hand—but, sometimes, it was impossible. Especially when I felt the sword strapped to my back. It was a needle driven into my very soul. *Alana's lucky she doesn't have to wear her family's sword. Not yet.*

The bell caught me by surprise. I'd zoned out so completely that...I shook my head, glancing around the room. No one stood. They'd been at the school long enough to know the period didn't *really* end until the monitor said so. I frowned as I noticed Kate—she was *still* writing lines—then turned my attention to the rest of the group. They looked back at me nervously, like deer caught in a hunter's light. A word from me could send them back to their desks with extra lines.

"If you've finished your lines, bring them here," I ordered. "If you haven't—or if you have assignments—scram."

I resisted the urge to rub my eyes as a small line formed in front of the desk. I took a third-year student's punishment book, checked the lines and dismissed him with a nod. It didn't really matter what he'd written, as long as he'd written actual *lines*. I'd managed to slip a handful of fake lines into *my* punishment book, when I'd been younger. Francis had pointed out that very few upperclassmen would deliberately make an enemy of an Heir Primus, back then, but now I rather suspected they hadn't noticed. They would have had to look closely to spot the lines that didn't match.

Kate was *still* writing lines. I dismissed the remaining students, then peered at her. She'd been told she could go...normally, students who didn't have to have their work checked would have been out of the door before I finished speaking. The days were still long, but they'd be getting shorter soon enough. Better to enjoy the sunshine while it lasted.

I cleared my throat. "Kate?"

Kate looked up at me. "Yes, Senior?"

"You can go," I said, mildly. "Unless you *want* the pleasure of my company."

Kate's eyes flickered from side to side. I frowned, feeling a twinge of concern. No lowerclassman ever born would want an upperclassman's company—and, if he did, he certainly wouldn't admit to it. The social gulf between lowerclassmen and upperclassmen was wider than the gap between Louise's parents and mine. Kate should have left the room at once, before I took official notice of her presence. I could have given her more lines.

I saw her rubbing her wrist and winced, inwardly. "Give me your punishment book."

If she'd fled, I would have let her go. I wasn't supposed to *know* her. But Kate didn't seem to realise it. Or maybe she thought that running would just get her in more trouble. She stood, smoothing down her skirt in a manner that was recognisably aristocratic, and walked over to the desk. She walked so gingerly that I couldn't help thinking she thought the floor was nothing more than very thin ice, that the slightest false move would send her plunging into freezing water. My eyes narrowed further. Penny was clearly teaching her poise as well as manners. And yet...

I took the book and opened it to the very first page. It hadn't been *that* long since Kate had started school, but she already had several *dozen* entries in the book. Penny had written most of them—there was a constant liturgy of lines for talking back, as well as other things—yet a handful came from the teachers. Magister Tallyman had written a sharp note about laziness that struck me as odd. What had she done? Fallen asleep in class?

Kate fidgeted nervously as I glanced through the next few pages. I hadn't earned so many punishments in my *entire* first year—I didn't know anyone who *had*. Francis had the record for lines, detentions and infractions in our year, I thought, and even *he* hadn't collected so many punishments in a *single* year. Although...there were punishments that weren't recorded. The sports masters often handed out push-ups and cross-country runs instead of formal punishments. Francis had argued otherwise, but there was no way I'd believe that a cross-country run *wasn't* a punishment. What sort of lunatic would do *that* for fun?

Francis, I thought.

I smiled. Kate flinched. I kicked myself, mentally. She thought I was smiling at *her*. I wanted to apologise, but I had no words. Upperclassmen did *not* apologise to lowerclassmen, even if they were in the wrong. It struck me, suddenly, that that particular social protocol might be a mistake. If the lowerclassman *knew* we'd made a mistake...

She reached for the book before I even offered it to her. I winced, again. She was lucky she'd done that to *me*, not Alana. Or Penny.

"It's only been a few weeks," I said, holding the book in one hand. "How did you manage to earn so many punishments?"

Kate looked stricken, caught between two upperclassmen. I shouldn't have asked. I should have…I shook my head. I had to ask, even though I didn't think I wanted to know the answer. And someone else *would* ask, eventually. The punishment books were charmed, linked to our permanent records. There was a point, I'd been told, when the staff would get involved. That would end very badly for Kate. They wouldn't bother to ask *why* she'd earned so many punishments. They'd just throw the book at her.

"I…ah…I…"

"I order you to tell me," I said, quietly. "And if anyone gives you any trouble over it, you can send them to see me."

"The Senior has been teaching me manners," Kate said. "But they're so hard to learn…"

"You have years *to* learn." I supposed that explained the change in her. Penny was bullying Kate even as she taught Kate manners. "You're doing very well."

"Thank you, Senior," Kate said.

I blinked as it finally hit me. Kate was calling *me* Senior? And Penny? *Senior* was an honorific given to older members of the family. It was rarely given to outsiders, even haughty and domineering upperclassmen. It would be like calling a complete stranger my father or older brother or…I scowled. Penny shouldn't be urging *anyone* to call her Senior.

"You're welcome." I hesitated, then made a note in her punishment book that she'd completed the whole exercise. Penny really *was* overdoing things. Kate had had so many lines to write that it was no surprise her wrist was cramping. "You can have a few hundred lines off for good behaviour."

Kate's eyes went wide. "Thank you," she stammered, as she took the book back. "I…"

"There'll be someone in the year above you who'll be producing pain-relief ointment on the sly," I told her. The healers wouldn't give her anything, not if her wrist was cramping through writing lines. But there was always someone who was trying to make a little money through brewing potions for the lower years. "They won't charge you very much, if anything. And you can look up how to make it for yourself in potions class."

"Thank you." Kate hesitated, as if she was on the verge of saying something else. "I..."

She bobbed a curtsey, then hurried out of the room. Technically, she should have waited for me to dismiss her...I shook my head. There were no witnesses. In hindsight, I should have made certain that Penny and I were somewhere private before I berated her. Penny...probably felt humiliated, even if Kate had had the sense to keep her mouth shut. I wondered if Kate had asked her what she'd been doing...no, I doubted it. Kate knew better than to ask Penny anything.

And what, I asked myself, *am I going to do about it?*

I rubbed my eyes as the bell rang for dinner. There was nothing I *could* do about it, not without revealing far too much. Last time, I'd stumbled across Penny's bullying by accident. Now, it would be all too easy to give Kate a reputation for being a sneak. Her peers would blame her for telling me, even if she *hadn't* told me. And even if I ordered her to tell me...

Better to keep one's mouth shut and take whatever you get like a man than sneak on someone, even your worst enemy, I reminded myself. The code had been drilled into me from my very first day at school. It was supposed to be good preparation for later life, but...I couldn't help feeling there was something wrong with it. *It's one thing to lie to keep a friend from getting into trouble, yet quite another to cover up a superior's misdeeds.*

I let out a long breath. What could I do? I could keep an eye on Penny and Kate, but...I could only watch them when they were outside the dorms. Whatever happened in the dorm *stayed* in the dorm. That, too, was part of the code. But...I shuddered. There should be limits. Of course there should be limits. And yet, it was a bit much to expect twelve year olds, half of whom had come from outside the city, to know where those limits rested.

The newcomers weren't raised in the aristocracy, I reminded myself. Rose had had etiquette lessons for the last six years, but it was still easy to tell that she hadn't been born in Shallot. Kate hadn't even had *that. They don't know how society really works.*

The door opened. Alana stepped into the room. "Your guests await you," she said, with heavy sarcasm. "You owe me big, you know."

I smiled, putting Penny and Kate out of my mind. "Yeah," I said. "I know."

CHAPTER
TWENTY-ONE

It was a pity, I reflected as I entered the suite, that Francis had other engagements after dinner. There was a football game, one of a series intended to determine which team would be representing the school in the national league the following summer. It didn't strike *me* as very important, but Francis swore blind he had to be there. If he wasn't...utter disaster would result. Or so he said.

Louise and Saline sat on the sofa, waiting for me. I nodded, then waved for them to follow me into the kitchen. A table had been placed in the middle of the room, laid out as it would have been in any Great House. I heard Louise mutter an oath, just loud enough to be heard; I tried to look at the scene through her eyes. Good manners and etiquette might hold society together—I'd heard that, often enough, from my aunties—but there was something about the table that was faintly ridiculous. It was a great deal of effort for a simple dinner.

"If you look at the children of the Great Houses," I said, "you'll notice that most of them—us—are treated as miniature adults. Their clothes are adult clothes, their meals are adult meals...even their *toys* are often adult toys. We are taught how to be adults from the moment we are old enough to walk, drilled mercilessly in social etiquette before we are old enough for our mistakes to be more than a source of humour. Our childhoods are often quite restrictive."

"My heart bleeds," Louise said, dryly.

I ignored her. "When I was a little boy, my sister and I were taught how to behave through a series of ritualised social events. Sometimes, we learnt alongside the other children; sometimes, we were taught alone. This dinner"—I waved a hand at the table—"is as close as I can come to a reproduction of how we were taught to dine. It is a little more complex than merely putting food in one's mouth."

"A little," Louise repeated.

"Quite." I drew out a chair. "In a formal dinner, each gentleman is paired with a lady. He is expected to help her into her chair, which can be a little challenging if the lady is wearing a long dress. Here...well, we have one gentleman so I'll help both of you. Saline?"

Saline sat and smoothed out her dress. "Thank you."

"I can pull out my own chair," Louise pointed out. "Why do I need *you* to do it for me?"

"It's a way of saying you're welcome here," I said. I pulled out a chair for her, then motioned for her to sit down. "And also a way of saying that I will be a good host."

Louse raised her eyebrows as she sat. "You've done this before?"

"Yes." The memories weren't very pleasant, even when the dinners had gone perfectly. "There were times when I would be paired with an older lady, who could be quite demanding."

Saline winced.

"Hah," Louise said. "And then what?"

"There's a bottle of wine on the table." I picked it up and undid the cork. "It's not wine, of course, but we'll pretend it is. Would you do me the honour of taking a glass?"

"Of course," Saline said.

I poured her a glass of cranberry juice, then offered the bottle to Louise.

She frowned. "What if I don't *want* wine? You might be trying to get me drunk for nefarious reasons."

"It's customary to take a little," I said. "But if you don't want to drink, don't drink."

I poured her a glass, then sat facing her. "It's also customary to make small talk with your partner before the food actually arrives," I continued. "These conversations are about nothing in particular—some people babble endlessly about the weather, others will show off their knowledge of the vintage. Sensitive matters are not discussed at the dinner table."

Saline took a sip. "Ah, I believe this was laid down a thousand years ago, a truly magnificent vintage. Ripe, full-bodied, full of flavour, mature… and a lot of other words I don't really understand. Babble, babble, babble."

I chuckled. "There'll always be *someone* with a far greater knowledge of wine than you," I told Louise. "Don't try to bluff them. It's a sign you're faking it."

"I could learn everything I needed to know about wine from books," Louise pointed out, sardonically. "Couldn't I?"

"Not quite." I met her eyes. "It's one thing to know the words, but quite another to practice. And you'll find it quite difficult to cheat."

I shrugged. "But outside the *real* wine snobs, you probably won't have to worry about it."

"Thank the Ancients," Louise muttered.

"Once everyone is seated, the servants bring the first course," I explained, as I stood and reached for the tureen. "In all the best households, the very first course is almost always soup. Families compete to see who can produce the most extraordinary recipe—last year, House Bolingbroke served turtle soup—but we're having chicken. The servant will bring a bowl and serve you at your seat—if you don't want soup, simply leave your napkin on top of your place."

Louise frowned. "Why can't I simply refuse?"

"It's rude not to take food when it's offered," Saline said, quietly. "By putting your napkin in plain view, it's a clear sign they shouldn't be offering you soup."

"And so offense is avoided," I continued. I served the soup, then sat back down. "Don't touch your spoon, let alone your soup, until everyone at the table has been served. Seeing as we have…."—I grinned—"tuck in."

"I don't even know which spoon to use," Louise complained.

"As a general rule, work from the outside in," Saline said. "There's a set of cutlery for each individual course. The servants will take them away as the meal progresses."

I nodded. "From now on, you're only permitted to leave your seat in the event of a major emergency," I said. "My governess always told me to make sure I went to the toilet before I went to dine. Leaving the table early is almost always bad news."

Louise looked appalled. "What if it *is* bad news?"

"Then people will be talking about it for years," I said, bluntly. "And… well, unless you have a very good excuse, you won't be allowed to return."

I sipped my soup, gingerly. "Eat carefully," I added. "People *will* be watching your table manners."

"Joy." Louise scowled. "Do I *really* have to learn all this?"

"It depends." I met her eyes. "If you want people to like you, and to want to help you, you have to appeal to them. And aping their manners is a good way to appeal to them."

"If you say so," Louise grumbled. "What do we do when we finish our soup?"

"If you want more, place your spoon by the side of your dish," I said. "If you've had enough, place the spoon *in* the dish. The servants will remove it."

Louise grinned. "I'm being served by the Head Boy," she said. "What a *great* honour."

"You're more than welcome," I said. "There generally isn't conversation during the first two courses. If someone talks to you, be polite but vague. They're being very rude and people will notice if you reply."

"That's rude too," Saline said. "And if someone touches your leg, feel free to kick them."

Louise looked at me. "Does that happen?"

"It shouldn't," I said. I let out a long breath. "But it can."

I cleared my throat. "There's normally a gap between courses, which can be filled with conversation. If you want more wine, simply signal one of the servants. As we don't have time"—I stood—"I'll take the bowls and spoons now."

Saline winked. "How very rude."

"True." I nodded to her. "If someone is still eating, you have to wait for them to signal they're finished. And you're not allowed to hurry them along."

I collected the bowls and placed them on the trolley. "When a formal dinner is announced, you'll receive a menu with a list of food selections," I added. "You send it back with your choices outlined. The staff will make sure you get what you want."

"And you'll also get a dance card, if there's dancing afterwards," Saline commented. "If someone asks for a dance, you pencil them in…"

"I've seen them," Louise said. "What if you don't *want* to dance with a gentleman?"

"You tell him that the dance card is full," I said. "And yes, you are allowed to lie. He may not take it that well, but…you don't have to dance with him."

"That's good, at least," Louise commented. "Why don't we see dance cards here?"

"We do," I said. "*You* just don't see them."

Louise reddened. I felt a twinge of guilt. "If you spent more time at the formal dances, you'd see them. You'd have one."

"Why don't *you*?" Louise scowled at her hands. "You could go to the dances."

"I'm betrothed," I reminded her. "Right now, I could not go on the dance floor without Cat—even if she didn't dance herself, she'd have to be there. And I don't want to go without her."

"It wouldn't mean anything to her," Louise said. "Would it?"

I cocked an eyebrow at her as I served the next course. "Wouldn't *you* object if your betrothed was dancing with another woman? And you weren't even there to still the gossip?"

"I'd understand they were dancing—and dancing alone." Louise reddened. "I wouldn't expect them to get married on the spot."

"But people would talk," I told her. "If you do the wrong thing, in public, people will talk about it. Yes, they'll talk. And if I danced with you, at a dance Cat didn't attend, people would talk. And it would cause a great deal of embarrassment for both of us."

"Stupid," Louise muttered.

I sat down. "Again, you have to wait until everyone is served before you eat. But this time you're allowed to use magic to keep your food warm until everyone is served."

"And, if you're a *very* honoured guest, the lord of the manor may serve you personally," Saline added. "Be polite if he does."

Louise frowned. "Is that likely?"

"It depends." I considered it for a moment. "If you're marrying his son, for example, he will probably serve you himself. If not"—I shook my head—"you probably wouldn't be allowed to sit at the high table. That's for the guests of honour."

We ate in companionable silence for long minutes, savouring the food. Louise seemed to like it. I didn't have the heart to tell her that it had come from the school's kitchens, rather than a master chef. Rose had told me, once, that she hadn't understood why so many students complained about the food at school until she'd eaten with Cat's family. The food there was so much *better* than school food that there really wasn't any comparison.

And expensive, too, I reminded myself. I'd heard stories about Lady Younghusband, who'd promised her guests a *very* expensive dinner. At the culmination of the feast, she'd taken a pearl from her earring and swallowed it. *The food could be awful and no one would complain, as long as it was expensive.*

"There can be any number of courses," I said, "but a typical dinner normally consists of three; starter, main course and pudding. By the time the pudding comes around, most guests are full. But you should find room for the pudding."

I stood, collected the plates and placed the pudding bowl on the table. "Unlike the other courses, you are allowed—and expected—to serve yourselves. The ladies eat first, in strict order of seniority. If you don't know the order, don't worry. Someone will tell you."

"And I'll be right at the bottom," Louise guessed. "Right?"

"Not always," Saline said. "It depends on your connection to the Great House."

Louise eyed me. "Explain."

I passed her the spoon. "If you marry someone with a high rank—Francis, for example—you will share his rank as long as you remain married to him. If you have children, you will keep the rank for the rest of your life. If you actually start out with a higher rank, you'll give it to your husband instead."

"Really?" Louise scowled. "How does that work?"

"If Francis married Alana, he would be treated as an Heir Primus," I said. "But if Francis married you, you'd be treated as a Cousin."

"Madness," Louise said. "How do you keep it all straight in your head?"

I shrugged. "Arguably, we don't. There are a lot of Grande Dames who don't talk to each other because of something that happened when my father was a little boy. And then…there are sometimes disputes for one reason or another. A few pointless and petty arguments over who should take the lead…I suppose it saves us from fighting over something real. A decent event organiser can make *thousands* of crowns by making sure that enemies don't have to sit together."

Saline giggled. "They don't always succeed," she said. "I remember when Lady Johanna and Lady Constance were forced to sit together. They nearly hexed each other at the dinner table!"

"That would have been bad," I said. I grinned at Louse's shocked face. "You can chat about anything over pudding, although it isn't meant to be too serious. After dinner, the real conversations begin."

"And all the real deals are made," Louise said. There was a hint of bitterness in her tone. "And all of *us* are excluded."

"I thought you were planning to join," I said. "You have to learn to play the game by the rules if you want to win."

"And yet, we don't know what the rules actually *are*." Louise's voice was very quiet. "Both for the real world *and* for the Challenge."

"We figure it out by trial and error," I said. "And these practice dinners"— I waved a hand at the table—"help us figure out what we're doing wrong without public embarrassment."

I stood, again. "Once the pudding is finished, the guests normally move into the smoking rooms. The important guests, the movers and shakers, go into one room. Everyone else goes into the other. Kids are excused, if they wish to go; everyone else has to stay, unless they have a pressing engagement. Again, it's a good idea not to leave too early. People will talk."

Louise scowled. "Do they do anything else?"

"No," Saline said. She helped me pick up the dishes and stow them under the trolley. "They talk and talk and talk..."

"I get the idea," Louise growled. She shook her head, slowly. "Is it just me or...or is most of High Society absolutely useless?"

Saline looked offended. "Hey!"

I considered the question for a long moment. She had a point, as uncomfortable as it was to admit it. There were a *lot* of aristocrats who seemed to do nothing but attend parties, make catty remarks and generally look down their noses at anyone who didn't have good breeding or the right connections. But…there were also aristocrats who did good, from my father to Cat's father to…

"They're just like anyone else," I said, fully aware that Father would be angry if he heard me saying it. "A certain percentage of them *are* useless, but not *all* of them."

I led the way back into the sitting room. "We can talk about more serious matters now," I said, pretending not to notice the look of boredom on Louise's face. "What would you like to talk about?"

Louise let out a long sigh. "How many of these dinners do we have to attend?"

I shrugged. "If you want to get anywhere in society, you'll have to attend dozens…"

"Hundreds," Saline corrected.

"… And if you don't attend, or if you make a fool of yourself, people will judge you harshly," I continued. "And then…"

The door opened. Alana stepped into the room. Her dark face was unreadable as she looked at me. I felt an odd little shiver running down my spine. She looked as if someone was in trouble. I had the nasty feeling it was me.

"Akin," she said. "A word? Outside?"

I nodded and stepped through the door. "Alana? What…?"

Alana met my eyes. "You need to go to Room 14-6B, now. You really do."

I felt…I wasn't sure *how* I felt. Room 14-6B was near the sports complex, right on the other side of the school. To go there, now…why?"

"Why?" My mouth felt dry. "What's…"

"Go," Alana said. "I can't say anything else."

She looked so much like Cat, in that moment, that I didn't bother to argue. I turned and hurried down the corridor, passing a pair of students on their way back to the dorms as I picked up speed. Most of the students would still be outside, if they weren't in the library or trying to earn a little extra credit. Room 14-6B hadn't been abandoned, but it might as well have been. It wasn't used very often. I'd used it as a study room once, during a group project, but I'd never had any formal classes there. It was...

I heard a sound as I approached. Instinctively, I slowed, slipping forward as quietly as I could. The sound grew louder as I reached the door and peeked inside. Francis stood there, his arms wrapped around a girl...they were kissing. They were kissing and...

I couldn't help it. I gasped.

CHAPTER
TWENTY-TWO

For a long moment, we all stood as still as statues.

I stared, unable to take my eyes off them. Francis was kissing…Francis was kissing *Lindsey*! He was doing more than kissing, too. Her shirt was unbuttoned—I caught a glimpse of more bare flesh than anyone other than her husband should see—and his hands were up her skirt, stroking her bottom. I could see him…Lindsey let out a yelp, jumping back from Francis so quickly she almost tripped over herself, and threw a hex at me. The sword was in my hand almost before I knew it, cutting the spell out of the air with casual ease. Her eyes were wide with horror as she hastily buttoned up her shirt to cover herself. Beside her, Francis gave me an odd little smile.

I tried not to look at her, even though I didn't dare turn my back. Lindsey was beautiful, with long auburn hair and…and…I felt a flash of envy, mingled with horror. Francis was dating Lindsey? Francis *shouldn't* be dating Lindsey. She was *betrothed!* What was he *thinking*?

"I…" Lindsey stared at me as she hastily buttoned up her shirt. Guilt was written all over her face. If I hadn't caught them in the act, I would have known what they were doing. "I…"

She stumbled forward, hurrying past me and out into the corridor beyond. I glanced after her, then turned my attention back to Francis. I felt the sword trying to pull me forward, an alien bloodlust demanding that I behead him without delay. It took all of my willpower to force myself to return the sword to the scabbard, cutting off the effect. And yet, it still seemed to be pushing at me. I wanted—it wanted—blood.

"Well," Francis said. "What brings you here?"

I found it hard to speak. Francis...Francis had lied to me. He'd said he had a sporting event...I'd believed him. It hadn't occurred to me that he might have been sneaking off to be with his girlfriend...his girlfriend? Lindsey was his girlfriend? Francis was playing with fire. He'd be safer insulting my mother in front of my father. He might be banished, but...

"Well?" Francis smiled at me. "*Cat* got your tongue?"

I found my voice. "What...what are you doing?"

Francis's smile grew wider. "What did it *look* like I was doing?"

I glared at him. "Are you crazy?"

"I don't believe so." Francis inspected his fingernails. "What brought you here?"

I ignored the question. "You and Lindsey are...are dating?"

"Of course," Francis said. "She's a hot little honey, isn't she?"

"She's *betrothed*, you..." I couldn't think of anything nasty enough to fit. "You bloody stupid idiot. She's betrothed to Lord Richard!"

Francis shrugged. "So what?"

I stared at him, unable to believe what I was hearing. "Francis, Lord Richard is the finest duellist His Majesty commands," I snapped. "He'll kill you."

"I can take him." Francis didn't sound like he cared. "Such men are always overrated..."

"He's been at the top of the league for the last three years," I reminded him. Even *I* had heard of Lord Richard. "He didn't get that ranking because someone pulled strings on his behalf."

I took a breath. "And even if her betrothed doesn't kill you, what about her family? There's a lot riding on her betrothal, isn't there? What happens if the betrothal shatters because of this?"

Francis pretended to think. "Nothing?"

"Nothing?" I shook my head. "Nothing?"

I had to fight to compose myself. "His family will blame you," I told him. "And they'll try to take it out on your family. *Our* family. And then... you'll probably be kicked out, just for being so"—I made an incoherent noise—"stupid that you shatter a betrothal just for your selfish pleasure!"

Francis's face reddened. He took a threatening step towards me. "Selfish?"

"Yes." I met his gaze evenly, refusing to back down. "Didn't you think about anyone else before you"—I couldn't put it into words—"before you locked lips with her?"

"And did a little more besides," Francis said.

I had to force myself to keep my voice steady. "And if you'd been caught by someone else," I said, "you would have done immense harm to the family."

Francis glared back at me. "Just like your sister?"

"Yes, just like Isabella!" I stood my ground as he moved closer. "You could have shattered *everything*."

Francis looked, just for a second, as if he wanted to punch me. "Do you really think it matters?"

"Yes!" I took a breath. "The family doesn't need *another* scandal. Not now."

Francis stepped back. "Tell me," he said. "Are you really angry? Or are you just jealous?"

I felt myself redden with a mixture of anger and embarrassment. I didn't want to admit it, but he was right. I *was* jealous. There was a bit of me that *wanted* to be free to date, to kiss, to go further—perhaps—with a girl of my choice. And there was a larger bit of me that wanted to go further with Cat, that knew we *would* go further if we were left alone. Francis knew me better than I cared to admit. It was easy to envy his freedom. But I couldn't believe what he'd done.

"She's betrothed," I said, again. "What were you thinking?"

Francis leered. "She came on to me, you know."

"I don't care," I snapped. "It doesn't matter, not now. If Lord Richard finds out…"

"And who," Francis asked, "is going to tell him?"

I considered it, just for a moment. Lindsey was betrothed, not engaged. She would have to be out of her mind to tell anyone what had happened, not when it would shatter the betrothal beyond repair. Lord Richard might not care—it had to have crossed his mind that the betrothal would not turn to marriage—but her parents would be furious. And Francis wouldn't tell anyone…I swallowed, hard. Was that actually true? Francis had done something pretty stupid just by kissing her, much less everything else. And Alana…

My mind raced. Alana had told me…had she been trying to help? Or hinder? I didn't know. It could easily be both. She was clever that way, careful enough to make sure she came out ahead whatever happened. And…I wished, suddenly, that Isabella was here. She would have seen the implications, long before I did. My sister was clever that way too.

"You're insane," I said, quietly.

"And you're jealous." Francis sounded pleased. "Come with me. We can chase girls together…"

My temper began to rise. "And then…what? Some of us have to think about the future."

Francis snorted. "Let the future take care of itself."

"The future *cannot* take care of itself," I snapped. How could he be so obtuse? Francis wasn't stupid, far from it. "If I do anything, now, it could have consequences…"

"So what?" Francis held out a hand. "Come with me."

I was tempted. Yes, I was tempted. I knew—even though I wasn't supposed to know—that there were places we could go, if we wanted to find girls. And those places would be discreet…perhaps. I'd heard my uncles talking, when they didn't know I was listening. Francis had already been…I swallowed, hard. It was so hard to think straight. And yet, I knew Francis could always talk himself out of trouble. I'd never had that talent. Father would kill me—perhaps literally—if I threw everything away.

"It must be frustrating, sometimes," Francis said. His face twisted into a leer. "To be betrothed, yet to be unable to *do* anything with her…"

"Shut up!" I clenched my fists, ready to throw a punch. "Just…shut up!"

"Come with me," Francis said, again. "You can forget her and…"

"You're a stupid idiot!" The words slipped out of my mouth before I could stop them, months and years of bitter frustrations—frustrations I didn't want to admit existed—boiling out of me. "You don't think, do you! You just don't think!"

Francis's face went very cold. "Say that again. I dare you."

"You don't think about the future," I snarled. "All your bloody life! You just…get on the field, kick a ball around and everyone admires you! You don't have to work to get everything you want in life…you don't even *want* very much in life. You just"—I found myself reduced to incoherence—"you just want to have fun."

He smiled. "And what's wrong with fun?"

"Some of us have to work to earn our inheritance," I snapped. "I've been entered in the Challenge because Father thinks it will convince the Council to take his place. And you…you could have blown everything right out of the water."

Francis smirked. "But it didn't happen, did it?"

"*It could have done that easily, you dolt!*" I wanted to punch him. No matter how annoying Francis had ever been, I had never wanted to *kill* him until now. "You're not the only one at risk, you selfish prat! You could have brought the entire family crashing down!"

"Don't be silly." Francis crossed his arms. "They'd kick me out before anything *really* bad could happen."

"You don't even think about your own best interests," I told him. "How far do you think you'll get without the family name?"

Francis's face darkened. "Further than *you*."

I scowled. He was probably right. Francis had a gift for making people like him…and a fairly complete education. He could change his name, move to a different country and make a new life…perhaps. I had the feeling he wouldn't be playing competitive sports. Or…or whatever he wanted to do. What did he really want?

"If Lord Richard doesn't kill you," I reminded him. "You *know* how betrothals work. No one is allowed to do *anything* that might call the betrothal into question. Lord Richard could kill you."

"I could take him," Francis said, again. "I…"

"You're not even listed in the league tables," I reminded him. "Lord Richard is at the very top! He won't even have to break a sweat blowing you to bits. Or were you planning to insist on choosing the weapons? The finest smile? The sharpest dress? The…"

"It doesn't matter," Francis said. "Lindsey isn't going to tell anyone. I'm not going to tell anyone. You're not going to tell anyone. And…how did you find me here?"

I thought, briefly, about telling him the truth. But who knew what he'd do if he knew *Alana* had told me? Would he try to bargain with her? Or threaten her? Or…I felt my heart sink as I realised the danger. Alana could blackmail both of us, now. She could demand we threw the Challenge as the price for our silence. I didn't dare tell Francis what had happened. I had no way to know what he'd do.

"I received a vapour note," I said. The spell was used for sending anonymous messages. "Someone knows, Francis. Someone who isn't *me*."

Francis shrugged. "Let them try to prove it."

"You don't need solid proof for nasty rumours to get started," I snapped. "And Lindsey might be pressured to break the betrothal if the rumours were nasty enough."

"So what?" Francis asked. "Does it matter?"

I hit him. His face snapped backwards, his eyes going wide with shock. I wasn't a sportsman, not by any means, but I *was* a forger. People often forgot that forging required physical strength. Cat was no taller than her sisters, but she was a *lot* more muscular. Francis caught himself, somehow, and threw himself at me. We crashed to the ground, rolling over and over as we tried to fight. It wasn't easy. He was the better fighter, but I was used to physical discomfort. And we were too close together for either of us to do anything clever. The fight might have gone on for a long time if he hadn't cast a shock hex. The blast picked us up and threw us in different directions.

He stared at me. I could see blood trickling down his face. I ached…he'd hit me in the chest, hard enough to break a rib. I gritted my teeth, ignoring the pain. It wasn't as bad as being hit with fragments of molten metal. Or a torture curse. I'd had worse.

"The *family* matters," I snapped. I sounded just like my father. "The family gives us everything, from a place to live to a proper education and training in magic that is *millions* of miles ahead of anything the commoners get. The family gives us everything! And we are expected to work for it in return. Anything, for the family!"

"Anything, for the family," Francis mocked. He touched his jaw. It didn't *look* broken, and I hadn't felt it break, but I didn't *know*. "Are you really that naïve?"

"Are you?" I stared at him. "What would you be without the family?"

I felt cold and grim and…unsteady. I'd traded hexes before, with dozens of people, but physical violence? I'd never hit anyone before, not even Francis. The idea of hitting Isabella or Penny—no matter how much she bullied her charges—was horrifying. Better to turn someone into a frog than slam my fist into their face. And yet…I could feel the sword at the back of my mind, reminding me that I'd killed. I felt sick. I didn't want to kill again.

"I would be fine," Francis growled.

I looked at him for a long moment, feeling my anger slowly being replaced by despondency. I felt…I felt cold and bitter and…how well did I know Francis, really? How well did I know anyone? Isabella's betrayal had caught me by surprise too. I should have seen it coming.

"If you say so," I said. I didn't have the energy to push it. "But you know what?"

"Enlighten me, oh great master," Francis said.

I felt a flash of anger, even through the fog that was settling over my thoughts. I wanted to wound him. I wanted to *hurt* him. I wanted…Francis, who shrugged off everything, to *feel* something. I wanted…

"You're off the team," I said.

Francis gaped at me. "What?"

"You're off the team," I repeated.

I turned, squared my shoulders and marched away. I'd seen team captains do the same—I'd seen *Francis* do the same—whenever they kicked a teammate off the team for poor performance. It was a ritual, Francis had explained, to make it absolutely clear that the unlucky player wasn't worthy. *He* had never been kicked off a team, of course. Not until now.

My back itched. I felt the sword snarling against its bonds, demanding… blood. It felt as if Francis was going to throw a hex at my back. I tensed, bracing myself to counter a spell or simply dive out of the way. But nothing happened. I marched through the door, slammed it behind me and headed down the corridor. It wasn't quite as easy to hold the pose as it looked.

I glanced around as I walked back to the suite, feeling dazed. Everything had turned upside down so *quickly*. I couldn't believe it. I'd known Francis was capable of being an idiot—I'd done enough idiot things to make me violently cringe, in my younger days—but courting a betrothed girl? He was mad. Even if nothing happened, even if Lord Richard and Lindsey's family never found out…I swallowed, hard. There would be no guarantee of that, whatever happened. Who knew how many others might have seen Francis and Lindsey kissing and kept it to themselves? Or put it in a letter to their parents? I honestly wasn't sure what I should do. Tell my father? Or would that simply start the avalanche rolling?

And without Francis, I asked myself, *can I win?*

I stopped and sighed. Louise and Saline would stay, but what about Tobias and Harvard? They'd been *Francis's* picks. Tobias might stay—he needed my patronage—but Harvard? I wasn't so sure. He might easily quit, if *his* patron had been kicked off the team. Or if Francis brought pressure to bear on him. Francis *was* Sports Captain. A word in the right ear could destroy Harvard's hopes of succeeding him.

Idiot, I thought, nastily. I wasn't sure who I meant. Francis or Harvard... or me? *He really should have known better.*

I half-expected to run into Lindsey as I entered the upperclassman dorms, but there was no sign of her. What was she doing? Would she come to me and plead for my silence? Or would she rely on Francis to convince me to say nothing? Or...I shrugged. Perhaps she'd reason I couldn't say anything. Francis was my friend, as well as my cousin...right? I'd hardly do anything to harm him...

Hah, I thought. What sort of cousin betrayed the family? *And what have I just done?*

Putting the thought aside, I stepped into the suite. There was no sign of Louise and Saline. Alana must have sent them back to their rooms. I was almost relieved. I was in no state for talking to either of them. But Alana herself was sitting on the sofa, sipping a mug of hot chocolate. She waved to me, cheerfully, as I entered.

"Akin," she said. She'd changed into a comfortable white nightgown that clashed oddly with her skin. "I think we should talk, don't you?"

CHAPTER

TWENTY-THREE

"It's too late to talk," I said, as if I had a choice in the matter. "Can we talk tomorrow?"

Alana took a sip of her chocolate. "Tomorrow is another day," she said. "Tonight."

I groaned. "Let me get a drink," I said, resignedly. It felt late, even though it wasn't firstie bedtime yet. "And then I'll join you."

Alana nodded her assent. I walked into the kitchen and heated a mug of milk, taking my time as much as possible without slipping into blatant rudeness. I needed to think. It couldn't be a coincidence that Alana wanted to talk now, after she'd…after she'd ratted out Francis to me. It had to be important. Alana couldn't want to be branded a sneak, even though she was in her final year. Father had warned me, more than once, that what we did at school would haunt us for the rest of our lives.

I picked up the milk and headed back into the sitting room. Alana was still sitting on the sofa, waiting for me. The white nightdress drew my eye without ever quite revealing anything…I bit my lip, hard. She was going to be my sister-in-law. She was already my rival, my competitor…my lips quirked. Our relationship was going to be complicated…it was *already* complicated. In hindsight, perhaps we should have worked together from the start.

"It's been an interesting day," Alana said. Her dark eyes rested on mine. "Don't you think?"

I shrugged. "It's been a very long day," I said. "What do you want?"

Alana smiled, very slightly. "I thought we should talk," she said. "And I thought you'd want to thank me."

"I suppose I do owe you some thanks," I said, dryly. "How many other people know about Francis and Lindsey?"

"As far as I know, just us." Alana shrugged. "But they picked a stupid place for their tryst."

I nodded. Francis had been lucky, luckier than he deserved. *Anyone* could have walked in and seen them…and not *all* of them could be convinced, through force or bribes, to keep their mouths shut. We would have been in *real* trouble if the McDonalds had caught him. *They* could have blackmailed him into…anything. I didn't fancy Francis's chances if Lord Richard challenged him to a duel.

And we still are in real trouble, I thought. *Alana knows.*

I took a breath. "What do you want?"

"In exchange for my silence?" Alana smiled. "I don't want anything. I merely thought we should…help each other, just a little."

"A little," I repeated. If she didn't want anything…I didn't believe it. Everyone wanted *something*. Father had said that, time and time again. And he'd made a point of warning me that not everyone would *say* what they wanted. Sometimes it was just embarrassing. Sometimes it was banned even to people of *our* high rank. "How should we help each other?"

Alana sat upright, resting her hands on her lap. "You and I will rule our houses," she said, flatly. "And you are going to marry my sister. There are too many…*things*…resting on the match for it not to go ahead. You and Cat will get married if our families have to use compulsion spells to force you to exchange vows."

I flushed. I knew just how much was riding on the marriage, but hearing it put so bluntly…I shuddered. I hadn't known, not really, what I was doing when I agreed. The marriage had seemed so far in the future that it might never happen. And now...now the marriage was looming in the very near future. I wasn't sure how to feel about it. Cat and I were close—or as close as we could be, given our chaperones—but did we want to get married? Did she want to marry me?

"You can't compel someone into a marriage," I said, playing for time. "And you can't force us to..."

My face reddened. Alana smirked. It struck me, suddenly, that she was lucky. She could blush all she liked and no one would see it, not on her dark skin. I swallowed hard, burying my anger and schooling my face into a mask. Alana could probably see through it, but...I gritted my teeth. She was right. We would be working together, closely together, after we inherited our respective houses.

A thought struck me. "Is your father planning to die? Or retire?"

"Dad has been talking about retiring soon," Alana said, calmly. "And... you never know what might happen tomorrow."

"No." I eyed her for a long moment. It had been a point of faith in my family that our rivals lived in a den of vipers, ever ready to backstab each other for a smidgeon of power. Stregheria Aguirre had certainly stabbed her entire family in the back in a desperate bid for power...power she could hardly have enjoyed for long before old age finally caught up with her. "And you're right. We have to plan for the future."

"You and I and Cat will discuss it, soon," Alana said. "She really does like you, you know."

I looked down, feeling...I wasn't sure *how* I felt. Cat wouldn't have been allowed any more freedom than myself. She wouldn't have been introduced to any eligible young men...she didn't even have any friends at the Workshop, no men who shared her talent or her zest for forging. Did she like me for myself? Or did she like me because there couldn't be any other men in her life as long as the betrothal was in effect?

Alana pointed a finger at me. "And if you hurt her, I'll show you something terrible."

I cocked an eyebrow. "You think *Cat* can't take care of herself?"

"She's too decent." Alana smiled, but it didn't touch her eyes. "*She* won't punish you as you deserve."

"You were horrible to her." Cat had told me a few things, all horrific. Alana had put her sister in mortal danger, time and time again. And she might not even have *realised*—sometimes—what she'd done. "And you presume to lecture *me* on morality?"

Alana's eyes narrowed. "I know what I did," she said. "I…I know."

She smiled, suddenly. "And what are *you* going to do when people start courting *your* sister?"

"Isabella can take care of herself." I yawned, helplessly. "And she'd be angry if I suggested otherwise."

And very few people will want to marry her, not now, I added in the privacy of my own mind, although I was sure Alana knew it as well as I did. Isabella was disgraced. She was unlikely to inherit anything when our father died. *Anyone who goes courting her will draw a lot of attention to himself.*

I rubbed my eyes. I was out of my depth. And I knew it.

"I have to go to bed," I said. "Chat tomorrow?"

"Of course." Alana gave me a sweet smile. "And you can swap detention shifts with me tomorrow, as a sign of your thanks."

I snorted. "I don't know if I should be thanking you or hexing you."

"Both, probably." Alana stood, brushing down her nightgown. I tried not to look. "I'll see you in the morning."

She strode away. I looked down at my hands, my thoughts churning. Francis had done something stupid, Alana had tipped me off to it…my head spun as I tried to understand the implications. Was Alana trying to help? Or hinder? Or…I felt a flicker of reluctant admiration as I realised just how well everything had worked out for Alana. She'd helped and hindered me at the same time. And I couldn't even be angry.

I need help, I thought.

I stood and walked into my bedroom, closing and locking the door behind me. My original privacy wards were still in place—no one had tried to breach them, as far as I could tell—but I took ten minutes to strengthen them anyway before sitting down at my writing desk. It was a curiously feminine design, very similar to my mother's private desk...I wondered, suddenly, if the rooms had been swapped at some point. Or if no one outside the very highest families really cared. There was no real *need* to buy separate desks for separate tasks.

Shaking my head, I produced a piece of charmed notepaper and wrote out a short message to Isabella. I didn't dare write *too* much down—I didn't know who *else* would be reading the letter—but it was easy enough to invite her to the potions fair. It was, technically, outside the bounds of Shallot. Isabella could travel there, if she wished...in theory. It depended on just how much of a fuss the family council made about it. Father wouldn't be pleased.

I need help, I reminded myself, as I finished the letter. I'd pay a younger student to post it, somewhere outside the school. *And she might be the only one who can advise me.*

My heart was pounding like a drum as I sealed the letter in an envelope and added a handful of charms that were borderline dark. No one, save for Isabella herself, should be able to open the envelope without destroying the contents. She and I shared blood...in theory, even Father wouldn't be able to open the letter. In theory...I swallowed, hard. I could get in real trouble for trying to communicate with Isabella covertly, rather than sending the letters through the family council. It would be hard to deny that I'd set out to keep them from reading the letter first.

I need help, I thought, again. *And I need advice.*

I placed the letter on the desk, then undressed, showered and went to bed. It felt as if no time had passed before the alarm charm jerked me awake at seven o'clock. I rubbed my eyes, wondering if I could get away with skipping my early-morning classes. I wanted to go back to sleep. But I was Head Boy. I had to set a good example. And besides, Magister Grayson would probably march up to my room, drag me out of bed and carry me back down to the classroom. He rarely tolerated excuses for skipping class. If you were on your deathbed, you'd better bring your deathbed with you.

I chuckled at the thought, then hastily sent vapour messages to the rest of the team. Francis might have told them...told them what? He wasn't stupid enough to tell them what he'd been doing, was he? Who knew *what* they'd do, if they knew? But he could have told them a lie? I shaped the spell, asking the team to meet me in a study room after breakfast and then went for another shower. There was no sign of Alana when I dressed and left the room. I was relieved. I didn't have the time for another round of conversational combat. I'd never really had the patience for subtle compliments, insults and barbed *bon mots.*

There were two firsties in the study room when I arrived, desperately flicking through their textbooks before class. I told them to go to breakfast—it was clear they hadn't eaten anything—and took a chair, waiting. The rest of the team slowly gathered, their faces puzzled. Francis hadn't told them anything, I guessed. Even Harvard seemed bemused. He didn't know what was going on.

"Sit down," I said, as I cast a privacy ward. It was a brute-force spell—my ears popped as the spell flared into life—but it would keep us from being spied on, at least for the moment. "We have to talk."

I allowed my gaze to wander from face to face. Louise looked unsure of herself...and alarmed. Beside her, Saline looked unperturbed. Tobias was glancing around, as if he expected a blow to fall at any moment; Harvard looked calm and composed, his face an unreadable mask. I felt a flicker of pity, mingled with irritation. Francis could bring a *lot* of pressure to bear on Harvard, if he wished. Harvard would wind up being caught between us.

"Francis is off the team," I said, flatly. "The details are none of your concern."

"Yes, they are." Louise leaned forward. "If he's gone, I want to know why."

I silently kicked myself. If there was *anyone* who would ask the obvious question, it was Louise. The others…the others might understand there were things I couldn't say. But Louise would demand an explanation. Of course she would.

"He was doing something…indiscreet," I told her. I turned away before she could demand specifics. "He's off the team."

Harvard gave me a sharp look. "For how long?"

"Forever," I snapped. I wasn't in the mood to be questioned. "He won't be coming back."

"I've heard that before." Harvard looked unconvinced. "Time and time again, from team captains who…"

I cut him off. "This isn't a sports match," I said. I was *sick* of people who got away with being jerks because they were good at sports. "And I will not deal with someone who…"

"You may not have a choice," Harvard pointed out. "All of our plans assumed we'd be fielding six people, not five. And there's no time to search for a replacement."

"If Francis was indiscreet," Saline said, "can we trust him?"

I scowled. I hated to admit it, but Harvard had a point. And so did Saline. We wanted to win. We needed to win. *I* needed to win. And for that, I might need Francis. And yet…I didn't know if I could *trust* Francis. I'd sooner deal with a declared enemy than someone who was dangerously reckless…and unpredictable. Francis and Lindsey could have been a *lot* more discreet. The risk of being caught had probably added to the thrill.

"Right now, it doesn't matter." I looked from face to face. "For the moment, Francis is off the team. That puts *some* of you in an awkward spot. If you want to stay, you are welcome; if you want to quit, then quit now. I swear to you"—I allowed my voice to harden—"that anyone who decides to quit *later*, over this, will *not* be forgotten."

Tobias coughed. "Promises were made…"

"I'll keep the ones made to you," I told him, as his voice trailed off. Those promises would, thankfully, be easy to keep. "Louise, Saline…I can and I will keep the promises made to you two. Harvard…I can't guarantee anything, not the position you wanted or the other things. If you want to quit, then do so."

"I'm not a quitter," Harvard said. I could hear the pain in his voice. "And I don't give up easily."

I allowed myself a moment of sympathy. Francis could make life very difficult for Harvard, if he wished. Harvard was Francis's *client*, to all intents and purposes. Harvard would have no recourse if Francis decided to nominate someone *else* to succeed him as Sports Captain, unless he claimed Scholar's Rights and bested Francis in a duel. And even then…there was a good chance he wouldn't get the position anyway. Francis would *still* have a great deal of power.

"You have until the end of today," I told him. Perhaps I was being generous, but…no one would be able to say I hadn't given him a chance. "If you want to quit, I won't hold it against you. Afterwards…if you quit later, I swear I *will*."

"I understand," Harvard said. I could see the struggle on his face. "And…I'll let you know."

He left, closing the door behind him. I guessed he'd gone to find Francis, to get *his* version of the story. Francis would tell him…I had no idea *what* he would tell him. The truth? A lie? Or a slanted story designed to cast him as the hero and me as the villain? Or…I shook my head. It didn't matter.

"I'll stay," Saline said. She smiled, brightly. "We don't need him."

"No," Louise agreed. She gave me a wary look. "Can you assure me he won't be coming back?"

I opened my mouth, then stopped. I couldn't give any assurances, could I? Not really.

"I don't know," I said, honestly. "And I really don't know what's going to happen next."

Louise looked down. "Of course not," she murmured. The bitterness in her voice surprised me. "No one does, do they?"

Saline took her arm. "We'll join you later, for more training," she said. The bell rang, warning us to be ready for class. She stood, brushing down her skirt. "And if you have to reinstate him, then do it."

"If you have to," Louise muttered.

I watched them go, convinced I'd missed something. But what?

Worry about it later, I told myself, as I took down the privacy charm and tidied up the room. It was the kind of job I should have given to a lowerclassman, but I wanted something mindless to do. *Right now, you have other problems.*

I put the thought aside as the second bell rang. It was time to go. I hurried down the corridor, pausing long enough to give the letter and a crown to a passing fifth-year, then put the matter out of my mind. If Francis wanted to be reinstated, he'd have to grovel. And hopefully, by then, I'd have some advice from my sister. And...

And even if she can't tell me anything useful, I thought, *it will be good to see her again.*

CHAPTER
TWENTY-FOUR

I had expected, on some level, that Francis *would* have come crawling to me, sooner or later, and begged to be reinstated on the team. I'd had plenty of time to think of what I was going to say to him, when he grovelled to me; I'd come up with all kinds of sarcastic remarks, intending to give him the kind of dressing down my father meted out whenever he got really angry. But Francis hadn't come crawling to me. He kept his distance, saying nothing the few times we crossed paths. I knew he was stubborn, but... by the time half-term rolled around, we were *still* not talking. It was...odd.

The atmosphere in the carriage, as we rattled our way back to the mansion, was so thick I could have cut it with a knife. Francis and I were sitting on one padded bench, facing Rose and Penny. Penny was carefully *not* looking at me, Francis was staring out of the window...poor Rose was caught in the middle, no doubt feeling hopelessly out of place. I was glad of the quiet—I wasn't in the mood for Penny's chatter—but I couldn't help feeling sorry for Rose. She didn't know what was going on, yet...

I let out a sigh of relief as the carriage rattled to a stop, the door snapping open a moment later. The footmen were putting the steps in place for the ladies to descend, but I jumped down without waiting. Francis followed me, walked past me and strode into the mansion without looking back. I felt an odd little pang. Francis and I weren't *that* close, but still...it hurt, just a little. I held out a hand automatically to help Rose step down, then nodded sharply to Penny. *She* could get down on her own.

A maid was waiting for us at the top of the steps. "Lord Heir, your father would like to see you in his office."

"Thank you." My heart sank. "Please escort the Lady Rose to her chambers."

The maid curtseyed. "Of course, My Lord."

I shrugged apologetically at Rose, who didn't look happy to be left alone with a maid, then hurried into the building. My father would have sensed my presence the moment the carriage crossed the wardline and entered the grounds. He'd know if I dawdled. A handful of children were playing on the stairs, laughing with glee as they slid down the banisters. I felt a pang of envy, mingled with amusement. Life really had been *so* much simpler when I'd been a little boy. I hadn't known just how much was going on behind the scenes.

And you still don't, I reminded myself, as I reached the top floor. *Father is always one step ahead of everyone.*

My heart began to thump uncomfortably as I made my way down the corridor. I'd only just got home for the holidays. Father normally gave me a few hours to recover and change into something more comfortable before he summoned me. Now...I wondered, grimly, what I'd done. What did Father know? The fight with Francis? The story *behind* the fight with Francis? Or Penny? Or that I'd been writing to Isabella, planning a meeting? If he chose to be angry, or if the council *forced* him to be angry...

I swallowed, hard. Isabella was my sister. I had every right to communicate with her. And if the family council thought otherwise...I didn't care. Isabella and I had been close, once upon a time. I wanted to be close again, to know there was at least one person in the mansion I could rely on. And yet...I knew what Isabella had done. She could have brought the entire family crashing down.

The door swung open, silently. I stepped inside. My father was sitting behind his desk, looking grim. I shuddered, inwardly, as I schooled my face into a mask. The last time Father had looked like that, I'd been in *real* trouble. And yet...this time, I had the odd feeling he wasn't angry at *me*. Who had angered him? Isabella? Uncle Davys? Or...who?

"Akin," Father said. "How are you coping with the Challenge?"

"The team is training hard," I said, carefully. I didn't want to say *too* much. If he didn't know about Francis, I wasn't going to rat my cousin out. "We're hampered by...by not knowing what we're actually training *for*."

"Yes." Father's voice was distant, as if he hadn't really heard what I'd said. "That's always the way."

I took a gamble. "Father...what was *your* Challenge?"

Father looked angry, angry and...some emotion I couldn't identify. "It went spectacularly wrong," he said, curtly. "And I'm not allowed to talk about it."

"If I knew, it could give me a clue..." I started. "Father..."

"I believe that's the point," Father said. "And I'm still not allowed to talk about it."

He met my eyes. "And how is being Head Boy?"

"Busy." I wondered if I should ask him about Penny. "Father...can I ask for some advice?"

My father surprised me by laughing. "When I was your age, my father knew nothing. The old man was so ignorant that it was just...*embarrassing*. By the time I turned twenty-five...by the Ancients! It was astonishing how smart the old man had become."

I blinked. "Father?"

Father smiled. "Ask for advice, if you trust me to give it to you."

"There's a...a dorm monitor who's bullying his charges," I said, carefully. "What should I *do* about him?"

"Never an easy question," Father said. I couldn't tell if he knew who I was *really* talking about or not. "Back in my day, of course, it was a lot easier."

I shuddered. I'd made the mistake of telling my older relatives, once, that I was excited about going to school. The horror stories they'd told had given me nightmares, although...Uncle Malachi had pointed out, rather dryly, that no one would have *survived* such treatment long enough to graduate. Cold showers, bad food, beatings every day and twice on Sundays...it sounded awful. Things had apparently improved since my father had graduated.

Father met my eyes. "You can rebuke him in private or you can deal with him publicly," he said. "In private, you will spare his pride...but, at the same time, you may accidentally convince him that it isn't *that* serious. In public, you will humiliate him. You may feel he deserves it. Maybe he does. But he will be humiliated and angry and that will drive him to find a way to strike back at you."

"Yes, Father," I said. In hindsight, it had definitely been a mistake to humiliate Penny in front of Kate. It wouldn't have been *hard* to drag her into a classroom. "I see."

"And you have to solve the problem fast," Father added. "If someone realises you knew—and did nothing—that will come back to haunt you, believe me."

"Yes, Father," I said.

"You'll be going to the fair tomorrow for a week." Father changed the subject with astonishing speed. "We've already booked rooms for you and Rose. You'll be seeing Cat there...remember, you will be chaperoned. Her mother will be there too."

And Isabella, I thought. *Do you know Isabella will be there?*

If he did, Father said nothing. "I expect you to behave yourself," he warned. "We cannot afford a scandal. Not now."

"No," I agreed.

Father shrugged, dismissively. "Piglet wants a word with you," he added. "You can find him in the library."

I blinked. "Piglet?"

"Malachi." Father turned his attention back to his paperwork. "He wants to talk to you too."

"Yes, Father." I turned to leave, then stopped myself. "Do you…"

I shook my head and hurried out of the room. I didn't want to ask him what he knew. I wasn't sure what I wanted to tell him. Instead, I practically *ran* down the corridor and threw myself down the stairs. Rose and I were going to set out early, tomorrow morning. I intended to have a good night's sleep, in my own bed, before we left.

And we'll be riding for hours before we arrive, I reminded myself. *The sooner Cat rediscovers teleport gates, the better.*

The library was empty, save for Uncle Malachi, when I arrived. He sat in a comfortable chair, reading a newspaper. The front page had a picture of someone I vaguely recognised, someone who was famous for being famous. Isabella would have known who she was, right off the bat. Louise, on the other hand, had probably never heard of her.

Uncle Malachi folded his newspaper. "Akin."

"Uncle," I said. I dropped into the chair next to him. "What can I do for you?"

"You're a third of the way through your final year," Uncle Malachi said. "How are you finding it?"

"… Tricky," I said. "One moment, everything is fine; the next, I'm drowning in quicksand."

Uncle Malachi smiled. "There are spells for that, you know."

"I can't go around casting spells on everyone," I pointed out. "Wherever I go, whatever I do, I think there's an unsolvable problem in front of me."

"Welcome to adulthood." Uncle Malachi chuckled. "It doesn't get any better."

"Really?" I wasn't sure I wanted to know that. "There are no lives of ease and pleasure?"

Uncle Malachi shrugged. "Perhaps. You could fritter away your inheritance, if you wished. Spend the whole thing on wine, women and song. But you wouldn't have much left afterwards."

"I suppose not," I said.

"Or you might be dependent on someone else," Uncle Malachi added. He tapped his newspaper. "Lady Felicity is in the papers again, making a beautiful fool of herself. It won't be long before her father cuts her off or marries her off to someone who can take her in hand, someone who will... point is, she's dependent on her father. She isn't in control of her own life."

"Maybe that's why she acts out," I mused. Even *I* had heard of Lady Felicity. "You're saying you can either be in control or give *up* control?"

"Quite," Uncle Malachi said. "She has quite a lot in common with Francis, doesn't she?"

I blinked, feeling cold. "Francis came to you, did he?"

"I like to give advice." Uncle Malachi shrugged. "It makes me feel useful."

"Oh." I was tempted to press for details—there was no reason why Uncle Malachi should feel useless—but I didn't have time. "What did he tell you?"

"That you kicked him off the team." Uncle Malachi met my eyes. "And he told me *why*."

"Did he?" I didn't think Uncle Malachi would lie to me, but...Francis could have easily lied to *him*. "What did he say?"

"That you caught him making out with Lindsey of House Arthur," Uncle Malachi said, flatly. "Or is the truth even *worse*?"

"That's the truth." I was surprised. "He actually *told* you?"

"I had to cajole him a little," Uncle Malachi said. "He came to my townhouse, a couple of weeks ago. We...chatted."

I let out a long breath. "Do you understand...do you understand how bad it could have *been*, if Lord Richard found out? Or if Lindsey's *family* found out?"

"Yes." Uncle Malachi looked at me, evenly. "And I also remember just what it was like to be a teenage boy, simply rancid with hormones."

"Really." I found it hard to believe. It was easier to think that Uncle Malachi—and his peers—had all popped into existence as adults. Cold logic told me they'd been children, once upon a time; emotion told me it was impossible. "What were you *like* as a boy?"

"A truly terrible person," Uncle Malachi said, dryly. "I put my foot in it so many times. But I remember what it was like."

"So, Francis told you the truth." I stood and started to pace. "Do you understand just how…how *irresponsible* he was?"

"And you have never done anything stupid?" Uncle Malachi's gaze followed me as I paced the room. "Anything that might have led to disaster?"

I remembered the feel of Ayesha's lips against mine and shuddered. If things had been different…

"Maybe." I shrugged. "What does this have to do with the price of tea in Hangchow?"

"Francis is a young man with few prospects," Uncle Malachi said, flatly. "He is permanently caught between the demands of his station and the limitations his station imposes on him. He wants to play sports professionally, not…work for the family or do anything we might consider socially acceptable. And he rebels against social convention because social convention is constantly pushing him down. It never works in his favour."

"Really, now." I met his eyes. "And if he'd been caught"—Francis didn't know who'd tipped me off, I recalled— "social convention would have destroyed him."

"A self-destructive impulse is not uncommon amongst young men in his position," Uncle Malachi said. "If they cannot win, they will often try to lose as spectacularly as possible."

"I weep for him," I said, sarcastically. Yes, I could see—and understand—Francis's frustrations. "That doesn't justify betraying the family."

Uncle Malachi lifted an eyebrow. "Did he betray the family?"

"He would have done so, if he'd been caught." I turned away, angrily. "It would have been disastrous."

"Maybe. You don't know that." Uncle Malachi shrugged, expressively. "For all you know, Lindsey and Lord Richard have no real *intention* to get married. There's five years between them. They're pushing the legal limits as it is."

I nodded. There weren't many laws covering betrothals, but one of them insisted that there could be no more than seven years between the partners. Even *that* was iffy. Custom decreed that the partners should be far closer in age, like Cat and I. Our birthdays were only four months apart. Yes, it *was* possible that Lindsey and Lord Richard's betrothal was a legal fiction. But…

"Uncle…" I swallowed and started again. "Please…get to the point."

"Francis deeply regrets what he did," Uncle Malachi said. "And he regrets the effect it had on you—and your team. He would like to rejoin, but he's too prideful to ask you directly."

"Hah," I muttered, although I knew he had a point. Francis would sooner swallow poison than his pride. "And why should I take him back?"

"Everyone makes mistakes." Uncle Malachi's voice was suddenly serious. "Yes, they *do*. It's astonishing how easy it is to back yourself into a corner, claiming all the while that you're not doing anything of the sort. If you refuse to take him back, Francis will only grow more bitter, more set in his ways. If you refuse to offer him the prospect of redemption, you will leave him with nothing but damnation. And that can be disastrous. A person who feels he has nothing to lose can be very dangerous."

"Francis has a *lot* to lose," I pointed out, tartly.

"Less than you might think," Uncle Malachi said. He leaned back in his armchair. "He's not the Heir Primus, is he? He doesn't stand to inherit much of anything, does he?"

"No," I conceded.

"So you have a choice," Uncle Malachi said. "You can leave him to sulk, to wallow in his bitterness until it curdles and he does something *really* dangerous. Or you can accept that he was an idiot, accept his promise to do better and…take him back, giving him the chance to recover from his mistake. He'll thank you for it."

I stared at my hands. "It wasn't a minor mistake."

"Maybe not," Uncle Malachi agreed. "You're right. It could have had disastrous consequences. But it didn't. And all he can think about, right now, is that you're punishing him for consequences that didn't materialise."

"Really." I wasn't sure I believed him. "Francis thinks *I'm* punishing him?"

"Yes," Uncle Malachi said.

I didn't look up. I had to admit—privately, if nowhere else—that none of the bad consequences had materialised. Lord Richard hadn't appeared at the school, screaming and shouting and demanding revenge; Lindsey, as far as I could tell, had behaved herself. And Alana had kept the truth to herself too. But there would be a price to pay, I was sure, for her silence. Francis had put me, deliberately or not, in a very sticky situation.

And yet, I could see Uncle Malachi's point. Did Francis deserve to spend the rest of his life paying for a mistake? A stupid mistake, but one that hadn't had any *real* consequences? I didn't know. What would my father say, if he knew? I wished I could ask, but I couldn't. It would tell my father far too much. And he'd have to take official notice of whatever I told him.

And how many problems will he cause me, later on, I asked myself, *if I let matters rest where they are?*

"I'm off to the fair tomorrow," I said, bluntly. "You can tell him that I'll give him a second chance, if he behaves himself. Yes, he can have his chance. And if he misbehaves…there will be no third chance. I won't ever trust him again."

And when I'm Patriarch, I added silently, *he can go kick balls around for a living somewhere on the other side of the world.*

Uncle Malachi nodded. "I will inform him," he said. "But the two of you should have a talk…"

"No," I said. I didn't want to talk to Francis, not yet. It could wait until I'd calmed down—and written to the others to tell them that Francis was going to be rejoining us. "You can tell him."

CHAPTER

TWENTY-FIVE

"This is amazing," Rose breathed, as the open-topped carriage crested the hilltop and drove down into Riverside. "I never dreamed…"

I glanced at her. "Surely, you've been to fairs before…haven't you?"

"Not like this," Rose said. "This is…"

Her voice trailed off. I smiled at her, then turned my attention back to the town. The fields surrounding Riverside were crammed with pavilions, tents and open-air stalls, each one flying flags to show who owned them and what they sold. I spotted House Aguirre's pavilion and smiled, suddenly consumed with the desire to order the driver to stop right next to it so I could run inside. Cat would be there, with her mother…I could go to her. I pushed the thought aside, angrily, as the driver headed on towards our townhouse. All the Great Houses had establishments in Riverside, although they pretended otherwise. It was the kind of place they could pretend to be normal, just for a while.

I sat back in my chair and forced myself to take a deep breath. I'd be seeing Cat in the evening, but first…I glanced at Rose, silently grateful she'd been so understanding. If she'd decided to cause trouble, it would have made my life so much harder. I'd probably have to pay a price for that too…I shook my head, rebuking myself. Rose hadn't grown up amongst the

Great Houses. *She* didn't feel the urge to demand repayment for her help, freely given. I almost envied her.

The carriage rattled to a halt outside the townhouse, a modest three-story building on the edge of town. Father had said we'd be alone there... for a given value of *alone*. The servants didn't count, clearly. I snorted at the thought as we clambered out of the carriage, the driver silently levitating our trunks to the ground and sending them up towards the waiting staff. I would have bet half my trust fund that one or more or the servants were quietly keeping an eye on us for Father. He wouldn't take the risk of leaving us genuinely alone.

As if we couldn't look after ourselves, I thought, as we were shown to our rooms. *It isn't as if we couldn't cook—or go out to eat.*

I showered, changed into a suit and waited. It felt as if I was waiting for...I wasn't quite sure, but—whatever it was—the family council would not approve. Rose spoke briefly to me, then headed out to meet Cat. I tried to read, but I couldn't. I was too tense. I hadn't been so nervous the first time I'd attended a formal ball.

The serving girl knocked on my door. "The Honourable Lady Kirkhaven, My Lord."

I stood as the door opened and a cloaked figure was ushered into the room. The servant curtseyed and withdrew, leaving us alone. I hesitated, suddenly unsure what to say, as the figure pulled back her hood. Isabella... stood in front of me, looking as unsure of herself as I felt. It was the first time I'd seen her in five years.

"I..." I couldn't help myself. I hugged her tightly. "It's been too long."

"Definitely." Isabella's voice had more than a hint of the north around it now. The Grand Dames would say she was excessively countrified. "I've missed you, brother."

I let go of her and took a step back. Isabella had grown up, coming into her full height. Her hair was in two neat braids, framing a heart-shaped face that was no longer a feminine version of my own; her loose dress framing a form that was definitely taking after our mother. And *she'd* been a great beauty, in her day. Isabella looked striking, even in a dress that had gone out of fashion when our *grandmother* had been alive. I couldn't help thinking that it would go right back *into* fashion if Isabella wore it on the dance floor.

"It's been too long," I said again, stupidly. "What have you been doing with yourself?"

"Oh, this and that." Isabella placed her cloak on the hook, then took a seat. "A lot of correspondence courses, really. Keeping up with my potions. Growing a lot of potions ingredients for myself. That's my excuse for coming here...I need more seeds and cuttings for my garden. You'd be surprised at how much it costs to get some of the *really* rare ingredients up there."

"It wouldn't surprise me," I said, darkly. "What *else* have you been doing?"

"Surprisingly little," Isabella said, vaguely. "Lots of little mysteries around Kirkhaven, things dating back hundreds of years. I've been studying them."

"Old magic?" I raised my eyebrows. "What *sort* of old magic?"

"It's hard to tell," Isabella said. "But there are...*things*...there that pre-date Uncle Ira. I keep wondering if there was a *reason* the hall was largely abandoned, so many years ago. Something that didn't get written down at the time."

I met her bright blue eyes. "Are you *safe* there?"

Isabella let out an odd little laugh. "As safe as possible," she said. "But I never really realised the depth of my ignorance. If I hadn't made a few friends..."

She shook her head. "And how about you? What made you so desperate to see me again?"

"Long story," I said.

I poured us both cups of tea, then started to speak. I told her everything, from the Challenge itself to the problems I'd been having with Saline, Francis and Alana. Isabella listened quietly, sometimes asking a question to elicit more information. Father had taught her well, I decided.

I wished—bitterly—that she hadn't made her own little mistake. Even if she *couldn't* be Heir Primus, she could have been my advisor. There were few other people I trusted not to steer me wrong.

"Francis always was a bit of a fool," Isabella said, when I'd finished. "And Alana"—her face twisted—"is cunning. She'll definitely find a way to make you pay for tipping you off."

"I figured as much," I said. "But what does she get out of it?"

Isabella snorted. "You'll be Patriarch, one day. It could be anything. A vote, swayed in a certain direction…it could even be money. She doesn't know herself, not yet. She'll keep the favour in reserve until she needs it."

She cocked her head, like a hawk that had just seen its prey. "And you should have reported the McDonalds to the staff. Or blackmailed them."

I frowned. "Why?"

"Ayesha McDonald put you in a changing room," Isabella pointed out. "You looked like an idiot—which is true, by the way—but she's the one who made it happen. She should be expelled. And then she used a spell intended for self-protection aggressively, which will come back to haunt her—and everyone else—sooner or later. And…*Ancients*! She kissed Cat's betrothed! And nearly ruined his prospects at the same time."

She smiled, sharply. "And you didn't even *see* anything. You'd *still* look like an idiot, yes, but no one could imply you were a pervert."

"I'm sure someone would try," I said, dryly. "I'd also look like a sneak."

Isabella looked pained. "If someone raids the kitchen for a midnight feast and you rat them out"—I winced, remembering that *she'd* been accused of doing just that—"yes, you're a sneak and everyone should give you the silent treatment. If someone sets you up for the biggest pratfall since Harry Enigma ran straight into a wall while waving to the crowd…you don't have any obligation to be *nice* to them."

"Too late now," I said.

"Maybe." Isabella shrugged. "You can use it later, though. It won't go away in a hurry."

"I'll remember that," I promised, before changing the subject. "Do you remember Saline?"

Isabella nodded. "Only by reputation. She was smart…"

"And now she's…not stupid, but slow." I described what I'd seen as best as I could. "I don't understand it."

"She could be under a curse, or forced to drink a potion," Isabella said. "Have you tried to check?"

"I found nothing." I took a sip of my tea. "And…if she was drinking a potion, wouldn't it have set off alarms?"

"Perhaps." Isabella didn't look convinced. "There *are* spells that bed into someone's magic, spells that can be really hard to detect, let alone remove. Have you considered…?"

I shuddered. "Who'd do that? I mean…really?"

"If Saline is deemed…*unfit*…to serve her family," Isabella said, "who benefits? And why?"

"She's not the Heir Primus," I pointed out. "But…yeah. Someone might benefit."

"Then figure out who," Isabella said. "And find a way to get rid of the curse."

"If there *is* a curse," I said.

Isabella looked calculating. "A *really* deep curse would be tricky to remove, either directly or through a Device of Power. Have you asked Cat for an *Object* of Power?"

"I'm not allowed to ask Cat for help," I said. "*Someone* will use it against me, whatever my intentions. They'll say I did it for myself, not for her."

"Quite so." Isabella studied me for a long moment, her expression just a little shifty. "And if you asked *me* for help?"

"You're not a Zero," I said. My sister was a powerful magician. I'd been on the receiving end of her magic often enough to know it. "You couldn't forge an Object of Power."

"I can get you one." Isabella met my eyes. "But there will be a price."

"Of course," I said, before I quite realised what she'd said. "You can *get* me one?"

"Yes." Isabella smirked. If I hadn't known her so well, I wouldn't have seen the nervousness under her smirk. "If you meet my price."

"Where from?" I couldn't believe it. Objects of Power were *expensive*, if they were still in working order. A ruined Object of Power was little more than scrap metal. "And…for how much?"

Isabella sipped her drink. "I searched the hall thoroughly, after I… *inherited*," she said. There was something in her voice that told me not to pry. Father had told me that *something* bad had happened, but he hadn't given me any details. The rumours ranged from absurd to truly terrible. "In one room, there was a collection of Objects of Power."

"Working?" It was impossible. "I don't believe it."

"Most of them were junk, stuffed away." Isabella nodded. "The family never throws anything away, as you know. But a couple were still functional. One of them is an extremely powerful spellbreaker. I brought it with me."

I swallowed, hard. It was possible, I supposed. Kirkhaven Hall *had* been abandoned in a hurry. Something important could have been left there, something…I found it odd to think that someone might have left behind a spellbreaker, but…I couldn't think of any alternatives. Isabella was no Zero. She couldn't have forged the spellbreaker herself. And she didn't have anywhere near enough money in her trust fund to *buy* the spellbreaker. It would be worth hundreds of thousands of crowns.

"I see." I let out a long breath. "And what do you want in exchange?"

Isabella met my eyes. "I want my exile to end. I want…I want my freedom."

I looked back at her. "Do you miss it? I mean…?"

"I don't know." Isabella looked, just for a second, like the younger girl I'd known. "You know, it's funny…but there's a bit of me that wouldn't go back, if they said I could. The country is so much simpler and there are things to do, while the city…"

She brushed one of her braids to the side. "In the city, my life is dictated by social convention. You know what I wear in the hall, most of the time? *Trousers.*"

I blinked, astonished. "Trousers?"

"They really are so much more practical when you're seeding potion beds," Isabella said. "Or walking through the woods, looking for hints of just what was happening"—she shrugged—"I don't think I'd want to go back, but I'd like to be *able* to. I'd like to go home, just for a short while, before going back to the hall. Does that make any kind of sense?"

"If they knew you were wearing trousers…" I shook my head. "They'd say you were walking around naked."

Isabella scowled. "Do you know how *cold* it is up there? This is summer"—she waved a hand towards the window—"and it is *still* bitterly cold."

"You know what I mean," I said.

"Yes, I do." Isabella nodded. "It isn't the only thing, either. I've been walking around with my hair down—who's going to notice? Or care? But if I did that in Shallot…"

I held up a hand. "I can't promise anything," I said. "But I can try. You have my word."

"I don't want much," Isabella said. "I just want to come home. Just for a little bit."

"I know," I said.

I thought about it. It wasn't going to be easy. Father couldn't bring Isabella home without starting a fight with the family council. He'd have to cut a great many deals to get her home, something that could wind up costing him…far more than he was willing to pay. And when I became Patriarch…I'd have the same problem. Perhaps I should just turn a blind eye to Isabella returning to Shallot for a few days. As long as she didn't enter the mansion itself, I wouldn't have to take official notice of her presence.

I'd have to find something to force them to get out of the way, I mused. *But what could that be?*

"You have my word that I'll try and find a way to bring you home," I said. If I won the Challenge…I could ask. I'd be due a reward from the family, for bringing glory to the family name. They could hardly say no if I asked for Isabella to be allowed to visit, if not to return home permanently. "You do realise that Father will immediately start looking for prospective husbands?"

Isabella coloured. "The poor sucker he finds will *not* find me a joyful bride."

"That poor man," I said, dryly.

Isabella poked me. "And yourself? When are you and Cat going to get married?"

"I don't know," I admitted. "But everyone seems to think it will be soon."

"It probably will be," Isabella said, bluntly. "You'll be declared an adult after you graduate. I'm sure of it. Cat…do you think they'll give her a Season? Or will they skip the formalities, seeing she's already betrothed, and move straight to the marriage? I wonder if that will bother her…"

"It probably wouldn't," I said. "She hates those affairs as much as I do."

Isabella gave me a pitying look. "You don't know much about girls, do you?"

I coloured. "Some of my best friends are girls."

"Ah, but you still don't know much about them." Isabella smiled. "Every single girl, myself included, wants a Season. We want a summer where we can swan around in our finest dresses, where every young man wants to dance with us, where we—just for a short month—are the centre of attention. Cat wants it. And if she says otherwise, she's lying."

Her smile faded. "Cat's family must have worried about her," she added, after a moment. "I wonder if *that* was why they agreed to the betrothal so quickly."

"They wanted to stop the war," I pointed out.

"Yes. But that couldn't have been their only concern." Isabella considered it for a moment, studying her fingers. I couldn't help noticing that they were covered in faint scars, traces of potions experiments gone wrong. "She needs protection."

"She can protect herself," I said.

"Strip her naked, remove all of her toys…then what?" Isabella shook her head. "She'd be defenceless. And she's already been kidnapped once. It could easily happen again."

"And she's unique," I said. "The King might want her in Tintagel."

Isabella twitched, just slightly. I wondered if she was *jealous* of Cat. The sole known Zero could get away with practically *anything*, as long as she delivered the goods. *Her* family would never send her into exile. They'd be cutting their own throats. But Isabella wasn't wrong. Without her Objects of Power, Cat was terrifyingly vulnerable. She'd outwitted one group of kidnappers. The next might be a little more dangerous.

And if someone wanted to save the balance of power, I thought, *they might simply try to kill her.*

I changed the subject, quickly. "What's life like in Caithness?"

Isabella shrugged. "I've only visited a couple of times," she said. "Hardly anyone there worth knowing. High Society…what *passes* for High Society… is composed of misfits and exiles, people who have been told to go away and not come back. There isn't anyone my age, not there. The youngest is old enough to be my mother."

"Oh dear," I said. "No young men, then?"

"Hah." Isabella seemed oddly surprised by the question. "No. Not in Caithness. It's a boring city."

She shrugged. "When are you meant to be meeting Cat?"

"This evening," I said. "And we're staying for a couple of days."

"I'll bring the spellbreaker here, this evening," Isabella said. "And then… try and come up to see me, if you can."

"I will," I promised. I felt a stab of guilt. I wanted to spend more time with her, but…I didn't *have* the time. I couldn't even ask her to join us for dinner. People would notice. *Father* would notice. "Did you come alone? I mean…?"

Isabella grinned, but there was a sharp edge to it. "What do you think?"

I thought about it, then decided I didn't want to know.

TWENTY-SIX

It was no great surprise to me that House Aguirre had one of the largest pavilions in the potions fair. All the Great Houses experimented with potions, to some degree, but House Aguirre had taken it further than anyone else. Auntie Sofia—Lady Sorceress Sofia Aguirre, Cat's mother—was a renowned Potions Mistress in her own right, yet she was outshone—fairly or not—by her daughter. Cat couldn't make potions on her own, but—with a handful of Objects of Power—she could brew recipes that hadn't been made successfully since the Fall of the Thousand-Year Empire. It was astonishing to discover just how *many* of them couldn't be modified so a regular Potions Master could brew them.

I followed Rose through a private door and into the backroom, trying to ignore the razor-sharp wards brushing against my awareness. The rear of the pavilion was reserved for Auntie Sofia, her daughter and her *private* guests. It felt odd to be there, even though I knew I was welcome. Five years ago, I would have been about as unwelcome as Stregheria Aguirre herself. I put the thought aside as I reminded myself to be on my best behaviour. If I slipped up in front of Auntie Sofia, Father would never let me hear the end of it.

Auntie Sofia was standing in front of a bubbling cauldron, counting out loud as she stirred the brew. She didn't acknowledge our presence, but I took no offense. Distracting a Potions Mistress at work was a bad idea. Instead, I stood and watched as she finished brewing the potion. She was impressive. She'd been brewing potions for longer than I'd been alive and it showed. I hadn't met many Potioneers who brought so much precision to their work.

She stepped back and smiled at me. "Akin."

"Auntie Sofia," I said. It was hard to tell what she was thinking. "Thank you for inviting me."

Auntie Sofia's smile grew wider. "You didn't come to see me." She raised her voice. "*Cat!*"

I blushed as the rear curtain swung open and Cat made her appearance. The sight of her took my breath away. She'd changed into a long green dress—I couldn't believe she'd been forging and brewing while wearing an expensive gown—that flattered her figure and brought out her eyes. It showed little bare skin, below the neckline, but it didn't matter. She wore a single glowing amulet around her neck. Her hair hung in a single long braid…

"Akin," Cat said. She glanced at her mother, clearly embarrassed. "It's good to see you again."

Auntie Sofia laughed. "The three of you can go have dinner," she said. "Cat, I'll want you back here at nine."

"Yes, Mum." Cat didn't show any of the petulance I would have expected from Alana—or Isabella. "I'll be back by nine."

She touched her amulet. Her face blurred, just for a second. Anyone who didn't already *know* who was under the glamour wouldn't have a hope of recognising her. Cat was probably fairly safe—I was certain she had quite a few surprises concealed within her rings and necklaces—but it was probably for the best. She *was* the single most interesting target for kidnappers for hundreds of miles. Who knew *what* sort of threats would come out of the woodwork if she was walking around openly?

I held out a hand. Cat took it. Her skin felt warm against mine. I wanted…I wanted to take her in my arms and hold her. But I knew better than to show any trace of *that* in front of Auntie Sofia. Instead, I led Cat back through the door and out into the field. Rose followed us. I couldn't see her face, but I *knew* she was smirking. We probably made a funny sight.

"Mum booked a private room for us at the Grand," Cat said, as we made our way through the crowds. "I'm afraid she insisted on paying for it."

"I'll survive." I grinned, despite myself. It was good to know that Auntie Sofia approved of our relationship. There were plenty of ways she could have signalled her disapproval without ever crossing the line into open rudeness. "What did she tell the manager?"

"I'm Bella, for the evening," Cat told me. She winked. "Sorry to disappoint you."

"Poor Bella," I said. "Having to put up with *me* for the evening."

Cat laughed and squeezed my hand. I smiled back, enjoying her company. Auntie Sofia had thought of everything. No one would bat an eyelid if I took my future sister-in-law out to dinner, particularly if Rose accompanied us; no one would wonder, at least openly, if I'd taken someone else instead. Cat had to find it a little irritating, but I suspected she understood. She'd already been kidnapped once.

"So," Cat said. We strode into the hotel, where a bowing manager showed us to our room. "I hear you're taking the Challenge...?"

I heard the faint surprise in her tone and winced. Cat wasn't the sort of person who would be *impressed* by the Challenge. Neither was I, of course. Francis and Alana might enjoy the thought of being crowned Wizard Regnant, but what did it mean? Really? The winner might reap the rewards for many years to come, but...he wouldn't get everything. And the losers would have to live with being losers. I wouldn't have taken the Challenge if I'd been offered a choice.

"It was Father's idea," I said. "Did *your* father tell *Alana* to take the Challenge?"

"No." Cat shook her head. "She's been talking about it for years."

"She must have been laying the groundwork ever since she became an upperclassman," I said, ruefully. "Your sister is very smart."

"She's the sort of person you appreciate more when she isn't picking on you." Cat winced, expressively. "It's good she's finally putting her talents to use, but…"

I nodded as the waiter entered the room, carrying three menus. We ordered quickly, then sat back in our chairs. Cat produced a tiny Object of Power from somewhere within her dress and placed it on the table. It glowed, an eerie light that sent shivers down my spine. I'd seen it before. No one could spy on us, not now. The most powerful scrying spell I'd managed to produce had been unable to see through the bubble. Even a lip-reader would find it impossible.

"She said you'd been having problems," Cat said. "Do I want to know the details?"

I frowned. "What did she tell you?"

"Very little," Cat said. "You know Alana. She prefers to keep as much as possible to herself."

"For future blackmail," I commented. "I caught Francis kissing a girl."

Cat opened her eyebrows in mock surprise. "Really?"

I had to laugh. "A *betrothed* girl," I clarified. "He could have landed the entire family in hot water."

"That could have been bad." Cat sobered. Her dark eyes met mine. "Do you trust him? I mean, *really* trust him?"

"Francis?" I was surprised by the question. "He's my cousin."

"And she-who-will-not-be-remembered was my great aunt," Cat reminded me. "Just because someone's *family* doesn't mean they're a good person."

I felt a twinge of discomfort. It felt *wrong* to hear outsiders criticising my family…I told myself, firmly, that Cat was practically family. And yet, it still felt wrong, as if I was being disloyal even *listening* to it. The family had to hang together, I'd been told time and time again, or we'd all hang separately. Our internal disagreements had to remain private. In public, we had to present a united front. And yet…

236

"I know," I admitted. "Do you *know* Francis?"

"I only met him once." Cat lowered her eyes. "It was one of those gatherings…"

I nodded in silent understanding. The gatherings were intended to let aristocratic children mingle, meeting the kids who would be their friends, allies, rivals and enemies before they reached an age where they could take part in the constant struggle for power. In practice, they often turned into magic contests, where kids showed off their magic by casting spells on each other. I'd never liked them. Cat had hated them, with reason. She couldn't hope to defend herself.

"He struck me as cruel," Cat said, softly. "Someone who was always mean to people below him. He reminded me a lot of Alana, to be honest."

I leaned forward. "Did he do anything to you?"

Cat shook her head. "But he was…unpleasant to the staff. I think you should be wary of him. Alana's bright enough to know to pick her battles. I'm not sure Francis is anything like as smart."

"He's Sports Captain," I protested, torn between the urge to defend Francis and a grim understanding that Cat had a point. "He isn't a complete idiot."

Cat shrugged. "The only qualification for being Sports Captain is being able to kick a ball into a net without magic," she said. "It's a booby prize."

I had to laugh. I'd had the same thought myself. It *was* a booby prize…

The door opened. The waiter entered, pushing a trolley of food. He placed the dishes on the table, poured the wine—it wasn't alcoholic, I noted—bowed and left, as silently as he'd come. If he noticed the Object of Power, he gave no sign. I clasped my hands, muttered a short prayer to our ancestors and bowed my head. Cat nodded, curtly. I rather suspected she didn't take the custom too seriously. I didn't blame her. She'd thought, for the longest time, that her ancestors had abandoned her.

"Try not to die," Cat said, between bites of chicken. "I don't want to lose you."

"I wish I could promise it," I said, seriously. I quoted a line from an old story. "But it would hurt my pride to be forsworn as well as dead."

Rose snorted. "Talk about something more cheerful, why don't you?"

I looked at Cat, then laughed. "Did you read the joint research paper by Magisters Grayson, Von Rupert and Tallyman?"

"I read it." There was an odd little edge to Cat's voice. "What did you make of it?"

"It's...*interesting*," I told her. "They believe they can actually *generate* magic. That...they can infuse magic into Devices of Power—and spellforms in general—on a far greater scale than anything we'd done before. That..."

I shook my head slowly. I'd worked hard to keep current with magical theory, but I had to admit that parts of the paper were well above my head. Magister Tallyman hadn't had time to discuss it with me, when I'd asked. And really, I didn't have time to press either. I was having a very busy year.

"They think that's how the Ancients crafted their flying cities," I continued, after a moment. "There are problems with scaling up Devices of Power to levitate a clipper ship, let alone an entire *city*, but if they manage to create a source of infinite power...they could do anything."

"So they believe," Cat said. "Given infinite power, they could do anything."

I eyed her, puzzled. "Do you think it's possible?"

"In theory, you can do anything," Cat said. "In practice, there are limits. And I wonder..."

"We still don't know what happened to the Thousand-Year Empire." I remembered the Eternal City—the badly *misnamed* Eternal City—and shuddered. A thousand years had passed since the Fall and the ruined city was *still* incredibly dangerous to unwary visitors. We'd been lucky to survive long enough to escape. "Perhaps they had a little accident..."

"Perhaps." Cat looked down at her hands. "They're talking about sending more research teams to the Eternal City. They asked me to accompany them."

I blinked. "The Magisters?"

"And a handful of others," Cat said. "They want to figure out what actually *happened* to the city."

I shuddered, remembering the ruins...and the sense of warped and twisted magic wafting through the air. I'd never felt anything like it, not even in the experimental laboratories the family had established in the countryside. Something had gone horrendously wrong, something that had affected the entire empire...I couldn't imagine it. What sort of accident would shatter the peace of the world, and send *all* of the flying cities crashing to the ground, without wiping out the entire empire? The devastation seemed to have been oddly limited. It simply didn't *work* that way.

Unless we're missing something, I mused. *But what?*

I met her eyes. "Are you planning to go?"

"I don't know." Cat seemed oddly reluctant. "I'd like to go—and I should be immune to the tainted magic—but...I have bad memories of the place."

"No one is going to *make* you go," Rose said. "Are they?"

Cat laughed. "Mum and Dad would prefer me to remain in the Workshop," she said. "Even after..."

She glanced at me. I found myself blushing. Again. I forced myself to ask a different question. "How *is* the Workshop?"

"It's fantastic," Cat said. "Although...it's quite frustrating, sometimes, to realise just how much I don't know. I've been reinventing a great many concepts from scratch."

I blinked. "Reinventing?"

"The Ancients left quite a few things out of their textbooks," Cat said. "Things they considered no-brainers, I imagine, but to us...we have to figure them out before we can proceed. I think a number of designs were supposed to be jointly forged, by two or three people like me...and, of course, I can't do them on my own. And then a bunch of *really* weird stuff turned up. There's... *something*...that seems to be doing *something*, but I can't figure out *what*."

She frowned. "It's actually quite disturbing, to be honest. I keep thinking I should discard it."

"Perhaps you should," Rose said. "If it's bothering you…"

"I want to know what it *is*." Cat chuckled, rather humourlessly. "It's *very* weird. I can't even describe it properly. And all my investigations keep producing wildly absurd results."

She met my eyes. "Come see it, over the summer. See what *you* make of it."

"I will," I promised. "Are you having fun?"

"It would be nice to have another pair of hands," Cat admitted. "I've been trying to find ways to…*limit*…the damage caused by magic, during the forging, but so far I haven't been able to devise something reliable. Another Zero, even an untrained Zero, would be very helpful."

I felt an odd flicker of…*something*. If there *was* another Zero, if he worked closely with Cat…I felt a twinge of jealously, even though I *knew* I was being silly. There was no other Zero, male or female. And yet…I missed being able to work with Cat. I'd envy anyone who had the freedom to spend time with her, experimenting with forging and potions as they delved into the mysteries of the Ancients…

"It would be," I said, finally.

Cat shot me a look, as if she knew what I'd been thinking. I wondered, suddenly, what she thought of me staying at school. I was surrounded by girls, all the time…did she wonder if I'd break my word? Did she…? It would have been so much easier if she'd stayed at Jude's, but it would have been pointless. Cat was so much happier, and more effective, in the Workshop.

We chatted for hours as we finished our dinner and put the plates to one side. I told her about Louise and Saline, neither of whom Cat knew very well; she told me about her experiments with Objects and Devices of Power. I had the oddest sense there was something she wasn't telling me, although I had no idea what it was. If she was afraid to discuss it here, even with an Object of Power protecting us from listening ears, I wasn't sure I wanted to know. A family secret? Or something more fundamental?

The clock chimed, once. "It's nearly nine." Rose stood, brushing down her dress. "I think I have to take you home now."

Cat stood, looking pained. I didn't blame her. She was seventeen, nearly eighteen, and yet...she had to be back at nine, a *childish* time. Isabella—and Francis—would have been horrified if they'd been told they had to be back any earlier than eleven. But then, Cat was uniquely vulnerable. I stood too, feeling a twinge of pity mingled with admiration. Cat had turned her disadvantages into a strength.

"Gosh, this *is* an interesting painting," Rose announced. She turned away from us. "The colours, the lights, the colours..."

Cat and I leaned forward and kissed. Her lips felt warm and soft and *right*. I felt my heart begin to race as I embraced her, my arms slipping down her back. She kissed me back, her eyes shining...I wanted to do more, so much more. I understood, more than I cared to admit, why Francis had gone so far with Lindsey. It was easy to forget propriety—and common sense—when a girl was in my arms, her lips touching mine...

Rose raised her voice. "I'm running out of arty-farty babble," she said. "And I'm turning..."

Cat drew back. I let go of her, reluctantly. Rose was only doing her job. Anyone else would have been *far* less permissive. The thought of being chaperoned by our parents—or our aunties—was horrific. And yet...

"I'll see you soon," Cat whispered. She picked up her Object of Power. "And thank you for coming."

"I wouldn't have missed it for the world," I told her. I stole a quick kiss. "And thank you too."

Rose cleared her throat, loudly. "Shall we go?"

I held out my hand. Cat took it. "Sure. Why not?"

CHAPTER
TWENTY-SEVEN

I'd intended to go straight back to school, as soon as I returned from Riverside, and spend the rest of the half-term training, but Father had other ideas. The moment I reached the mansion, I was plunged into an endless series of social engagements, from polite chats with relatives I barely knew to formal introductions to Shallot's movers and shakers. Father put me through my paces, testing my knowledge and ruthlessly correcting me whenever I got the wrong answer. He even let me cast a couple of votes when we attended Magus Court.

It was almost a relief to return to school, when the holiday finally came to an end, and resume my normal life. I'd been terrified that *someone* would notice the box Isabella had given me, even though I'd slapped enough concealment and obscurification charms on it to hide a small army. Indeed, it was quite possible—I'd remembered, too late—that doing too *much* to conceal something might alert any watching eyes to the simple fact I had something I thought worth concealing. I had no idea what Father would make of the Object of Power, if he found it. He'd certainly ask a few sharp questions about where I'd found it. And I really didn't want to tell him the truth.

There had been no time to find Louise and Saline when I returned to school. I'd written to them—and the rest of the team—to inform them that Francis had been reinstated, on probation, but they hadn't bothered to reply.

I wasn't sure if that was a good sign, or a bad sign, or…they might simply not have received the letters. Louise and Saline both had families within the city. They could have gone home, rather than remaining in an empty school. I wouldn't have blamed them if they had.

I went to breakfast, the following morning, feeling tired and worn. I hadn't slept very well and I'd had to be up early. I was in no state for conversation as I munched my breakfast, drank enough coffee to float a boat and headed down to Magister Niven's classroom. I cursed whoever had drawn up the schedule under my breath. The first day of schooling should be spent doing something mindless, not something that forced me to *think*. I had the uneasy feeling that I wouldn't be able to put together an answer to a question if I were asked.

"In our preceding classes, we discussed the government of Shallot and how it is pervaded by the patron-client system," Magister Niven reminded us. "We turn now to the *downside* of the system—the near-collapse and reformation of the Craftsman's Guild. Who amongst you can tell us what happened to the Craftsman's Guild?"

I tried not to cower as his gaze swept around the classroom. I knew the answer—Father had made me study the decline, fall and rebirth of the Craftsman's Guild—but I was in no state to actually give it. I kicked myself, mentally, for not taking a refreshment potion before going to breakfast. I could have swallowed it and…I would have paid for it later, of course, but I would have felt better while I was in class. Instead, I'd just have to tough it out.

"The guild grew too big, too fast," Alana said. She sounded disgustingly fresh. "The internal rules weren't suited to purpose and the whole edifice collapsed."

"Correct." Magister Niven shot her a brief smile. "Why did this happen, you might ask?"

He paused, then continued instead of calling on someone to answer. "The Craftsman's Guild was originally founded by a team of craftsmen who didn't belong to any of the Great Houses and, therefore, couldn't call on their protections. It was formally incorporated as a guild after the craftsmen proved their value to the city by withdrawing their labour and given a seat on Magus Court. Indeed, the following years would see the guild expand rapidly—too rapidly—and thus sow the seeds of its own near-destruction. Why did that happen?"

Louise stuck up her hand. "The Great Houses conspired to bring the Craftsman's Guild crashing down?"

"No." Magister Niven sounded more amused than annoyed by her answer. "The problem was considerably more fundamental than that."

"The guild didn't *think* before it set up its entry requirements," Francis drawled. I wondered how *he* managed to sound so fresh. I knew for a fact he'd gone to bed after me. "And then it couldn't change them."

"Correct," Magister Niven said. "The guild's founders wanted— needed—to represent as many craftsmen as possible. They therefore set the entry requirements very low, counting experienced master craftsman as equal to apprentices and amateurs. This worked, in the sense that membership rose at an astonishing rate; this failed, in the sense that it actually undermined the guild. Masters could be outvoted by their apprentices, when they banded together; the apprentices, unsurprisingly, voted measures that favoured them, not their masters."

"Dumb selfish apprentices," Francis commented.

Magister Niven shot him a sharp look. "The average person is not *selfish*, young man. He is, however, *self-interested*. The apprentices voted for measures that were in *their* self-interest, not those of their masters. Individually, there was nothing wrong with any of the measures. Indeed, they helped to prevent abuse—which could be quite serious, in those days. But collectively, they made it harder for the guild to operate. Mistrust rose, leading to masters refusing to take apprentices…and then apprentices voting for measures that *forced* the masters to take apprentices. The quality of their instruction dropped sharply."

I winced. I'd seen enough accidents—in potions as well as forging—to fear the consequences of poor instruction. If my teachers had hated me, or resented me, it would have been very easy for them to arrange an accident...or simply let it happen. And there *would* have been accidents. I'd had enough—with good teachers—to know that accidents happened. There was no way to keep people from making mistakes.

"The masters attempted to deal with the problem by rewriting the guild's rules," Magister Niven explained. "They believed that only masters, and qualified journeymen, should have the vote. The apprentices saw this as a threat, with reason. A formal reassessment of who had the right to vote, and therefore steer the guild, would undermine their position as the masters clawed back their power. Legally, rewriting the rules required a two-thirds majority; practically, the masters were *never* going to muster even a *third* of the voters to support them. Why should they?"

He paused. "The situation rapidly snowballed out of control. Masters started flatly refusing to take apprentices, *whatever* the rules said. Apprentices retaliated by harassing merchants who wanted to deal with masters, taking the issue onto the streets. It looked as if the Great Houses were going to have to intervene, which would have been disastrous. The baby would have been thrown out with the bathwater."

"A charming metaphor," Louise muttered.

Magister Niven scowled. "Perhaps *you* should tell us what happened next."

Louise flushed as the class tittered. "Common sense took over," she said. "The guild reformed itself."

"In a manner of speaking," Magister Niven said. "It would be more accurate to say that the masters—the *majority* of masters—were permitted to form a new guild. The new guild had different entry rules, with apprentices denied the vote until they passed their exams and became journeymen. It wasn't perfect—it was quite possible for an apprentice to be held back indefinitely—but it worked. The smarter apprentices made their way to the new guild and pledged themselves to be obedient, in exchange for instruction. And instruction they received.

"The old guild rapidly found itself deflating. Street violence rose as desperate apprentices, the ones who would have been rejected in a rational system, tried to fight for their very survival. This time, however, they had overplayed their hand. The ringleaders were rounded up, punished and expelled from the city. The remainder either adapted to the new reality or sank into the underclass. Hardly anyone was sorry to see them go."

"But they wanted to..." Louise shook her head. "They thought they were doing the right thing."

"A common delusion," Magister Niven said, gently. "From their own—limited—point of view, they were indeed doing the right thing. But from an outside point of view, they were selfish idiots who were threatening to collapse the entire edifice. Indeed, even *they* came to realise that their positions were dangerously stupid. There was no way they could force a master to give them decent instruction, whatever the rules said. All they *really* succeeded in doing was devaluing the guild's certificates. The smart ones learned to adapt."

Francis laughed. "And the stupid ones died."

"Correct." Magister Niven's eyes swept the room. "The core of the problem was that the guild put the helm in the hands of people who had not even learnt to row. The apprentices were, in many cases, willing and eager to learn. They did not, however, understand just how much they *had* to learn. Some of the realities—and practical limitations—of their art could *not* be learnt, save through experience. They therefore voted for things that either could not or *would not* be delivered. And they didn't want to listen to the masters, the people who *did* have the experience, because they weren't telling them what they wanted to hear."

Louise leaned forward. "Sir...why was there so much distrust?"

Magister Niven let out a long sigh. "In those days, young lady, there were far fewer protections for apprentices. By law and custom, the apprentice belonged to the master until he received his journeyman papers. It wasn't uncommon for apprentices to be abused, violently beaten for failures real or imagined…yes, there *were* a lot of unscrupulous masters out there. Even the decent ones believed that apprentices were wild animals who needed to be beaten into submission, not youngsters who could be taken in hand and trained. The apprentices…some were lucky, some rather less so. Many of them believed the masters would exploit them, given the chance. They might well have been right."

He shrugged. "On one hand, the masters did not endear themselves to the apprentices. On the other hand, the apprentices didn't endear themselves to the masters either."

"But the masters were right," I said, before I could stop myself. "Weren't they?"

"In this case, yes." Magister Niven smiled, thinly. "But in other cases, no."

He looked around the room. "It is illegal, as a general rule, to arbitrarily—and retroactively—change the admission rules. Very few motions to change the rules have succeeded, even if the change seems—on the surface—entirely reasonable. Why would that be the case?"

"Because you could start excluding people who met the former qualifications, simply because you didn't like them," Alana said. "And then everyone else would start doing it too."

"Correct." Magister Niven nodded to her. "If someone meets the qualifications, they have to be allowed to join. And vote, if they meet the qualifications for doing that too. You don't get to change the rules simply because you fear an influx of newcomers. If you can't exclude someone legally, you can't exclude them at all.

"The system works because it is basically *fair.* Not fair in the absurd sense that everyone gets what they want, when they want it, but fair in the sense the rules apply to everyone. They provide a framework for entering the guild—if possible, if you meet the requirements—and rising within the guild, to the point where you can cast a vote and help to steer the ship. And, by then, you should have enough *practical* understanding of the guild to know what you're doing when you vote. One of the few *successful* changes to guild rules—for example—took place when the Fishermen's Guild rewrote the rules for nominating officials. Why did *that* succeed when so many other attempts fail?"

There was a pause. Louise—finally—put up her hand.

"This ought to be funny," Francis whispered.

I glared. I wasn't in the mood to put up with him, not now. And if he was going to rejoin the team, he could start by treating Louise and the others with a little respect.

"The original set of rules stated that elected officials had to have ten years of experience within the guild itself," Louise said. "Over the years, those officials had become more interested in running the guild than taking fishing boats out to sea. They were steadily losing touch with the realities of the trade. The revised set of rules stated that elected officials could run for office after *five* years of experience, but they also had to have at least ten years of sailing experience...all very recent. They weren't allowed to lose touch. And the majority of guildsmen thought it was a good idea, so the motion passed."

"True enough," Magister Niven said. "It's also worth noting that the Fishermen's Guild grants voting rights after two years of sailing experience, before or after the voter joins the guild. Careerism was actually quite rare within the Fishermen's Guild, even before the rules changed. It's quite an interesting case study."

He paused. "For your homework, tonight, I want you to draw up a scenario in which one of the major guilds could be subverted—legally. And then I want you to think about how it could be countered, also legally."

I had to smile. Magister Niven *loved* pushing the limits. Father had told me, once, that—every year—there were dozens of complaints about him. But pushing the limits—and forcing us to think about why the limits existed in the first place—was his job. No wonder he got on so well with Cat. Cat herself was a striking example of what happened when someone learnt to think outside the box.

And this exercise will raise more than just a few eyebrows, I reminded myself. *There will be hundreds of complaints, when the parents hear about it.*

Magister Niven grinned, as if he knew what I'd been thinking. "Dismissed."

I sat in my chair and watched as my classmates rose and hurried out of the room. There was just enough time to get a drink and use the facilities before the next class began. Magister Niven lifted his eyebrows as he saw me sitting there, then nodded to the door. It closed with an audible *thud*. I sensed privacy wards sliding into place a moment later. I stood, as he walked back to his desk. I needed advice, but...Cat trusted him. I'd place my faith in her.

Magister Niven sat on his desk. "Can I help you with something?"

I nodded. "Many years ago, my father took part in the Challenge," I said, carefully. If there was anyone who would defy the Castellan on the matter, it was Magister Niven. "Something happened, something bad. Do you know what?"

"I suggest you ask your father," Magister Niven said. His face was artfully blank. "It's hardly *my* story."

"Father refused to tell me," I said. I'd asked three times, in three different ways, but Father had refused to answer. "And it might be important."

"It could be," Magister Niven agreed, blandly. "But tell me...if your father wanted you to know, wouldn't he have *told* you?"

"My father might not want me to know." I tried not to clench my fists in frustration. Why *did* Cat like Magister Niven again? "But that doesn't mean I *shouldn't* know. Sir."

"Quite." Magister Niven seemed more amused than annoyed by my tone. "Does he have a habit of hiding things from you?"

"He didn't discuss the facts of life with me when I was a kid," I said, bluntly. It would be interesting to see how he reacted. "How was *I* supposed to understand the changes in my body?"

Magister Niven showed no visible reaction. "There are some issues that can only be handled by one's parents. It isn't *my* job..."

"Yes, it is." I was surprised at my own daring. Magister Niven might be one of the more easy-going teachers—anyone else would have kicked Louise out of the class by now—but there were limits. "I have to know, sir, and Father isn't telling me..."

"There are things I *can't* tell you," Magister Niven said, dryly. "What I *will* tell you is that you should do a little research. Educate yourself! Do you know we have copies of society pages and newspapers in the library dating back over fifty years?"

I blinked in surprise. *That* was an approach I simply hadn't considered. If something had leaked out to the newspapers, it might still be in the archives. I groaned, inwardly. I should have thought of it. I had relatives who collected newspaper cuttings about themselves and bound them up in giant scrapbooks. I...

"Thank you, sir," I managed. "I never thought of that."

"Learn to think for yourself before you rely on others to do your thinking for you," Magister Niven told me. "And learn to question everything you're told."

"I thought that was what you were trying to teach me," I said.

"Yes. And, every year, there's only one or two students who really get it." Magister Niven smiled, although I didn't understand the joke. "Everyone else...? They simply don't think for themselves. And then they wonder why they get into trouble."

He shrugged, just as the bell rang. "You'd better get to class," he said. "You don't want to be late."

"No," I agreed. Magistra Loanda would be unhappy if I came in late. There was no point in asking Magister Niven for an excuse note. She wouldn't accept it. "I'll look up the references later."

CHAPTER
TWENTY-EIGHT

"Well," Louise said. "Are we even supposed to be here? Together?"

I shrugged. I'd found the abandoned study room years ago, back when Rose and I had been exploring the corridors under the school, but I'd never had a use for it. It was just too close to the school itself to be used as a secret lair, close enough that someone had stripped out everything—desks, chairs, blackboards—and left the room empty. But it would suffice for what I had in mind.

"It should do," I said, as I unslung my carryall. "Take a seat, please."

"That's not what I meant." Louise crossed her arms under her breasts. "Are the three of us—you, me and Saline—meant to be together?"

"There are three of us," I pointed out. I opened my carryall, digging through the bag to retrieve the box Isabella had given me. "You can swear I didn't do anything with Saline and she can swear I didn't do anything with you."

Saline sat on the wooden flooring and crossed her legs. "She got out of bed on the wrong side this morning," she said, confidingly. "And she didn't eat much for dinner."

Louise glared at her friend. "You don't have to tell him *everything*."

"I didn't tell him everything," Saline said. "I could have told him…"

"Shut up." Louise's face was as red as a tomato. "Just…shut up!"

I looked from one to the other, then shrugged as Louise sat next to Saline. The box felt suddenly very heavy, as if it contained secrets beyond imagination. I wondered, suddenly, if I was making a mistake. If they told anyone else what I'd brought to school...it wasn't illegal to own an Object of Power—the sword strapped to my back was hardly illegal—but people would ask questions. I was walking around with a small fortune in my bag. They'd want to know where I got it.

"I've been thinking," I said, as I sat down. "And..."

"Always a bad sign." Louise's eyes narrowed. "What were you thinking when you allowed Francis to rejoin?"

"That he deserves a second chance," I said, bluntly. I'd spent enough time second-guessing my decision to allow him to rejoin. I didn't want her snapping at me too. "And that's not what I called you here to discuss."

I rested the box on my lap as Louise scowled at me. "Saline is...*odd*," I said. "She's bright, but slow. Powerful, yet...she has trouble shaping advanced concepts and grasping spellforms that a second-year should be able to handle. And all of this started fairly recently. She wouldn't have got through the lowerclassman exams if she hadn't been able to pass them."

"We know," Louise said, impatiently.

"It's not uncommon for magicians to peak, to reach a limit to how much magic they can channel," I continued. "But that wouldn't affect their comprehension. They should still be able to follow the spell notations and suchlike, even if they can't craft a spellform or cast a complex spell."

"So you said," Louise snapped.

Saline put a hand on her arm. "Let him finish."

"I think Magister Niven likes you," I said, to Louise. "He's *very* forbearing with you."

Louise coloured. "Get to the point."

"I think someone cast a curse on Saline," I said. "Not one that kills or controls, but...one that impedes her ability to cast magic and work spells. I saw a handful detailed in a book of curse-reversing spells. Once it embeds itself within the victim's magic, it's very hard to detect and harder still to remove."

"And you think someone cast this spell on Saline?" Louise said. "Why?"

"If we knew who cast the spell, if there really *is* a spell, we might know why." I looked at the box, resting innocently on my lap. "Saline? Do you know who cursed you? If anyone cursed you?"

Saline shook her head, wordlessly.

"It isn't easy to remove such a curse," I said. "A skilled Healer would have to be hired. And one *hasn't* been hired"—and I thought cold thoughts about *that*—"and so…"

Louise scowled. "Can *you* remove the curse?"

"No," I said. "But we can cheat."

I opened the box and removed the spellbreaker. It was surprisingly small, for a device of such potential. It looked like a piece of clockwork, with three tiny silver discs arrayed together…there was no magic on it, as far as I could tell, but it felt…*odd*…against my bare skin, as if it was just *waiting*. There was something curiously crude about it, as if it had been put together by an apprentice. Cat would have done a far better job. Perhaps *that* was why it had been overlooked, when Kirkhaven Hall had been abandoned. My ancestors might have reasoned it was broken and simply not bothered to check.

Odd, I mused. *If nothing else, they could have melted it down for silver.*

"This is a spellbreaker," I said. "It breaks spells. All spells."

Louise shot me a sharp look. "Is it safe?"

"It should be," I said. I'd run the calculations myself, twice. There shouldn't be any real risk to us. Or to the school. Any spell caught within the area of influence would fade away, as if it had never been there at all. There should be no risk of a magical backlash or feedback loop that might prove deadly. "Saline? Do you want to take the risk?"

Saline looked pale, despite her brown skin. "How will it feel?"

"I don't know," I said. "Lie flat on your back, place it on your chest and spin the disc."

I watched as Saline stared at the spellbreaker, her expression torn between a queasy kind of fascination and outright disgust and fear. I understood. An Object of Power, in the wrong hands, could do a great deal of damage. A spellbreaker could make the difference between life and death. Someone who depended on magic to keep them alive would be doomed, if they stepped within the area of influence. The device was small, but alive with the potential for good—or evil. I understood, suddenly, why so many people had been terrified, when they'd realised the truth about Cat. Her mere existence was a harbinger of something that might bring their world crashing down.

Saline reached for the spellbreaker and took it, holding it as gingerly as a live scorpion. I glanced at Louise, then motioned for her to stand up and step away as Saline lay on the hard, wooden floor. I wanted to be closer, but…I didn't want to be too close to the spellbreaker when it activated. I was afraid, too. I wasn't sure *what* Cat had done, when she'd stopped the Crown Prince and Stregheria Aguirre, but it had terrified me at the time. Now…I hoped I was doing the right thing. The theory was sound, everything should work…

Saline's voice shook. "I'm ready."

Louise took my hand and squeezed it. I blinked in surprise, then realised she needed comfort and reassurance. She was as nervous as Saline, as I…

"Spin the first disc," I said. The Object of Power was very simple to activate. Isabella's notes stated that it worked for somewhere around five minutes, then simply stopped. Sometimes. She didn't know why. "Now."

Saline touched the disc, lightly. It took her two tries to get it to move, but the effect was immediate. The world seemed to darken, as if it was going to sneeze; I had the weird sense of something *rushing* past, even though the air was still. I couldn't help myself. I stumbled back until I hit the far wall, dragging Louise with me. I couldn't take my eyes off the scene. Saline was there…and she wasn't there…her form blurring and not-blurring and… my head spun, unable to make sense of what I saw. The room was growing darker, the light spells we'd cast slowly fading... I kicked myself for not extinguishing them myself, first. They were just a waste of magic now...

I heard Saline cry out—Louise squeezed my hand so hard it hurt—and then the effect snapped out of existence. The room was dim, so dim that I couldn't help wondering if my eyes were failing before I realised the truth. The room was dim because the light spells had dimmed, where they hadn't failed completely. I cast a pair of spells, then winced at the light. There was something *wrong* about them, as if the light was digging into my very soul. I blinked furiously as I inched forward, half-expecting to run into... *something*. Saline was lying on the floor, crying.

Louise ran past me and knelt beside her friend. "Saline? What happened?"

I followed, more carefully. There was nothing *physically* wrong with Saline, as far as I could tell, yet...there was *something*. She looked somehow... *lesser*. Her hair had come loose—I felt dirty for even looking—her face was streaked with sweat and...her hand was pawing the air in front of her. I couldn't tell if she was going into shock or...or what? I wished, suddenly, that I knew more about healing. Perhaps I should have asked Rose to join us too.

"Take it," Saline gasped. Her voice was light and breathy, as if she'd run a marathon. "Please."

I picked up the spellbreaker and looked at it. There was...*something*...an aura, perhaps, surrounding it. I felt uncomfortable even *holding* the Object of Power. I put it back in the box, sealed it with a handful of charms and returned it to the bag. I wanted never to look at it again, but I knew I'd have to remove it eventually. Maybe we could find a way to use it for the Challenge.

Saline shook, her entire body dry-retching. "I thought...it was him!"

"Him?" I was instantly alert. "Who?"

"Uncle Redford," Saline said. She retched again, violently. She didn't throw up, but that seemed to make the retching worse. "He...he cast a spell on me and...and...I..."

She swallowed, hard. I watched, feeling a surge of burning rage. An uncle casting a spell on his niece...there was no way *that* could possibly be good. If he'd damaged her ability to use magic…why? And if he'd wiped her memories too…what in thunder had he been doing?

"I didn't remember," Saline said. She sounded like she was pleading, although I wasn't sure who she was pleading *with*. "I didn't know what I'd forgotten, what he'd made me forget, until the spell broke."

My anger grew stronger. I wanted to *kill* her uncle. I wanted to hurt him, I wanted to make him suffer before I killed him. The sword hummed its agreement, its presence suddenly very strong. I could draw the blade, march to Saline's house and behead her uncle before anyone even knew I was there. I was halfway to drawing the sword before stopping myself. I needed to know why.

"I just couldn't *think*," Saline said. "My thoughts…they didn't come. I couldn't think and I couldn't…"

I forced myself to think rationally. What had her uncle been trying to *do*? I wasn't sure I wanted to know. He'd done a lot more than merely suppress her memories…dangerous, I told myself, if he'd been abusing her. I felt sick at the very thought. There were all sorts of dark rumours about some of society's outcasts—the stories about Reginald Bolingbroke were too outlandish to be credible, I hoped, although no one quite knew how he'd died—and some of the rumours…I felt my stomach churn. I told myself that some of the stories *had* to be false. They had to be. I knew that Isabella was not well on the way to becoming a warlock…

Saline sat up. "He wanted me to fail the exams," she said. "He told me that and…I forgot. How did I forget?"

"The curse wouldn't let you remember," I said, tonelessly. A curse cast by a blood relative…yes, it would go unnoticed, unless the caster got *very* unlucky. "Why?"

Saline looked down at her hands. "I don't know, but…I had an apprenticeship lined up, for when I graduated. It was a family thing…I don't know the details. But if I didn't qualify, *his* daughter would be next in line."

Louise hissed. "*That* petty?"

I shook my head, slowly. "The right kind of apprenticeship could open a *lot* of doors," I said, dully. "It might pay off for him."

I couldn't believe it. And yet…I'd never heard of anyone outright *cursing* a relative to ensure that someone else got an apprentice, but I could see the logic. The awful logic. It was one hell of a risk, but…if it worked, it would bring vast rewards. And, once the apprenticeship was claimed, the curse could be quietly dispelled. There would be no evidence left. No one would ever be able to prove what Saline's uncle had done.

Except us, I thought, vindictively. *She got all her memories back and then some.*

Saline raised her hands and cast a spell. I saw magic sparkling in the air, taking on shapes and forms as she cast spell after spell. I had to admire her control, now the curse was gone. Magic danced around her as she stood, power flickering in and out of existence. The aura left behind by the spell-breaker evaporated. She smiled at me, holding out her hands. I took them and allowed her to swing me around. Her laughter echoed through the room.

I stepped back as her power slowly faded. "What do you want to do?"

"Nothing, yet," Saline said. "I need to think."

"You can't let him get away with this," Louise said. "Saline…"

"I know," Saline said. "But I have to decide how best to handle it."

I cocked my head. She sounded different…I scowled, inwardly. Of *course* she sounded different. The curse was gone. It was no longer influencing her thoughts or tampering with her magic or…anything. I saw her smile grow even wider and grinned back at her. She was so happy. I wanted to reach for her, to let her pull me back into the dance.

"Don't tell anyone, not yet," Saline said. She looked from me to Louise and back again. "I need to *think*."

"You'll be safe here, for the moment," I said. Saline's uncle wouldn't notice any change in her until she went home. By then, she'd have a plan. I hoped there'd be a place for me. I would be *delighted* to help her send him to his ancestors. "And we will respect your decision."

Louise didn't look happy, but she nodded.

"Thank you, both of you," Saline said. "I...thank you."

"It was Akin," Louise said. She sounded annoyed with herself. "I never thought of using a spellbreaker."

Saline turned to me, her eyes shining. "Akin, I..."

She leaned forward and kissed me. Hard. I felt my heart begin to pound as I felt her breasts, pressing against my chest. It was the kind of kiss that Cat could never have given me, not when we were chaperoned...I forgot that Louise was there, as I fell further into the kiss. I wanted it, I wanted *her*. I wanted...I wanted it never to end. I wanted...

I pulled back, breaking contact. Saline stared at me; her face stunned, her chest heaving. She knew I wanted her, she knew...

"I'm betrothed," I said, quietly. "Saline..."

Bitter shame and guilt overwhelmed me. Ayesha McDonald had kissed me by force, but this...I'd wanted her as much as she wanted me. I could have done it, too. I hated myself, in that moment. How could I blame Francis for making out with Lindsey, despite the risk? How could I blame him when I'd come so close to making the same mistake? Maybe I *had* made the same mistake. I hadn't tried to escape when she'd kissed me.

Saline stared at me. "Akin..."

"I'm betrothed," I repeated. Cat was going to kill me. Her family was going to kill me. *My* family was going to kill me. "We can't."

"Why not?" Saline stared at him. "I...I *like* you, you..."

My heart twisted as I saw tears in her eyes. I wanted to take her in my arms and kiss the tears away and...I told myself, firmly, that I couldn't. Not now, not ever. Saline would find someone else and...I hoped she'd be happy. The *new* Saline...maybe she'd date Francis. I had the odd feeling they had more in common, now, than either of them would be happy admitting. Maybe...

"Never mind," Saline snapped. She wiped the tears from her eyes, then wrapped a glamour around herself. It was so strong that even *I* couldn't see through it. There was no sign she'd been on the verge of crying, only a moment ago. "Just...never mind."

She turned and stormed out of the room, slamming the door behind her. I watched her go, feeling utterly conflicted. My thoughts ran in circles. I'd wanted her. I'd come far too close to throwing everything away for her. I'd...Francis was going to laugh his head off, when he found out. He'd make *very* sure I never forgot what I'd done. And Cat...

A moment later, Louise slapped me. Hard.

CHAPTER

TWENTY-NINE

I tasted blood in my mouth as I stared at her, shocked.

She'd slapped me. I couldn't believe it. My thoughts ran in circles as I reached for my magic, my mind unable to quite comprehend what had happened. I'd never been slapped before. I'd rarely even been *hit*. Francis and I had traded blows, but…normally, disputes between magicians were settled with magic. And Louise had slapped me…I knew lower-class women were allowed to slap men, but upper-class women? They used magic.

"You utter…" Louise sounded furious. I could feel her magic boiling, as if she was on the verge of losing control. I'd never seen anyone *her* age on the verge of a magical temper tantrum. "Akin, you utter…*louse*."

She drew back her hand to slap me again. I stepped back, hastily raising my hands. If she slapped me again…my jaw throbbed, reminding me that she packed a punch despite her small size. I felt something trickle down my chin. I hoped it was blood.

"She likes you," Louise thundered. "*Liked* you. And you just rejected her…"

I stared at her in shock. "I didn't…"

"Of course you didn't," Louise snapped. "Men! You're all the same! You don't see what's under your very nose! Saline was in love with you and you… you pushed her away."

"I…" I caught myself and started again. "She's not in love with me…"

"You showed her kindness and understanding and patience," Louise said. "You helped her, you taught her…you even figured out what was wrong with her and *cured* her! She *fancied* you, you…halfwit! And you pushed her away. You…"

She raised her hand. I reached for my magic, my mind reeling. How had things gone so bad so quickly? I couldn't believe it. I'd never had any reason to think Saline liked me, to think…I would have felt like I was taking advantage of her, if she'd kissed me before the curse was dissolved. I'd helped her, yes, but…I would have done it for anyone. Francis was right, I supposed. I liked people who needed me. Saline really was my type.

"And you pushed her away," Louise said. "Why?"

I found my voice. "I'm betrothed," I said, carefully. "I can't give her anything…"

"You're betrothed," Louise repeated. "Does that even *matter*?"

"Yes." I felt a surge of anger, mingled with guilt and shame. I'd kissed Saline…no, she'd kissed me, but I'd kissed her back. Just for a moment, but more than long enough to cross the line. "Louise…I love Cat."

"Do you?" Louise met my eyes, challengingly. "Have you spent time with her, alone, for the last five years? Or have you always been chaperoned, unable to talk freely?"

I winced. That struck a nerve. My firstie year had been dangerous, but…I'd enjoyed being with Cat, working with Cat…sharing our mutual love of forging even as the world around us went mad. Afterwards, with Cat at the Workshop…we'd never been truly alone. We'd never been able to completely relax. We'd never been able to talk freely, to share our hopes and dreams. Even our letters were read by both sets of parents. There was no way either of us could put anything *intimate* into them. Who knew who might wind up using it against us?

"I know her," I said, finally. "And I…I like her."

"Really?" Louise didn't seem impressed. "Really truly?"

My temper flared. How old was she? Sixteen? Seventeen? She was talking like a girl who hadn't even entered her second decade. She was mocking me. I knew she was.

"Yes." My voice was very flat. "I know her. We have a lot in common. We can build a life together"—I winced, remembering one of my father's rare lectures on married life—"and work towards the future together. And I'm not going to throw that away for…for anyone."

Louise rested her hands on her hips. "And how do you know you don't have more in common with Saline?"

I found myself speechless. I'd never thought to put it into words. Cat and I had just…*clicked*, back when we'd first met. We'd worked together well, even though we were from rival families. She was brilliant and imaginative and…and I'd loved working with her. I missed that, more than anything else. The days when we could slip into the forgery or discuss new designs over a cup of tea were gone. They wouldn't come back until we were married.

"You don't." Louise caught my eyes and held them. "You don't know."

I took a breath. I honestly didn't know what to say. I'd barely *known* Saline, even though we were in the same year. I hadn't paid much attention to *anyone*, beyond Francis and a handful of others. In hindsight…I shook my head. Hindsight might be clearer than foresight, but it wasn't much use. There was no way anyone, even Cat, could produce an Object of Power that would allow me to go back in time and do it again.

"Cat and I were betrothed at the end of the House War," I said, instead. "The peace between our families *rests* on the match. We cannot betray it—I cannot betray it—because of…of anything. And I don't *want* to betray it!"

"That's horrific." Louise sounded shocked. "Were you and Cat *forced* into the match?"

It had been Cat's idea, but I had a feeling Cat had understood as little about the realities as I had, back then. She couldn't have *really* understood what she was giving up—and what she was asking *me* to give up—any more than I had at the time. And then the grown-ups had latched onto the idea, as if it were the answer to all their problems. It might well have been. Five years of peace between our houses had solved a *lot* of problems.

"We chose it," I said.

Louise snorted. "How could you possibly understand what you were agreeing to?"

"I knew," I said. It wasn't entirely true, but…I didn't care. "Louise…"

Louise cut me off. "Saline likes you and you…you kissed her back. I *saw* you."

"And I shouldn't have." Cat was definitely going to be angry. I really *shouldn't* have kissed Saline back. "And she shouldn't have kissed me either."

"Hah," Louise said. "You *liked* it."

I coloured. "It doesn't matter…"

"Yes. It does." Louise took a step closer. "You wanted her and…"

My temper snapped. My magic boiled within me, demanding release. "Enough!"

"It isn't enough," Louise said.

"Yes, it is." I controlled my temper with an effort. "She shouldn't have kissed me. I shouldn't have kissed her back. It was"—I tried not to think about the feeling of her body pressed against mine—"a moment of weakness. It was…"

I shook my head. "I like Cat. I like being with her, working with her…and even if I didn't, I wouldn't be selfish enough to throw it all away and jeopardize the peace between our two families just because"—I caught myself, on the verge of saying the unsayable—"I wanted someone else. And…"

Louise jabbed a finger at me. The spell struck me before I could react. My entire body locked solid, my muscles aching painfully as they were jammed in place. I tried to muster a counterspell, but her spellform was too precise. She must have learnt the spell from Saline, I realised numbly. It had a lot in common with the spell Ayesha had cast on me.

"Your system is evil," Louise snapped. "Evil and monstrous and…"

She clenched her fists. For a moment, I was sure she was going to hit me. "You and Cat are being forced to sacrifice your happiness, your chance at a future of your own choice, merely to keep the peace between your families. Neither of you *knows* what you want. You were *children* when you made the agreement. You didn't know what you were agreeing to, did you? How could you? And now you're being forced to keep the agreement when you're not sure if you *want* it!"

I wanted to protest, to say it wasn't like that at all, but I couldn't move. I struggled desperately against the spell, yet...it twisted and turned, *just* like Ayesha's spell. I couldn't break free. I was at her mercy. And she was angry. I could feel her magic, pulsing on the air. She might turn on me at any moment.

"And Saline likes you and you like her." Louise's voice hardened. "I saw the way you looked at her, from time to time. You found her attractive. I know you did. And yet, you rejected her...because your family *needs* you to marry a girl you barely know. Can you not see how inhuman that is? Can you not see how *monstrous* it is?"

She went on, her voice rising. "You're not evil, Akin, but you're trapped within an evil system that turns people into monsters. Your sister nearly destroyed your entire family because she was trapped, because she had to take power for herself or spend the rest of her life at someone else's mercy. And Francis..."

Her face twisted. "How *could* you let him back on the team?"

I couldn't answer. My lips were locked solid. But...I wasn't sure what I would have said, if I could. The team *needed* Francis. It needed as many competent and capable magicians as it could get. And Francis had been there for me, when I needed him. I'd forgive him a lot, just for being there.

And yet, he was threatening the entire family too, my thoughts reminded me. *What would have happened if someone else had caught him with Lindsey?*

Louise's voice was shaking. "He's an ass," she snarled. "He looks at Saline like she's a piece of meat. Me...he looks at me like I'm an object, like I'm so lowly I don't even qualify as a piece of meat! He laughs at me, pokes fun at me...pokes fun at you too, when your back is turned. And the girls! I know he's been courting girls, lots of them. How many natural-born children do you think he has?"

Her voice rose until she was practically shouting. "How many *bastards* do you think he has?"

I flinched, nearly tumbling over as my body jerked reflexively. I was in shock, too stunned to take advantage of the brief opportunity to break the spell. A properly brought up young woman did *not* use that word. She just didn't. And...my mind ran in circles. Could Francis really *have* gone that far? It would have been the scandal of the century if he *had* managed to impregnate another student, but...he wasn't that stupid. He would have used contraception spells. Wouldn't he?

Louise paced the room. I saw tears glistening in her eyes. "I should have known better," she said. "Blood will out, right? That's what you lot always say. And even the decent aristocrats get pulled down by the rest. Your system is corrupt, as foul and fetid as a cesspit; it makes monsters out of decent men and makes monstrous men even *more* monstrous. And it sucks in people like me, taking their magic and blood and giving them delusions of grandeur and acceptance in return. But they're just delusions, aren't they?"

No, I wanted to say.

It was true. Common-born magicians like Rose, the ones who showed immense potential, were brought into patronage networks, even married into the Great Houses. Of course they were. There was no point in letting such people go to waste, simply because they didn't have aristocratic blood. Cat's *mother* was common-born. And her daughter was remarkable...I wondered, suddenly, if we were looking in the wrong place for Zeros. Perhaps we should be looking amongst the commoners instead...

"I should never have agreed to join your team." Louise wiped tears from her eyes, then turned to face me. "But I gave my word."

She stared at my frozen face for a long moment. She looked...pitiful, and yet terrifying. I wanted to hug her and hex her, at the same time. Her hair was coming loose, falling around her face. She might never be classically pretty, not like Isabella or Alana or Saline herself, but she was striking. Her face had raw character. I...I told myself not to be silly. I had enough female troubles right now.

"I gave my word," Louise repeated. "I'll talk to Saline. I'll tell her...I don't know *what* I'll tell her. I'll tell her something. And we'll be at the training session, later today. We'll do everything in our power to make sure the team wins, that *you* get crowned Ruling Wizard of Wizard."

Wizard Regnant, I thought.

"And *you* will keep your word to *me*," Louise continued. "You *will* continue to tutor me. You *will* teach me how to behave. Because I'm going to go into politics, I'm going to reform the system, I'm going to fix the problem or bring the entire system crashing down. And if you don't, I swear by all of my ancestors I will make you pay. I'll tear your life to shreds."

I stared at her, too numb to be shocked. I'd known Louise resented her station in life, but this...I wanted to tell her that she was being stupid, that she was pitting her frail body against the might of the Great Houses and Magus Court itself. I wanted to tell her that she could make things better, if she tried. But I couldn't speak. She wouldn't let me speak.

"Don't give Saline a hard time, either," Louise added. She sounded calmer, now she'd given voice to her frustrations. She knew, I suspected, that she'd crossed a line. There was no going back now. "And watch your back. I wouldn't trust your cousin any further than I could throw him."

She walked out of my field of vision, her footsteps retreating. "The spell will wear off, sooner or later," she said. "See you at training."

I heard the door open, then close. I stood there, helplessly. I could *feel* the seconds ticking by, each one as long as a minute...I tried to concentrate, summoning my magic to break the spell. But...I cursed Louise and Saline and Ayesha as I worked, even though I knew I was being unreasonable. If

Ayesha hadn't enchanted me, Louise would never have known the spells existed...my head spun as I realised the implications. If Louise hadn't been taught the spells, when she was a little girl, how safe had she been on the streets?

The spell broke. I dropped like a sack of potatoes, hitting the ground hard enough to hurt. The muscle spasms caught me a second later...I nearly screamed in pain as pins and needles jabbed into my body, my muscles protesting. I forced myself to cast a general painkilling spell, even though it was dangerous. The pain faded to a dull ache, then vanished. I rolled over and forced myself to lie flat. There was no point in trying to stand, not yet. The painkilling spell might have banished the pain, but it wouldn't have done anything for the damage...if there *was* damage. Locking someone's muscles could be dangerous, if the spell wasn't done properly. Most magicians preferred more generalised freeze spells.

I stared at the ceiling, wondering what I was going to do. I'd known Louise was resentful of her station in life, but...I hadn't realised how deep her resentment ran. And that worried me. I hadn't realised at the time just how deeply *Isabella* resented her position, let alone how far she was prepared to go to claim the power she thought should be hers. And she hadn't been wrong. I thought about Alana, so calm and confident and capable, and shivered. What would Isabella have been, if she'd been Heir Primus? If she'd had something to work towards, instead of watching helplessly as it was dangled out of reach?

A part of me wanted to run after Louise, to hex her again and again until she begged for mercy. Another part understood her, though, all too well. And yet another part knew I couldn't afford to kick her off the team, let alone push her away. And...I swallowed, hard, as I remembered what she'd said about Francis. Did he have other girls? I found it easy to believe, even though... surely, there would have been rumours? I didn't know *what* to believe. Francis wasn't betrothed. No one would care as long as he was careful.

I forced myself to stand, slowly. Louise had promised to stay on the team...I had the odd sense she meant it, that I could trust her that far. After all, I'd promised her something too...I scowled as I realised I might be in some trouble. If Louise told everyone that Saline had kissed me...she'd land Saline in hot water too, but she might not care. I'd have to keep my promise to her, just like I'd intended to do. I hadn't had any intention of betraying her.

My thoughts wandered as I packed up the bag, checked to make sure I'd collected everything and headed for the door. Things had changed, for better or worse. And I had no idea what would come next...

And I have to talk to Cat, when I have a chance, I thought, glumly. I'd have to tell her what had happened, before rumours started to spread. *She deserves to hear it from me.*

CHAPTER
THIRTY

If things hadn't been so tense, between…just about everyone, the training session would have been a great success.

Saline was powerful—I'd known she was powerful—but she was also brilliant. Without the curse, she was almost a different person. Magic crackled around her like a living thing, flaring in and out on command. It was beautiful, just like Saline herself. And her control was so fine that even *Francis* complimented her. She was practically dancing as she cast spell after spell, pitting herself against Francis and Harvard and almost coming out ahead. Her control…even *Alana* wasn't so controlled. I had the strangest feeling that I understood, perfectly, why her uncle had wanted to cripple her. *His* daughter hadn't stood a chance.

And yet, the air was tense. Saline looked at me, her expression wistful, whenever she thought I wasn't watching. Louise, beside me, seemed to be having second, third and fourth thoughts about remaining part of the team, after everything she'd said and done to me. I wondered if I should be hexing her, or—at the very least—invoking my authority as Head Boy and giving her a lecture on casting powerful spells on her fellow students. There were limits, after all. And pranks stopped being funny very quickly.

"That was amazing," Francis said, after Saline caught a spell he hurled at her and sent it back. It crashed into his shield charm and vanished in a shower of sparks. "It really was."

Saline blushed. "Thank you!"

I eyed Francis warily. He'd been subdued, at least in my presence, since I'd returned from Riverside, but…I'd caught him watching Saline, a hungry expression on his face. He hadn't said anything, nothing I could object to, but…I understood, I thought, why Louise disliked him so much. I wouldn't have liked someone looking at *me* like that. And, in hindsight, his open disdain for Louise could easily come back to bite us. I wondered how he treated Tobias, when I was not around. Tobias was common-born too.

"We're doing much better," I agreed, putting the matter to the back of my mind. I'd just have to keep an eye on it and hope for the best. "Tobias? How do we stand on potions?"

"I've brewed up a dozen vials each, of various different potions." Tobias sounded gruff, but confident. "We should have more than enough to keep us going."

"If we manage to keep the vials intact," Francis pointed out. "What's to stop the other teams raiding our supplies?"

I shrugged. Preparing for the Challenge would be a great deal easier if we knew what we had to do. But…there was no point in crying over it, not now. We had to cover as many bases as possible, carrying as much as we could without being weighed down. I had a feeling there were limits to what we would be allowed to take onto the field. I still didn't know if I'd be allowed to take the sword.

"They will." Louise sounded very definite. "They'll start running short too."

"Then we'll stop them," Francis insisted. "We charmed all the bags shut, didn't we? And hexed them, to give anyone who tried to open them a nasty surprise."

"That won't stop them for long," Saline warned. "They're upperclassmen, not firsties."

"If they manage to steal the bags long enough to remove the hexes, we've probably lost anyway," I said. "Right now, we have other problems."

"Yep." Saline grinned, practically jumping in the air. "We have to practice our *spells.*"

I allowed myself to relax, a little, as we started an impromptu duel. We *had* gotten a lot better, even Tobias and Louise. And Saline was *brilliant.* I wondered, briefly, if I could convince her to pretend the curse was still there, in class. If the other teams didn't realise how good she was, they might underestimate her. If…I shook my head. It wouldn't be remotely fair on her. Saline had too many marks to make up before the final year exams rolled around. I couldn't ask her to throw that away for me.

Particularly as I hurt her deeply, I reminded myself. The thought nagged at my brain, mocking me. I'd tried to remember every little interaction I'd had with Saline, but…there had been nothing, no hints that she liked me. *She has to feel as bad about it as I do.*

A hex slammed into my chest. My body twisted and shrank into a mouse. The world suddenly loomed very large. I heard Saline giggling as I concentrated on breaking the spell, feeling a flicker of panic. If she'd used one of *those* spells…the spell broke, almost effortlessly. I rolled over and snapped out a hex of my own. Saline jumped to one side, allowing the spell to expend itself uselessly against the far wall. She was smiling, an open honest smile. I found it oddly reassuring. She didn't hate me.

"You snooze, you lose," Saline called. "You should have been moving."

"Yeah," Francis said. His words lacked their usual bite. "You should have…"

He broke off, one hand raised. "Can you feel the wards?"

I frowned, reaching out with my mind to touch the wards. They were strong—we'd put them together carefully, after the last set had been torn down—but…they were starting to go down. No, they were being *taken* down.

I felt a flash of alarm, mingled with dull admiration. Whoever was probing their way towards us was good. Very good. They would have sneaked up on us if we hadn't taken so much care with our wards. And they might not realise they'd tripped an alarm.

"They're coming," I said. I tried to get a sense of how *many* were coming, but it was impossible. They'd weakened the wards they hadn't taken down. There would have to be at least three people, by my estimate, but... there was no way to be sure. "We have to get ready."

Louise looked pale. "They're coming here?"

"Yeah." For once, Francis didn't sound sarcastic. "And we can grab them." He looked at me. "What do we do, fearless leader?"

I felt my stomach sink. I didn't *want* to give orders...but I had no choice. I was the one in charge.

"Louise, Tobias, stay behind," I said. They were our weakest duellists. I didn't want to put them in the front line. "Everyone else, come with me."

I felt the air grow colder as I led the way out of our secret—not so secret now, I supposed—lair and down the corridor. We'd spread the wards out as widely as possible, accepting the danger of someone tripping them by accident in exchange for early warning of any intruders. I checked their path, then motioned for my team to take up places in another abandoned classroom. We still couldn't get a good look at the invaders, but...we'd know if they changed their plan and circumvented the ambush. They'd have to start taking down more wards if they wanted to come at us from another direction.

Unless they've found a way through the wards, I thought. It should have been impossible, but I knew better than to believe it. There was always a way though, even with Objects of Power anchoring the wardlines. It was just a matter of finding the weak spot and forcing one's way through it. *If I obtained an Object of Power, why couldn't they?*

I lowered my voice as we spread out and took cover. "Don't hex until I shout," I ordered, slowly. "Saline, you and I will bring down their defences; Francis, you and Harvard hex them."

"Got it," Francis said. "What do we do with them afterwards?"

Put them in the locker rooms, the nasty part of my mind whispered. *Or...*

I shook my head. Ayesha and Zeya McDonald had been lucky, very lucky, that their little joke hadn't led to outright disaster. The consequences...no, I wasn't going to risk that, not for a prank. Better to merely humiliate them than...I braced myself, sweat prickling down my back as I heard a shuffling sound in the distance. I cast an obscurification charm over our positions, then stood still. I could *feel* them coming towards us. Their charms were strong, but I'd spent hours getting a feel for the room's background magic. They might be able to keep me from sensing them directly, yet...it didn't matter. I knew where they were because I knew where they *weren't*.

My lips twitched. Magister Harmon had said that, years ago. I hadn't understood him at the time. Now...now, I thought I knew what he meant.

I glanced at Saline as the intruders came into view. They were inching forward, holding long metal wands—Devices of Power—as they advanced. They'd planned it carefully, I noted; one inched forward, then the other two would come forward in turn. There didn't seem to be any more than three of them, as far as I could tell, although that meant nothing. A whole army could be following them and, as they'd already taken down the wards, we'd have no way to sense them. I shook my head. There wouldn't be a whole army. There would be ten of them at most.

Unless two teams have decided to ally, I thought, as I peered into the semi-darkness. *That would give them a major advantage.*

I took a breath, then gave the command. "Now!"

Saline and I cast the spell together, tearing into their protective webbing of obscurification and concealment charms. I heard someone shout in surprise as their cover vanished, an instant before Francis and Harvard hurled their first hexes. A dark figure melted—I heard croaking a second—later, but the other figures jumped reflexively to the side, dodging the spell. I was unwillingly impressed. They hadn't known they were walking into an ambush, but they'd reacted with admirable speed. I saw the frog grow back into a man, a second later. I hexed him in the back before he could react.

"Yield," Harvard shouted, as he threw another hex. "We've got you."

A flare of light almost blinded me. I half-covered my eyes and ducked, sharply, as a hex flew over my head. Someone—I thought it was a girl, but I wasn't sure—ducked behind an old piece of sporting equipment, so old and degraded that I wasn't certain what particular kind of torture it had been used to inflict. Perhaps students had been forced to clamber up and jump to the ground...or something. I'd never liked gym and I'd dropped it as soon as I could. I didn't care if the wretched monstrosity got destroyed in the crossfire.

I glanced at Saline. "When I give the command, yank it away."

Saline nodded, her dark face almost invisible in the half-light. "Ready."

"Now," I ordered.

She cast the spell. The climbing frame—or whatever it was—hurled itself away from the wall and crashed somewhere on the far side of the room. The person hiding behind it was caught by surprise, desperately trying to get her wards up before it was too late. I didn't give her time. I slammed a shatter charm into her wards—I almost shouted as I saw Ayesha McDonald illuminated in the glow—and then hit her with a transfiguration hex. She shrank into a tiny doll, no larger than my arm. I kept a wary eye on her— she was strong, more than strong enough to break the spell—as I layered another charm on her. It should be enough to make breaking the charm difficult, if not impossible.

Francis whooped. "I think we won!"

I cast a light spell into the air. The chamber was suddenly filled with light. Ayesha was lying on the floor, helplessly. One of her companions was a frog, croaking pitifully in Harvard's tight grip; the other, sensibly, had beaten a hasty retreat as soon as she'd realised they'd walked into an ambush. Ayesha's sister? It was odd, not to see the two McDonalds together. Or was Zeya the frog? I didn't want to check.

Saline laughed. "I think we won too."

I looked down at Ayesha. The doll was immobile, but...I could *feel* the magic, mine and hers, pulsing around her silent form. She was looking back at me, somehow. She knew I had no reason to be *gentle*. Maybe I wouldn't take the risk of putting her in the locker room. There were plenty of other embarrassing things I could do to her, without the risk of being expelled. It was all part of the game.

Francis nudged me. "We should ransom them back to their team."

"Maybe they'd pay us to *keep* them," Harvard said. The frog croaked in protest. "What happens if the team leadership is permanently transfigured?"

"It doesn't matter," I said. "We can't keep them permanently anyway."

"I'm sure we could get *something* for them," Francis persisted. "Perhaps a guarantee that they wouldn't try to sabotage us again. Or..."

I shook my head. There were limits. We couldn't keep them prisoner indefinitely...and they knew it. Sooner or later, the teachers would notice they were missing and we'd all be for the high jump. Ayesha's comrades weren't going to pay any ransom. They simply had to wait us out. I looked down at the doll, wondering just what she was thinking. Was she trying to break the spell? Or was she waiting, biding her time until she could change back without interference? I had no way to know.

"I'll deal with them," Saline said. She cast a spell on the frog, freezing it into immobility. "I'll take them to the upper levels. They can change back there."

"And who knows who will see them?" Francis smirked, openly. "They might be very embarrassed indeed."

"I'll see to it," Saline said. She took Ayesha and studied her for a long moment. "She was often very unpleasant, you know."

"Don't go too far," I said, warningly.

Saline winked at me, then took the frog and hurried off into the distance. I watched her go, then picked up the abandoned Devices of Power. They'd been forged very well, although...it was clear they hadn't been designed for the Challenge. I had the feeling they'd held their better work in reserve. They wouldn't have wanted to waste *those* on a sabotage raid, not when it could cost them their change to win. *That* would be amusing.

Francis nudged me. "So...what happened between you two?"

I gave him a sharp look. "What do you mean?"

"She can barely look at you and you...can barely look at her." Francis's grin widened, until it looked like the last thing a particularly unfortunate swimmer might see before his death. "Have you been fooling around when you're betrothed?"

"No." I felt a hot stab of white-hot anger. Why did Francis have to be so perceptive, particularly now? "She made her interest clear, but I turned her down."

Francis whistled. "You turned her down? That's some impressive will-power, my man!"

I glared at him. "And what about you and Lindsey?"

"Well..." Francis shrugged. "We talked and decided it would be better to go our separate ways. No harm done, no hard feelings...you know the drill."

"How suspiciously mature of you," I muttered, darkly. It was stupid, but I envied him. "And what about the other girls?"

Francis eyed me. "Other girls?"

"Be careful." I didn't really want to know *what* he was doing, but...if it could impact the family it was my *duty* to know. "And..."

I stopped as Saline ran back down the corridor to join us. "Done," she said. "They'll revert to normal in a few hours, unless they break the spells themselves. And when they do, they'll have witnesses."

I frowned. "Where did you put them?"

"By the statue of Tempest the Terrible," Saline said. "The firsties use that corridor all the time. *Someone* will trip the ward and break the spells… and see them snap back to normal."

"Ouch." I was torn between unholy glee and the uneasy sense we might have stepped over a line. "And what *else* did you do?"

Saline gave me a long look. "What makes you think I did *anything*?"

"Instinct," I said. I wasn't sure I could put it into words. "What did you do?"

"Oh, just a little charm I learnt when I was a firstie," Saline said. "It makes someone think they're naked. Completely untrue, of course, but…"

Francis laughed. "You couldn't have made their clothes fall off?"

"Of course not." Saline gave us both a brilliant smile. "*That* would have been a bit obvious. This way…they'd have to admit they were pranked by a firstie spell if they wanted to make a complaint. And they'd have to work out what we'd done before they could remove it."

Or use a spellbreaker, I thought. Saline's prank would work. I was certain of it. Ayesha and Zeya would waste time looking for an upperclassman-level spell, instead of realising they'd been hit with a mild compulsion. Once they did, of course, they'd have no trouble at all getting rid of it. *And then they'll start plotting revenge.*

I shook my head. "I've created a monster, haven't I?"

Francis blinked. "What do you mean?"

Saline jumped in before I could formulate a reply. "I think we should all go out to dinner," she said. "We have a lot to celebrate, don't we?"

"Yes," I said. I had a lot to do, too, but it could wait one night. "I suppose we do."

THIRTY-ONE

I should have gone straight to bed, after we returned from dinner, but I couldn't sleep. I simply didn't feel tired. Instead, I checked in with Alana—she was on night duty, as she didn't have any classes in the early morning—and made my way to the library. It was on the verge of closing—it was practically Lights Out—but I did have some privileges as Head Boy. The librarians ignored me as I slipped through the door and made my way down to the archives, ignoring a pair of lowerclassmen who were frantically trying to finish their homework before the bell rang.

The sight took my breath away. The archivists had filed away *everything*, from outdated copies of *The Practical Potioneer* to *Society Pages*, a newsletter covering the doings of High Society. I rolled my eyes, thinking about how my aunts cursed the paper—sometimes literally—and yet were delighted when *they* appeared between its pages. The only thing worse than having one's dirty laundry splashed across the front page, it seemed, was *not* having one's dirty laundry on display. I snorted at the thought. They couldn't complain about being featured if they went out of their way to make sure they *would* be featured.

I made my way to the rear of the room, looking for newspapers and broadsheets from fifty-one years ago. The stacks were crammed with dust, despite arrays of protection spells. The archivists had done their best, but there were limits. I was uneasily aware the paper might crumble in my hands. I tried not to cough as I found a handful of scrapbooks. Someone—a very long time ago—had cut up the newspapers, then folded the cuttings into giant scrapbooks. I wondered if they'd been trying to make things easier for their successors or harder. There were so many spells woven into the scrapbook that I didn't dare try to use magic to lift them. I had to carry them to the desk with my bare hands.

Brushing dust off the cover, I slowly started to work my way through the book. It rapidly became clear that nothing had really improved over the last fifty years, at least when it came to reporting. A third of the articles were full of fluff and nonsense, another third were practically obscene...I read a description of a dress worn by a society beauty and shuddered by how much attention the reporter paid to her figure, rather than the dress itself. He was practically slobbering over her. I wondered what the poor girl had thought, at the time. *My* mother would have turned the reporter into a pig, if it hadn't been so completely redundant.

The remaining articles were more informative, but I still had to flip through them to find the ones I wanted. Some crawler of a reporter had written a piece of backstory on Master Carioca Rubén—it was hard to connect the description with my father, who would have been about fourteen when the article was written—that *had* to have been approved by the family. It was so fawning that even the most contemptible social climber I'd met would have been repulsed. I wondered just how much the reporter had been paid to write such things with a straight face. Did they need surgery to remove his tongue from my grandfather's buttocks?

I snickered at the thought, then flipped through the pages. There was another puff piece on Sofia Cameron—Cat's mother, I thought—about her graduation; she'd gone into an apprenticeship with a *very* experienced Potions Master. Beyond that, there was another brief piece on a handful of names I barely recognised, families that had been falling below the poverty line for years. I wondered, as I kept turning the pages, if I'd gone too far into the future. Perhaps I needed an earlier scrapbook.

Or perhaps they're not in very good order, I thought, as I scanned another puff piece. It insisted that Lady Younghusband would go far. I supposed the writer had been correct, although not in the sense he'd intended. *Or they didn't know what might be considered important, fifty years later.*

My blood ran cold as a thought struck me. Could the details have been removed? The Librarians and Archivists Guild would fight tooth and nail to keep information from being destroyed, but...they might have failed. Or...they might never have been told. If someone had wanted to destroy the records, or hide them, they *might* be able to circumvent the protective charms. I could see a couple of ways to do it, particularly if the information was hidden instead of being destroyed. It could be...

I kept thumbing through the pages, moving with more urgency as time ticked by. My father would have graduated...I stopped and read the description of the graduation ceremony again, line by line. There was no suggestion my father had been crowned Wizard Regnant—I already knew he hadn't been—but there was also no suggestion he'd taken part in the Challenge. And then...I read it again, slowly. It was hard to be sure, but it sounded as if someone had *died* during the Challenge.

"And who," I asked myself, "could it have been?"

Someone cleared her throat. "Can I help you?"

I looked up, sharply. A librarian—one of the student assistants—was standing there, her hands clasped in front of her. She was a lowerclassman, too lowly for me to notice...it couldn't have been easy for her to approach me, even if she *was* a librarian. I glanced at the clock and frowned. Her boss had probably told her she couldn't leave the library until I did.

"I'm not sure," I said. I glanced at the next couple of articles, but they seemed to date from the following year. "Is there a way I can get a class list for fifty years ago?"

"The lists are in the archives, over there," the librarian said. "I'm afraid they didn't do yearbooks, back then."

I nodded and let her show me how to find the lists. It wasn't *hard* to deduce who'd died, simply by comparing the class list to the graduation list. Malcolm Sweeny...I frowned, puzzled. The Sweeny Family lived in North Cairnbulg, on the other side of the Inner Sea. I didn't think I'd ever met one. Relations with North Cairnbulg had been icy ever since Crown Prince Henry, who'd married the Princess of North Cairnbulg, had called on his father-in-law to provide troops for his attempted coup. And Malcolm Sweeny had died? I looked for a copy of *Who Is Who*, but found no trace of him. There would be a record, I was sure, if he'd graduated. Anyone who graduated was a gentleman by default.

"Odd," I mused.

I could practically *hear* the librarian wringing her hands behind me. She wanted to tell me to go, but...I could give her lines, if I took offense. And she couldn't go to her boss, either. It would be a sign of weakness...I shook my head as I glanced down the list, looking for familiar names. My father, Uncle Davys, Uncle Malachi and...

Ice washed down my spine. Magister Grayson?

I let out a long breath. "Thank you," I said, returning the book to the shelf. "I'll show myself out."

My mind was spinning as I made my way out of the library and down the stairs. Magister Grayson had shared classes with my father? He'd never said anything, not once. And most teachers *would*, if they had ties to a student's parents. Technically, I probably shouldn't be in his class at all, but...he *was* one of the best teachers in the world. He was harsh, and often savage when he pointed out our mistakes, yet...I'd learnt a lot from him. Cat preferred his partner, Magister Von Rupert, but I didn't. Von Rupert didn't have the presence to command a class.

Not that anyone gives him any trouble, I reflected, as my feet carried me down to the charms classroom. *Magister Grayson is vindictive enough for two.*

I paused as I reached the classroom and peered inside. Magister Grayson was sitting at his desk, drinking a cup of coffee with one hand and marking papers with the other. It didn't look as if he was having much fun. I was tempted to walk away, even though I knew I had to ask before I died of curiosity. Head Boy or not, Magister Grayson could make life very difficult for me if I interrupted him.

He snorted, without looking up. "Do you know what time it is?"

"Yes, sir." There was no point in trying to deny it. "Ten in the evening."

"Right." Magister Grayson snorted, again. "And do you have something more *interesting* for me than this piece of...cowpat?"

I entered the room and approached the desk. Someone—I hoped it was a firstie, because anyone older should have known better—had written an essay that had to be at least two or three times as long as it should have been. From what little I could see—the handwriting was terrible too—the writer had *also* made a whole string of fundamental errors and then corrected them, instead of going back and starting again. Maybe they'd just been in a tearing hurry. There were times when we were meant to show our working, if only so we could see where we'd gone wrong. This was not one of those times.

"I'm almost tempted to let her *try* this," Magister Grayson said. "But the Castellan would have my head if I let someone blow herself to bits."

"Yes, sir." I didn't know who he was talking about, but it didn't matter. "Can I ask you a question?"

Magister Grayson eyed me for a long moment. "Sit down," he growled. "What do you want to know?"

I hesitated, then took the plunge. "You were at school with my father," I said, carefully. "I wanted to ask you if you remembered him..."

A flash of anger crossed Magister Grayson's face. "Yes, I remember him. Your father was very difficult to forget. What *about* him?"

I wondered, suddenly, if I'd put my foot in it. But it was too late to back out now.

"He took the Challenge, in his final year," I said. "I was wondering if you remember what happened."

Magister Grayson grunted and turned his attention back to the essay. "Ask your father."

"He refused to tell me," I said, pleadingly. "And I don't know who else to ask."

"How astonishing," Magister Grayson said. "Your father finally developed some common sense."

I blinked. I hadn't expected *that*. "Magister...I don't have anyone else to ask," I said. "The reports...there are hints that a student died during the Challenge..."

Magister Grayson looked up, sharply. "And there I was thinking it had all been covered up."

"I need to know," I said. "What happened?"

"No one knows." Magister Grayson looked down. "And no one really cares..."

"Please," I said. "*I* care."

"Do you?" Magister Grayson smiled, humourlessly. "I'll tell you what little I know, if you wish, in exchange for you marking these papers. You'll have to pour yourself some headache potion. You're going to need it."

I hesitated. I hated marking papers, particularly when it wasn't my best subject. If I made a mistake...I'd be in deep trouble. Magister Grayson would make sure I suffered for it. And yet, if it was the only way to get him to talk...

I met his eyes. "When do you need them?"

"Tomorrow afternoon," Magister Grayson said. "You should have enough time."

Perhaps. If I skipped class...or got up very early or...I nodded, slowly. It was doable. I'd hate it, but it could be done. And yet...I frowned. I had the oddest sense I was missing something. What?

"I can do it," I said. I sat down, resting my hands on my knees. "What can you tell me?"

"Your father and your uncle were close friends, once upon a time." Magister Grayson's tone was dark, suggesting he'd disliked both of them. "They did everything together, more or less. They broke quite a few hearts, back in the day. And then they did the Challenge. They put a team together and…"

He shrugged. "Something went wrong. Malcolm Sweeny died. No one is quite sure what happened to him. Or why. The details were covered up, but the rumours…your father and your uncle were never so close again, after that. They spent the rest of the school year hating each other. Everyone else thought it was a bit of a relief."

I leaned forward. "A relief?"

"Your father was not a very nice man." Magister Grayson gave me a cold smile. "Let us just say that there were people who danced a jig when he finally left school."

"That can't be right." I swallowed, hard. I didn't believe it. I didn't *want* to believe it. "No one ever *said* it to me…"

"He was Heir Primus, then Patriarch," Magister Grayson pointed out. "How many people dared call him out for his sins? And how many people would dare to tell his heir that, perhaps, his father shouldn't be placed on a pedestal?"

He shrugged. "Oh, your father grew up a lot. I'll give him that, even though he was a right pain in the unmentionables. He hasn't done a bad job with you, I suppose, and he went to bat for his daughter when many others would simply have disowned her. Perhaps he's even a decent man at heart. I don't know. But there were a *lot* of people who had good reason to hate him. Their hatred probably hasn't gone away."

I stared at him. "What about you?"

"Maybe, if things had been different." Magister Grayson shrugged. "Hugh took me on as an apprentice, after I graduated. I became a journeyman, then a master…somehow, we managed to keep working together. There's no reason to dig up old bones, not now, not until someone came calling…"

"Thank you," I said. I wasn't sure what to make of it. Had my father been a bully? I didn't want to believe it. "And…what happened?"

"I don't know," Magister Grayson said, sharply. "The only thing anyone knows for sure, anyone outside the charmed circle, is that Malcolm Sweeny died. There were rumours, of course. There always are. Some people think your father killed him. Some people blame your uncle instead. Some people think he had a terrible accident and it was all covered up because it might have been blamed on the school. And some people were happy to tell even wilder stories. We just don't know."

"And nothing leaked out?" I shook my head, slowly. "Why not?"

Magister Grayson snorted, again. "Your family is rich and powerful. Malcolm Sweeny's family was a long way away, on the other side of the ocean. The king himself—our king's father—had a keen interest in keeping things quiet, at least until a series of trade deals were concluded. Very little was actually printed, outside the school…there was chatter, of course, but eventually it went away. It always does. Someone got married, someone else got separated, someone died, someone was born…by the time *you* were born, it was old news. I dare say you would never have heard of it, if things had been a little different."

I nodded, shortly. That made sense. I knew just how much time and effort Father expended on making sure the society pages printed the right things, often rewarding reporters who praised him and condemning journalists who asked awkward questions. It would have been easier, back then, to keep something out of the papers. There hadn't been so many newspapers fifty years ago and almost all of them had been owned, directly or indirectly, by the Great Houses.

My mouth was dry. "I never knew. Not until now."

"I don't know for sure *what* happened," Magister Grayson informed me. "And I don't know who you could ask. Everyone who took part will be inside the charmed circle. There will be limits on what they can say, now. If your father can't or won't tell you…well, that's probably a sign."

I shook my head. "I never even wanted to take the Challenge."

"Then quit. Quit now." Magister Grayson started to gather his papers. "Or, if you feel you must continue, then stop whining and continue. Most students survive."

"*Most*," I repeated. "I like the sound of *that*."

"I've been a teacher for the last ten years," Magister Grayson said, ignoring my sarcasm. "In that time, there has only been *one* death during the Challenge. I don't think there have been more than five or six deaths in the last hundred years. Statistically speaking, you're in much more danger in Potions or Charms. The odds are firmly on your side."

"Thanks," I said, dryly. No one was *trying* to kill me in Potions or Charms, although it sometimes felt that way. "And..."

I hesitated. "Whatever my father did to you, I'm sorry."

Magister Grayson shrugged. "Do you think it matters?"

He passed me the papers. "I want them all marked by tomorrow afternoon," he said. "And I expect them to be marked properly. And if they're not"—his eyes bored into mine—"I will take great delight in giving you detention for the rest of the year."

"Yes, sir." I wanted to yawn. I had to swallow hard to keep from actually yawning in front of him. "I won't let you down."

"See that you don't." Magister Grayson smiled, humourlessly. "And try not to let your father down too."

CHAPTER

THIRTY-TWO

It didn't take me long, the following morning, to start regretting the deal I'd made. Magister Grayson had given me dozens of papers, all of which had to be marked intelligently. His students weren't allowed to guess. They had to show their work, put forward coherent explanations of what they'd done…and the poor sucker marking them had to give them intelligent responses in return. I was starting to think, by the time I ground through four papers, that I'd been overcharged. I had so much to do that I might have to skip my afternoon classes too.

And that would set a very poor example, I thought. The Head Boy could not be allowed to skip classes, unless something important came up. Even if it did…I shook my head. I might not get into any *formal* trouble if I missed one or two classes, but it might cost me later on. If I missed something I needed to hear…*I'll have to borrow Francis's notes and hope he did a good job of scribbling down everything the teacher said.*

I was midway through the fifth paper when a vapour message flickered to life in front of me. I looked up, sharply. Everyone I knew should be in class. Was someone else skiving? It was hard, somehow, to feel indignant about *that*. How could I give lines to some poor unfortunate skulking in the corridors when I was guilty of skiving too? Easily, I supposed. It was my job.

The vapour message opened when I touched it. "I've caught an intruder in the thickets," Skullion's voice said. The groundskeeper's voice was gruff, as always, but I thought I could detect a hint of surprise in his tone. "She requests you deal with her personally."

What? I stared at the vapour message as it repeated itself, then blinked out. An intruder? Cat? No, Cat could simply have walked in the front door. She wouldn't have wasted her time trying to climb the walls or sneak through the gardens, not when there was an easier option. But who else could it be? Everyone who might want to see me was already inside the building. *Who?*

I looked at the pile of paperwork, then sighed as I stood, pulled on my jacket and headed towards the stairs. The thickets were a dense collection of shrubs, planted along the west wall...they looked safe, the perfect place to sneak in and out of the school, until an unwary student actually *entered*. And then they came to life, trapping their victim until the groundskeeper arrived. Francis had been caught a couple of times, I knew. The smarter students tended to give the thickets a wide berth.

But they look so tempting, I reminded myself. By custom, anyone caught *outside* the school had to be officially ignored. It was only when someone was caught in the act of sneaking in or out of the school that they could be formally punished. *They look as if they provide cover to anyone foolish enough to venture inside...*

The warm air blew against my face as I left the school and walked around to the thickets, unsure what I'd see. I just kept drawing a blank. Skullion was standing by the edge of the thickets, a firstie standing next to him...Kate? I blinked in surprise, then schooled my face into impassivity. Kate looked terrible. Her uniform was torn in a dozen places, her hair was a tangled mess and her feet were charmed to the ground. The thickets had had a *real* go at her. I recognised the signs. Her bloater hat had practically been disintegrated. She'd be in some trouble if Penny spotted her...

And she'll have to pay for a new one, I thought, numbly. Rose had taught me that school uniforms were expensive, to the commoners. *That won't be easy.*

"She was carrying this, My Lord." Skullion held out a bottle. "I thought it should be brought to your attention."

I eyed Skullion, sharply. The groundskeeper was at the bottom of the school's hierarchy, but only a fool would take him lightly. He was a competent magician in his own right as well as the undisputed master of all who lived below stairs. They were respectful to the teaching staff, but they kowtowed to Skullion. He took care of them. I was fairly sure he wasn't the ogre he pretended to be—he would have been quite within his rights to frogmarch Kate to the Castellan—but I wasn't inclined to test it. There were limits.

"Please," Kate whispered. I wasn't sure who she was talking to. "Please..."

I took the bottle and blanched. Shallot Homebrew. I'd tasted it once, during a midnight feast that had ended with us all in detention. Cheap, nasty, and alcoholic. *Very* alcoholic. And...I frowned as I mentally counted the pennies. Cheap for me, perhaps, but Kate? She shouldn't have been able to afford it, unless she'd somehow earned herself a stipend. I doubted it. She shouldn't have been buying it at all, let alone bringing it into the school. She was in very hot water indeed.

"Thank you, Skullion," I said, flatly. I dispelled the charm holding Kate in place with a flick of my finger. "Kate, come with me."

Kate didn't move until I touched her shoulder. She jerked under my touch, then followed me like a lost puppy. I tried not to show any trace of my feelings as we walked back into school—thankfully, the corridors were mostly empty—and up the stairs to my office. There was no sign of Alana, for better or worse. She should have been in class. My lips twitched. For once, *Alana* was the one who was honouring the rules.

I put the bottle on the desk and sat down. "Why did you try to smuggle *that* into school?"

Kate looked away, unwilling to meet my gaze. I was starting to have a very nasty feeling that I *knew* the answer already. Penny. Penny had to have told her to buy the alcohol...I swallowed hard, feeling a surge of raw anger. Kate was *twelve*. She shouldn't even be leaving the grounds without permission, although I knew some firsties were happy to try sneaking in and out of the school from the very first day. And she certainly shouldn't be buying alcohol. She could have gotten expelled.

She still might, I reminded myself. *And...*

I cleared my throat. "Why?"

Kate's voice stammered. "I...I wanted to drink it."

"I know you're lying," I said. I couldn't help feeling pity, pity and anger. "Kate, I need you to tell me the truth."

Kate shook her head. I cursed under my breath, cursing her and Penny and the system itself. Kate should have been free to come to me—or Alana—and tell us what was happening, but...she couldn't, not without being branded a sneak. And then her life wouldn't be worth living. No one would like her, no one would trust her...even though she'd done the right thing. Perhaps Louise had a point. Perhaps the system needed to be changed.

I closed my eyes as I wove a spell. "Kate, tell me what happened."

Kate's eyes jerked open wide as words spilled from her mouth. "Penny told me to buy the alcohol for her or she'd hex me to death. I had to do it, but I couldn't pay for it; I had to take money from Emma and Fiona to pay for it and then slip out of the school and..."

She started to panic. "What...what did you do to me?"

"A light compulsion spell," I told her. "No one can possibly blame you for telling me everything, not now."

"Penny will," Kate said. Her legs buckled under her. "She'll kill me."

"No."

I shook my head. Father was going to kill *me*. Or the Castellan. Casting compulsion spells on one's peers was perfectly fine, but casting them on a firstie—someone who didn't have a hope of resisting—was borderline bullying. No, it *was* bullying. Father had ordered Cousin Bertram whipped, once, for casting such spells on the maids. I wondered, sourly, if he'd order that for me too. I deserved no less, even though I'd meant well. And the Castellan might take my badge. I probably deserved that too.

My heart sank as I thought through the implications. Penny could *not* be allowed to get away with this. It was…it was so far beyond acceptable that it would be a major scandal if it got out. And it *would* get out. One of the girls would talk, eventually. And then…

I reached for a sheet of paper. "I'm writing you an excuse note," I told her. "I want you to go to the study down the hall, the one normally reserved for upperclassmen, and stay there. If anyone tries to kick you out, show them the note. They should leave you in peace."

"Thanks." Kate sounded bitter. "But what…?"

"I'll deal with it," I promised. The only way to avert a scandal would be to deal with it myself, as quickly and decisively as I could. "Go. Don't leave the study until I come back."

I watched her go, then cast a vapour message into the air. Penny would report to me at once—or I'd know the reason why. She probably wasn't in class, not if she expected Kate to return with a bottle of cheap wine…I felt my blood boil as I realised just how badly Penny had treated Kate. How *could* she? If Kate had been caught by anyone else than Skullion, she would have been expelled—or worse. No one would go to bat for a commoner girl with no close friends. Penny had probably seen to it that Kate had *no* close friends.

And if Cat hadn't been so close to Rose, I thought as I waited, *Rose would have been expelled in her first year too.*

The door opened, without knocking. Penny stepped into the room, looking surprisingly calm and composed. Was she *that* confident she could talk her way out of trouble? Or had she not realised she *was* in trouble? Kate wasn't *that* late, not yet. I wondered how she'd intended Kate to explain her absence to her teachers. There wasn't *much* that could draw their attention, but a firstie skipping class definitely *would*. Perhaps she'd had a plan…or perhaps she simply hadn't cared. I didn't know. Really, I didn't care.

"Stand." I pointed to the space in front of my desk, then the bottle. "Explain."

Penny blanched, almost losing her balance. "I…it's a bottle of wine."

"Yes." I met and held her eyes. "I confiscated it from Kate, when she was caught sneaking back into the school. She refused to tell me why she had it, why she'd left the grounds to *buy* it, until I cast a spell to make her talkative. And would you like to know what she told me?"

"She's lying," Penny said, immediately. "She's..."

I glared. "Do you think a little firstie girl could shrug off a spell cast by an upperclassman?"

Penny swallowed, hard. I wondered if she *was* going to try to make that argument, crediting Kate with a level of skill that neither I nor Isabella nor Alana—or Penny herself—had possessed when *we* were firsties. We'd had the benefit of years of training, both direct and indirect. Kate hadn't cast many spells—if any—before she'd been given a scholarship to attend Jude's. My heart sank still further. If Kate was expelled, her family would be on the hook for her school fees. And they'd be unable to pay...

"She misunderstood," Penny said. "I was joking..."

My temper snapped. "You sent a firstie girl, one who hadn't even *seen* a big city before she came here, out to buy alcohol for you. A firstie! How did she even know where to go? She could have been arrested or"—I shuddered, remembering whispered horror stories about things that happened to the unwary in Water Shallot—"she could have been expelled."

"It was for a midnight feast," Penny whined. "I..."

"You should have gone and bought the wine yourself," I snapped. "You should have taken the risk yourself. You're an upperclassman! They might have looked the other way if they'd seen *you* smuggling alcohol into the school. Yes, they might! But Kate? What were you thinking?"

"I wanted to show her where she stood." Penny tried to gather herself. "Akin, she's an arrogant little..."

"No, she isn't." *Arrogant* was not a word I'd apply to Kate. "And even if she was, you should have been giving her lines. Not...assignments that could land her in very hot water indeed. What next? Did you order her to steal from her fellow students? Raid classrooms for answer sheets? Pay you for the privilege of sleeping in her own bed, in her own form? Ancients! What were you thinking?"

Penny dropped to her knees. "Akin, I…"

"Get up," I snarled. I had no time for false humility. "You've gone too far."

Penny looked up at me. "Akin, if you tell everyone…"

I laughed. "Penny, do you think you can keep this a secret forever?"

"The family name will be dragged through the mud, again," Penny said. "Just like Isabella…"

"Be silent." I wanted to reach out and strangle her with my bare hands. How dare she? How *dare* she? "Penny, how many of your charges know what you're doing? How many of them are likely to keep their mouths shut, forever? How many of them won't tell their parents or older siblings what you've been doing? And how many of them have connections who will take full advantage of what they've been told?"

"I can silence them," Penny pleaded. "I can…"

I made a rude sound. "Kate got *caught*, Penny. Don't you think there'll be an investigation? Don't you think they'll ask her questions, under truth spells a thousand times more powerful than the one I used? They will force her to talk and she'll finger you. She won't be able to help herself."

"Please," Penny said. She was still on her knees. "I…"

"No." I took a long breath. "You will go to the Castellan. You will confess to everything—and I mean *everything*. He will give you your punishment and, whatever it is, you will take it without a fight. And, afterwards, you will take whatever punishment the family deems fit to hand out too."

Penny glared. "But…the family name…"

"Will be redeemed by us punishing you for your crimes," I told her, curtly. I hoped that was true. "We discovered there was a problem and we moved to fix it."

I met her eyes. "If you don't go, I'll make sure everyone knows. I'll tell the Castellan myself. I'll go to Father and tell him. I'll even go to *your* father and make sure he punishes you. Or do you think he won't listen, if the Heir Primus tells him what to do?

"... No," Penny said. "I...mercy. Please."

"I don't understand it," I said. "How did kindly old Uncle Malachi raise a daughter like you?"

Penny glared. "You leave my father out of this."

"I didn't involve him," I reminded her. "You did. You involved him—you involved everyone—when you crossed the line. You were given a responsibility, a sacred trust. And you broke it. You should have been Kate's big sister, not...a bully."

"She's a commoner," Penny muttered. "I don't see what the big deal is..."

I stood. "She's a little girl. An innocent little girl. A *defenceless* little girl, without family or friends to hold you to account. And you...you should have been there for her, not...*Ancients*, Penny! What were you thinking?"

"She's not innocent," Penny mumbled. "I..."

"Be quiet," I snapped. "What's it to be? Are you going to go to the Castellan yourself? Or do I have to drag you there, kicking and screaming? Because if I do..."

"I'll go," Penny said, quickly. "I'll go and...I'll go."

"Good." I met her eyes. "I will, of course, be writing a full report. And I'll make sure Kate is interrogated too, along with any of her dormmates who might have been...mistreated...by you. You will have no space to hide anything, anything at all. And if you do..."

"I get it," Penny said. "I..."

"Good," I said. I allowed my voice to harden. "Because this is the sort of crap that starts vendettas. And *that* could really get out of hand. Go."

I watched her go, then rested my head in my hands. Penny was right. The family name was going to take a beating, even though I'd handled it. And Kate...I made a mental note to make sure that everyone knew I'd forced her to confess. I'd probably get in trouble for using such spells on a firstie, and it might cost me my badge, but no one would blame her for talking. She wouldn't be branded a sneak.

And Penny will get her just desserts, I told myself, as I stood. I had to talk to Kate, then write a full report for the Castellan before I went back to the essays. *She'll get what's coming to her…*

But I still didn't understand. Uncle Malachi was a good man, a kind man. He'd always been there for us. How had he managed to raise such a daughter? How?

In truth, I didn't want to know.

CHAPTER
THIRTY-THREE

The following morning, we were called to the Great Hall.

It wasn't *common* for upperclassmen to be summoned to the Great Hall, certainly not without ample prior warning. Schedules had to be changed, classes postponed...I'd done a little work as a hall monitor, last year, and I knew how many problems could be caused simply by cancelling or rescheduling a class. I heard my classmates chatter as we walked into the hall, puzzling over what had happened. A couple of students I barely knew insisted that it had to be something to do with the Challenge, but I wasn't so sure. *Every* upperclassman had been summoned, not just the ones taking part in the Challenge.

I looked around as I took my seat at the front of the room. Penny should have been with the other fifth-years, at the back of the hall, but there was no sign of her. I had no idea if that was good or bad. She could have been suspended last night, sent home or...I really had no idea. Alana sat next to me, her face expressionless. I'd told her a little of what had happened, at least partly to make sure she kept an eye on things too. There was no way to know how Penny's classmates would react.

The Castellan strode onto the stage. "Be quiet," he ordered. The chatter, already muted, died away. "This won't take long."

My heart sank as his eyes swept the room. It wasn't going to be good. I knew it.

"Yesterday, it was discovered that Penelope Rubén, a fifth-year dorm monitor, was abusing her position and mistreating the firsties who had been placed in her care. Her conduct was completely unacceptable. We acknowledge that mistakes can be made, and that it isn't easy to switch from being a lowerclassman to an upperclassman, but we feel she went well beyond making *mistakes*. She was given a chance to plead her case, yet she was completely unable to justify her conduct."

The room was so quiet that I could practically *feel* the silence, pulsing around me like a spell. I needed to know what else she'd done, but—at the same time—I wasn't sure I wanted to know. It was enough to know that Penny was in trouble, that she was finally going to receive justice for her crimes. And they *were* crimes. Her conduct would have been unacceptable even if Kate had been the *only* victim.

"Accordingly, we have been forced to take steps."

The Castellan paused, long enough for his words to sink in. "Penelope Rubén has been formally stripped of her status as both dorm monitor and upperclassman. She will continue to attend her regular classes, throughout the remainder of her time with us, but she may no longer comport herself as an upperclassman. She will be considered, for all intents and purposes, a lowerclassman. Her belongings have already been moved to Raven Dorm, where she will stay for the rest of the year. She will be right at the bottom of the dorm."

I winced, despite myself. Penny might think she'd got off lightly, but that wouldn't last. She might wind up wishing she *had* been expelled. In Raven Dorm, she would be treated as a firstie…she'd have to go to bed at Lights Out, she'd be the last to use the showers or…I shook my head, feeling a twinge of pity. Penny's enemies in fifth-year wouldn't hesitate to give her lines, meting out punishments that were normally given to firsties. The humiliation alone would be more than she could bear.

And Father won't be pleased either, I mused. *What will he say to her father?*

"Penelope will also be spending the next two weeks in the stocks, after classes," the Castellan continued. "I expect each and every one of you to look at her, at least once, and remember it could happen to you too. We grant you wide authority. We expect it not to be abused."

"Hah," Alana muttered.

I winced, again. Penny was in for a *very* rough two weeks. Students— particularly lowerclassmen—were going to be throwing everything from stinging hexes to rotten eggs at her. And she wouldn't even be able to seek revenge. If they were careful, she would never even know who'd struck her. She would *definitely* prefer to be expelled. I wondered, idly, if she'd pleaded to be kicked out, when she grasped the scope of her punishment. Or if she'd been too relieved to care.

And I'll have to account for my own role, I mused. *Father will not be happy with me either.*

"Those of you who are taking part in the Challenge, remain behind." The Castellan gazed at us for a long moment. "The rest of you, morning classes are cancelled. I suggest you spend your time wisely."

Alana looked at me as the room steadily emptied. "Are you going to be covering Penny?"

"No." I shook my head. The punishment was harsh, but it wasn't unjust. "She brought it on herself."

The Castellan cleared his throat. "There are five teams taking part in the Challenge," he said, bluntly. "Well, four teams and a lone competitor. We've numbered you from one to five, for various reasons. Name yourself something else if you wish."

Francis nudged me. "The Greatest of the Great?"

Alana overheard. "The Big Heads, more likely."

"Maybe later." I'd never thought of naming the team. Perhaps I should have thought of something clever—or amusing. Some of the sports teams had names no one dared write down. "Right now, I think we have other problems."

"From this moment on, there must be no more sabotage," the Castellan said. "Go collect your gear, then take it to your rooms and wait. Do not speak to anyone outside your team on the way. I'll be with you as soon as I can."

He dismissed us with a wave of his hand. I looked from face to face—Francis and Harvard looked confident, Louise and Tobias nervous, Saline impassive—and nodded at the door. My stomach churned. I tasted acid at the back of my throat. This was it. The Challenge was about to begin. In hindsight...I recalled Magister Grayson's words and kicked myself, silently, for not paying closer attention. He'd practically *told* me the Challenge was about to start.

"Here we go," Francis sang. "Here we go..."

"Shut up." Louise sounded terrified. "I..."

"Too late to back out now," Francis mocked. "We're committed."

"And we'll see it through," Saline said, firmly. "All of us."

I smiled at them as we made our way to our lair, collected our supplies and headed over to the barracks. We'd filed six bags with various pieces of gear, from food and drinks to potions vials and Devices of Power, but...it felt as if we hadn't packed anywhere near enough. I placed the spellbreaker in my pouch, then felt the sword on my back. No one had *told* me I couldn't take the sword onto the field. I intended to hang on to it as long as possible.

The barracks looked to have been freshly cleaned, probably by lower-classmen working off their punishments. Someone had placed mattresses and blankets on the bunks, along with a handful of supplies. I peered into the toilet and noted that it had been cleaned too. I wondered, as I sat at the table and waited, just how long we were intended to wait. An hour? Or a day? Or...or what? I wished, once again, that I knew what was about to happen. It could be anything.

"Whatever happens, we did our best," Louise said. "That's all that matters, right?"

Francis snorted, but he didn't have his normal bite. "*Winning* is what matters," he said, dryly. He sounded as if he didn't really believe himself. "Better to be a winner than a loser."

"Hey." Saline rested a hand on Louise's shoulder. "We'll have tried, if nothing else."

"Yeah," I said. "We will have tried."

I allowed my eyes to wander around the room, feeling an odd surge of comradeship. We'd worked together, we'd formed a team...no one, whatever happened, could take that from us. It would be good to win, but even if we lost...I winced, inwardly. My father wanted me to win outright, for the family. Anything, for the family. I wondered if victory would be enough to balance the scales, after Penny had been caught bullying younger students. It was lucky it hadn't been *Isabella*. That might have been enough to bring our father's position crashing down.

The door opened. The Castellan stepped into the room, carrying a bag slung over his shoulder. We rose.

"Be seated," the Castellan ordered. He walked to the table and sat down. "For what it's worth, this is your last chance to back out. If you don't want to compete, you will be placed in seclusion until the Challenge is over, after which point you'll have to live with yourself."

I shivered. I wanted to back out, but...I had to compete. I didn't have a choice. The others...I watched, wondering if anyone would leave. They all looked back at me, evenly. I could tell they were all scared, some more so than others, but...none of them left. I told myself that was a good sign. We'd had our problems, but we'd come together as a team. Win or lose, that was all that mattered.

But winning would be good too, I told myself.

"Very good," the Castellan said. His voice was very even. "You are now committed."

He met my eyes. "After this discussion is over, you will each drink a potion. It will put you to sleep. During that time, you and your competitors

301

will be transported to the field, where you will wake. The Challenge is generally considered to begin once you open your eyes. Don't worry. It will take some time for the other teams to get their bearings and come after you."

I shivered. That didn't sound good.

"You have three objectives," the Castellan said. "First, you must make your way to the castle at the centre of the field. Second, you must hold the castle—against both your competitors and your enemies—until the former have been eliminated. And third—finally—you must convince us you've won, that you *deserve* to be Wizard Regnant. You'll have to think hard to put forward a good answer."

Francis looked disappointed. "So it's basically a more advanced version of Capture the Flag?"

"You could say that," the Castellan said, evenly.

Louise had a more pertinent question. "When you say *eliminate*, you mean...?"

"You are allowed to stun them, freeze them, transfigure them or put them under compulsion spells," the Castellan told us. "Should all members of a team be eliminated, the team itself will be deemed to have lost; as long as there's one member still active, the team is still considered active. That person can easily free his comrades."

"If he can find them," Francis muttered.

The Castellan opened his bag and handed out a set of armbands. "Each of you will wear one of these," he said. I took one and studied it, thoughtfully. "You'll notice there's a simple spell woven into the gem. As long as that spell is active, your team is active too. The light"—he snapped his fingers, bringing the gemstones to life—"is your team colour. Should you wish to surrender, you may do so. That'll change the colour, binding you to the other team. Otherwise..."

He shrugged. "You are *not* allowed to remove your armband, while you're on the field, and you are not allowed to remove someone else's armband.

Trying to do so will mean automatic disqualification. Bear in mind that we *do* have ways of monitoring you."

"Of course," Saline muttered.

I leaned forward. "Do we have a time limit?"

"No." The Castellan smiled. "The Challenge continues until all but one team has been eliminated. If you really cannot continue, take off your armband. We'll come get you."

"I see." I wasn't sure *what* to think. How did the Challenge relate to the patronage-client system? Francis was right. It sounded like a glorified war game, not...not something serious. "You mentioned enemies...?"

The Castellan's smile grew wider. "You'll find the field itself is dangerous," he said. "There are a *lot* of traps in the area, from concealed hexes to animated golems. Should you be caught...well, you might lose. Teams have lost, at times, without ever facing their competitors. And yes, your competitors can attack you too."

"It appears to be the fastest way to win," Francis said.

"It does, doesn't it?" The Castellan produced six vials from his bag and placed them on the table. "These have been specially calibrated for you. Drink them when you're ready. We'll come and take you to the field."

He paused. "Do you have any other questions?"

"What about our classes?" Harvard looked irked. "I'm supposed to be duelling this afternoon..."

"Cancelled," the Castellan told him, bluntly. "Don't worry. It won't be held against you."

"Of course it will," Harvard said. "I'll be knocked down."

"There will be no suggestion that you rejected the challenge to the duel." The Castellan sounded very firm. "And you will have time to make up for your missed classes later."

"How very understanding," Louise said. "We'll still be behind."

"You'll have more than enough time to catch up," the Castellan assured her, calmly. He passed out the vials. "Put on your armbands, if you haven't already, then drink the potion. I have to go speak to the others...unless, of course, you have any more questions."

Francis grinned. "What is the price of sliced ham, per portion?"

The Castellan gave him a sharp look. "Save your witticisms for the enemy, young man. You might *just* distract them long enough to escape."

"Yes, sir." Francis sounded calm, but I could tell he was nervous. "I'll crack jokes like no one has ever cracked jokes before."

I had a different question. "What about our supplies?"

"Put them there"—the Castellan pointed to the floor—"and they'll be shipped out with you."

Francis whistled, softly. "Good thing you asked."

"Quite." The Castellan stood. "And now, if you don't mind, I'll see you afterwards."

"Thank you, sir," I muttered.

I stared at the vial in my hand as the Castellan left, the door swinging closed behind him. I didn't need to test it to know there was a locking spell in place, keeping the door firmly shut. The only way we'd be leaving the room, at least before the challenge was over, was unconscious. I hesitated, unwilling to open the vial and take a sip. There was something about the concept of deliberately putting myself to sleep that worried me, even though I was surrounded by friends. I'd never liked sleeping potion when I'd been a child.

"Well, it was nice knowing you guys." Harvard stood and made his way over to the nearest bunk. "I'll see you on the flip side."

Tobias opened his vial and took a sniff. "Basic sleeping potion," he grunted. "Not dangerous, unless you *really* overdose."

"Thanks." Louise didn't sound reassured. "Are we just to go to sleep?"

"It certainly sounds that way," I said. It felt like Winter's Night, where children had to be in bed and asleep before the Ancients delivered their presents. Isabella and I had tried to stay up, when we'd been kids, but...

somehow, we'd always fallen asleep and woken to discover a pile of presents at the end of our beds. "We don't have a choice."

"I didn't know I was going to have to put myself to sleep," Louise protested.

"None of us did." Saline helped Louise to her feet and led her to the bunks. "Better to get it over with."

"I guess so." Francis looked at his vial. "Akin, I…"

He shook his head. "What do you think happens if we don't go to sleep?"

I shrugged. "I have no idea," I said. "Maybe they enchant us to go to sleep instead. Or…"

A snore split the air. I glanced at the bunks, surprised. Harvard was snoring loudly, the empty vial clasped firmly in his hand. It must have been a strong potion or…I had to smile. A person as sporty as Harvard probably didn't *need* potion to get a good night's sleep, not on a regular basis. He could wear himself out on the sports field.

Maybe there's something to be said for sports after all, I thought.

"Well, goodnight," Francis said. "If I die, tell my father that I loved him."

I rolled my eyes. "I'm sure he already knows it."

"Hah." Francis stood and stumbled towards the bunk. "Night, night."

He lay down and drank his potion, his eyes closing a moment later. I stood and looked around. Everyone was asleep, everyone but me. They all looked so innocent, so untroubled by the coming ordeal. I felt a frisson of fear as I made my way to my bunk, wondering what I'd see when I opened my eyes. The Castellan had said much, but…I had the weirdest sense I'd missed something. He'd told us something important, something I needed to remember, yet…what was it?

I lay down and opened the vial. The smell alone was enough to make me dizzy. I wanted to throw it away, but…bracing myself, I put the vial to my lips and drank. It tasted cloying, a far cry from the sleeping potions I'd taken as a child, the ones I had later learnt to brew for myself. The world started to spin around me, no matter what I did…

An instant later, I was fast asleep.

CHAPTER
THIRTY-FOUR

Something had crawled into my mouth and died.

I...I jerked awake, coughing to get the taste out of my mouth. The others were no better, coughing and sputtering like firsties fleeing their first potions accident. I rolled over and sat up, one hand reaching for the spellcaster on my belt. If we were attacked...I fumbled with my bag, silently blessing the person who'd insisted we pack water. I took a long drink to wash the taste out of my mouth, then passed the bottle to Saline and looked around. We were lying on an earthen floor...a shack, I guessed. Light was streaming in through the open windows and the doorway. The actual door itself had been removed long ago.

"Where are we?" Francis looked as bad as I felt. "And what's outside?"

"It could be anything," I said.

I peered outside. The shack—it was definitely a shack—was surrounded by foliage. A handful of paths led into the distance, all vanishing into the woods. Birds flew through the trees, undisturbed by our presence; I could hear insects buzzing in the distance, the sound so pervasive that it started to blur into the background. I stepped outside, one hand raised to cast a shield charm, but there was nothing beyond warm air. I closed my eyes and reached out with my senses, but there was nothing beyond vague hints of magic somewhere in the distance. Or…I wasn't sure *quite* what I was sensing. There was something *muffled* in the distance.

"Look," Francis said. "That's our destination."

I followed his pointing finger and saw a castle, rising in the distance. It looked to be at least a mile away, perhaps two…I wasn't sure. It wasn't familiar either, even though I thought I knew every castle within twenty miles of Shallot. Where *were* we? I glanced at the sky, trying to determine how long it had taken to get us to the shack? It *looked* to be just after noon, but it was hard to be sure. Once we'd taken the potion, they could have kept us asleep for days if they'd wished. It wouldn't have been that hard.

They can't take us out of class indefinitely, I told myself, as I brushed down my uniform. In hindsight, perhaps we should have changed into something a little more suitable. *Our parents would kick up a fuss if we missed more than a couple of days of class.*

Louise joined us, looking out of place. "Where are we?"

"I don't know." Francis sounded concerned. "We could be anywhere within fifty miles of the city."

He nudged me. "Well, fearless leader? Which way do we go?"

"We attack the nearest team," Harvard suggested. "Take them out before they can take on us."

I shook my head. We weren't in any shape for a fight. The other teams probably weren't in any better shape, but…we didn't even know where they were. And they might hear us coming, if we started crashing through the bushes. I turned to study the shack as the rest of the team stumbled out, dismissing it as a possible base. I'd played enough games of Capture the Flag and Storm the Fortress to know it would be next to impossible to defend, even against firstie spells. Our enemies could simply set the building on fire, then hex us when we came stumbling out.

"We'll go to the castle," I said. "Grab your kit. We have to be off before they come looking for us."

I forced myself to think as I hefted my bag and slung it over my shoulders. The Castellan—and his staff—wouldn't give any of us an unfair advantage. Logically, the other teams would be scattered *around* the castle, giving us all roughly the same distance to travel before reaching its walls. And yet...I frowned, turning the matter over and over again. There was definitely something simplistic about the whole affair, as if...the game wasn't complex enough. I was sure I was missing something. But what?

"We should have changed into sports kit," Louise muttered, as we regrouped outside the shack. I could see sweat glistening on her forehead. "Or worn something a little more suitable."

"None of us knew we were going today," I reminded her. I cleared my face. "Francis, Harvard; I want you to take point. Watch for traps. Saline and I will stay in the middle; Tobias and Louise will bring up the rear. If they attack us, remember to counter their spells as well as hexing them back. We don't want to be wiped out in the first engagement."

"Do it like we practiced and we should be fine." Francis sounded edgy. "If not..."

I met his eyes. "Let's go."

The air seemed to grow warmer as we started to make our way towards the castle. I reached out with my senses, time and time again, but sensed nothing beyond the faint haze of everyday magic. This didn't *seem* to be a high-magic zone, yet...something kept bothering me. It might not be a good idea to take the shortest path, I told myself, but we didn't have a choice. Alana and the McDonalds had better teams, when it came to trading hexes and curses. We needed to get into a position we could defend before it was too late.

It might be too late already, I mused. *As we get closer to the castle, the odds of encountering them go up sharply.*

I peered from side to side, trying to see what lurked within the foliage. The path was growing narrower, forcing us to walk in single-file. The undergrowth was too thick to let us slip into the forest itself. I was *sure* we were being watched, I was sure we were being monitored…I glanced at the armband, wondering just how many spells had been infused into the gemstone. The Castellan might be watching us…I shook my head as I brushed sweat from my forehead. Of *course* he would be watching. They needed to see how we coped with the Challenge and…

"We're walking in circles," Francis announced, suddenly. "We've passed that tree"- he jabbed a finger at an innocent-looking tree—"twice already."

I blinked, then reached out with my senses once again. This time, I saw it. A simple misdirection charm, so low in power that it barely registered. And yet, it had twisted our minds…how long had we been walking in circles? I glanced at the sky, but the sun didn't seem to have changed position. Or was that part of the spell?

Francis glanced at me. "What now?"

"We burn our way through the foliage," I said. "Unless you have a better idea…"

"No," Francis said. "Do it."

I pointed my spellcaster at the foliage and muttered a spell. The foliage caught fire quickly, the flames spreading rapidly until we had a clear path into the forest. I led the way through, cursing under my breath as I felt the misdirection charm shatter into pieces. The smoke was likely to tell the other teams where we were, if they had a chance to look for it. I glanced up, but it was hard to tell how much of the sky they could actually *see*. We were lost beneath a canopy of leafy branches.

"This way," I said. "And watch for further traps."

It got hotter, somehow, as we kept advancing towards the castle. There was no path now, forcing us to pick our way through a complex network of tree roots, little streams and gullies that might—once upon a time—have channelled water to the distant ocean. I wondered, again, just where we were. One of the Royal Preserves? Or an estate that belonged to the school? Or…I couldn't think of anywhere that had matched what we'd seen. The entire area looked to have been untouched for hundreds of years.

"Watch out," Francis snapped. "There's something ahead!"

I followed his gaze. There was a hex, neatly concealed within the roots... I swallowed, hard, as I carefully plotted a way around it. Whoever stood on the hex—whoever stood too close, perhaps—would be caught and then...and then what? I had no idea. I glanced up, sharply, as I heard an explosion in the distance. One of the other teams? Or...or what? There was no way to know.

The traps grew thicker, forcing us to slow down as we evaded or disarmed them. I felt tired, my arms and legs protesting bitterly at their mistreatment. Louise and Tobias looked as bad as I felt. They'd both taken off their jackets and slung them into their bags. I tried not to notice how Louise's shirt clung to her skin. She was as sweaty as me. The others seemed to be taking everything in stride, even Saline. I supposed that five years playing sports had done wonders for their endurance. Who would have thought that *that* would come in handy?

Francis did, I thought. *And he wasn't exactly wrong.*

I listened, carefully, as we crossed another path. It was tempting to just turn and walk down it, but that would probably lead us straight into another trap. It was harder to pick our way through the foliage, yet...it did have the advantage of forcing us to be careful. I heard crashing sounds in the distance, suggesting that *something* very big and clumsy was moving within the trees. Some of my relatives hunted—they had entire forests set aside for hunting—but I'd never joined them. I'd never liked the idea of chasing foxes or hunting wild boar on horseback. And magic made the game much too easy.

Francis nudged me. "We're going to have to take a break."

I blinked in surprise, then nodded. We had to be *much* closer to the castle now. The ground was starting to slope down, as if the castle had been built at the bottom of a hollow. It struck me as odd, but...how old *was* the castle? Most castles had been built after the Fall, when the warlords had been trying to secure their holdings; this one, perhaps, might predate even the Thousand-Year Empire itself. It might explain why it had been abandoned for so long. The building wouldn't have protected its designers, not from the empire. They might have simply left it behind after they were conquered.

Tobias opened his bag and passed out a small selection of potion vials. I nodded my thanks and sipped the nutrient potion, silently admiring Tobias's skill. Most nutrient potions tasted utterly foul, so foul that people had to be desperate beyond words to drink them. Tobias's potion, however, was surprisingly nice. I was surprised other brewers didn't use the same recipe. It would be a great deal easier to get people to drink the potion.

"The castle isn't that far away now," Francis said. "You want to take point with me?"

I nodded, stiffly. I'd let Francis and Harvard take the lead for too long, even though they *were* the best at spotting traps and navigating around them. I finished my potion, then stood, brushing down my uniform. It was probably ruined. Mother would make sarcastic remarks, when she found out. There were a *lot* of things I could have done, if I'd known what I was facing. I hadn't, of course. That was the point.

"We'll scout out ahead," I muttered. If we were *that* close to the castle, we'd need time to recuperate before we tried to get inside. There was no shortage of ways to keep intruders from entering and...I wondered, suddenly, if we'd been encouraged to sabotage our rivals so we'd develop the skills to break into the castle. "Saline, you're in charge."

Saline saluted, cheerfully. "Right you are, My Lord!"

I expected Francis to make a snide remark as we slipped into the undergrowth, but he said nothing. I had the oddest feeling his mind was elsewhere. We picked our way down a gully, careful not to take the obvious route. It was dangerous to scramble down, but neither of us wanted to risk triggering a concealed booby trap. If we were turned into stones here...I shivered as I looked around, noting just how *many* stones there were in the area. Armbands or no armbands, we might never be found. Far too many horror stories I'd read had started with someone being transformed, and lost, and the spell wearing off hundreds of years later...if indeed it wore off at all.

They're just stories, I reminded myself.

"There," Francis said. "Look!"

I followed his gaze. There were a handful of shattered ruins—they were so badly damaged and overgrown that it took me some time to realise they'd once been houses—and, beyond them, the castle itself. I hadn't realised just how *big* it was until now. It loomed high over the canopy, so high that it reminded me of an iceberg, with most of its mass concealed below the treeline. I wondered, once again, where we were. I couldn't believe that the castle had remained concealed for hundreds of years, not until now. It was impossible.

The sense of *age* grew stronger as we inched towards the wall. I spotted a dolman, somehow untouched by trees and lichen alike; I shivered, remembering what little I'd read about the locals before the Thousand-Year Empire had conquered them. Very little *was* known for certain, save for the fact they buried their senior magicians and rulers under dolmans. The invaders had done an excellent job of wiping out their culture and replacing it with their own. I wondered, deep inside, if I should feel a little guilty. My ancestors had done the wiping.

But that doesn't mean they did the wrong thing, I reminded myself. *For all we know, the culture deserved to be destroyed.*

"We'll have to bring the others here," I muttered. I scanned the wall, but I couldn't see any doorways. There had to be a doorway somewhere... didn't there? I wondered if the designers had *flown* in and out of the castle. It was possible, at least in theory. Levitation spells would suffice. "Francis..."

I heard a scream, behind me. A feminine scream...Louise? Or Saline. It didn't matter. I turned and ran, drawing my spellcaster as I hurried back the way I'd come. They were under attack. I had to...

A spell slammed into my back. The force of the impact picked me up and hurled me through the air. I barely had a second to realise I was going to hit the ground hard before I did, the force of the impact knocking the wind out of me. Someone was on top of me a second later, his magic slamming into mine. Strong hands gripped mine and yanked them behind my back. I could barely focus, could barely struggle, as I felt my hands being tightly bound. A moment later, my legs were bound too.

Francis's voice was thick with heavy satisfaction. "Got you."

I was stunned. "What…"

"You always were slow on the uptake," Francis jeered. I had to twist my head to see him. "I suppose you could call this a mutiny. Or a coup."

"What…" I tasted blood in my mouth and spat. "What are you *doing*?"

"Winning," Francis said. "Getting what I want, for once."

"Francis…"

"I have been told, time and time again, that I have a duty to the family," Francis said, as if I hadn't spoken. "But what has the family given me in return? Tell me…what?"

I stared. It was hard, almost impossible, to *think*. What was he doing? Betraying me…why? Betraying the family…?

"Everything," I managed. I struggled against my bonds, but Francis had tied them tight. Very tight. The knots were already cutting off my circulation. I'd been frozen and transfigured more times than I cared to remember, but this…? There was something humiliating beyond words about being tied up. "Francis, the family gave you…"

"It showed me what I could have," Francis said. "And then it took it away."

"No," I said. It hadn't been like that. It hadn't been *anything* like that. "I…"

Francis ignored me. "They won't be able to deny me, when I am crowned Wizard Regnant. Not that there was ever any chance of *me* forming a team, was there? Never mind—I'll take yours. I already *have* taken yours. And I will be the winner and all the doors that were closed in my face, for an accident of birth, will open. And *you* will be my ace in the hole."

I thought I understood, then. Francis had found a loophole in the rules. If he stunned me or froze me or turned me into something, I would be eliminated…and, if the rest of the team was taken out too, he'd lose. But if Francis left me tied up, I would never—technically—be eliminated. He'd have plenty of time to escape his captors, if indeed he was captured, while they searched for me.

"Francis," I began. I wanted to think of an argument that might convince him, but nothing came to mind. He'd already gone too far. He had to win, he had to be crowned Wizard Regnant, or he would lose everything. "Do you think anyone will let you get away with this...?"

"Your father will soon fall," Francis said. He stood, drawing his spellcaster and pointing it between my eyes. "And no one else will care."

He cast a handful of charms over me, then turned and walked away.

CHAPTER
THIRTY-FIVE

How could it have gone so wrong?

I asked myself that, as I lay on the ground. I knew a dozen spells that should have untied me in a jiffy, but none of them worked. Francis had charmed the air around me, casting a ward that fed on my magic and dispelled my spellforms. I was morbidly impressed, even though I was in a fix. He'd spent a *lot* of time figuring out how best to hold me prisoner...he must have been thinking about it for months. I couldn't even draw the sword.

I felt...I felt helpless. I knew now, deep inside, how Cat must have felt all those long lonely years. Even now...Isabella had been right. Take away her Objects of Power and Cat was helpless, vulnerable to even the *merest* spell. I was vulnerable too, now. If someone wanted to take me out of the game—or, worse, kill me—they could simply hex me in passing. And even if I somehow managed to escape...

Stop feeling sorry for yourself, I told myself, sharply. *Francis has to be stopped.*

I forced myself to think. Francis couldn't get away with this, could he? I doubted it. I might be embarrassed—I might be effectively disinherited—but that didn't mean Francis would get away with it. His treachery would be known, even if he was crowned Wizard Regnant. Or would it? I'd never known my father had taken part in the Challenge. If we were all sworn to secrecy...Francis might just get away with it. And then...what? I burned with anger and helplessness. It was bad enough to lose, although I wasn't stupid enough to think I had to win all the time. I could cope with losing fairly. But treachery…

A thought crossed my mind. *But is that really the point of the Challenge?*

Gritting my teeth, I twisted until I managed to roll over and press my fingers into my utility belt. Francis hadn't thought to take the spellbreaker. He hadn't even known it was there. I winced in pain as I cut myself on one of the discs, then pushed them into motion. It struck me, an instant too late, that it might be a bad idea to trigger an Object of Power that had my *blood* on it, but I couldn't think of any other way to escape. My magic flickered and failed, leaving me feeling weak and drained. It was hard, so hard, to move. I couldn't understand how Cat coped. I muttered a spell, but nothing happened. The spellbreaker was stealing magic…

I realised my mistake, too late. The spellbreaker had destroyed Francis's spells, but…it was also preventing *mine* from working. As long as I remained within the field, I wouldn't be able to use magic…and the wretched Object of Power was attached to my *belt*. I couldn't roll out of the field, not without taking it with me. And it wasn't stopping. I hesitated, just for a second, then forced myself to roll over, crushing the Object of Power under my weight. Isabella was *not* going to be pleased. The spellbreaker was irreplaceable. I silently promised myself that I'd ask Cat to make her a replacement, if she could. Of course she could. But would she do it for Isabella?

Later, I told myself.

The magic came back, slowly. Very slowly. It felt like hours before I could focus enough magic to make my bonds untie themselves. My hands and feet ached as I pulled them free and forced myself to stand up. I rubbed them frantically, trying to rid myself of the uncomfortable pins-and-needles sensation. My uniform was a muddy mess. Mother would be furious, if she saw me. I laughed at myself a second later. That was hardly my major problem, not now. I had to stop Francis, even if it cost me my chance to be crowned Wizard Regnant myself. I was *not* going to let him get away with it. If he'd do it to me, he'd do it to *anyone*.

I looked around, carefully. The trees loomed as close as ever. It was impossible to see what might be hiding in the foliage. I could hear birds and insects in the trees, but…but nothing that might be human. I wondered if Francis had already gained entry to the castle. It was possible. I hadn't seen any doors, but that was meaningless. There had to be a door somewhere, unless we were meant to climb the walls. Francis probably could. He'd been a sporting enthusiast for years. There was nothing fake about the trophies *he'd* earned. I gritted my teeth as I turned and started to make my way back towards where I'd left the rest of the team. Francis might have told them that I'd been eliminated. Or…

My blood ran cold. Francis had found both Harvard and Tobias for me. Or had he found them for *him*? Francis could offer them both sizable rewards, particularly Harvard. What if they had turned on me? Or…I couldn't believe that either Saline or Louise would have turned on me—neither had anything to gain through treachery—but it might not matter. If Francis had lied to them, they might have gone with him quite willingly. Or…I could easily see Francis and Harvard beating Louise and Saline. They were both experienced duellists *and* they would have the advantage of surprise.

I picked my way through the trees, watching carefully for traps. It would be ironic as hell to escape my bonds, only to fall prey to a hidden spell. A flash of magic rushed through the trees, making me duck before I realised it wasn't aimed at me. I stayed low, watching and listening for threats, but there was nothing. Whatever was happening, it was outside the range of my senses. Had two teams gone to war? Or…or what?

My fingers grasped the sword's hilt as I reached the clearing, but I didn't draw it. The moment I did, everyone with *any* sensitivity to magic would know where I was…and Francis would know I'd escaped. Instead, I slipped forward and into the clearing. It was empty…no, a body was lying on the ground. My blood ran cold as I inched forward, raw terror clutching at my heart. Someone was injured? Someone was dead? I felt a flicker of relief—and then a surge of guilt—as I realised it was a man. Louise and Saline had been wearing skirts…it was Tobias. He was lying on the ground, held frozen by a spell. And, in his hand, he held his armband.

I stared at him, puzzled. He'd taken off his armband…why? I looked at his frozen face and thought I knew the answer. He looked like a man straining against a spell, a *compulsion* spell. Someone had *forced* him to take off his armband. I tested the spell holding him in place, ready to jump back in case it snapped at me, but…I couldn't break the spell. It wasn't a standard freeze spell. It was something more sinister, keeping him trapped in a moment of time…unaware, even, that he *was* trapped. I looked at the armband on *my* arm and shivered as I realised what had happened. The armband was charmed to freeze the wearer if he took it off, holding them suspended until they could be removed from the field.

"I'm sorry, Tobias." I knew there was no way he could hear me, but I couldn't help myself. "I wish I'd kept him off the team."

I turned slowly, surveying the clearing. There was no sign of anyone else. I wondered, grimly, just what it meant. Had Francis turned the girls into animals or objects? I reached out with my senses, but felt nothing. There was so much background magic—it felt as if it was getting stronger—that it was impossible to sense them, if they were there. Or were they with him, willing or not? Francis could have enchanted them, if he'd wished. Or Harvard…

Another flicker of magic flared up in the distance, only to be lost in the haze. I took a final look at Tobias—beyond my help now, until the Challenge came to an end—and started to walk, heading back towards the castle. The magic kept flickering and flaring, suggesting…what? Trouble? I wasn't sure if I *should* be heading towards it, but…I needed to find and stop Francis. Everything else came second. I said a silent prayer to my ancestors that they wouldn't forget the betrayal, whatever else happened. I'd never really taken my ancestral rites seriously, but now…I promised myself that, if I survived, I'd keep them in mind. And Cat's. I'd pay enough homage for both of us.

I kept my head low as I slipped through the trees, feeling the magic growing stronger and stronger. It was almost painful to my senses, as if I could *feel* it tearing into my very soul. My father had taught me how to block my sense for magic, if I had no other choice, but I didn't dare take the risk. I would be a blind man picking his way along a treacherous path, blind to the traps that might remove me from the game. I ground my teeth in silent frustration. An hour ago, I'd known that I might lose—that I might be eliminated—and still win, if the team won. Now...if I was eliminated, my cause would be lost. I didn't want to be Wizard Regnant—and I still wasn't sure I wanted to be Patriarch—but I sure as hell didn't want *Francis* to be either. I dreaded to think what he might do with my father's power.

But the family council would know what he'd done, I told myself. *Wouldn't they?*

I wished, suddenly, that I'd paid more attention to family politics. Or that Isabella had stayed in the city, where she could advise me. Were there uncles and aunts who would sooner see Francis as Patriarch, rather than me? It was possible. Francis wouldn't make a good Patriarch, but that might be the point. Our family required a strong hand, a *heavy* hand...Francis was neither. And yet, I could see why some of my relatives might want him in charge. He wouldn't be able to bring them to heel. He wouldn't even see the need to *try*.

The castle wall came out of nowhere, hidden within the bushes until I was right on top of it. I grunted as I walked right into the stone. My fingers brushed bare stone, feeling hints of metal—and magic—woven into the walls. It felt oddly familiar, reminding me of something...something I'd seen before. But where? I forced myself to think as I made my way along the wall, looking for a door. Something familiar...

Understanding clicked. Once, years ago, Father had taken me to see the founding stone, concealed underneath the family mansion. The stone itself was a Device of Power, rather than an Object of Power...I'd always wondered why my ancestors hadn't obtained an Object of Power for their wards before the Fall. It should have been possible, back then. But the stone—and the magic running through it—had felt *just* like the castle walls. What did it mean? I didn't know, but I found it oddly reassuring. I was starting to feel as if I knew what was going on around me.

I heard someone cry out, someone female. I hurried forward, even though I knew I could be running straight into a trap. The flickers and flares of magic grew stronger as I pushed my way through the bushes and peered out into a clearing. Magicians were fighting, outside an open door. Alana and Bella fought, back to back, against Francis, Saline and Harvard. Louise was standing by the door, her face blank. Saline...she was fighting, but her face was a struggling mask. Tears ran down her cheeks, even as she fought. I knew, beyond a shadow of a doubt, that she was under a compulsion. A *strong* compulsion. I was no duellist, but even *I* knew she was making mistakes, hoping—perhaps—to give Alana or Bella a chance to take her out. But every opening she gave them was closed—quickly—by Francis or Harvard. They were good. Very good. I'd never realised just how *much* time Francis had spent duelling. He was better than me.

But not good enough, I told myself. My fingers grasped the sword's hilt and pulled it free. I felt the blade come to life, shimmering with deadly energy. *Not good enough to stand against an Object of Power.*

I stepped forward, into the clearing. The sword strained at the leash, pulling me forward. It wanted blood. It wanted *Francis's* blood. I had to fight to hold it back as the combatants parted, Saline's face twisting between relief and a blank, soulless mask as she struggled against the compulsion holding her in place. Alana and Bella didn't even exchange glances as they backed off, moving in perfect unison. I felt a stab of envy. Twins and triplets were *meant* to work together as one. Would Isabella and I have developed the same skill if we'd stayed together? In hindsight, I wished...

Francis's face darkened. He jabbed a finger at me. The sword leapt up, blocking the curse effortlessly. I felt magic spiral around me as the curse broke on the sword's blade. I grinned savagely, feeling my legs start to move.

The sword was practically *forcing* me forward. It was all I could do to keep it from launching itself out of my hands and into Francis's neck. Visions of a beheaded Francis danced in front of my eyes. I wanted him dead...

"Now," Francis snapped.

He cast a spell. I barely had a moment to recognise it before the ground shook, violently. I jumped back, just in time to avoid having my legs fall into a newly-opened fissure. It was smart, I acknowledged. Francis couldn't beat the sword, so he wasn't going to try. I wondered if he'd spent hours planning how to stop me, if I drew the sword, or if he'd simply forgotten it was there. I found that hard to believe, but there were times when *I* forgot the sword even though I was *wearing* it. And then I ducked, again, as Saline hurled a series of hexes at me. Behind her, Harvard and Francis blasted Alana and Bella with freeze spells...

I cursed under my breath. Saline was fighting desperately, but she couldn't break the compulsion. I inched back, trying to think of a way to stop her without actually *hurting* her. She was going to impale herself on the sword if she kept coming like that...my mind raced, trying to think of *something*. I was barely aware of Francis turning and running into the castle, Louise following him like a dog on a leash, as Saline kept coming. I knew a handful of powerful counterspells, but she wasn't giving me time to cast them. The sword was blocking her hexes, yet...it was a killer. I didn't dare strike her with the blade...

Bracing myself, I shaped and cast a lightspell. There was a blinding flash of light, just enough to disorient her. The compulsion wouldn't let her cover her eyes, but as long as she couldn't see—as long as she didn't know where I was—she couldn't fight. There was an opening, just for a second. I lunged forward and punched her in the jaw, feeling oddly guilty as she tumbled to the ground. It wasn't her fault Francis had put a spell on her. I *knew* she'd resisted it as hard as she could.

Harvard's eyes went wide. I pointed the sword at him, ready to cut him in half if he tried to fight or bury it in his back if he tried to run. He did neither. Instead, he pulled a device from his belt and pointed it at me. Strange lights flickered, drawing my attention like a moth drawn to a flame. My strength started to drain, again. The sword was suddenly very heavy. I wanted to put it down...

A compeller, I thought, numbly. It was all I could do to keep my grip on the sword. No *wonder* neither Saline nor Louise had been able to break the compulsion. *He brought a compeller onto the field.*

"Put the sword down," Harvard ordered. In my dazed state, it was hard to understand why I shouldn't do as I was told. "Put the sword down..."

I bit my lip, hard. The pain gave me a little focus, just enough to cast a summoning spell. Harvard laughed, unkindly. The spell was hardly a *duelling* spell. It was harmless, unless the caster was imaginative...Harvard would have blocked anything more dangerous, but not a summoning spell that had missed him. He lifted the compeller, then stumbled forward as the fallen tree I'd summoned crashed into his back. I heard—or thought I heard—his bones break as he hit the ground, screaming in pain. The tree had tried to take the shortest path to me. Unfortunately for Harvard, it had had to go right through him to get to me.

My head cleared, instantly. I shook myself, then hurried forward. Harvard was still alive, but his back was bleeding heavily. I reached for his armband, then stopped myself. We'd been warned not to try taking them off. I had no idea what would happen if I did. Instead, I cast the strongest stasis spell I could. He'd be safe enough until the Challenge was over.

"Akin." Saline's voice was weepy. I turned to see her sitting on the ground, hugging her legs. "I'm sorry."

"Don't be," I told her. "The fault was mine. And his."

CHAPTER

THIRTY-SIX

There was a flash of light. When it cleared, Alana was moving again. She eyed me warily, her eyes flickering to the sword in my hand. Cat had repaired the sword, years ago. I wondered what she was thinking, if she was cursing her sister or silently thanking her for repairing the blade. It had saved all of us, back when Stregheria Aguirre and the Crown Prince had tried to take over the city, yet…we were on opposing teams. I felt the spell blinding Bella unravelling, a second before there was another flash. They'd woven powerful cancellation charms into their uniforms. I wondered, grimly, what had happened to the rest of their team. Alana had had five teammates, hadn't she?

"Akin," Alana said, slowly. I saw her hand twitch, as if she intended to hex me. I didn't really blame her. She had no idea what was going on, but… only *one* of us could be Wizard Regnant. "What happened?"

Saline shuddered, as if she was on the verge of crying outright. I had the urge to go to her and hug her…but I knew better. Not in front of Alana and Bella. "Francis…Francis *compelled* me to fight for him."

Alana and Bella exchanged glances. "Why?"

I listened, grimly, as Saline explained what had happened. They hadn't stood a chance. Harvard had hexed them when their backs were turned, then—when Francis had returned—they'd put a compulsion on the girls.

Tobias had been compelled to remove his armband, putting him in stasis. It made me wonder if Francis had *known* what would happen if someone removed the armband, if someone had briefed him on what to expect... someone...but who?

A nasty thought crossed my mind. I put it aside as Saline continued the story. The four of them had made their way to the castle, where they'd run into Alana's team. Francis had promptly ordered an attack, which had gone very well until I'd arrived with the sword. And then...my heart went out to her as she started to cry openly. Saline had already been abused by her uncle. She didn't deserve to be abused by Francis too.

I looked at Alana. "Truce?"

Alana blinked. "*What?*"

"I have to stop Francis." I met her dark eyes, silently wishing she didn't look *so* much like Cat. Cat would listen to reason. I wasn't so sure about her sister. "And you have to help me stop him. After that...we can fight it out for the title, if you still want it."

"You'd trust us at your back?" Bella sounded incredulous. "And you expect us to trust you?"

"If Francis wins the title, there will be consequences. Political consequences." I looked from one to the other, feeling the sword pulsing in my hand. It demanded action. I wanted to put it back in the scabbard, but I didn't dare until they agreed. "You have to help me stop him from winning or both of our families will suffer."

Alana and Bella exchanged another look. I wished I knew what they were thinking. What would happen if they refused? I didn't know, but...I wouldn't be able to turn my back on them. I wouldn't dare. Francis might win by default, simply because the four of us had eliminated each other. The sword was a powerful weapon, but it didn't make me invincible. Francis had already proven that to everyone's satisfaction.

"Truce, until we are the last on the field," Alana said. "Agreed?"

I nodded, stiffly. "Agreed. What happened to the rest of your team?"

"Francis got them," Alana said. "Do we have time to go find them?"

I shook my head. Somehow, I was sure we didn't have much time. The sword felt heavy as I put it back in the scabbard, then motioned for Bella to help Saline as I turned to the door. Alana stepped up beside me, her face grim. I glanced at her, then led the way into the castle. The interior was gloomy, but not dark. Burning torches hung from the walls, drawing us onwards like moths to flame. The shadows seemed to twist and turn around us as we inched into the castle, our senses straining for traps. There was only one way to go, as far as I could tell. No doors, no rooms...just a long stone corridor. I hated it on sight. No one would have any trouble guessing where we'd be going.

I glanced back out of the castle, looking up the featureless stone walls. Climbing them was out of the question, even for Francis. The magic currents surrounding the building were strong, too. If we tried to levitate, we'd lose control and plunge to our deaths; if we transfigured ourselves into birds and tried to fly, we might be dashed against the stone walls or simply find ourselves unable to change back. There were some magicians who wore an animal form as naturally as breathing, but I'd never tried to master the art. It had too many dangers, even for experienced magicians.

"We'll have to walk." Alana sounded no happier than I was. "Where will he be going?"

I shrugged. I knew nothing about the interior of the castle...or *did* I? My fingers brushed the stone again, sensing the same combination of magic and metal...cold iron, if I understood correctly. The faint tang of iron hung in the air, tasting metallic against my tongue. It was achingly familiar. I'd worked with enough iron, at the forge, to know the taste and smell was actually an illusion, but...I swallowed, hard. There would be time enough to return to the forge later, if there *was* a later. Francis had gone too far. His only hope to avoid being disgraced—Wizard Regnant or not—was to eliminate all the witnesses.

And pray we're not being watched, I thought, glancing at my armband. *Are we being monitored as we compete?*

The shadows seemed to grow darker as we made our way further into the castle, the space between the torches growing wider and wider. I gritted my teeth in annoyance. Whoever had placed them was an evil genius. There was too much light for the night-vision spells to work properly, yet too little for us to see normally. I couldn't help peering into the shadows, half-expecting something to jump out of them. I wasn't used to semi-darkness. Or being unable to see...

A shape loomed up in front of us, concealed in the shadows. Bella let out a gasp. Beside her, Alana stumbled against me. I cast a lightspell and recoiled in horror as a monstrous face looked back. I was halfway through casting a blasting spell when I realised that I was looking at a statue, a monstrous mutated creature that walked on two legs but was nothing like a man. The statue was so *real* that I had to resist the urge to blast it anyway. There was something about it that chilled me to the bone.

"I nearly wet myself," Bella exclaimed.

"Too much information," Alana said. "*Really.*"

Saline giggled. "What do you think it *is*?"

I smiled, relieved to hear that she was starting to recover, then turned my attention to the statue. It was...odd. Something from the Desolation, perhaps? There was so much wild magic there that someone unfortunate enough to *live* there might have been mutated into...into this creature. There were all sorts of stories about *things* deep within the Desolation, although none had been confirmed. People who travelled too far into the Desolation rarely came back. Those who did were often insane. The dreams of a land route to distant Hangchow were nothing more than dreams.

"I haven't the slightest idea." I touched the statue gingerly. It didn't feel like stone. It was...I wasn't sure *what* it was. "Someone's perverted dream, perhaps."

I cancelled the lightspell, then turned to lead the way further up the corridor. "Come on," I said. "I think he's going to go high."

The darkness enshrouded us again as we inched past the statue. There were others, a small army of statues lurking in the darkness. We glanced at the first two, then ignored the rest as the corridor suddenly widened into a darkened chamber. I glanced at Alana, motioning for her to be ready as I cast another lightspell. The shadows didn't part easily—they felt like living things—but, as the light grew brighter, we saw paintings on the walls. I studied the nearest as we looked around. It showed a magician locked in battle with monsters, like the statues we'd passed in the corridor. It looked as though the magician was losing.

Alana muttered an oath. "Look!"

I followed her gaze. Adam Mortimer, the student who thought he could compete on his own, was standing in the centre of the room, frozen in stasis. His armband was held in his hand. I swore under my breath—I supposed Father would forgive me for swearing, under the circumstances—as I inched forward. Adam was competition, and I was impressed he'd managed to get into the castle alone, but...Francis had to have gotten the drop on him. And then...I groaned, inwardly. Francis had inched one step closer to winning, simply by eliminating one person. I glanced from side to side, wondering what had happened to the other two teams. They could be anywhere. Perhaps it had been a mistake not to look for Alana's missing teammates. If they remained...wherever they were...they might count as *eliminated* if the rest of us were eliminated too.

"Idiot," Alana said. She made a face at Adam's frozen form. "You know he tried to ask me out, once upon a time?"

I shrugged. I had no interest in Alana's schoolgirl crushes. Or...perhaps I should listen, just so I could tell Cat. *She* might be interested.

"I always thought he was too full of himself." Alana sounded amused. "And now I know I was right."

I peered up at the roof, my eyes tracing out the metallic runes and sigils inserted into the stone. They were designed to channel magic...a *lot* of magic. I traced them out, then looked towards the door...where the logic of the building *told* me a door had to be. It was hidden in the shadows, but clearly there. I inched forward, peering into the darkness. There were no torches within the stairwell, no source of light at all. I allowed myself a moment of relief, then cast a night-vision spell as I started to climb the stairs. The stone walls were threaded with metal, leading up...I thought I understood, as we moved up, where they led. The entire castle was heavily warded...

Except it isn't, I thought. *We didn't meet* any *resistance when we walked into the castle.*

I slowed, thinking hard. I couldn't imagine the wards not *trying* to stop us, when we entered the building. Even commoner households had a few basic wards to keep out thieves, supernatural vermin and unwelcome relatives. I'd assumed we'd have to break into the castle—it was why I'd brought the spellcaster—but instead we'd encountered a marked *lack* of resistance. Had Francis already taken down the wards? Or had we put our heads in a trap?

A dull shiver ran through the building. I froze, one hand gripping the sword in the scabbard. If we were in trouble...I looked back at Alana and the others, then resumed the climb. There was nothing else we could do. On impulse, I cast a location spell, but the results were unclear. Francis had probably warded himself. We were cousins, not brothers. We had a blood tie, but it wasn't *that* strong.

Alana nudged me. "What do you think he's doing?"

I shrugged. "Something bad," I muttered back. "Something...I wish I knew."

The thought caused me a pang as I spotted the light at the top of the stairwell. What *was* Francis doing? Had he realised that he had to remove all the witnesses? Or did he think he could get away with everything he'd done? We'd been told, often enough, that all was fair in love, war and the

Challenge. If my father—and his father, I assumed—had been unwilling or unable to discuss the Challenge, perhaps...I shook my head. Whatever happened, Francis was *not* going to get away with it. I'd see to that, whatever the cost.

Saline pushed past me. "I'll go ahead," she said. "You keep yourself in reserve."

I bit my lip, but she'd gone past before I could muster an objection. Alana grinned at me, then told Bella to bring up the rear as we followed Saline up and out into the light. We were on top of the castle, staring at battlements that seemed too low to be useful...I couldn't feel any safety charms, nothing that might prevent someone from toppling over and falling to his death. The magic currents were stronger here, blowing with the wind...I felt uncomfortable, just standing on top of the building. The urge to step back inside was almost overpowering...

"Louise." Saline sounded relieved...and worried. "What are you doing?"

I followed her gaze. Louise, her face set in a blank yet tearful mask, was building...*something*...on top of the castle. My eyes traced it out...it was a Device of Power, but what *was* it? Francis couldn't have brought it with him, could he? No, it was impossible. I would have noticed if he'd brought more than his tools—*my* tools- with him. He'd found the components in the castle itself. My mind raced. He was trying to link his device, whatever it was, into the castle's wards...no, into its magic. I'd sensed the power the first time I'd touched the walls. Francis could have done the same himself.

A hex flashed towards us. I ducked, drawing the sword as the hex struck the stone wall behind me and flashed out of existence in a shower of sparks. Alana moved to the side, warily pacing the battlements. I stood in the centre, sword in hand, and looked for Francis. It took me a moment to see him, even with the sword aching for blood. He was standing on top of the device, a multitool—*my* multitool—in one hand and a spellcaster in the other. His face twisted in hatred when he saw me.

For a moment, I couldn't move. Did Francis hate me? Had he merely pretended to be my friend, all along? Five years…how had he kept it up? Or…had something else happened to him? I knew him, or I *thought* I knew him. Francis hated to lose. Even if I forgave him, even if *everyone* forgave him, he would still have lost. And he knew it.

The wind blew stronger as Francis hurled another hex at us and jumped down, landing on the far side of the device. I caught the spell on the sword's blade and hurried forward. Francis snapped a command and Louise hurled herself at me. I nearly cut her down before I realised who she was. Saline darted forward and slammed her palm onto Louise's chest. There was a flash of light—and a strange smell, hibiscus flowers—before Louise toppled to the ground, screaming. I hurried past her, hoping that Saline would be able to deal with her. I wanted—I *needed*—to catch Francis before it was too late.

"Stop," I shouted at him. "It's over. There's nowhere to run!"

Francis reached the end of the battlements, then turned to face me. His face was pale, sweat glistening on his forehead. And yet…I saw a hint of madness in his eyes, a grim determination to win whatever the cost. Magic crackled over his skin, arcing in all directions. The sword absorbed the charms hurled directly at me, but the others…I gritted my teeth as I was battered with ice-cold water and sleep. Mist and fog started to form in front of me, blocking my vision. I banished it with an effort as I moved forward. The sword wanted blood.

"Why?" I demanded an answer, even though I doubted I'd get one. "Why…?"

Francis laughed, hysterically. "Do you think I *wanted* to spend the rest of my life playing second fiddle to you?"

"You wanted to win?" I glared at him. "Everything you did…you just wanted to win?"

"Are you really that naïve?" Francis mocked. His words…something occurred to me, something bad. But…I didn't have time to think about it. "Of *course* I wanted to win!"

"But the family..." I couldn't wrap my head around it. The sword's hum grew stronger, demanding blood. "What about the family...?"

"Who cares?" Francis laughed. He didn't stop laughing, even as I raised the sword. "I just wanted to win!"

I heard a scream behind me, a scream of rage. I glanced back, just in time to see Louise on her feet, hurling a hex at me...no, at *Francis*. Francis blocked it with an effort, but the shock of the impact drove him back...and over the battlements. He fell. I yelled something and ran forward, trying to cast a spell to catch him. The magic currents flared around me, breaking up the spell before it could take shape. Francis laughed—I swear, he laughed—as he fell...

... And his body hit the ground, far below, with a sickening thud.

CHAPTER

THIRTY-SEVEN

For a long moment, I stared in horror.

Francis was dead. I had no doubt of it. He was a powerful and skilled magician, but he hadn't had a chance to cast any of the spells that might have saved his life. His unmoving body lay at the foot of the wall, blood slowly spreading out...I couldn't take my eyes off it. Francis had betrayed me—he'd betrayed everyone—but...we'd also been friends. Hadn't we? I'd always *thought* we were friends.

"I didn't mean to..." Louise was on her knees, babbling. Saline was kneeling next to her, one arm wrapped around Louise's shoulder. "I didn't mean to kill him..."

I looked at her, unsure what to say. Or do. Francis was dead. He'd betrayed me, but...he was dead. And...my head spun. I had a feeling I knew that someone had moved him, that someone had pointed him at me like a spellcaster set on *fire*...and I thought I knew who that person had been. But...that didn't matter, not now. Louise hadn't meant to kill him, yet... she might be blamed for his death. Uncle Davys would demand retribution, perhaps even a full vendetta. It could not be allowed.

"It wasn't your fault." I was fairly sure of it. Louise had every reason to hate Francis, but...she hadn't meant to kill him. "I'll swear to it, if necessary."

I looked past her, at Alana. The truce wasn't quite over, but...I met her eyes, wondering if she'd stab me in the back too. She looked back evenly, her dark gaze defying me to suggest it. She knew something of honour, I supposed. Cat had suggested otherwise, but...if nothing else, Alana was smart enough to realise that getting a reputation for breaking her word would make it impossible for anyone else to trust her. I felt a dull thud echo through the castle as I walked towards the girls, taking a moment to squeeze Louise's shoulder. She hadn't meant to kill Francis, but she might never come to terms with what she'd done.

"So." Alana nodded to me. "What now?"

"I have no idea." I thought, briefly. "We leave Louise and Saline here and go hunting..."

"Monsters," Louise whispered. "You're all monsters."

Alana gave me a puzzled look. I ignored it. There was no time to argue. We had to finish the game. "If we can eliminate the other teams..."

An idea crossed my mind. What if...?

A scream echoed from the stairwell. I jumped, lifting the sword. Bella had been down there, watching our backs. I heard something shuffling up the stairs as Alana ran forward, magic crackling over her hand. A dark shape emerged from the stairwell, inching towards us. It was one of the monsters...I cursed my oversight as it came into the light. We'd walked right past them, taking them for statues. It dragged Bella behind it, by the hair. Bella was gasping in pain, trying to hex it...

Alana blasted the monster with a powerful hex, at point-blank range. It staggered, but seemed otherwise unaffected. A moment later, it pulled Bella forward and pressed its hand against her cheek. Bella turned to stone, right in front of us. The monster let go, as soon as the transformation was complete. Bella's stone form dropped to the ground and lay there, unmoving.

I lashed out with the sword. The monster didn't move, didn't try to dodge, as the sword cut through it like a knife through butter. I stared as it was bisected, the two pieces falling to the ground. There was no blood, just an oily substance that started to dry up as soon as it was exposed to the outside air. I poked it, warily. I'd seen something like it, during advanced forging lessons with Magister Tallyman, but never in such great quantities. Magister Tallyman had said it was expensive, astonishingly so. And rare.

"A construct," I said. The monster looked like one of the training dummies, only tougher. I would have loved to take it apart, if we'd had time. Instead…"How many were there, downstairs?"

"Dozens, at least." Alana was bent over Bella's prone form, casting a handful of spells. "I can't free her."

"The Castellan said there'd be other traps," I reminded her. We'd walked right *past* them. I cursed under my breath. "And now…"

I heard a scratching sound and turned, just in time to see another monster climbing over the battlements and coming right at us. The sword guided me forward, slashing through the creature's neck and beheading it. The body kept coming…I shook my head in disbelief, then slashed the creature into a dozen pieces. Another appeared behind it, and another…I kicked one off the battlements and peered down. Dozens—perhaps *hundreds*—of the constructs were climbing towards us. I heard a scream from far below. Someone else—someone from one of the other teams—had been caught.

Alana turned and cast a blasting hex, aiming at the battlements under another creature. It fell backwards and over the battlements, just like Francis. Somehow, I doubted the fall would be enough to kill the creature. It wasn't really alive. My mind raced as I bisected another construct, trying to remember what I'd been told about them. They were practically unstoppable, as long as their spellform remained intact. They'd only gone out of fashion because they were, at base, Devices of Power…with all the vulnerabilities of every *other* Device of Power. A construct built around an *Object of Power*—or a construct that *was* an Object of Power—would be unstoppable. The Thousand-Year Empire had conquered two continents with them.

"Keep knocking them off the walls," Alana snapped. She hauled Louise to her feet and shoved her towards the stairwell. "Don't let them come up."

"They're just...*coming*," Louise stammered. She cast a spell—a blocking ward, I thought—but it didn't seem to work. Louise had never coped well with surprises and this...this was a real surprise. "What do we do?"

I forced myself to think as I heard a crashing sound from further down the stairwell. Louise was right. They were still coming, still advancing towards us...and there was nowhere to run. If we tried to go down the stairs, we'd be caught and petrified before we had a chance to escape; if we tried to go down the outer walls, we'd fall to our deaths. The magic currents were growing stronger. I had no faith in our ability to levitate ourselves down—or even put ourselves in stasis long enough to survive the fall. The currents were just too strong. I dismantled another construct as I tried to think...there *had* to be a way out.

"We can go down the stairs in a group," Alana said. "If I take the lead, you can..."

I held up a hand as a thought struck me. I pushed the sword against the floor, trying to cut a hole that would let us drop *into* the castle. But there was a surge of magic, strong enough to threaten even the sword itself. I gritted my teeth as I aimed a blasting hex at another construct, sending it plunging towards the ground. There was no way out, unless...

"Cover me." I tried to give the sword to Alana, arguing that she would be my sister-in-law soon enough, but it refused to go. "Watch my back."

"Try not to die," Alana advised. "Cat wouldn't like it."

I nodded and hurried towards the Device of Power Francis and Louise had been making. It was a siphon, as far as I could tell...no, it was more than *just* a siphon. The pieces had been left for us deliberately, a puzzle for us to put together if we wanted to win. I studied it for a long moment, working out how it went together. Francis had been wrong, I noted as I pulled out a handful of metal components. He'd taken forging classes, of course, but he'd dropped the subject as soon as he could. He'd certainly never shared my fascination. Or Cat's. It was how we'd bonded.

"Louise, come give me a hand," I ordered. "We need to put this together."

Magister Tallyman would not have been amused at how quickly I worked. Haste led to mistakes, he'd said often enough, when it didn't lead to serious injury or even death. But I had no choice. I put the Device of Power together at terrifying speed, knowing there would be no time to correct any mistakes. Francis, thankfully, had dropped the multitool on the battlements. It would have been one final irony if he'd taken it with him when he fell…

Magic crackled around us as the pieces fell into place. The constructs moved faster now, coming right at me. I lashed out with the sword, taking two apart…an instant before a third caught Saline. I heard her scream as she turned to stone, her face caught in an instant of pain…I shuddered as Louise stumbled to her feet, casting a series of spells. It wasn't enough to slow the constructs. Alana was caught by her jacket; she shrugged it off, an instant before she could be petrified too. It was slightly indecent, but…I laughed at myself. We had other concerns right now.

"Louise, cover us." I put the sword down, then motioned for Alana to take the other side as the magic grew stronger. "Alana, we have to work together…"

"Got it," Alana said. "On three…one, two, three!"

Our minds plunged into the Device of Power, into the wards running through the castle. They were weird, designed to torment people who *entered* the castle rather than simply keep them out. A chill ran down my spine as I realised just how old the castle had to be…the original lords and masters of the Post-Fall world had granted themselves total control over their mansions, with the right to do whatever they liked to anyone who entered, but that had fallen out of fashion long ago. I saw why, now. A person with such tight control of the wards could do *anything*, from peep into a maid's bedroom to ensure that *nothing* happened without his permission. It wouldn't do anything for mutual trust and respect…

My mind expanded further. I could see the constructs now, closing in on us…and the other teams. Ayesha and Zeya McDonald were still going, but they were trapped; I felt a flicker of sadistic glee as I reached through the wards, freezing them in place. Hamish Bolingbroke was already petrified, yet the rest of his team were still going. I froze them too, effortlessly, before turning my attention to the constructs. It was easy to stop them in their tracks.

I heard Louise scream. My mind jerked out of the wards before I could stop myself. A construct had caught her, an instant before I stopped them. Louise's face was caught in timeless agony…I shuddered, then turned to face Alana. She was holding her hand up, ready to cast a spell. I braced myself, ready to counter her spell. I doubted she'd give me time to grab the sword.

"Wait." I held up a hand. "Can we talk first?"

Alana stared at me, as if I'd started speaking in tongues. "What?"

"We can combine into a single team," I said, hastily. Never mind there were only two of us left, as far as I knew. "We can share the victory."

"We can't share the title," Alana pointed out. But she wasn't trying to hex me. I suspected she wasn't sure of victory, if we started fighting. She was tired…I was tired too, but I had the sword. If I grabbed it before she could stop me, I would win. "Or do you think otherwise…?"

"If we're both on the same team, as co-leaders, we would share the prize," I said. I had the feeling we'd misunderstood the Challenge, right from the start. "Right?"

"Right," Alana said, slowly. She touched her armband. "Green, perhaps?"

"Why not?" I changed my colour. She changed hers. "It's over."

I raised my voice. "It's over!"

Someone clapped, behind me. "Really?"

I jumped, spinning around. The Castellan stood there, looking bored. I couldn't understand how he'd reached us so quickly. Had he been there all along? Or…had he just been sitting on the battlements, watching and waiting for a single team to emerge victorious? He and his staff had designed the wards. He wouldn't have any trouble hiding within them if he wanted to conceal his presence.

"Yes, really." I met his eyes. "The Challenge is over. And we've won."

"Not quite." The Castellan looked back at me, evenly. "Convince me."

"We're on the same team now," Alana said. "We can't fight now."

The Castellan lifted an eyebrow. "Really? I seem to recall that *Francis* was on your team, Akin."

"I know." I felt my cheeks heat. "But we've won."

"Maybe." The Castellan studied me, thoughtfully. "Convince me. Please."

I took a moment to marshal my thoughts. "Francis was right. On the surface, the Challenge *was* a little disappointing. Capture a castle. Eliminate the other teams. He said it was just another version of Capture the Flag and he was right. There's nothing special about it. It certainly isn't a mirror of House Politics."

The Castellan didn't sound offended. "Indeed?"

"But that *wasn't* the Challenge, was it?" I leaned forward. "The *real* Challenge was to put together a team, to learn how to work together to compete. And we did it. We both put together teams, we survived...*fractures*... within the teams and, when the crunch came, we worked together against an overwhelming outside threat. *That's* the mirror of House Politics, isn't it? We had to learn to work together, not fight it out."

And Francis misunderstood completely, I thought. I knew, now, that he wouldn't have been able to win. His treachery alone would have been enough to disqualify him. *He didn't really know what he was doing.*

The Castellan smiled. "Congratulations, Akin. You win."

I blinked. "Sir...Alana and I won."

"But it was you who put the pieces together." The Castellan nodded to himself. "It was you who worked out the *true* nature of the contest. And it is *that*, Akin, which makes you Wizard Regnant."

"We should share it," I protested. I didn't dare look at Alana. "I would have failed if she hadn't worked with me. She made the choice to claim victory jointly..."

"That wasn't your choice to make," the Castellan said. "Do you understand what you are throwing away? If I told you that only one of you could be Wizard Regnant, would you give it to her?"

If, I thought. I looked down at my hands. Father would be furious, beyond words, if I simply gave up the title. I'd worked hard for it. But…I didn't want it to come at such a price. I wasn't Francis. I wasn't going to betray my future sister-in-law for a title I didn't really want. Besides…who knew? *When the rubble settles, maybe no one will care who won the contest.*

"We can share the title," I said. "I won't take it for myself."

"Nor will I." Alana crossed her arms under her breasts. "If we can't share, then…forget it."

I blinked in surprise. Really?

The Castellan looked from me to her and back again before cracking a smile. "Very well," he said. "Hail, Akin Rubén. Hail, Alana Aguirre. Wizards Regnant, from now until the end of time."

Or until someone wins the next *Challenge*, I thought.

Alana had a different concern. "What about the others?"

"They will be freed." The Castellan gave her a half-smile. "You two will, of course, have to explain what happened. They won't have been aware of anything, since they were frozen…"

His eyes met mine. "I'm sorry about your cousin," he said. "Even after…"

I nodded, too tired to feel much of anything. I'd come to terms with Francis's death later, after I'd tied up the loose ends. "Sir, I need to go back to the mansion. Please…can you let me go ahead of the news?"

"As you wish." The Castellan nodded. He didn't ask what I intended to do, for which I was grateful. Perhaps he assumed I wanted to tell Uncle Davys myself. Or perhaps give my father the good news. "And what about Harvard?"

"Give him medical attention, then…leave him." I shook my head. I didn't have time to worry about Harvard, not now. "I'll speak to him later."

Alana grinned as the Castellan hurried away. "You're giving Harvard a chance to run."

"That would solve a number of problems," I said, as I turned towards the stairwell. If Harvard fled...I wouldn't have to worry about him later. He could cross the border into Garstang and...well, who cared? He wouldn't be bothering me any longer. "Will you deal with the team? Both teams?"

"I suppose." Alana didn't look pleased. It wouldn't be easy to explain what had happened...and why. There would be people on both teams who'd feel cheated by the outcome. "But tell me...what are you going to do?"

I felt my heart clench. "I have to go back home," I said. The suspicions I'd had, earlier, had hardened into certainties. I picked up the sword and studied the blade, reading the motto woven into the metal. "I have an uncle to kill."

"Really?"

"Yeah." I could feel the sword's anticipation as I sheathed it. "Anything, for the family."

CHAPTER

THIRTY-EIGHT

It was getting dark by the time the carriage rattled through the gates and stopped in front of the main entrance.

I stood, brushing down my tattered uniform as I scrambled out of the carriage. I hadn't bothered to get a shower, let alone change into something fresh. The broadsheet boys were already hawking the news, their shouts filling the air as night slowly fell over the city. Something had already leaked. And, if it had reached the broadsheets, it had also reached the Great Houses. They all had sources within the school.

The housekeeper stared at me in surprise. "Master Akin. Your clothes…"

"Never mind." I cursed myself, a second too late, for snapping at her. "I'll change in a moment."

She looked shocked, as if I'd hit her. I promised myself that I'd do something to make it up to her as I reached out and touched the wards. They welcomed me—and the sword—home. I thanked them, silently, then asked a simple question. The wards answered, at once. I breathed a sigh of relief. Clearly, not *all* the news had leaked. I took off my muddy shoes and hurried up the stairs. There was still time to reach the library before the remainder of the news reached the mansion.

I pushed the door open and stepped inside. The wards crackled around me—they didn't like my muddy clothes—but made no attempt to push me out. Good. I wasn't in the mood to let them. I was quite prepared to draw the sword and cut my way into the library if necessary. The outer chamber was empty, a pile of books resting on the table; I glanced at them, wondered idly who was studying advanced alchemy, and strode into the reading room. Uncle Malachi was sitting on a chair, reading a broadsheet. He looked so affable that I almost thought twice. Maybe I was wrong. Maybe...

He looked up at me. His eyes went wide. I saw, just for a second, a flash of guilt and horror behind his eyes and I *knew* I was right. And yet, I was conflicted. Uncle Malachi was a kindly old man, a man who'd advised me as a child...a man who'd raised Penny, a girl who grovelled to her superiors while belittling and bullying her inferiors. In hindsight, I should have wondered more about how a seemingly kind old man had managed to raise a daughter like Penny. It said a great deal about him that he'd never even *tried* to check her behaviour as she grew up.

"Akin," Uncle Malachi said. "What can I do..."

I cut him off. "You did it."

Uncle Malachi's face became a mask. "Did what?"

"You turned Francis against me," I said. I reached for the sword and drew it as I stood facing him. The blade hummed in my hand, demanding blood. "You convinced him to turn on me."

"Indeed?" Uncle Malachi's face was still expressionless, but his eyes never left the sword. "And what makes you say that?"

He's not denying it, I thought. It would be dangerous to try to lie to me, when I was holding the sword, but...I knew, with a sick certainty, that I was right. *He'd be outraged if he was innocent.*

"You asked how I could be so naïve, back when Father told me I'd be taking the Challenge," I said. "And Francis used the same words."

Uncle Malachi paled. "Akin..."

"Francis is dead." I took a little pleasure from the look of shock that crossed his face. "He knocked me down, tied me up, cast mind-control spells on the girls and…and it wasn't enough to save him. He fell from a very great height and…he died. You sent him to his death. Why?"

My thoughts ran in circles. Uncle Malachi *had* to be the person who'd encouraged Francis to take the plunge. Uncle Davys knew better, not after… after whatever had happened between him and his brother. And yet, why? Uncle Malachi didn't benefit, as far as I could tell. Or did he? If Francis became Heir Primus…I shook my head. Francis would have had a lot of hard questions to answer before he was anointed Heir Primus. I didn't think he'd be able to come up with satisfactory answers. And he'd never *wanted* to be Heir Primus. He'd told me that and…and I still thought it was true. He could have done a great deal more to unseat me if he'd wanted the job for himself.

Uncle Malachi's face went very hard. "Don't speak of things you don't understand, boy."

I glared at him. "My father gave you everything. A wife, a place in the family, a position of power…"

His face flushed. "Shows how little *you* know, boy."

I stared, unable to reconcile the person I was seeing—now—with the kindly old uncle I'd loved. Uncle Malachi was…what *was* he? This sneering person wasn't my uncle. I wondered, just for a second, if he really *wasn't* my uncle. It wasn't impossible to fool the house wards, just very difficult. Someone could have taken his place and…I shook my head, mentally. It would be impossible to keep the deception going for very long. Too many people knew Uncle Malachi for an imposter to take his place indefinitely.

"Explain it to me," I ordered. I pointed the sword at him and watched as he flinched, pressing his back into the chair. "Why?"

"I did *everything* for your father," Uncle Malachi hissed. "*Everything.* And what was my reward?"

I blinked. "You're part of the family…"

"Hardly." Uncle Malachi snorted. "You think Petal cares *that* much for me? The match was arranged and…she didn't want me. She made her opinion quite clear, on our wedding night…oh, have I shocked you? Poor little boy."

I flushed. "You had a daughter."

"Our duty," Uncle Malachi shrugged. "And afterwards…she went off to the estate, leaving the daughter with me."

"And you did *such* a good job of raising her." I sneered. "I caught her bullying firsties, Uncle. Common-born kids who couldn't defend themselves, kids who couldn't fight back…funny how she didn't pick on any *aristocrats*."

"Quite." Uncle Malachi glared at me. "You want to know the truth? Can you handle the truth?"

He went on before I could think of an answer. "You know where I was born? Water Shallot! The very edge of Water Shallot, true, but Water Shallot nonetheless. Daddy was a merchant, permanently in debt to the loan sharks…no loans from the bank for us! I grew up without two pennies to rub together. If I hadn't won a scholarship, I would never have gone to Jude's. My father couldn't have afforded it."

I stared at him. "You grew up in Water Shallot?"

Uncle Malachi kept speaking, ignoring me. "I went to school and I met kids who'd never been hungry, kids who were protected and cosseted by society…kids like your father and uncle. They were the best of friends back then, allies even though they were expected to be rivals. I…attached myself to them. I did everything: I fetched and carried, helped with their homework, snuck food and drink out of the dining hall after hours, clapped and laughed when they bullied other kids…I even purchased alcohol and brought it into the school. I did everything, no matter how humiliating, because I wanted…I wanted them to find me indispensable. I wanted them to take me with them when they left school."

He glared at the floor. "Oh, there were people who hated me, of course. They called me an arse-licker and all sorts of other names, but…I told myself it didn't matter. I would have done anything, if it kept me from having to go back to Water Shallot. I studied hard, I learnt how to comport myself in society and pretend that I'd never even *heard* of Water Shallot. I certainly had no interest in *slumming*, no interest in dropping hints about roguish dealings in the rough side of town. They never let me forget, of course. Your father treated me like dirt, even when I was serving him. You know what he used to call me?"

I remembered. "Piglet."

"Oh, how we laughed." Uncle Malachi shook his head. "And their reward? A wife who doesn't love me, a place in society that can be yanked away at any moment and…and what? I have nothing."

"I loved you," I said, flatly. I met his eyes, daring him to look away. "And you set Francis up against me?"

Uncle Malachi laughed, humourlessly. "Your father has enemies, boy. People in the family who think he shouldn't be lording it over them. People who look at your betrothal and think he's selling the family out to its enemies. People who hate him because of what he *did* to them, when he was a child. And when it dawned on me that he had enemies…oh, it was easy to offer them my services. What loyalty did I owe your father?"

"He lifted you out of the gutter," I said. "Didn't he?"

"Your father was a bullying *bastard!*" The flash of anger on his face surprised me. "And when he had no one else to bully, he bullied me. I spent half my time finding new victims for him because when I didn't it was *me* who got stuck to the ceiling or turned into a frog or forced to humiliate myself for his amusement. And his uncle was even *worse*. Do you know how easy it was to push him into betraying his brother, just for a title he didn't really want?"

"Like Francis." I was reeling inside. I'd known my father was strict—I still cringed at the memory of the lecture he'd given me for stealing a book, unaware that it was Isabella who'd *actually* stolen the book—but I'd never thought of him as a bully. He didn't abuse the servants or…or anything. "You did all this for revenge?"

"And a position of power for myself," Uncle Malachi said. "You lucky brat, born with a silver spoon in your mouth...you can't understand what it's like to be powerless."

I remembered lying on the ground, my hands and feet tied and my magic gone and shuddered. I *could* understand, better than I cared to admit. And yet...maybe not. I might be stripped of my position as Heir Primus—even now, even after winning the Challenge—but I wouldn't be kicked out of the family. I'd spend the rest of my days in the forgery, developing my skills... it would almost be a dream come true. But Uncle Malachi? He would go straight back to the gutter.

"Your sister committed treason and *she* was merely exiled," Uncle Malachi said. It was almost as if he had read my thoughts. "But me? I can be stripped of everything I have at any moment."

"I don't know what Father did to you," I said. "But whatever it was, it doesn't justify everything *you* did."

Uncle Malachi shrugged. "Winners write the history books, young man. You would be astonished—and horrified—by how much is never written down, simply because the people in power don't *want* it remembered. And you know..."

I saw a flash of horror cross his face. "Everything I did proved worthless in the end. And everything I was given...it can be taken away."

"You said." I met his eyes. "Francis is dead."

"Yes." Uncle Malachi smiled, coldly. "It serves Davys right. He was always the worst of the pair. I could tell you stories, you know. Things he did, even as a young adult. *He* never learnt restraint. He would go to the brothels and trash women and...and do things you probably never considered possible. Hah. I always figured the family council would disinherit him if your father died without issue. He might even have ensured that your parents never had more children."

I stared at him. "Really?"

"It's possible." Uncle Malachi grinned, humourlessly. "I wouldn't put it past him."

I let out a long breath. How many monsters *were* there in High Society? Stregheria Aguirre, Saline's uncle...and now two of *my* uncles? Were we *all* related to monsters? I was starting to think that Louise had a point, when she said we were all monsters. But...I couldn't believe that Uncle Davys had cursed my parents after Isabella and I were born. Father would never have let him get away with it. Unless...Father had never realised what he'd done. It was possible...

Or he might be trying to provoke you into doing something stupid, I reminded myself, savagely. *Remain focused on him.*

A thought crossed my mind. "Uncle...years ago, Isabella borrowed—*stole*—a book from Father's private collection. I never understood how she managed to get into the cabinet without being caught by the wards. Did *you* give it to her?"

Uncle Malachi's face darkened. "I encouraged her, just a little."

I felt a flash of raw anger. "What *were* you thinking?"

"That I wanted to make your father *pay*." Uncle Malachi rose. I sensed magic crackling around him. "And now, *you* are going to let me walk out of the door and leave the manor."

I moved to block his way. "Why should I do that?"

"Because I *know* things," Uncle Malachi said. "Things you and your family—the *inner* family—cannot afford to have discussed in public. Things that will make you pariahs in High Society, things that will make Lady Caitlyn's family throw up their hands in horror and cancel the betrothal. You will let me go, in exchange for my silence."

He shrugged. "You can keep Penny."

I stared at him. "You..."

It was impossible to put my feelings into words. I had little love for Penny, after everything she'd done, but to have her father simply abandon her...Isabella had committed treason, yet *my* father hadn't abandoned her.

I clung to the thought as I raised the sword, ready to cut him down if he made one false move. Whatever my father had been in the past, he wasn't that person now. A man like the teenager Uncle Malachi had described wouldn't have hesitated to throw his daughter to the wolves. It was Uncle Malachi who'd never grown up.

He's old enough to be my father and he's still trapped in the teenage mindset, I thought, my emotions churning. He'd learnt to hide his true thoughts and feelings very early. I shuddered, wondering what would have become of Kate if I hadn't caught Penny bullying her. Would *she* have turned into a monster too? *I can't let him go.*

The sword hummed, demanding blood. I told it *no*. Uncle Malachi had to answer for his crimes. His allies had to be identified and…sent into exile. Or kicked out onto the streets to starve. It would be only fitting, even though…I felt an odd flicker of sadistic amusement as I realised Uncle Malachi had trapped himself. He might have sought revenge on my father, and he might even have succeeded, but it wouldn't have left him in a better position. His backers, whoever they were, would have no qualms about letting him take the fall. They might even kill him to bury their tracks…

"Sit down," I ordered. "You're going to answer some questions for…"

Uncle Malachi snapped a word. The books flew off the shelves and launched themselves at me. I ducked back, hastily casting a shield charm to protect myself. Francis had forced me to practice, time and time again, until I could cast the charm in less than a second. I hoped that, wherever he was, he was having a laugh at Uncle Malachi's expense. He'd done *something* to help catch the villain before he'd met his doom.

I lunged forward, the sword lashing out. It wanted to cut through Uncle Malachi's head—it sliced through his protective wards as though they weren't there—but I managed, somehow, to whack him with the side of the blade. He grunted, staggered to one side and collapsed to the floor. I took no chances and stunned him, again and again. He could be faking it. I had no doubt he'd *learnt* to fake pain and unconsciousness—even death—when he'd been a student. An aptitude for cringing and begging had probably come in handy, if half of what he'd done me was true.

The sword hummed. I returned it to the scabbard, then checked Uncle Malachi's pulse. It was steady, but...I shook my head. He'd have the very best of care until he awoke, whereupon he'd be questioned and then...I had no idea what my father would do. I doubted it would be anything pleasant. Uncle Malachi was an adult. He knew the consequences for treason. Or, at least, the consequences for being *caught*.

I heard the door open behind me. "Akin," Father said. His voice was very tired, as if he'd gone without sleep for far too long. "Well done."

"How much of that did you hear?" I asked, as I turned. Father looked... old. "Were you listening?"

"Enough." Father cast a spell over Uncle Malachi's body, then nodded to me. "I think we should have the rest of the discussion in my office."

"Yes, Father." I cleared my throat. "And what about him?"

"We'll take care of him." Father's voice was very flat. It suggested he was in no mood to brook defiance. "Now, *come*."

CHAPTER
THIRTY-NINE

F ather's office had changed.

I looked around, thoughtfully, but it was hard to tell *how* it had changed. The room seemed…*smaller*, somehow: otherwise, there weren't any changes as far as I could tell. And yet…it dawned on me, slowly, that I'd been a very different person, the last time I'd been inside the office. I'd been a boy, back then. Now, I was a man. I looked down at myself and smiled as I sat on the armchair. My body hadn't changed over the last few months, but…I'd grown out of childish attitudes. I was no longer *merely* my father's son.

"I heard the reports from Jude's." Father sat and poured us both some tea. "Francis's body has been recovered and is being held there, until we can decide what to do with it."

"Bury him with his ancestors," I said. "He *was* family, wasn't he?"

"Yes." Father passed me a cup of tea. "What happened? Tell me everything."

He'd given me the good china, I noted. The *adult* china. The cup was so delicate that the slightest mistake could break the handle. I handled it gingerly, taking a sip…it tasted wonderful. Father had never made me tea before, not as far as I could remember. It was yet another sign that I was an adult, that we were—almost—equals. I felt an odd little pang as I launched into the story. Uncle Malachi might have the last laugh, after all. I would never be able to look at my father in the same way again.

Father listened, saying nothing, as I told him everything. *Almost* everything. I left out some of the details—I wasn't going to mention Isabella's involvement, or how Ayesha McDonald had turned me into a frog and left me in the girls' locker room—but I told him almost everything else. He didn't ask any awkward questions as I outlined how I'd put the team together, how we'd embarked on our adventure, how we'd been betrayed...and how Alana and I had worked together long enough to understand what was *really* going on. Father didn't condemn me for sharing the victory. Indeed, I rather thought he was *pleased*.

"You won," Father said, when I had finished. "Or, at least, you shared the victory. Yes. We can spin that to our advantage."

"Yes, Father." I found it hard to care. "What about...What about Francis?"

Father sighed. "I'll have to discuss that with Davys," he said. "It won't be easy to cover it up, not after...everything."

I met his eyes. "Wouldn't it be better to tell everyone the truth?"

"Perhaps." Father looked back at me, evenly. "Not everyone will keep their silence. But...we don't need another scandal, not now. Let them remember him fondly, if they wish."

"Perhaps," I echoed. I looked down at my hands. "I don't know how to feel about it."

"I understand." Father rested a hand on my shoulder, just for a second. "He was family. He shouldn't have betrayed you. You should hate him for that, but there are so many good memories that you find it hard to hate. And that isn't a bad thing."

"Really?" I looked up. "Father, how did Malcolm Sweeny die?"

Father looked pained. "Back then, there were four of us. Davys, Malcolm, Malachi and myself. We thought we were the very best of friends."

"Uncle Malachi had a different opinion," I said, tartly.

"I know." Father met my eyes. "I never realised…I suppose I saw what I wanted to see, like so many others."

He shook his head, slowly. "We took the Challenge, the four of us. No one else needed, we thought. I didn't understand the true nature of the Challenge. You"—he gave me a proud look—"surpassed me there."

I beamed, feeling almost like a child again. I wanted my father to be proud of me. And now…I basked, even though I also felt a little guilty. I wanted him to be proud of Isabella too.

"My father—your grandfather—thought that I would prove myself, if I won the Challenge. I didn't realise that Davys was jealous, not then. I didn't realise that *he* thought *he* should be Heir Primus. And when we went onto the field, he betrayed me. Like father, like son…I suppose. Perhaps I should have warned you, but…"

He shook his head. "Malcolm got in the middle, between us. I don't know who fired the curse that actually killed him. It was an accident, I'm sure. Malcolm was the best of us, the one who would always try to tell us… well, he tried. We never listened. Malachi stood to one side and watched as we fought. Afterwards…the whole affair was covered up. Malcolm's death was officially classed as an accident. It was, I think. Neither Davys nor I *wanted* to kill him."

I shuddered. "And it was all covered up?"

"Yes." Father studied me for a long moment. "Grandfather wasn't happy. He took off his belt and ordered me to bend over for a thrashing, then told me I'd have to learn to live with what I'd done. I might not have fired the curse that *killed* him, but…his death was partly my fault. Even if no one else knew about it, I did. And it hung over me until…"

"You sent me to take the Challenge," I finished.

"Yes," Father said. "Oh, I was relieved when we had a son *and* a daughter instead of two sons. I didn't want you and your brother to fight it out for the title, not after…Davys was my friend, I thought. I hated to lose the closeness we'd once shared. I thought Isabella and you could be allies without ever having to come to blows."

"And she resented it," I said. "Father, she would have made a better Heir Primus."

"Would she?" Father lifted his eyebrow. "It was you, not her, who solved the Challenge. It was you, not her, who befriended people who could help. And it was you, not her, who actually *allied* with an enemy—a rival, I suppose—to win. Isabella...takes too much after me. It's you who takes after your mother. She was always the one who thought in terms of making friends, rather than trying to win all the time."

"It wasn't fair, though," I argued. "She should have had a fair shot at the title."

"I know," Father said. "I might even agree with you. But tradition cannot be gainsaid so easily."

"Father..."

Father held up his hand. "I will do what I can, as always," he said. A faint smile ghosted across his lips. "And, thanks to you, I may finally have the leverage to bring our enemies to heel."

"Uncle Malachi's backers," I said. "Father...what will you *do* to him?"

"It depends." Father looked pensive. "It never crossed my mind, you know, that he might not see things in the same light as I. I never thought that...he might fear me as much as he loved me. But then...I was a little monster back then. If I had the time again, things would be different."

"You can't," I said, quietly.

Father nodded. "We can only go onwards. And if Malachi is cooperative, if he names his backers and helps me gather evidence against them, I won't be *too* rough. Perhaps. Davys will want blood, of course. Francis is dead and he'll want revenge. Maybe we'll just send him back to the gutter, as he feared."

"It isn't fair," I mumbled.

"The world isn't fair." Father met my eyes. "And a lack of fairness doesn't justify treason, attempted murder and *actual* murder."

"No, Father," I agreed.

Father sighed. "I'll have to discuss the matter with Petal, too. She may have something to say about how Malachi should be treated. And Penny. You handled that well, although you could have done it better. No one would have blamed you if you'd hexed her into next week."

"Her victims needed to see justice done." I shifted, uncomfortably. "I'm not sorry."

"You're a better person than I was, at your age." Father reached into his pocket and produced a small box. "I have something for you."

The words slipped out before I could stop them. "You're going to propose?"

Father gave me a long look. "If only your generation was half as funny as you think you are," he said, crossly. "It's a very different kind of ring."

He opened the box, revealing a silver signet ring. I stared, feeling—just for a moment—as if I wasn't ready. The family crest shone, the magic embedded within the sigil responding to my father's presence. It was more than just a ring, I knew. It was a seal, something I could use to verify my letters and…

It struck me, all of a sudden, what was happening. What Father intended to do.

"I am proud of you, son." Father's voice was tightly controlled. "And it gives me great pleasure"—he held out the box—"to welcome you to adulthood."

I stared, my stomach churning. Adulthood…if I took the ring, I would be a legal adult, with all the rights and responsibilities of any young blade. I could do anything any other adult could, from drinking alcohol and quaffing pleasure potions to…getting married. It wouldn't be long, I knew with a sickening certainty, before Cat was declared an adult too. She and her sisters were *my* age. Traditionally, girls were declared adults in early summer… only a few short months away.

And then we'd be expected to get married, I thought, numbly. I wanted it and yet…I was nervous. How did *she* feel about it? I thought she wanted it too, but…I didn't know. Our families would not be amused if we didn't get married. *What will they say—or do—if we refuse?*

I took the ring and rested it on my palm, as I'd been taught. The glow grew a little brighter as the ring bonded to me, then settled. I placed it on my finger, feeling the charmed band tighten until it was firmly in place. I felt…I was an adult now, for better or worse. I wasn't sure *how* I felt. My father and I would never be equals, but…right now, we were on a more even footing than parent and child. I could talk back to him if I wanted.

"It's never easy to find out that your parents don't have all the answers," Father said, quietly. "You'll understand, when you're a father yourself."

I admired the ring for a long moment, then looked at him. "What about Isabella?"

"I don't know." Father sighed. "She is old enough to be declared an adult, now. I had always intended to declare her an adult after she finished school. Now…I don't know. I don't think she can have a Season, not now. And even if she did, who would want to dance with her? Or marry her? It wouldn't be easy to find someone suitable."

"Yes, Father." I found it hard to imagine anyone from High Society wanting to marry my sister, after what she'd done. Perhaps Isabella would be better off staying well away from Shallot. She'd be shunned if she came home, even if she was officially forgiven. "But it just doesn't seem fair."

"Like I told you," Father said patiently, "the world is not fair."

He shrugged. "There's a lot I have to tell you, secrets passed down from fathers to sons…we'll have that discussion later, when you come home for the holidays. And then…we'll plan your wedding."

"Not yet, Father." I met his eyes. "Let me graduate first."

"Of course," Father said. "But your mother would *love* a summer wedding."

"Cat might not," I pointed out. It would be too early. "She might want a Season."

"Strange." Father shrugged. "Who can she dance with, but you?"

"She might want it," I said. "And it isn't as if she could marry *everyone* she danced with."

"No," Father agreed. "But how many girls are actually betrothed before they reach adulthood?"

He stood. "We'll discuss it later," he said. "There are a lot of things we have to discuss. Until then…you'd better get back to school."

I glanced at the clock. It was nearly nine. Where had the time gone?

"Yes, Father." I stood too. "And thank you."

"Thank *you*," Father said. He cocked his head, communing with the wards. "I'll have the carriage brought 'round for you."

He held out his hand. I shook it, awkwardly, then turned and made my way out of the office and down the stairs. The housekeeper gave me a worried look as I passed, but said nothing. I knew she'd be reporting to Mother…I shrugged, inwardly, as I hurried down the steps and clambered into the carriage. My bones ached as I sat down, the carriage rattling to life a moment later. It had been a very long day.

I lay back and closed my eyes, trying to focus my mind. I needed a shower—no, I needed a bath. And then…I wondered, absently, how many classes I was going to miss. The Castellan had made it clear that the Challenge could go on for *days*. I'd missed one day, at least, and I'd probably miss another day tomorrow…I dismissed the thought, resisting the urge to let the carriage's gentle motions rock me to sleep. I had to get back to my room and shower before I even *thought* about going to bed. If I tried to sleep in my clothes…

The carriage rattled to a halt. I glanced up as the coachman opened the door, half-convinced I'd been dozing. I honestly wasn't sure if I'd fallen asleep or not. I put the thought to one side and stumbled out, almost falling to the ground as I picked my way down the steps. The school entrance looked warm and welcoming. I drew on my magic, just enough to keep me awake as I made my way into the entrance hall.

The scent of rotten eggs greeted me. I stared. Penny was trapped within the stocks, her uniform stained with food, drink and a handful of potions. A nasty mark on her face suggested that some of her tormenters had been hurling something a little harder than rotting eggs.

She glared at me. "Come to gloat?"

I felt a stab of pity, despite everything. Penny's life was about to be turned upside down...again. She might never see her father again. Her mother...I wondered, grimly, what Aunt Petal *really* thought of her daughter. Uncle Malachi had claimed that Aunt Petal had practically disowned the girl. Given how little time she spent in the mansion, I was inclined to believe it.

"No," I said. Penny deserved punishment, but this...this was public humiliation. It was too much. I eyed the piles of rotting food in disgust, wondering just how many enemies Penny had actually made. The stocks were charmed, I'd been told. Anyone unlucky enough to be put in them wouldn't be able to see who was throwing things at them. And that was just encouraging people to bully the bully. "I..."

I muttered a handful of charms, drawing on the last of my magic to clear up the mess. It wasn't much, but it would have to do. Besides, it was nearly ten. Penny would be sent to bed soon enough, with the rest of the fourth years. She was going to hate it. She'd never be a *real* upperclassman, not again. Her former friends and dormmates wouldn't hesitate to rub the point in as often as they could.

Penny gave me an odd look. "What are you doing?"

"Francis is dead," I said, as I sat next to her. "He died out there, on the field."

"No." Penny sounded shocked. "He can't be dead."

"I saw him die," I told her. It was hard, so hard, to keep the horror out of my voice. "They'll be burying him, soon enough."

Penny started to cry, great heaving sobs that shook me to the core. I'd never realised she was *that* close to Francis...they'd been friends, I'd thought, but there had been two years between them. They certainly couldn't have associated at school. People would have talked. But...she was crying. I patted her head, awkwardly, and stood, muttering a charm to get rid of the smell. Penny deserved punishment, but putting her in the stocks was wrong. I'd have to do something about that, when I became Patriarch. There would be time for a little political wrangling then...

Perhaps, I told myself. *And perhaps, when I reach that age, I will have other concerns.*

"I'll see you tomorrow," I promised. I wasn't sure why I said that, but I did. Penny had had a shock. Perhaps I could reach out to her now, to help her to get better. It wouldn't be easy, but...I didn't want Uncle Malachi to claim another wasted life. "And Penny..."

Penny looked up. "What?"

"You're one of the family," I said, gently. "Don't forget it."

She gave me an odd look. She didn't understand. I couldn't tell her, not then. Father would have to tell her *something*, when the time came. And then...who knew what would happen?

"Don't forget it," I repeated. I met and held her eyes, trying to make her understand that I was sincere. "Goodnight."

I nodded to her, then headed off to my room.

CHAPTER

FORTY

The awards ceremony was a subdued affair.

Alana and I sat on stage as the Castellan gave a long speech, then stood long enough to be jointly crowned Wizard Regnant. It felt meaningless to me, even though the entire school cheered as we held the talisman in the air. I understood, at that moment, why Francis had been so enamoured of the sporting life. It felt good to be cheered, to hear the school celebrate and know that it was celebrating *you*, but...Francis was dead. He'd ruined his own life—before losing it—just because he'd wanted to win. Sooner or later, I knew, the cheers would have stopped. And what would he have done then, in a desperate bid to win the adulation of the crowds?

The Castellan said nothing about that as he spoke a few short words for Francis, neatly glossing over everything he'd done and giving the very distinct impression—without ever quite saying it—that Francis's death had been a tragic accident. It had been an accident, of course, but...the Castellan never mentioned his treachery. Or Uncle Malachi. I had no idea what was happening, back home. Father had told me, the one time I'd asked after returning to school, to stay there and wait. It was better that I wasn't directly involved.

So I can't be blamed, if things go wrong, I thought. *He's only looking out for me.*

I sighed, inwardly, as the ceremony finally came to an end. I stood and headed back to my room, ignoring Alana's hint that I should join the post-ceremony party. I didn't feel like partying, not after everything that had happened. Besides, I had letters to write. Isabella had replied to my earlier message, telling me not to worry about the destroyed spellbreaker. *That* had puzzled me. Reading between the lines, I had the oddest sense that she was *relieved* the spellbreaker had been destroyed. She'd been quite insistent that I didn't ask Cat for a replacement.

The school felt empty as I walked up the stairs, although I knew it was an illusion. Classes had been cancelled, just for the day. The lowerclassmen would be running wild, while the upperclassmen celebrated the victory. I wondered, absently, what the teachers were doing...apart from putting a cover story firmly in place. The Castellan had definitely covered everything up, as neatly as possible. In a year, very few people at the school would know the truth.

And no one wants to admit it, I thought, as I stepped into my office and closed the door behind me. *The whole story will be buried in the archives.*

I sat at my desk and looked down at the letter, without ever quite *seeing* the words. My mind was elsewhere. Francis had betrayed me, but he'd been manipulated...Uncle Malachi must have found it easy, after practicing on Francis's father and uncle. And...I wished, bitterly, that I'd never heard of the Challenge, let alone accepted it. The family ring felt heavy, as if my hand were weighed down with responsibility. It was a responsibility, I understood now. I didn't really want it. I wasn't sure why Uncle Malachi *had*.

There was a knock on the door. I looked up, surprised. Who would come to see me *now*, of all times? "Come!"

The door opened. Louise stepped into the room.

I stood. "How are you feeling?"

"I've been better." Louise's hand was shaking as she pushed the door closed. "The healers said it would take some time before I recovered."

"I'm sorry to hear that," I said, as I pointed her towards the sofa. "I didn't realise that he'd…"

"No, you didn't." Louise's voice was hard. She clasped her hands together, seemingly reluctant to take the seat I offered her. "But you knew he wasn't a good person, didn't you?"

I swallowed, hard. "I knew he wasn't perfect…"

Louise snorted. "It's been a week," she said. "A week, and I *still* have nightmares about what he made me do. About what he *could* have made me do. He…he *enslaved* me."

"I understand." I hadn't been allowed to see the medical reports, but I had a fair idea of what charms Francis had used to control the girls. The longer they remained in place, the harder it was to shake off the after-effects. "And I…"

"No, you don't." Louise met my eyes. "You kicked him off the team. You should have *kept* him off the team, even though you thought you *needed* him. He was an arrogant bully with wandering hands and…and you left him alone, because he was *family*. Because he was an aristocrat. And it never crossed your mind that he might betray you."

"I wish it had." I was too tired to take offense at her words. Besides, she was right. If Francis hadn't been my cousin, I wouldn't have taken him back. "I'm sorry."

"Yeah. I know." Louise didn't look away. "You know what they say about lying down with dogs? You get fleas. And *you* lay down with a dog…you let him walk all over you, because he was your cousin and you thought you needed him. You ignored the warning signs…"

"I know." I felt a hot flash of anger. "Is there anything you can say to me that I haven't already said to myself?"

Louise rested her hands on her hips. "Just this," she said. "Your system is corrupt and evil and ultimately destructive to everyone, including you. You"—she bit off a word she might have gotten in real trouble for saying—"*aristocrats* are either monsters, like your cousin, or enablers. Like you. You let him get away with far too much, because he was your cousin and an aristocrat and…"

She glared. "You made me a promise. Are you going to keep it?"

It was on the tip of my tongue to say *no*. But I couldn't. I didn't want to break my word, not even to her. I didn't want to be known as an oathbreaker. It was one step towards becoming a warlock.

"Yes." I looked back at her, as evenly as I could. "I'll teach you how to blend into High Society."

"Good," Louise said. "Because I'm going to *use* that knowledge to tear it down."

I resisted the urge to laugh, barely. "You won't find that easy."

"No." Louise didn't sound like she was joking. "But it has to be done."

She relaxed, slightly. "What are you going to do about Saline? And her uncle?"

"I promised her my help," I said. "And I will…if she wants it. She may want to deal with him herself."

"Another evil monster," Louise said. "How many are there?"

More than you know, I thought. I wasn't going to discuss Uncle Malachi with her. *Every family has its own monster.*

She looked down at the floor, her expression sobering. "I'm sorry for slapping you," she said. "I mean…I'm not sorry. You deserved it. But… Saline pointed out that I shouldn't have done it."

"Yeah." I shrugged, expressively. I probably *had* deserved it, although not for the reasons she thought. "Right now, it's a very minor matter."

"Hah." Louise let out an odd little giggle. "I *will* reform the system, Akin. Or bring it crashing down."

She turned and walked away before I could say a word. I watched her opening the door, my thoughts churning. She couldn't do any real damage, could she? I doubted it. Shallot had survived for nearly a thousand years. A few more decades and the city would have lasted longer than the

Thousand-Year Empire itself. Louise couldn't do any real harm. Who knew? Perhaps she might even push us into making a few needed reforms.

Kate was standing outside the door, looking nervous. She flushed as soon as she saw me, seemingly torn between entering my office and running for her life. I was surprised she'd even *come* to my office, knowing that any passing upperclassman could give her lines for walking through upperclassmen territory. And she knew, better than most, just how many upperclassmen could abuse their power.

"Come in," I called. "Please."

"Thank you," Kate mumbled. "I just wanted to…"

"Come on in and close the door," I said. "Please."

Kate entered, her face reddening. "Sir," she said, as she closed the door. "I just wanted to say thank you."

"You're welcome," I said, dryly. "It was my duty."

"I…" Kate swallowed hard, then started again. "I wanted to ask, though. Why did you help her? I mean…"

I kept my face impassive, somehow. Someone must have seen me help Penny. Someone…or maybe she'd told her escorts, when they arrived to take her to her new dorm. Penny shouldn't have been able to work magic, not while she'd been in the stocks. She would have had to tell them something. Besides, it wasn't as if anyone *else* would have helped her. Any friends she had would have deserted her, as soon as they realised she'd fallen from grace. Isabella's friends had done the same. None of them had stood by her.

"Penny deserves punishment." I wasn't sure why I was answering the question. I could have told her not to be cheeky and sent her away with a flea in her ear—and lines to write—but instead, I was trying to answer. "But there are limits. Letting everyone throw rotten food at her is…it's wrong. It just turns people into bullies."

I wondered, suddenly, if Kate had been throwing rotting eggs herself. She certainly had better cause than most. But…I didn't want to know. Who knew what she might say, if I asked?

"What's going to happen to her now?" Kate leaned forward. "I mean... will she be reinstated?"

"No." I was sure of that, if nothing else. "You won't have to put up with her again. No one will. And no one can blame you for snitching."

Kate looked relieved. "Thank you."

I nodded in understanding. "Kate..."

"Yes, sir?"

"Penny wasn't very good to you," I said. It was the understatement of the century. "And I feel a certain obligation, because she is a member of my family, to make it up to you. If you need a favour, at some point in your life, you can ask. I'll do what I can."

Kate reddened. "What can you give me?"

"Patronage, perhaps." I frowned. Kate was a little young for a formal offer of patronage, but...at least she'd know the offer was on the table. "If you want an apprenticeship in later life, you can ask and I'll see what I can arrange. Or...there are plenty of possibilities. I suggest you wait and *think*, carefully, about what you want. It is a very rare coin indeed."

"Yes, sir." Kate looked conflicted. "I...I threw eggs at her. I did. I..."

I held up a hand. "Don't do it again," I told her. "I understand. Yes, I understand. But you could turn into a bully yourself..."

"It feels like she's gotten away with it," Kate said, slowly. "She wasn't even *covered* in muck."

I was tempted to ask just where Kate had grown up, but I resisted. Instead, I leaned forward.

"She hasn't gotten away with anything," I told her. "She'll be taken out of the stocks, eventually, but no one will forget. She won't ever wield power again. She won't ever be trusted, not really...to someone like her, that is the worst of punishments. I had an old aunt who muttered, angrily, every time she was passed over for a position of power. And you know why she was never offered the chance to show what she could do? Everyone already *knew* she'd abuse her power, if she was given a chance."

I shrugged. "She'll marry, perhaps. She'll probably build a life outside the city, where no one knows what she did…"

My thoughts darkened. I could be wrong. Who knew *what* would happen to Penny, once Father had finished with Uncle Malachi? I wasn't sure what I wanted to happen.

I put that aside. "You, in the meantime, will have a chance to build a career of your own," I added. "And when the time comes, ask me for a favour."

"I don't feel guilty," Kate said. "Is that wrong?"

"Perhaps." I remembered my father's words and shivered. "Sometimes, we just have to learn to live with what we've done."

I pointed to the door. "Go enjoy the rest of the day," I ordered. "Classes will restart tomorrow."

Kate dropped a curtsey—she'd been practicing, I noted—and practically skipped out the door. I watched her go, wondering—pointlessly—if I'd ever been so young. Of course I had, six years ago. It felt like an eternity. Kate didn't look *that* much like Isabella, not now. But *that* was obvious. They were very different people.

I smiled as I started to turn my attention back to the letter. Kate would be fine, probably. She had my promise of help, when she needed it. Perhaps I'd ask someone to keep an eye on her, although I had no idea who. And besides, asking someone to watch out for her might weaken her, in the long run. Kate had to learn to stand on her own two feet. It wasn't going to be easy. She really needed more friends in her year. Now that Penny was gone, maybe she'd find them.

There was another tap at the door. I looked up, irritated. "Come!"

Rose stuck her head into the room. "I've brought you a guest," she said. "Can she come in?"

I felt a surge of desperate hope, mingled with fear. "Yes…"

Rose stepped to one side, allowing Cat to enter. She looked stunning, clad in a long white dress that contrasted neatly with her dark skin. Her braids hung down, a reminder that she wasn't—yet—an adult. I felt myself flush as I stood, wondering if she was jealous. But then, neither of her sisters had been declared adults yet either. Traditionally, they'd have to wait until summer. Girls were rarely declared adults out of season.

"Akin." Cat gave me a warm smile. "Alana told me everything. Congratulations."

"Thanks." I motioned her to the sofa. Rose sat next to her, looking mischievous. "Do I want to know *what* she told you?"

Cat grinned. "She said you two managed to work together to win," she said. "And it was you who understood the *real* game."

"That's true." I was mildly surprised Alana had told the truth, although I suppose I shouldn't have been. She was a better person, these days, than anyone had ever given her credit for. "But Francis died..."

"I'm sorry to hear that," Cat said. It was hard to tell if she meant it. "Will your family hold a public funeral?"

"I suppose so, even though he betrayed us." I essayed a dark joke. "I'm starting to think it runs in the family."

"Every family has its own little secret," Cat said. "Some are just more serious than others."

"Yeah." I met her eyes. "It's been a hard few months."

Cat looked back at me. "Come join me in the Workshop."

I almost laughed, even though she sounded earnest. "I'd love to. But I don't think our families would like that, not...not now."

"No," Cat agreed. "But does it matter how well you do on your exams?"

"It matters to my family," I said, reluctantly. I would have loved to just walk away from school and join her, even though we would be chaperoned every waking moment...at least until we got married. "And we don't want too many people looking at us."

"We have them looking at us already." Cat looked disappointed. "Do you know Alana's already been sending out dance cards?"

I blinked. "Already?"

"Yeah." Cat shared a glance with Rose. "Dad's been talking about our Season…well, Alana and Bella's, at least. He wasn't sure about mine."

"Because we're betrothed," I asked, "or because they want to… delay matters?"

"A little of both, I think." Cat met my eyes. "I'll just be dancing with you, I think."

"How terrible," Rose said, dryly.

I shot her a rude gesture, then looked at Cat. "There's a lot I have to tell you," I said. "Do we have time?"

"A few hours, I think." Cat shrugged. "As long as Rose is with us, no one is going to say anything."

I took a breath, then started to talk. I told her about Francis, about Penny, about Ayesha McDonald and Saline. Cat listened, her face darkening slightly when I mentioned that Saline had kissed me. I braced myself, unsure what to expect. If she chose to be angry…

"She put you in the girls' locker room?" It took me a moment to realise Cat was talking about Ayesha, not Saline. "I never knew she was *mad*."

"I don't know," I said. In hindsight…had Francis trashed our lair? It was possible. "I got out of it before I could be caught."

"Or see anything," Rose said.

"Yeah. Still…" Cat looked at me. "Don't do that again, okay? Or let someone else kiss you."

"I won't," I promised. "I never even knew she liked me…"

Cat and Rose exchanged glances. "Boys never notice anything," Rose said, dryly. "You do have admirers."

"I don't think you should have told me that," I said. My father had pointed out, once, that being Heir Primus would make me irresistibly attractive. I could be as ugly as one of the constructs we'd fought and I'd still be attractive. *That* had been an awkward conversation. It barely beat out the sex talk for sheer unadulterated embarrassment. "I don't want to know."

Cat took my hand. "You did well," she said. "I understand why they like you."

I couldn't help smiling. "As long as *you* like me..."

"Just you wait." Cat winked at me. "Just you wait."

***

THE END

The Zero Enigma Will Continue.
Soon.

AFTERWORD

I originally wrote this—in a slightly different form—as an essay for *Fantastic Schools and Where to Find Them,* a blog about reading and reviewing magic school novels. Please feel free to search for the blog—if you like *The Zero Enigma* and *Schooled in Magic,* you might like some of the other books on offer.]

Boarding schools are evil.

That is not a word I use lightly.

When I tell people I went to a British boarding school, I am commonly asked about two things: the cane and sexual abuse. School corporal punishment was banned in 1987 and I was never sexually assaulted while I was at school. And yet, boarding school was a foretaste of hell. Being in boarding school—I had the misfortune to attend a particularly bad school for four years—was like being in prison, only with worse food.

It's difficult to explain this to someone who has never experienced boarding school. I've had people tell me that it must have been very exciting, shortly after reading *Harry Potter*; I've even heard kids ask to be *sent* to boarding school. (If someone read one of my boarding school books and decided they wanted to go to boarding school, my first thought would be *what have I done?*) It is simply incomprehensible to most people, save perhaps those who joined the army and went through basic training. And even *they* were older when they joined up (and they got paid).

The boarding school I went to would have been lovely, if it hadn't been a school. It was set within vast grounds, a third of which was devoted to a golf course and makeshift running tracks. The remainder was forest, which I would have enjoyed exploring if I hadn't lived in constant fear of being caught away from school. But the closest outpost of civilisation was a small village, nearly forty minutes away on foot. There were no buses to the closest town, no taxis one could use to get to the nearest railway station; there was, in short, no way to leave without permission. It was, to all intents and purposes, a prison for my twelve-year-old self.

When you go to regular school, you can go home at the end of each day and relax. You can leave the teachers and bullies and everyone else behind. You are not obligated to endure their company outside school. You also have a chance to think about what happened in relative privacy. But in boarding school, you *cannot get away.* You are forced to endure the company of your fellow inmates and the wardens…sorry, teachers…for weeks on end. Even if you are lucky (?) enough to enjoy a school with vast grounds, there is always the prospect of being caught by one of the bullies and beaten or humiliated. There is no *safe space.* You certainly don't have the chance to relax, take off the mask and think about the day.

It's easy to idealise this sort of environment. Enid Blyton certainly did, when she wrote *Malory Towers.* The series is sweet enough to rot your teeth: midnight feasts, jolly pranks and japes, etc. And yet, if you look beneath the surface, even Blyton admits that there is something fundamentally wrong with the average boarding school. If you fit in—if you play up and play the game—you have a jolly good time; if you don't, like Gwendolyn Mary Lacey, you're a social outcast right from the start. Guess which one I was?

Hogwarts, for all of its magic, is a very accurate depiction of the less pleasant aspects of boarding school life. The teachers turn a blind eye to bullying, spitefulness and even pranks that nearly turn into outright murder. (Sirius Black got away with a prank that could have resulted in two deaths: in hindsight, the years he spent in prison for a crime he didn't commit could easily be seen as a karmic punishment.) Fred and George are not harmless pranksters—they're outright bullies, who are responsible for crippling at least one fellow student and driving their older brother out of the family.

And the teachers, too, are quite unpleasant; Snape, for all of the sympathy he draws from people like me, is simply not a very nice teacher. I don't fault him for hating James Potter, but taking it out on Harry is unacceptable. Both Flitwick and McGonagall have their darker moments; Hagrid, as likeable as he is, shouldn't be teaching at all. And Dumbledore is clearly more preoccupied with the war than doing his job. My head teachers didn't have that excuse and they were *still* unwilling to actually do anything to change the school.

Boarding schools are simply not very kind to those who are different. This is true of all schools, of course, but boarding schools are the worst because *you can't get away.* I don't think there was a single day when I wasn't insulted or beaten or generally treated like crap—I even came to hate my surname, because it was an easy insult. Even writing this down brings back the feelings of helplessness and worthlessness that made it hard to adjust to normal life, after finally being released from prison...sorry, school. And I know that others never recover completely. Some of them even turn into school shooters.

You see, if you are trapped in boarding school—or any sort of school—it is easy to come to hate everyone. You hate the bullies because they bully you, of course, but you also come to hate everyone else; your fellow pupils, because they are silently relieved that *you* are the target of the bully, and the staff, because they do nothing. Indeed, I can testify that many of the lower-ranking pupils picked on me, while the staff found it easier to punish me than the bullies.

And so your development becomes stunted. You do not develop basic empathy—why should you, when no one has ever shown *you* empathy? I know, all too well, that I am not as empathetic as I should be—I can rationalise showing empathy, but not emotionalise it. Nor do you learn basic social skills, because you are ruthlessly mocked (or attacked) for being socially unskilled, ensuring you don't have a chance to learn from your mistakes. (Every geek knows he or she will not be given the benefit of the doubt, while a jock will be.) You tell yourself that you don't care—you cripple your own ability to feel emotion—and yet, all you can do is bottle it up. I've had all sorts of emotional problems over the last seventeen years because the emotions I thought were contained were starting to leak. I've had times when I've overreacted to something because it brought back emotional memories that *convinced* me I had to fight—or *flee*.

And while this is true of many day-schools, it is far—far—worse in boarding school. If you attend without a considerable degree of emotional maturity—and physical strength—you are in deep shit.

Going back to the Hogwarts example, it is clear that Harry benefited from going to school (not least because it took him away from an emotionally abusive home.) Hermione, too, might have benefited, although she never lost her less attractive character traits. Ron, Draco, Neville, Percy, Fred and George, on the other hand, did not benefit anything like so much. I would go so far as to argue that they were actually *harmed* by the school system. Ron and Percy had to endure the mocking of their twin brothers, resulting in Percy actually walking *away* from his family; Neville had to put up with Snape's bullying and a massive crisis of confidence; Draco got too much handed to him on a silver platter until he finally bit off more than he could chew. And Fred and George were allowed to have fun—boys will be boys—instead of having their more dangerous traits sharply curbed.

All of this, it should be noted, is probably the most realistic part of the series.

But why did this happen?

The English aristocracy believed, on one hand, that boys were wild animals who needed to be tamed, not sensitive snowflakes who needed to be coddled. And, on the other hand, they believed that adversity built character. A child brought up under strict discipline would be more easily able to handle the rigors of adulthood, in what—it must be admitted—was a very harsh era. Furthermore, as the vast majority of aristocratic children attended places like Oxford, Eton and Cambridge (nineteen future prime ministers attended Eton; twenty-seven went to Oxford; fourteen went to Cambridge) attending such a school/university would offer a chance to make contacts at a very high level. If you went to Oxford around 1968 or thereabouts, there is a chance you might have met Theresa May, the *current* Prime Minister. The merchant classes, therefore, had a very strong incentive to push their children into those schools.

It wasn't just education, you see. It was everything from social attitudes and manners to language and everything else one needs to fit in with the aristocracy. An Oxford 'Old Boy' would have something in common with every other 'Old Boy.' He'd see a Cambridge student as an equal, even if they attended different schools. He wouldn't say that of someone who attended the local comprehensive. Classism has always been a powerful aspect of British society. Indeed, you could argue that this is also true of the *fictional* Wizarding World. Everyone goes to Hogwarts or faces immense social exclusion. The students may be ethnically diverse, but they are not intellectually diverse.

The problem with these attitudes was not that they were necessarily *wrong*. A Drill Instructor would argue that recruits have to be broken down before they can be built up again. And yes, the world is a tough place. Learning to handle pain and disappointment is a skill best mastered before one is out of one's teens. The problem was that they were enforced on children/early teens who didn't have the maturity to handle it (or, if nothing else, the grim awareness that they signed up of their own free will.) And when it went sour, it went *really* sour.

Worse, the system is tailor-made for abuse. Apathetic teachers do as little as possible, particularly after hours. (Only one teacher remained on duty after classes in my school and he was often hard to find.) Bullying is rife because there is little real supervision, a problem made worse by the powerlessness of most of the teachers. Even suspending particularly unpleasant kids can be difficult these days. But predatory teachers can be a great deal worse; boarding schools offer all sorts of opportunities for preying on one's charges. I was not remotely surprised to hear about sexual abuse scandals. I know, all too well, just how much can be done in boarding school that parents never hear of. And when the facts do start to leak out, the impulse is often to circle the wagons and protect the school rather than the students.

I can see the appeal, in so many ways. Hell, I practically embraced it myself before I actually *went* to boarding school. (In hindsight, I should have committed some awful crime and got myself sent to jail instead.) But in reality, boarding schools are hell. I don't blame my parents for sending me—they were told there was no choice, if I wanted to overcome my problems—but, if I had my way, sending kids to boarding school would be classed as a form of child abuse.

Christopher G. Nuttall
Kuala Lumpur, 2019

PS.
And now you've read the book, I have a favour to ask. It's getting harder to earn a living through indie writing these days, for a number of reasons (my health is one of them, unfortunately). If you liked this book, please post a review wherever you bought it; the more reviews a book gets, the more promotion.

CGN.

Printed in Great Britain
by Amazon

41308401R00234